Crowned by Sacrifice

BOUND BY SIGHT

BOOK 1

ALEXANDRIA LONG

For Grumpy- Thank you for the endless amounts of ice cream, hugs, and adventures. Thank you for everything. Miss you bunches.

For my kids- you make everyday an adventure, and I am so amazed by you.

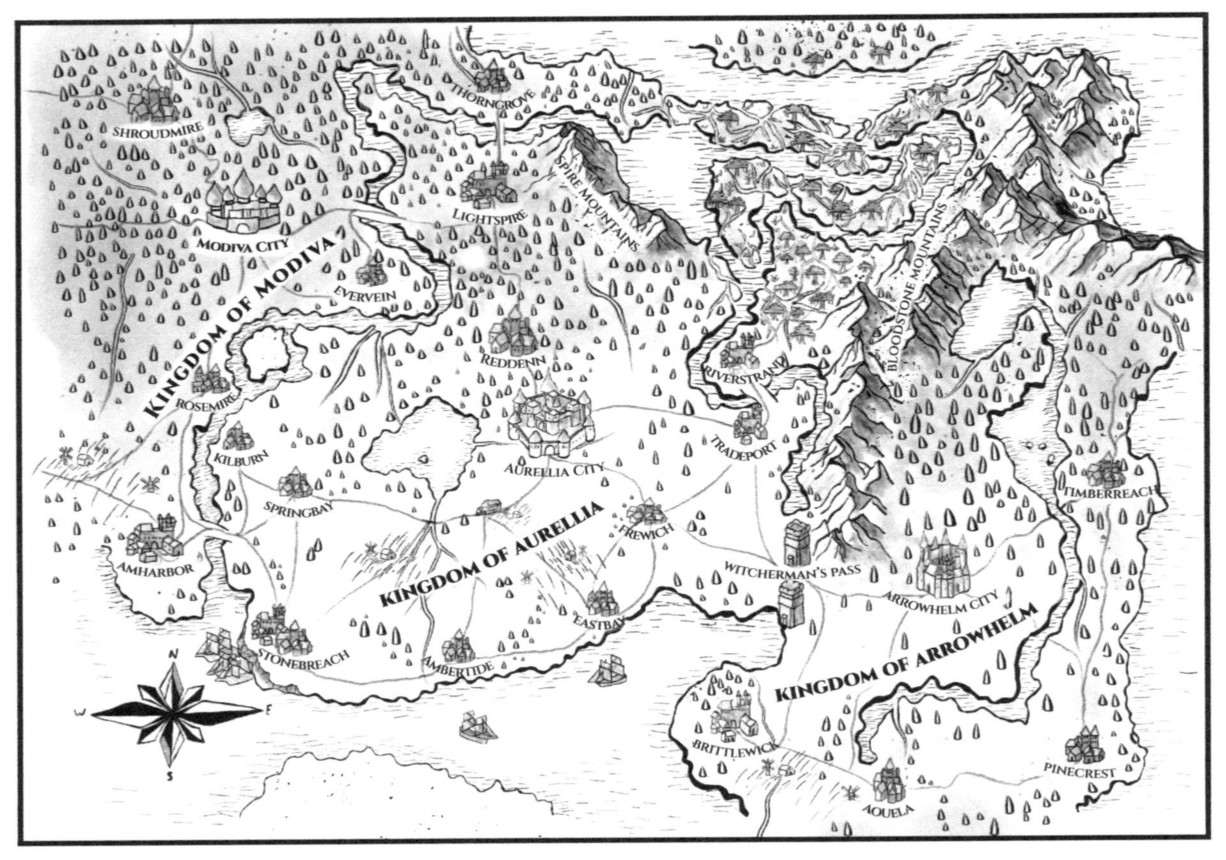

KINGDOM OF MODIVA
KINGDOM OF AURELLIA
KINGDOM OF ARROWHELM
SHROUDMIRE
THORNGROVE
MODIVA CITY
LIGHTSPIRE
SPIRE MOUNTAINS
BLOODSTONE MOUNTAINS
EVERVEIN
REDDENN
RIVERSTRAND
ROSEMIRE
TRADEPORT
KILBURN
AURELLIA CITY
TIMBERREACH
SPRINGBAY
FREWICH
AMHARBOR
WITCHERMAN'S PASS
ARROWHELM CITY
EASTBAY
STONEBREACH
AMBERTIDE
BRITTLEWICK
PINECREST
AOUELA
N
E
S
W

CONTENTS

PROLOGUE

Clara

8 Years Ago

The sharp pain as feeling returns to my fingers makes me stop twisting them as I pace through the room trying to make sense of everything that I thought I knew. One, my daughters have inherited the sight. The shrieking giggles of the girls float up through my open balcony door. Andria will be okay— my cousin will step in when the time comes and train her. She will thrive in that environment, and I hate that I won't be here to see it. Katerina, however, will need to face this head-on and alone.

Second, I would do anything, *anything* for them to survive and live long, happy lives. Even if it means I need to remove myself.

I turn from the window, my eyes lingering on the chest at the far end of the room and I know what I need to do. I cross the room, the wood planks of the floor warm on the soles of my feet from the summer air. The gentle creak from the chest hinges fills the room as I kneel in front of it and rummage through the belongings thrown within over the years. Where is it? My fingers find the old, cool leather, and I pull it from underneath a shawl my mother gave me when I married Joel. The worn, red-leather journal is partially filled with visions and thoughts from when I was pregnant with Katerina, but there are enough pages to still be large enough for what I need it for. I lean back on my heels, and allow the lid of the chest to fall closed. The low thud echoes in my mind like a knell. I don't have much time. I glance out of the open balcony doors. The sun is still high, the sky clear. The giggles have faded into non-existence, and I would bet Kat is likely spending time with the Gold boy. My chest aches with the knowledge that I hold but cannot share. Everything that is to come? It must come to pass.

Sighing, I rise and walk slowly to the table on the balcony. The sun breaks through the clouds and the sea crashes into the shore in the distance. The sound is a comfort, and I lose myself momentarily in the rhythmic lull as I sit in one of the chairs, crack open the journal and begin to write. I write about everything— our history, where our family originated, my visions, thoughts I remember having during important moments in my life. I warn her of everything without giving anything specific away. She will have to figure as much out as she can on her own. I spill out everything that I wish I could tell her myself, and everything that I hope she will be. Time passes quickly; the crickets sing as the fireflies come out to chase each other in the growing darkness.

The sky is dark and the stars twinkle above by the time I close the journal and lay down the pen; essentially cutting off my words. Feeling myself deflate, I rise to head back inside. I am thankful that Joel is working late tonight— my mind and heart are heavy with what I need to do. I wrap the journal in the shawl from the chest, leaving a folded note on top for Joel with another explaining Andria's role in what is to come. My fingers linger on the fabric, the paper crinkling slightly under the weight. The letter for Joel explains everything that is to come and what steps he will need to take to ensure that things unfold the way that they must. I leave the bundle on the foot of the bed, sitting beside it and try to clear my mind of the memories, visions, and what needs to be done. My hands shake as I reach forward to the small end table beside the headboard, pull open the small drawer, and withdraw a small vial of clear liquid. My heart pounds in my chest and I feel my shoulders tighten and my palms go clammy as I place the vial on the pillow. I don't want to do this, but this is the only way.

I devour the room; taking in the floor to ceiling shelves that make up the wall alongside the door that leads to the rest of the house. My eyes linger on the shelves, on the books filling them, and I shake my head. I rise, trailing my fingers along the spine of each book, my fingers gliding on the leather until they stop almost of their own accord. I pause, looking around the rest of the room before turning back to the shelf. My mouth opens when I see what tome my fingers rest on— *Seer Society: A History and Societal Importance of Seers.* I pull the book from the shelf, feeling its weight in my hands. There is one last thing I need to do.

CHAPTER 1

My mother died because of the things that she saw. This sentiment has been playing on repeat in my mind these past few months, and no matter what I do, I can't shake it. There are about a million reasons why I wish I could still talk to her, but lately, it's been a constant battle between my upcoming nuptials and the visions that started plaguing me about four months ago. My mind is a mess as I walk along the halls in the upper right wing of my family home in an attempt to clear it for the first time in weeks, and the rhythmic patter of quick footsteps of someone running down the hall towards me works to break me from the memories. I don't have to turn as I'd recognize those footsteps anywhere.

"Katerina! Oh, Katerina!" Andria sings as she runs after me, not taking long to reach me. The house may be large, two wings with a staircase in the middle off of the foyer with a large formal dining room behind on the main level, but it still only takes minutes to reach one end of the house from the other. Especially if running.

"Hmm?" I stop and look at her. Her cheeks are slightly flushed from chasing after me and her green eyes sparkle in excitement. "What's going on?" I ask.

"There's someone downstairs for you, a man. I've never seen him before, but Peter is freaking out. I'm not sure why, but it must be someone he doesn't like very much," she giggles.

I barely nod in her direction before I take off down the hall. Who would be coming here? Not once have I had anyone call on me outside of Peter. My father has kept us in the dark when it comes to both society and the world around us. The only glimpses I ever received of the world outside of our territory came from the letters I received over the years from Peter, and the few stories Andria and I could get our father to share. There were a few of my father's sailors who would tell us stories as well; tales of far away places, countries across the sea, and of the other territories along the coast.

Then of course there was Ian, my father's ambassador to the King's council when he is unable to be in attendance and essentially an older brother to my sister and myself. Ian is our window to the outside world, the goings-on at court and in the country. He has been at court for some time now, since my father has been home more frequently as of late. I assume it is due to both Andria coming of age and the arrangement of my own marriage. As it is, my father waited several years after I came of age to set up my engagement to Peter. Two years to be exact. Andria is sixteen now and should be getting engaged within the next couple of years.

My feet fly down the hall, the portraits on the carved panelled walls blur in blotches of color as I race back the way I came to the staircase in the center of the home. While eager to see who awaits at the foot of the stairs in the foyer, I stop once I reach the top, taking in the scene for myself. Peter is fuming by the bottom step staring defensively at the stranger— arms crossed, and his stance wide. I have never seen him so hostile. Turning to inspect the newcomer, I feel all of the air leave my lungs as my fingers dig into the warm wood of the banister. The stranger is the man from my visions.

I try to ground myself by gripping the banister tightly and digging my fingers into the sturdy railing. The stranger's dark hair curls at the nape of his neck, longer than it had been in the visions that have been plaguing me for months. His face is tight as he glares at Peter; his pursed mouth and hands resting on his hips speak to a level of annoyance, but his presence seems to command respect and authority, almost as if the very idea that he exists demands to be recognized and revered. Who is he? Why is he here? Why now?

I slowly head down the stairs with Andria following close behind, my feet silent as they slowly move from step to step. The wood is worn, but sturdy and quiet under foot. Not even a creak escapes under our weight. My breath and body are shaky, and I hope no one notices. My hand still clenches the banister, and the other is balled into a fist at my side. I glance between both men, not sure what to make of the scene in front of me, or what to think. The stranger seems to sense my presence because he glances up almost immediately. Peter, noticing his distraction, also glances up to find me assessing the situation. He allows me to make it to the bottom of the stairs before he takes a single stride to my side, but his eyes return to the stranger. He stands close enough I can feel his chest move with every breath he takes. He stands tall, his body hard and tense as he puts a hand on my elbow in an attempt to stop me when I take a step forward out of his shadow.

I shake my head at Peter's soft, "Kat, don't," and step closer to the stranger. I can feel the tension within Peter radiating outward to fill the room, but there isn't really anything I can do to help alleviate it, and my own curiosity takes hold of me. I need to know who this man is and why he is so ingrained in my visions.

"Hello, may I help you?" My voice is soft, and my lips tilt up in the corners in welcome to the stranger— always playing the role of Lady, just as I've been taught.

The man smiles and dips his head in my direction as he lets his hands fall from his hips and clasps them together in front of him. "I have business that I must speak with you and your father about. Is he available?" he asks, shooting a quick glance at Peter. Peter steps forward until my back is against his chest once again. He is breathing hard, and I realize just how much he is holding back. He feels the need to protect me, to keep me close, and I can't imagine why. Who is this man? What does he want?

"Alaric, why are you here?" Peter cuts in before I can respond. A name to put to the face, and it suits him. Alaric. It is regal, memorable, and I recall that the eldest son of King Henry has the same name. It can't be him, can it?

Alaric's deeper voice cuts with a slight echo in the open space, "a private matter that doesn't concern you." Alaric turns from Peter and addresses me again, "my Lady?" He brushes Peter off so casually, almost as if he's done it a million times before.

Peter steps closer toward Alaric, causing me to take a tiny step forward myself as he pushes me slightly. "Doesn't concern me? I'm sorry, *your highness*, but she is my fiance. Anything you have to say to her actually does concern me," Peter jumps in, spitting the title at Alaric, using it as an insult rather than the command of respect a title usually carries. The utterance of his title makes my heart skip and stutter. What is he doing here? I reach behind me slightly to grab Peter's fingers and squeeze them gently, silently telling him that it is okay before I step forward out of his reach.

"Yes, sir, my father is in his study down the hall. Let me go grab him. I'll be just a moment…"

Our eyes meet, those blue eyes that have been haunting me for weeks stare into mine, and I can't help but stand there frozen. I have to admit that he is handsome, but that doesn't draw me to him as much as the glimpses I have seen in the visions that haunt me daily: my first time seeing Alaric in the woods, a palace through the trees, a guard swinging a sword, the ringing clang of metal on metal, and the salt-and-iron scent of blood. I've been trying to piece together their meaning, and it is clear that I should have seen this moment coming. Or at least known that he might become real to me at some point, and not simply remain a vision, since he is the focus of everything I see over and over again. Alaric strides toward me and offers me his arm. "Shall I go with you rather than wait here?"

I dip my head in a nod, not trusting myself to speak. Before I realize what's happening, Alaric is surrounded by a garden within palace walls, almost as if he is lying in the grass. His calm exterior cracks with a grin that feels familiar, and he holds a hand in his. My hand? As quickly as the image appears, it disappears, as does everything else.

I must not have lost consciousness for very long, as I feel the stairs digging into my lower back. I feel a warm embrace, and I relax into the arms that hold me. Peter whispers in my ear, and I simply nod in response. I look around me, and Alaric kneels in front of me, his brows drawn together and his jaw clenched in a frown of concern. My father rounds the right corner into the foyer, followed closely by Andria. She must have run to him when I collapsed. I sit up, and bring myself to stand; breathing hard with one hand on the banister, the other firmly grasped by Peter's.

"I apologize for the scare, I am alright." I nod at Alaric, Peter, and I turn to my father, my chin high, playing off the heat of embarrassment that threatens to overwhelm me. I know my cheeks are flushed, but I refuse to show any other sign of weakness. My heart pounds in my chest, and it is a fight to remain on my feet. My head throbs with every beat of my heart, and I fight off the exhaustion that threatens to pull me under its spell and into unconsciousness. The visions haven't been getting any easier, demanding a toll on my body as well as my mind. My father meets my gaze, and I shake my head subtly. I am fine, or will be, with nothing more than a bruised ego, and my eyes plead that he drop the situation and move forward. He clears his throat with a small jerk of his head, and his eyes go to Alaric. He bows deeply, and gestures that we all follow him to his study. He turns on his heel, his shoes scraping on the stone floor as he does, and he leads the way back down the hall to the right of the stairs.

"Are you okay? I'm sorry about showing up unannounced. I know there is a protocol. I should have sent a messenger ahead to inform you I was coming," Alaric says as we make our way down the hall to the right of the stairs toward my father's study. Peter opens his mouth to argue, but closes it before squeezing my hand. He doesn't bother asking if I am okay, and instead remains at my side as a source of comfort and stability.

I glance up at Alaric and give a curt nod. "I'm fine, thank you."

The conversation is thankfully cut short as we reach the study. The door is already open, and my father leads the way inside, lingering in front of the fire, his arm held out to us as a gesture to enter and find a seat. I sink into the same armchair I use every time I'm in here— the oversized chair directly in front of the fire. The room looks the same as always, the flowered tapestry my mother bought for him the year she died hanging behind my father's desk. A decently-sized map table sits to my right. It stands about waist-high, and spans about three feet in length. The face of the table shows our war ships in the harbor with our trade ships in various ports along the coastline and different military men scattered across the realm. Not much has changed on this either, and from this vantage point, the country doesn't seem very large, but I know it takes about three weeks on horseback to get from one end to the other, and about a week to reach Aurellia City from here.

I look away from the table and take in the rest of the room. The fire flickers vibrantly in the fireplace, chasing away the early spring chill. Peter takes the chair directly beside mine, and Alaric paces slightly in the small space to the right of my father's desk and in front of the doors that lead to the garden. I glance first at Peter, then at my father, waiting for someone to tell me what is going on. I watch my father glance first at Alaric, then at me. He lifts an eyebrow, as if to say that he knows he is the one from my visions, and knows that I may need this push to move forward with anything involving the visions. A knot forms in my gut, and my teeth sink into my lip.

My father clears his throat before speaking. "Katerina, this is His Royal Majesty, Prince Alaric. He, uh," he pauses, considering his words a moment before he plunges forward. "He wants to marry you."

How could he possibly know this? Unless Alaric wrote to inform my father of his intentions, and he simply did not share the information with the rest of us. Either way, this should have been my decision, and we should have been made aware of any change in my status when he knew. My father ignores Peter, who, in frustration, runs his fingers through his hair before crossing his arms over his chest. My father clears his throat again and turns toward the fire.

Peter kneels in front of me and gently brushes my hair away from my face and makes sure I'm okay. My eyes search his; fire burns in my veins, hotter than I even knew possible in response to the anger that burns through me. Peter traces a thumb over my jawline, and my mind races with the knowledge the visions have provided me thus far. Which frankly hasn't been much more information than there is some sort of threat to the kingdom. I don't know how widespread, or what role I will play when it comes down to it, but somehow I'm supposed to be okay with taking a leap of faith and leaving everything that I have ever wanted behind? No, it is too much.

"A pleasure to meet you, Prince Alaric." The lie tastes sweet on my tongue, almost like honey. I bow my head, my eyes fluttering and my breath searing my throat as I clench my jaw and raise my head to meet his gaze. The bow is necessary for the respect deserved for the title he bears, but I quickly start to despise the man brandishing it like a weapon. "As for your request, I'm sorry, but I'm already engaged."

Alaric takes a moment to consider what I'm saying. "I'm aware of your situation; however, since I outrank everyone here, I can overrule your previous engagement," he pauses briefly, his eyes sliding over to Peter before continuing, almost to emphasize the point to him. "You *will* be my bride. Your father has spoken highly of you every time he has been at the palace, and since he is one of my father's advisors, that is quite often." He nods toward my father, and turns back to me. "My father tried to contact yours to cancel your engagement when he realized that I was interested in a match. Somehow, those letters never seemed to arrive."

He looks pointedly at Peter as if he had something to do with the missing letters. I want to jump up and argue, but I steel myself against the words pouring out of his mouth. "So, I went ahead and came here instead. I hope you will forgive my intrusion." He bows his head and turns to my father. "Joel, I would very much like to marry your daughter. As heir, and Prince of Aurellia, I don't need your permission, but I would appreciate the honor of becoming your son-in-law if you would dissolve the engagement between Katerina and Peter. Out of respect for you, I am asking, but I will not ask twice."

At this, Peter finally loses it. He rises to his feet, begging my father to forbid the arrangement, but I don't think he has much of a choice. Alaric is the heir to the throne, what he says goes. I bury my face in my hands trying to figure everything out. The world spins around me, the dizziness threatening to pull me under, but instead drown under the cacophony of the voices raised in argument around me until they finally disappear, and I am left an empty shell. The ringing in my ears lessens and I claw the wall that I have built around myself. I know anger towards Alaric is futile, but the situation is different. Everything I have wanted, everything I thought I knew has shifted and the anger I've pushed aside for months comes bubbling to the surface.

How has everything come to this? I never anticipated this sort of thing to happen; that my visions would destroy everything that I hold dear. I hoped and prayed that my mother would be the last victim of the curse the female line holds, but I am wrong. I am only the next in line.

I finally look outward and notice that my father has remained silent, staring at the fire. He is well-aware that Peter is everything I have ever wanted in a partner, and I don't even know anything about this man in front of me besides what my visions have shown me, which isn't much. I watch my father's shoulders sag slightly, and I can't help but wonder if my mother foresaw this moment, if she knew the possibility of my world imploding around me. My father finally turns from the fire and makes eye contact with Alaric.

"You are the future king and I have to allow it. You know this." My father holds up a hand, stopping Peter's protests. "You make the rules, and we must obey; but please, is there nothing we can do to sway your mind? This engagement has been in the making since they were eight."

Alaric shakes his head, and that simple movement shatters the wall I had scrambled to put up around myself since hearing his intention. "Perhaps we can create some sort of arrangement for your younger daughter. She is only two years away from being able to marry." My father looks taken aback, but before he can say anything Peter jumps in.

"Alaric!" Peter glares daggers as sharp as the ones thrown through his tone. "You seem to forget that it is your nobles who give you your power. You have no right coming in here and demanding my fiancée."

Alaric laughs and shakes his head, bemused with Peter and the invisible crumbling of worlds he is causing. "I have every right. I am heir to the throne."

Peter looks like he has more he wants to say, his mouth opening and closing silently, but instead shakes his head, turns on a heel, and leaves the room, leaving the three of us remaining staring after him. The door slams against the doorframe, shaking the door on its hinges so much that it doesn't latch and instead bounces back open. My father breaks the charged silence, "I will figure out an arrangement for my youngest daughter when the time comes, but for now, Katerina is enough. I beg you, please take care of her." His voice is quiet, strained, and I know he is apologetic for how things are going, but it isn't enough to diminish the flames that have arisen in response to everything crumbling around me.

"I will," Alaric starts, but before Alaric can turn his attention to me, I finally speak. "Excuse me, but is this not my life that you are taking control of? Do I truly not get a say in any of this?" I rise out of the oversized chair, bringing myself to appear bigger than I am, but am well aware that I am unsuccessful as both men tower over me in both size and power.

Alaric starts to speak, but my father interrupts, glancing briefly at Alaric and only continuing when Alaric nods his head and takes a small step back, providing him the space to speak. "Katerina, I apologize, but that is just how it is. You must say goodbye to Peter. You will be Alaric's bride."

I ignore the cracking feeling within, and cross my arms over my chest both to hold myself together and to close myself off to them. I cannot and will not go willingly. The visions be damned.

"Kat," my father pleads, while defeat makes his shoulders sink and his head tilt slightly down. He appears more tired and unsure than before, yet he still stands tall and stands by the decision that was made in my stead. I know what he sees as he looks at me. He sees my mother, looking like the day he met her— flaming hair with wild curls, grey eyes hurt and accusing as my entire world is flipped upside down. He avoids me, has for years once I grew older and the uncanny resemblance to the love and loss of his life became more prominent. He can't bear to look at me for long without seeing her. He clears his throat as he continues, but his voice is gruff, and I know he is feeling the pain that I am sure emanates from me like an aura. "He is the future king. What he says, goes."

Alaric looks almost smug, his eyes almost sparkle in the victory of stealing me as his bride. A smile works wonders to his features, and I hate that I even notice. I shake my head vigorously, refusing to let this happen and refusing to let the tears fall. My father must sense what I am feeling because I hear a whispered apology as I run from the room. I don't care that the door is left ajar, and that they expect me to lay down and take the news like the "gem" my father claims me as. I will not go willingly.

I run up the stairs and down the hall to Peter's room. The hallway is empty, thankfully, but there really isn't anyone else to run into. We keep the house sparse of dignitaries and soldiers, but that is likely to change with Alaric's purpose here revealed. In the meantime, it is only the family and Peter in the house since his family left a few days ago. His room is not too far down the hall from the kitchen and the smell of fresh bread baking fills the air— I close my eyes briefly, remembering a time my mother snuck us into the kitchen to eat the freshly-baked bread and cookies. We also tried our hand at kneading dough but ended up wearing more flour than accomplishing anything else. I open my eyes, and hesitantly open Peter's door.

"Peter?"

I hear a rustle across the room, near the door to the balcony. I quietly close the door behind me and observe the room before me. The room has two doorways, one leading to a small washroom, the other to the balcony. The room is a decent size, but seems small with the large bed against the wall to my right, and a small armoire beside the double balcony doors. There is a writing desk directly to my left just inside of the door. Peter's clothes are scattered everywhere, haphazardly balanced on the chair in the corner, one shirt away from tumbling to the floor. The bed is in disarray; the pillows are sideways, and the blanket is laying half off the bed as if he just got out of bed and didn't care to make it afterwards.

Through the already open balcony door, I see Peter by the railing, his head bowed and can tell by the set of his shoulders that his knuckles are white against the thick wrought iron railing of the balcony. My shoes barely whisper against the ground as I pick my path through Peter's belongings to the balcony where he resides. I reach out to him, longing for more than simple touch and instead for the future I know we both desire as my hand brushes against his shoulder, causing him to jump and turn toward me. His eyes trace my face, and I feel every spot they linger as if they were a caress. My body trembles with electricity under his gaze.

I step closer. My eyes trace his features before I meet his lips with mine. He gasps, surprised, but it doesn't take him long to become an active participant. I feel his hands slide to the small of my back, his hands wrapping my ribs as he pulls me closer. My hand rests on his cheek, the stubble scratching my palm. Before long, he pulls away, watching my face closely. His eyes are shrouded in pain and I hate that I am the reason.

"You're marrying him, aren't you?"

I don't say anything, not wanting to give him hope when I have none myself. He has to know it isn't my choice. I wouldn't be marrying Alaric if I had things my way. He releases me and takes a small step back as if the distance is what is needed and stares at me, waiting. I watch his hands clench into fists at his side as his eyes drill into me. I don't even know where to begin. I don't want this anymore than he does, and I know that he is angry and frustrated at the turn of events and he doesn't mean to take it out on me, but I can't help but feel the sting of the accusation that subtly implies that I sought this arrangement out.

"Alaric…" My thoughts race as I try to organize what I want to say—thoughts that have not stopped spinning since Alaric's appearance in my foyer. Thoughts that have been spinning since the visions began four months ago, and honestly for much longer. How did we get here, and how do we go back? Back to the two children that skipped rocks in the bay, and learned to swim and climb trees in the small wooded area at the north of the property line? The teenagers that snuck into the village and the docks, everywhere we knew we weren't supposed to be. How do we go back to that?

"Damn him!" he interrupts before I can wrap my head around what I even want to say. I watch as he turns from me and faces the open air. The light breeze flutters his hair, and his balled fists slowly unclench. He breathes deeply and musses his hair by running his fingers through it before speaking. "You know I've been at the palace lately, spending a lot of my time negotiating with the royal family regarding trade and the men my family will be providing from my territory. I serve on the council in my father's place. Because I hold more power than most of the other nobles in the King's inner circle, besides your father of course," he nods toward me as he continues, "they don't like having me around. Although Ian has been a real friend and he is slowly turning the others toward my side. Anyway, it's incredible how quickly the royals forget that it is us, the nobles and the inner circle, that give them their power. It is us that give them our men for their military, and who provide the materials for trade," he shakes his head, his fingers wrapping around the railing again as he looks out toward the sea.

"My father hoped that Alaric and I would become friends, he claimed that having the favor of the future king could be nothing but beneficial. But for as much as I have tried to see past his failings, it is not easy. He is so stubborn and is so unlike his father it is unbelievable. Alaric and I constantly disagree— both in and out of the counsel room. Alaric firmly believes that he is the source of his own power and needs to be constantly reminded of his people and that he needs to work as a part of a team, not dictate everything as it happens and as he needs." Peter sighs and rubs the back of his neck before leaning against the railing with his side, one elbow resting on the railing. He doesn't meet my eyes, but watches the world just over my head. Seagulls float in the breeze overhead, only flapping their wings once every minute or so.

"My father obviously doesn't know or didn't realize the type of person that Alaric is. Or he simply didn't care. The friendship never took off, and while we are typically cordial with one another, there have been a few times in the sparring field that we have taken advantage of our general *dislike* for each other," he grimaces, "I give him props though, he is strong, and a fierce opponent on the field, but other than that, he is arrogant and not someone I care to be around. When it comes down to it, Alaric is young and untried, yes, but his younger brother, Lucas, understands all of the roles and where he stands when it comes to the counsel and the people. He takes our advice into consideration. But not Alaric. I'm sure with the right motivation, he can be a great ruler, but as it is right now, Lucas may be the better choice." He is quiet for a moment, but his eyes find mine and pain laces his gaze, mirroring my own. "I hate that I have to go back to being a member of the counsel after this whole thing is over. Especially if he takes you from me. I don't think I can stand by and watch you be with someone else."

He holds my gaze, his eyes bright with unshed tears and he gently takes my hand in his and brings it to his lips. My own part slightly, as my heart leaps in my chest, and I wish I could stay in this moment forever. I long for the future I've dreamed with him and hate the direction the visions seem to be pointing me. I hate that I have no say in my own life, visions or otherwise. If only there was another way. If only. My other hand trails his cheek, but I let it fall feeling small and hopeless.

"I won't let this be the end of us. I will fight for you, Kat. I can promise you that," he says, looking me in the eye. I fight back the tears that threaten to fall as I hope for the future we want but know we can't have.

"I know you will." I keep his gaze until his lips close over mine once more, our fingers tightening around each other's.

CHAPTER 2

My mother told me that our people came from Arrowhelm, in particular, the city Aouela. Seers are revered by the people there. Even the royal family keep a few on staff. As for the city itself, she told me there is a group of them that will train those with the gift. They will help you learn how to wield it in a way where you control the visions, not them control you. There are further powers in each of us that are mostly untapped, but are possible with the right motivation. My mother went to Aouela as a young girl— before she met my father. She tried to teach me everything that she learned, but none of it worked for me. I still fumble and fall after each vision, and I can't do half of the things that she could. I wish she had sent me to train in Aouela. Maybe then I wouldn't have to let go of everyone and everything. Maybe then I could save my girls and my Katerina wouldn't have to sacrifice everything in order to survive and save everyone.

All of the answers lie in Arrowhelm.

Perhaps I can make the journey with my girls. Convince Joel that this is what is necessary. That we will need the seers in Arrowhelm to train us and show us the way to make a difference. I never did understand how the greater power my mother wielded worked, and from what I have seen, somehow my daughter will know although she will need no training to do so. She will be so much more than me.

The golden honeysuckle on the trellis nearby glimmer faintly in the growing moonlight. Their sweet scent mixes with the briny sea air, and my bare toes dig softly into the dirt and grass underneath them. The bluffs line the outer rim of the property, and remains my favorite spot after everything, and likely always will be. The house sits slightly above the bluffs and is a ways back— the garden reaching through the expanse leading to the bluffs. There are steps carved into the face of the bluff to my left, but there is a softer inclined walkway to my right that winds down to the beach at the bottom and the docks the royal fleet occupy. The fishing docks sit near the mouth of the river to the west of the property, on the edge of town. From where I stand, I can see the slight glow of the town in the distance. The town sits right on the water, on stilts that keep it elevated and safe when tide ebbs and flows.

I watch the fleet bob gently in the bay below. They look like the little toy boats that Andria and I would play with in the small pond just outside of our father's study. The gentle breeze ruffles my loose hair. I have always loved the feeling of the wind blowing through my hair, and the smell of the salt in the air. It has always sent a warm feeling into the core of my being, the warmth of home, the warm feeling of belonging somewhere in the world. For me, that place is here: standing on the top of the hill, where the sea meets the edge of the land. It is a place of wonderment, a place full of longing for travel, of something more than what I've always known. I remember as a child I wanted nothing more than to board one of the ships in the harbor, and just sail away, and I wanted that more and more after my mother died. Or at least I did, until I came to realize that this is the only place she can still be found.

The sea reminds me of her; her smile and the grey of her eyes, like a storm brewing over the water. God do I miss her. And somehow, even though I know she is gone and never coming back, I feel as if she is with me. As if she is standing here by the sea, holding my hand, praying that I am not like her.

I know I should be getting back to the house, but being here surrounded by my mother brings back good memories from before. I need this, the feeling of the dirt between my toes and the wind in my hair to ground and center me from the reeling that still overwhelms me. Everything I have ever wanted has come to a shuddering halt, and I don't know if I want to go through with this new engagement. There is no saying that my involvement will solve the problem my visions are warning me about, nor do I know if there is truly anything that can be done anyway. But if I don't do something, will I regret it? I tilt my face to the sky, begging for her, for my mother to send a sign that I am doing the right thing. That I am on the right path. A warm wind embraces me, which is as much of a response as I'll ever get, and a tear escapes from my closed eyes.

I can feel Peter come up behind me; his breath tickles the nape of my neck and his woodsy scent envelops me as if in a cocoon. "There you are. I wondered if I'd find you here," he murmurs as he slowly wraps his arms around me, pulling me against him. I rest my head against his chest behind me and continue watching the boats below. He kisses the side of my neck, and my breath catches in my throat.

"When in doubt, I'm usually here."

"I've noticed," he rumbles against my neck. I can't help but to tilt my head slightly, giving him more access to my throat. He nuzzles into the crook of my neck. "Kat?"

"Mmm?" My eyes close as his fingers trace circles on my hips and he leaves a small kiss on the top of my shoulder.

"Before things between us have to disappear, and I don't have the chance to really tell you, I just want you to know that I have fallen completely in love with you. I fell a little more with each letter you wrote. You give so much of yourself so freely in your words. Your soul was left bare to me in every single one," he pauses, trailing his nose up my neck to my ear. "These past few weeks have solidified what I already knew. It has been years in the making, but I am yours. Completely," he leaves a kiss just under my ear, "Utterly," he nips at my ear, "Yours."

Twisting in his arms to meet his gaze despite the shiver of

liquid flame that goes through me as he breathes in my ear, I look up into his face. The raw vulnerability I find in his eyes makes my breath catch and I can't help but to stare in amazement, my eyes etching every inch of his face into memory. He already lives there, but I want to remember him in this exact moment. I want to remember how his sandy hair flicks back with the gentle breeze, making it messier than it already is; the way his mouth is slightly open as he gazes at me, and how I'm at a loss for words, not because I don't feel the same, but because I know I'm going to sound like a blubbering idiot in comparison to his eloquent soliloquy. His forehead pushes into mine in a need to be close, but his eyes dim as he patiently waits for a response. I know I need to say something, but the words evade me. If this were a letter, the words would come easily.

"Kat?" he breathes my name, and I close my eyes and try to settle my racing heart as I nuzzle my nose against his as I formulate the words and finally release them.

"I think I knew about a year ago when you started talking about all of the parties and balls and all the women and people you were meeting. As much as I loved hearing from you and reading your letters, I hated reading them. I was jealous." I scoff and shake my head slightly, remembering the burn that would linger in my gut when reading his letters. He tilts his head back slightly to look at me, and I have to clear my throat to continue. "*I* wanted to be the woman that was there, the one that you were dancing with, the one stealing all of your time." I flick my eyes upwards to meet his with a small smile, losing myself. "I hated that I only had you in letters that I would read and reread day after day, simply to get a glimpse into your life and mind. I wanted everything." Our breath mingles as he starts to tilt his head closer to mine. "I still do— want everything. Every moment, every dance, *everything*."

His lips on mine cut off any further conversation. They are

soft, gentle, like the petals of the roses in the garden, but passion drives us both and the kiss soon becomes a dance, a twining of stems growing together so tightly it is hard to tell the difference between them. He holds me closer, and my fingers wrap themselves in his hair. One of his hands is in my hair, holding me even tighter and closer to him, so that we essentially become one. Every breath we take is of the other, and I no longer know where he ends and I begin. I don't care if anyone sees us; let them. This is the path that I choose. What moments I have left, I am jumping head first into. Let them see. Peter breaks away first, rubbing his nose against mine as he pulls back. He grins, as I gaze into his eyes, the green darker than normal, reminding me of the sea during a storm. I lose myself in them, sucked beneath the waves until I am breathless and reeling. I never knew I could feel like this, that something as simple as a moment shared with someone could leave you feeling full of life and as if you had never lived a day before this moment.

"I pictured you in place of every girl I met. It was always you I wanted to spend my days, my time, and every moment with. I kept rushing back to my room every day wondering if your next letter had arrived, if I had gotten another moment of your time. I craved your touch, your hand in mine with every dance at every ball." His left hand slides from my waist to take my hand in his. He suddenly spins me then pulls me close, dancing slowly to the sound of the waves crashing into the shore below us. I giggle softly as we move, breathless and happy. His voice is soft and he leans his forehead on mine as we circle slowly, "everytime someone would make me laugh, I wondered if you would find it funny too. I would go back to my room and write down every joke, every important thing that happened, so I would remember to tell you in my next letter. It has always been you, and I regret that it took until now to tell you, Kat. You are everything. Everything." The moon shines above us, the stars twinkling in the clear sky. Home is here, in his arms, and I am a fool to ever let this go.

My fingers linger on the soft petals of various flowers as I pass on my way back to the house. I wish everything were as simple as they seemed to be when I was a child. I glance toward the clouds that begin to cover the moon and stars— there must be a storm blowing in from the sea. Usually they are quick squalls that come and go, but nonetheless I hurry into the house before it begins to rain. I watch the first drops fall from my balcony doors which I leave cracked to allow the breeze in. I turn, glancing around. I glance at my bed, longing to curl up there and never leave and instead I find a small, red, leather-bound journal on my pillow.

The fire is still going in the fireplace, likely from a servant stopping in here while I was out, so I take the book and curl up in my armchair near the fire. I open the cover, and my mother's handwriting glares up at me. I hold the small book up to my chest and fight back tears. I didn't know my father still had anything that was authentically hers. I feel as if I'm holding a small piece of her, and it makes me incredibly happy. I bring the book back down to my lap, opening to a random page and I peer at the small delicate characters that cover the page.

> *Self-projection, the ghost*
> *of what should be real, standing*
> *alone before the crowd, her lover*
> *dead beside her, bringing her*
> *foe to his knees with her hand*
> *in his chest, destroying*
> *the thing that makes him human.*

I slowly lower the book to my lap. My thoughts race. She must have used this as a way of recording her visions. I reread the poem, my fingers tracing the indent the letters create on the page, and no matter how many more times I read it I'm not sure what to make of this one. Self-projection? Is that possible? Then again, if anyone had told me they were having visions I wouldn't have believed them. I search the next few pages, but there is nothing more about this. I will likely never know who she is talking about, or whether this came to pass or not. I sigh, rising and gently put the book on the small bedside table before stepping out onto my balcony. The sea breeze billows my loose hair behind me, and I close my eyes. I ignore the light rain that had begun to fall once I stepped outside, and just enjoy the feeling of the breeze and imagine it's my mother holding me in her arms.

I stand there until I'm soaked through and shivering. I head back inside, lift the journal from the table, and sit on the edge of my bed, my feet resting on the frame below me. The bed dips slightly under my weight. I let the book fall open in my lap and I flip through a few pages, waiting for something to jump out at me. I know that over time, I will come to read and dissect the entirety of the journal, but for now, I glance through randomly. I don't notice myself rise and begin pacing since I'm too absorbed in my mother's words. The words float around me, embracing me and I imagine my mother's voice reading each entry aloud.

A small folded sheet falls from the back of the book and onto the floor. I pause, gently closing the book and putting it back on the table before bending down to grab the paper. The minute my fingers graze the folded page, I know that I was meant to find the folded note. The outside of the paper doesn't give anything away, so I unfold it as the old paper crinkles softly. My eyes follow the curve of my mother's script and a small gasp escapes my lips before I slide to the floor beside my bed, one hand covering my mouth, the other clutching the paper like it is a lifeline. It is a wonder that the paper stays intact and doesn't rip under the pressure of my shaking fingers.

My dearest Kat,

You must understand why I did what I did.

The visions…they became too much. I know you will eventually know exactly what I mean when I say this. This journal is all I have to give you that may help you. Most of the visions outlined in this book involve you. Every word I've written, use to your advantage. There are histories, family ties, and things that I have learned over the years that may be helpful for you. Katerina, you have so much ahead of you.

Remain strong. You will make it through. But please, please, remember where it is you come from. No matter what happens, you will always have a home to come back to. Or somewhere to escape to. Somewhere to run if it comes down to it. There are options made available to you.

I don't want to say too much, but you need to know that you are in danger. Everyone is in danger. Evil and darkness lurk in the shadows, slowly poisoning those he believes stand in his way. Be mindful of his trap—but his brother will light the way. Your whole life is going to be turned upside down, and it will become clear that you will need to fight for yourself and those you will swear to protect. You will survive, baby girl, but it will be difficult. You need to stay strong. In a way that I never could. I know that you will be able to do this. You are stronger than I ever was. And when the time comes, protect your own little girl better than I protected you.

You are my pride and joy. Both you and Andria. I hate that I had to go, but I couldn't handle it anymore. I wanted to remember you as you were, as children. I couldn't watch either of you fall victim to the visions in the way that I have.

All of my love,

Clara

She knew something was going to happen, yet she abandoned everything and everyone? How could she do this to us? I thought I had forgiven her for what she had done, but this brings all of the hurt and anger back. At least I have her journal, her words to comb through. Maybe then I can start to understand not only the woman that left us behind, but the visions as well. My fingers drop the letter, and when I remove my hand from my mouth, it comes back wet with tears.

I turn and fall back onto my bed, my hair fanned on the pillow beneath me with my arms spread wide. I lay like that a moment until the grief overwhelms me for the first time in a long time and my fingers cling to the pillow at the head of my bed and tug it into my chest as I curl around it on my side. I allow the tears to fall, letting time stretch past as I remember every detail of my mother. Her auburn hair, darker than mine, curled down her back, left loose more often than it was tied back, her blue-gray eyes that seemed to pierce through whatever or whoever was on the receiving end of her glare. She was bold, but quiet. She kept to herself and now I wonder if that was due to the visions. I miss the moments she would sit with me, her fingers running through my hair as I lay beside her. She would tell these stories of a city in another place. A city full of light and laughter. A place where women were talented and revered for those talents, a place of belonging and where all were welcome. She would talk about taking us there one day, when we were older, or old enough to understand. I never knew what she meant by that, but now I think I finally do. Is there somewhere out there where there are others? Somewhere I could learn about what it is I can do? Is this faint memory what she left for me, or was she trying to tell me without telling me? I wonder if these stories were something that she included in her journal for me, or if they were simply that; stories.

About an hour later, I climb out of bed and cross the room to the balcony door, open it and go out into the night. I almost forgot Andria was coming tonight so I can finally tell her the truth. She should be here anytime, but I look up at the sky and try to count all the stars to pass the time, before realizing it's impossible. I give up on even trying to count the twinkling lights above and instead look for shapes and pictures until I hear a voice behind me.

My name is said as a whisper, almost a haunted song in the

night. I turn, and freeze when I see Alaric. With the little light shining through my door, he looks hazy, not fully corporeal, yet his eyes, his blue eyes glitter like the stars above. His dimples flash with every movement of his mouth, the corners of which lift in a smile. Dark stubble outlines his strong jaw line, and his dark hair falls into his unnatural eyes. Tonight, he is wearing a dark green tunic, so dark it is almost black and white trousers. The outfit is embellished with gold; a gold chain that hangs from one of the buttons and disappears into a small pocket, likely holding a small pocketwatch.

He lingers in my line of sight and behind him I notice a grand ballroom filled with people dressed in finery. Alaric holds a hand out as if to offer a dance, and a small hand with a small crescent shaped scar takes his outstretched hand. I recognize it immediately. Peter and I had been exploring the woods when we were 9, and my dress had gotten caught in the jagger bushes. In the process of getting it unstuck, I caught my hand and sliced it up pretty good. I was a crying and blubbering mess, and Peter ended up having to cut my dress in order to get me free. I remember the pain, and the five tiny stitches that our nurse had to do to close the wound, causing the small crescent shape on the flesh between my thumb and pointer finger on my left hand.

The vision continues as Alaric pulls me to the dancefloor, and I watch as we dance. Spinning and twirling among the nobles, I seem happy. But just as quickly as he appears, the scene disappears. I feel my knees start to give in, but I will myself to remain strong and continue to watch.

I stare out into the dark, trying to find him. I hear him chuckle quietly and my eyes search desperately for him. He chuckles again and reemerges into the light, but this time I don't see him, I see a man who looks similar but slightly younger with darker, fiercer features. A feeling of despair, hopelessness, and suffering swarms me and the sounds of clanging swords and screams come with him. It becomes hard to breathe. The man disappears and Alaric returns, reaching a hand out to me, his face desperate. I back up toward my room and shut the door, leaving the visions on the other side.

My body grows heavy, and I barely make it to my bed before my knees give out. I sit there, on the edge of my bed, my thoughts circling around the images still playing in my mind. Alaric is definitely involved, but so is this second man. While the helplessness that radiates off of the version of Alaric in the visions, I am still unsure of the source of the destruction to come. Something about the second man makes me itch with a blackness that seeks for release and sends a shiver creeping down my spine. I don't like the feeling, but I know I have to go through with this engagement, even if it goes against everything I desire for myself. With a sigh, I head back out onto my balcony, knowing now that the vision has passed and no one waits for me in the darkness. I stand with my hands dangling in the air as I watch the stars above me. A chill shakes me and I turn to head inside to fetch my small white blanket that sits on the small chest just inside of the doorway. I cocoon myself in the blanket and pace across my balcony, back and forth, again and again, nervously waiting for Andria.

It is beyond time to tell her everything. I should have said something as soon as I found out about our mother, or at the very least after I started to have the visions myself. We have always told each other everything; every single thing that has happened in our lives. She is my best friend. I hug my small blanket closer around me, trying to squeeze everything back inside of me. This has to have been the longest day of my life. I know Andria was too young to remember much when everything happened with our mother, and even when our father told me about the visions and the suicide, she was still too young. I didn't want her to lose the innocence and love she felt in the memory of our mother. One of us deserves to remember her in this way, and not just harbor anger and resentment that we weren't enough for her. Tendrils of my hair that have broken free from my blanket cocoon tickle my cheek when the gentle breeze picks up. Even through the nerves and unease I feel surrounding me at every turn, the breeze is comforting. It is almost a whisper saying everything is going to be okay.

Eventually, I hear Andria's soft voice call me from inside. I release the breath I didn't realize I had begun to hold from the utterance of my name, and head through the door. My palms slide on the doorframe as I peer inside the open balcony door, and I unconsciously smooth them down my side. Andria has already made herself comfortable on my bed, and I can't help but smile despite the fluttering in my stomach and pounding of my blood in my ears. She lies sprawled on her back, her blonde hair fanning the bed underneath her. Her arms are spread out beside her, almost as if she is falling.

"Just make yourself comfortable," I laugh. She giggles and rises on her elbows, looking at me.

"What did you want to talk about? It sounded serious."

"That's because it is serious."

Andria rises, sitting up fully and crosses her legs in front of her without untangling them from her dress. She runs her fingers through her long straight hair, her fingers catching slightly on a couple of unnoticeable tangles, and I momentarily forget everything and instead think about all of the times we have had through the years. Andria smiles before asking, "Kat? What's going on?"

I sit beside her on the bed, rubbing my legs as I lean back against my headboard. My left hand feels along the bed beside me, searching until my fingertips feel the pillow, and pull it into my chest. I curl around it, drawing my knees up against the pillow tucked into my chest with my arms wrapped around it to keep the pillow in place. "Do you know how our mother died?"

Her head tilts slightly to the side. Her eyes narrow, the skin scrunching around them and her brows furrow as she blinks at the ceiling a few times while chewing on the inside of her cheek. "Everyone said she died in her sleep. That she simply never woke up. I have had a feeling that isn't exactly what happened, is it?" She looks at me from under her lashes and still picks at the ends of her hair. Her teeth sink into her lip, and sadness emanates from her, and I wish I didn't have to be the one to tell her everything.

"Do you know about her visions? How she saw and knew things that were going to happen?" I hug the pillow tighter and will myself to continue, steeling myself against the outlash that is sure to follow here soon. Andria shakes her head, her eyes widening briefly as if startled by the news. Her eyes flit from me to the door, then to the floor almost in denial, defeat, or avoidance. I get the sinking feeling that she may know more than she is admitting to. "She saw something or the visions became too much and she couldn't cope. Either way, she killed herself, Andi. Our father hid it from us because he didn't want us to know, and honestly, I don't blame him for that. It would have made the whole situation worse if we had known the truth considering how young we were." I know I can't downplay the situation or the hurt of knowing our mother felt that we would be better off without her, and I don't try to. Andria is going to have her own thoughts and feelings about it all, just as much as I do. I don't want to influence her feelings in any way, so I choke back any emotion of my own.

"How long have you known?" She sniffles, studying the ends of her hair in her hands- her way of putting up a wall to hide her true emotions. It is easy to see through her, it has been just the two of us for a very long time and I know her better than I know myself most days.

"Father told me a couple of years ago, when I hit the age where he was told the visions could start manifesting. He warned me that the visions could be inherited, and to be careful if I ever did start having them," I stop, looking toward my open balcony door. There is still a slight breeze coming in, and the sheer curtains dance slightly. The breeze also teases the fire in the fireplace, making it flicker and pop more fiercely than before. The air in the room is thick, though not from the heat of the fire, or any humidity that may be in the air, but simply from the tension between the two of us.

"You've kept this from me for years? You don't think I should have known about this?"

"I had no choice, Andi. Father made me swear." I glance back at her. Her arms are crossed over her chest and the betrayal is clear on her face; her eyes glisten with tears and her cheeks are flushed. I reach a hand out but pull back at the glint of steel in her eyes. I want to beg her to let me in, tell me what she is thinking. "Please understand. I wanted to tell you sooner."

"Then why are you telling me now?" She unfolds her arms and plays with the ends of her hair again. It is a nervous habit she picked up a few years back. I know she thinks it makes her appear nonchalant, but I know she is just putting up a front. Her jaw clenches and unclenches, and her nostrils flare with the effort of holding back tears. She blinks hard, and I know that she is hurt and angry but is somehow maintaining her composure. I continue to watch her as she stares at her hair in her hands. She definitely knows something more than she is saying.

"Because it is happening to me. You need to know that it could happen to you too." My voice breaks and I look away, my eyes burning, but I quickly glance back, waiting for her to look at me. I let my tears fall silently, refusing to crumble to pieces even though it is all I've wanted to do today. These visions are costing me everything I have ever wanted. I wish I didn't have this burden, but I find myself hoping even more that Andria never has to face them.

She freezes, dropping her hair before her eyes meet mine. "Wait, you are having visions too?"

I nod, burying my face in the pillow. I feel the bed dip as she moves closer and puts her hand on my shoulder, rubbing comforting little circles into my flesh. The tears slip into the pillow, and I take a few shuddering breaths to settle myself.

"For how long?" she whispers, her voice has a hard edge to it but I ignore it, thinking it is the lingering hurt and anger.

I prop my chin on the pillow, my face splotchy and swollen from the tears. "A few days before Peter came back. So, maybe three or four months?" I look at her, and I can tell she is deep in thought. She looks worried, her brows furrow and she chews on her bottom lip, but she doesn't voice her concerns aloud.

"Does father know?"

"Of course, I went to him the morning after my first vision. I didn't want to keep it from him, not after everything he went through with our mother." I watch her nod and she continues to rub my shoulder absentmindedly. "There is something you should see." I rise from the bed and open the chest at the foot of my bed, pull out the red leather book, climb back into the bed, and I hand the book to her. She takes it, her fingers brushing mine as her eyes ask what it is. I nod for her to open it. When she does, her response is similar to mine when I realized whose book it was. Her mouth opens slightly, and her hands tremble, the book shakes slightly in her grasp.

"This was hers, wasn't it?" she asks as she slowly flips through the pages. "Where did you get this?" She looks up at me, her eyes shining with unshed tears. I know the emotions she must be feeling because I felt them too. Every last one of them.

"I found it this evening. I'm guessing she wrote down what she saw in order to figure things out. I assume that was father's intention in leaving it for me; he thought it might help to do the same."

She looks back down at the journal, carefully caressing the pages. A tear streams down her face, and I tear up as well. If our mother left this for me, what did she leave for her? I rest my head on her shoulder and silently cry about the visions, our mother, and the twist of fate that has become my life. We read through some of the entries, acquainting ourselves with the woman we didn't know; the version of our mother that was hidden from us. We comfort each other without speaking, and eventually we both fall asleep, our mother's book lying on the bed between us.

CHAPTER 3

I wish Joel would just leave me alone. He thinks I need a break from everything, but how can I take a break when I can't stop seeing death and destruction? He wants me to let go and try to move past everything, but he doesn't know anything that he is talking about. Maybe if he was in my head he would actually understand. But until then, he won't. He says I'm going crazy, but I'm not. There's no way that he even knows what crazy is. My own mother went crazy in the end, even with the training she went through she couldn't control anything that was happening and now neither can I, but then again I never had the control that she did.

No. He is wrong. I'm not going crazy. I am not my mother. I am not going to be anything like her. I can barely be in the same room as Joel right now. I can't. I just can't.

But my girls, my beautiful girls, they are all I have left that makes any sense. If I could wrap myself in them and never deal with anything else again I would.

I just don't know what to do anymore.

What if Joel is right?

I continue to lie in bed, staring at the ceiling when I wake. Andria left in search of food not too long ago. I think about last night, and how well she seemed to take the news. The only thing she seemed taken aback by was my having visions. How did she phrase it? 'You are having them too'. Almost as if she, too, were experiencing them. I sit up quickly. Is she having visions too? Why wouldn't she tell me if she was? I jump, my heart leaping to my throat and my head whips toward the door when someone knocks. I slowly climb out of bed, crossing my arms over my chest and realizing I fell asleep in yesterday's clothes, and head to the door.

"Father?" He is certainly not who I expected to see standing in my doorway.

"Katerina, may I come in and speak to you for a moment?" I nod and open the door wide enough for him to come through, then I close it behind him. He takes a seat and gestures for me to do the same. I curl into my favorite chair by the fireplace, drawing my feet up underneath me, tilted sideways slightly to face my father in the chair catty cornered to mine. "Katerina. I understand this must be very difficult for you," He starts, his eyes drilling into me. I am not sure what he expects from me, so I nod and he continues, "I wish there was something I could do. I know you care deeply for Peter, and that is all I've ever wanted for you, but I hope you can learn to care for Alaric. From what I know, he and his family are good people. He was raised right, and I know he will treat you as an equal."

He looks sad, regretful. He refuses to meet my gaze, and instead looks at his hands. The hands that have helped guide me over the years. The hands that held mine when we would walk in the woods or explore the shore, and the same hands that will give me away when I marry in a few months. His face is drawn, and I can't help but notice how much older he looks lately. The lines that mar his complexion seem more pronounced, deeper somehow than they did even yesterday— as if he is feeling the weight of my visions and the choices that have been made for me, and he wishes there was something else he could offer. His sandy hair is starting to go white at the temples, and his normally close shaven beard is longer today and offers small speckles of white to offset the reddish blonde. I wish he would say anything that would imply I even had a choice, but it is clear that he won't and knows that I am at an impasse. There is no going back, only forward.

I lower my head, allowing the silence to linger for a few

moments before softly speaking. "Alaric is the man from my visions." I watch him from below my eyelashes, wondering if he had already put two and two together, or at least had some suspicion. He nods but doesn't say anything, which is exactly the reaction I was expecting.

He didn't seem surprised when Alaric showed up, or put up much of a fight when it came down to it. Did he know all of this would happen? That I would fall in love then have to sacrifice it to change the outcome of the visions? He wouldn't do that to his own child, would he? My mind whirls at the thought, and I mentally shake it from my mind, and focus on the conversation at hand. Alaric is the key to everything, and based on last night's vision, I am almost positive he is the answer. My mouth opens and words pour out on their own accord, so I plow forward, "but I don't know for sure if he is the cause of the war, or the key to stopping it, but I believe he is the key to figuring it out because of how central he is to everything that I have seen." I explain some of the things that I have seen, and express my thoughts regarding what I interpret them to mean. He listens, and adds insight when I leave things open ended, and I begin to feel a little more comfortable with the way things are heading, but I still heat in frustration about the marriage arrangement and the depth of what is going on. "I want out; I don't want this."

Nodding, he states, "I understand your resentment, but it is something you need to work past. There is nothing you can do about it but try and stop whatever your visions seem to be warning you against. Maybe this is your destiny," he pauses, glancing at the leather bound book on my bed. "has the journal helped?"

His eyes meet mine, but I lower my gaze. I hadn't considered this being my destiny, and I'm not sure I want it to be. I shrug, then speak, "It has helped some. If not with the visions themselves, at least it is helping me understand her and who she was." I let that linger in the air a moment, and taste the metallic tang of regret and pain before I continue, "I found a letter that was hidden in the back of the book. It was addressed to me." I wait, wanting to see if my father will admit to knowing about it. His silence and his lowered gaze is all the confirmation I need.

Even though he knows about the letter, I plow into the contents; "She warned that I was in danger and that I needed to be careful. I didn't get much else out of it, beside the knowledge that I needed to be strong, but that I would survive whatever is coming. I just wish she was around to tell me that herself." I stare into the flames, watching them lick the wood, curling upwards before disappearing into smoke that rises into the chimney. Roughly wiping away a stray tear with the back of my hand, I think about my mother. I picture her laughing, she used to laugh so freely when we were young, throwing her head back and I remember how her eyes would sparkle with the joy, the freeness she would feel in that moment. Her laughter had been contagious. I didn't realize at the time how dark she had become the older I became. She lost that freeness about a year before she died.

"I wish she were here too." His voice is soft but gravely, sounding almost broken. Part of me wonders if he really does wish she were here, or if he is just saying that for my sake. He never did move on from her or remarry, and I never questioned it. I watch as he rubs his hands together, cupping them slightly as he leans forward to rest his elbows on his thighs. He looks at me, tilting his head enough to catch my eye. I meet his gaze, and he clears his throat, the sound sharp but makes the point I think he is aiming for. "I just want you to be careful. I don't want to lose you. Come to me if anything changes." He pushes to his feet and rests a hand on my shoulder on his way out. I turn to watch him go, but speak once his hand is on the doorknob.

"I'm worried about Andria. She," I search for the right words, "she seemed to know about the visions. I think she might have them too." My eyes flutter and my tongue darts out to moisten my lips.

He freezes one hand on the knob, the other by his side as he is half turned toward me. His eyes are dark, and I can't quite read his face. "I can't lose you both. Please talk to her. See if you can find out. Please." He sounds broken, defeated.

"I will."

He nods, and slowly walks out of the door, softly closing the door behind him. I begin to wonder if he does know what my mother saw that pushed her over the edge and if that is why he is so worried about us.

Later that afternoon, with my mind full of my own memories mixed with the visions from my mother's journal, I find solace in my garden at my usual perch at the fairy fountain. The chilly sea air helps soothe my uneasiness and anxiety surrounding my path when I see Andria stroll through the flowers just starting to come back from the winter cold. She wanders aimlessly, lost in her own thoughts but eventually makes her way over to me, carefully following the little path that we designed when they put the garden in when we were young. It curves one way then another, almost a maze without walls. It moves much like the waves as they crash against the shore. I can't help but grin as she breaks through the outer rim of flowers surrounding the fountain. She walks on her tiptoes. She has always done that, and none of us have really known why. It is just something that makes her who she is. Watching her tiptoe her way through the garden sets me at ease; at least something hasn't changed.

She sits down next to me on the stone outer rim of the fountain. For all of the memories and tears we shared the night before, she seems happy, but then again, she has never not been. Her green eyes are our father's as is her pinstraight sandy colored hair. I used to be envious of how straight her hair is before I learned to love my auburn curls. I look out towards the depths of the garden. There aren't very many animals or anything out, but it is still a little too chilly for them to run around. They will start to come out in a couple of weeks as the weather finally warms. Behind me, the fountain's gentle bubbling reminds me of days I would spend out here with our mother. She used to say that the fairy that sits at the top of the fountain was sent to watch over us, to make sure we were safe. It is a comforting thought, and I can't help but to wonder if she is watching now, and has been all of these years.

Neither Andria or I speak for a while, and I'm okay with that. She knows everything and is well aware that I don't want to go through with marrying Alaric, and that I want the certainty and life that Peter offers. She is so sure of what is going to happen, and so sure of herself and that is something I wish I could say about myself. I wish I knew who I am supposed to be, I only know this isn't it. I only know that I want to stand up and fight, but I don't know how or where to start. I watch as she looks out toward the path to the sea, almost as if she can see the ships in the harbor and they call out to her.

"Do you ever want to run away?" She avoids my gaze. It's obvious that she is hiding something, and I don't know how I didn't see it before.

I study her for a moment, wondering what she wants to run away from. "All the time."

She nods, then rises to her feet. She starts to walk away, but I call out, "Hey Andi? Do you have them too?" My voice is soft, almost as if I am trying to soothe a cornered animal. I don't want to spook her, and make her run, but I need to know. I need to know I am not alone, and I don't want her to go through it alone either.

She glances down at her feet, still not meeting my gaze, and I feel her uneasiness like a wave crashing into me as it comes into shore. She continues to stand there a few minutes, not answering, but not running either. I think she is trying to sort through her thoughts, but she doesn't give any indication of what is going on behind those green eyes of hers. She finally meets my gaze, and my heart sinks. Her eyes are big and her mouth is slightly parted in fear. She gives a very small nod of her head. She reaches a hand out to me, and I take it in mine and squeeze it tightly.

"Mom was right. You will survive what is to come, but nothing is going to pan out in the way that you expect. I cannot say more. I can't—" she breaks off with a shiver, and she looks back over her shoulder towards the harbor. "I wish I could tell you to board a ship and not look back. But things need to pan out the way that they will. It has been months of this. Months." Her voice is quiet. I can barely hear her over the bubbling of the fountain. Her head tilts back watching the clouds above us. The stone beneath me digs into my palms and I release the rock with which I have started to cling to unconsciously. "I thought I was crazy, that I was sick. To know that I am not alone, that this isn't all in my head, eases some of that fear, but Kat," she meets my gaze again and squeezes my hand tightly before releasing it and letting her hand fall to her side limply. "I am so sorry for everything. For absolutely everything." Her voice cracks, and I hear her sniffle as I start to push myself off of the stone to come to her, to ask her to explain further, but she leaves as quickly as she came. I let her walk away, and I lose myself in the footsteps that she takes. Months? She has been having them for months? What is coming? If I only knew, maybe I can make a difference, change something sooner.

Peter is waiting for me at the docks when I arrive. The sun has dipped below the horizon, the sky still clinging to the pinkish purple hue left behind. The sea is calm, and the sky is clear of the few scattered clouds that lingered overhead this afternoon. The ships of the naval fleet creak as they bob in the gentle waves entering the harbor. There are sailors milling about, calling out to each other in camaraderie, and nod at me as I pass. I know they will not mention to my father that I am here, they stopped reporting my whereabouts a few years ago when I came of age. For that, I am grateful. These men treat me as Lady of the house; In their eyes, I hold as much power over them as my father. He was gone so often when Andria and I were young, and these men watched us turn from girls to women, and they began to feel more like family than not. My footsteps echo on the old, saltridden, wooden planks anchored a foot or so above the water. Each step feels like a funeral knell, signaling the ending of Peter and I, and I hate every one I take.

Peter waits at the end of the dock, looking out at the empty sea in front of him with his hands dangling loosely at his sides. There is a small fishing boat bobbing to his left, and nothing but the ocean in front of him. The air is full of the smell of brine and clean air, and I breathe deeply until I can taste the salt. I pause beside him, glancing up. His face is tear-stained, and he refuses to meet my gaze. He very rarely shows any kind of weakness, but everything with Alaric has put a strain on us, and I wish there was something that either of us could do to avoid letting each other go. I want more than anything to confess everything about the visions to him. He has always been my one person outside of Andria that I could tell everything to. The one person that I could trust to hold my secrets and bare my soul to. His hand finds mine and he holds it tight, his fingers twining with mine as he brings it up to his lips to leave a kiss on my knuckles. The touch of his lips causes the flutter to reignite in my belly.

"I leave tomorrow." His voice is deeper than normal, strained with the deep seated emotion that drains his face and makes him blink hard and glare out at the ocean in front of us.

"But—" I begin, but he continues, cutting off my reply.

"I tried talking to your father and Alaric, but no one would listen. I don't think there is anything that will change their minds. I don't know what else to do," his voice finally breaks, and his face crumples as he breaks down in tears again. I turn fully to face him, and hold him close. He buries his face in my neck as he clings to me. We cling to each other, fracturing beneath the weight of what we are forced to let go. Tomorrow? It's too soon.

"I can't do this. I can't just let you go. I won't." I whisper, tasting the salt of my own tears intermixed with the salt in the air. My hair flutters against my cheek, and I long to board the boat beside us and disappear with Peter by my side.

Peter lifts his face out of my neck and kisses me hard. The absolute need that consumes me ignites in my core, and I can't help but to kiss him back just as fiercely. He crushes me to him one arm wrapped around my waist while the other bunches my dress and grabs my behind, and my fingers curl in his hair, holding him to me and pulling at the tendrils. I bite his lip and he gasps but recaptures my mouth as he lifts me up, and I wrap my legs around his waist. I feel him against me, and I know I should stop this, but I can't. I don't want to stop.

Peter steps back with me in his arms, and turns to the small fishing boat to his left and he easily steps down into the boat from the dock while clutching me to him. I need him like I need air. He spins us around, and my back meets with something solid. He keeps me pinned there, my legs around him, and he is pressed against me; holding me against the door with his hips as his hands rest on the door on either side of my head. His mouth recaptures mine, our tongues battling for control. My hands remain locked in his hair as I tighten my legs around him, grinding against him slightly. The fire burning within me rises further to envelop me completely. He quickly grabs me once more, and opens the door behind me, carrying me into the small cabin.

Next thing I know, I am lying on a bed and Peter looks down at me. The cabin is small; empty aside from a small chest at the foot of the bed that takes up a bulk of the room. The door is closed behind Peter, and I can't help but bite my lip as I look up at him. My desperation for him blinds all reason, and I can sense a similar desperation from him. My fingers trail up my body to my bodice. It has a front laced corset, and I gently, slowly tug on the strings to release the tie. Peter moistens his lips and watches my every move. The corset loosens as does the dress and I can easily slide it off of my shoulders. They slide down my shoulders as I rise to a seated position, my eyes never leaving Peter's face. The sleeves and my dress slips down little by little until it pools at my waist leaving me bare to him from the waist up. Peter swallows hard as his eyes trail my body. He swallows again, and quickly removes his shirt, his muscles rippling in the process.

He takes a step towards me, until he stands between my knees. He puts a finger under my chin and lifts my face to look up at him. He bites his lower lip and slowly lowers his lips to mine. The kiss is soft, more of a caress than anything. I grab his hips and my touch is his undoing. His hands are in my hair, and his body presses into mine, pushing me down into the bed. He holds himself above me on his elbows, but our bodies press against each other, and the friction of his skin against mine burns me even hotter. My legs wrap around his waist, my dress bunched up around my waist. He grinds himself against me as he kisses me harder, full of every desire and need we have for each other.

He pulls away slightly, breathing hard. "I love you, more than anything." He nuzzles my neck, leaving trailing kisses there and down my collarbone. Venturing into new territory. I try to catch my breath, but find it difficult with each new place his lips find.

"Peter," I breathe, my hands fisting the blankets beneath me. He trails down my chest, my stomach, kissing around my belly button as he looks up at me beneath hooded eyes. I arch my back, throwing my head back as his hands roam across my breasts, palming them gently and rolling each nipple as he continues kissing down my body. He releases my breasts, and grabs my dress from around my waist, pulling it off of me completely. I lie there, completely bare to him.

"Kat, do you want me to stop?" Peter asks, watching me, breathing hard.

"Don't stop," I breathe, gripping the blankets beneath me as he obliges. My body ignites as we connect and our bodies become one. We lose ourselves in each other; living in each breath, moan, and whispered caress.

I pull my dress back on, tying the corseted front as Peter pulls his shirt back on.

"Peter," I turn to face him. "What does this mean? Do we go to my father? He can't let me marry Alaric now."

He runs his fingers through his hair, thinking. "Alaric will not let this be the end of it. He will retaliate against me in some way for 'taking what is his.' I've seen him do it before." His eyes meet mine, and I must have a look on my face because he comes to me and cups my face in his hands. "Maybe I am wrong, but I can't risk you. I can't…" he trails off, his voice growing soft and sad. His eyes fill with tears as he searches my face. "Katerina, I am unbelievably lucky to be loved by you. Tonight was a dream. One that I wish we could linger in. I would give anything. Anything if we could stay here, sail away and forget everything," he pauses, choking back his tears. "but we can't."

He kisses me long and hard. He breaks away, kisses me gently on the top of my head, lingering a moment there before pulling away. His thumb rubs against my cheek before he releases me and with a look full of longing, regret, and unbelievable pain, he opens the door and leaves me standing there alone. The air is cold without him there. I choke on a sob. He is just giving up on us? He said he was going to fight for me, where is that fight now?

"Peter, wait!" I choke, trying to call out to him as I rush out of the door and onto the bow of the small boat. The boat and the dock are empty. Peter is gone. He left me. I stand there, shattering into a million pieces that I have no clue how to put back together.

When I hear the commotion downstairs early the next morning, I know it means Peter is leaving, and I regret not running to my father after he left me on the boat last night and force him to release me from my engagement to Alaric. Instead, I devoured entries in my mother's journal trying to find a way out, a way to run to Peter and leave all of this behind. At the very least I should have gone to Andria to get answers from what she knows, but instead I found nothing in the memories laid out in the journal, and am stuck in this engagement to a man that I vow I will never love. Never in the way that consumes me. After watching Peter simply leave last night, I won't put myself in a position to shatter like that again. I know I have to let Peter go, but I can't. He is a part of me, now and forever, and nothing will ever change that. I have to see him, have to talk to him one last time. This can't be how we end.

I bolt out of bed, grab clothes, pull them on, run a brush through my hair, and run out the door and into the hustle-bustle of moving people. The hallways are filled with servants carrying trunks and Peter's things out of the house, onto the front lawn, and to the stable where the carriage awaits. My eyes search frantically for him, darting one way then the next. The front lawn is empty aside from a few of the servants coming back in the house from taking belongings to the carriage. I scan the cobbled path that leads to the stable, and start to make my way in that direction when I finally spot Peter. In my desperation, I missed Alaric standing against the faded stone of the house until he steps in front of me and I lose sight of Peter. I rise to my tiptoes and try to look over or around Alaric, craning to the side, but he moves with me and I growl, my fingernails dig into my palms as my hands fist tightly.

"What are you doing down here?" His voice is gruff, and I glare at him, without responding, and his brows furrow as he frowns. "You are here for Peter," he snaps, his words biting. Why does Peter get under his skin so much? Why is Alaric so possessive over me? He doesn't even *know* me! "Why? Why make the break worse on him?"

"Not now, Alaric. Please." My shoulder breaks through his wide footed stance as I push my way past, making him take a step back all the while staring at me bewildered, but I don't have eyes for him, and pay him very little attention as I ignore him calling after me and rush to where I last saw Peter. The world around me blurs as I turn full circle, searching. Where is he? How did he disappear? How do we even have so many servants? The house can't possibly hold them all. Then I spot him at the far end of the stable illuminated by a ray of sunlight that escapes the rafters above. He is talking to the carriage driver, and isn't aware of my presence. I make it four strides through the stables when Alaric blocks me again. My hands raise from my sides and work themselves into my hair as I snap, "Alaric!"

He holds his hands up defensively, "Think of what you are doing. You're just going to make it worse for him. Just stay away." He shakes his head, and I am baffled by the arrogance that emanates off of him. I scoff, leaning back slightly while shaking my head, my lip rising in a snarl of defiance.

"I'm allowed to say goodbye."

"Not if I say you can't."

"Who the hell do you think you are? You may be the heir to the throne and outrank me, but if you want me as your wife, you need to get over yourself. You don't own me, and you never will. Now move!" I try to get around him, only to have him grab me by the wrist, pulling me against him while pinning my arms by my side. I struggle, bucking like a wild horse in his arms, squirming and doing whatever I can to get away. I see red, and my breath comes faster and shallower.

"Let me go! Peter!" I cry out. Peter spins on his heel, his hair whirling around to hit him lightly in the face as he searches for me. "Peter!" I cry again, and time seems to slow. His eyes finally find mine, and the pain that flares in his eyes nearly kills me. "Alaric! Let me go," I sob, my voice hoarse and guttural, otherworldly. I see flashes of myself in a similar hold, but one made of rope rather than flesh. My own cry lingers in the air as I watch Peter push his way through a crowd, fighting his way through the throng to get to me. A steel ringing fills the air, and before I can see me, I am transported back to the present and find myself hanging limply in Alaric's arms while I stare through my tears and tendrils of curls that have escaped into my face, at the one and only man that belongs to my heart.

"No. See? You're only making it worse for him." The servants finish loading the carriages, and Peter nods absently as the coachman murmurs something to him before climbing onto his perch at the front of the carriage. Peter lingers, looking torn; like he wants to stay and rush to me, but knows that he can't. He ducks his head, breaking free of my gaze before he glances up, and I watch as he lifts his chin, and takes those few steps to the carriage.

"No. No. No. I have to say goodbye. I have to tell him—" My voice disappears and I watch as Peter climbs into the carriage and the door closes with a click that slices through the air in a way that solidifies the last words he uttered last night; *we can't.* He left me alone, and as the carriage starts to leave, and Alaric finally lets me go, I sob as I take the last few steps to the road before my legs give out and I collapse into a heap, sobbing, staring after the carriage. Splintering apart in ways that I know will be irreparable.

CHAPTER 4

My mother used to have me sit with her and practice skills that she learned in Aouela.

Focus. Breathe deep, feel each breath deep in your belly. Clear your mind and close your eyes.

Good.

Now imagine yourself outside of yourself, standing at the other end of the room. Send your mind there, into this image of yourself.

This is where I would always fail. Every. Single. Time.

I could never replicate what she could do.

When it came to controlling the visions, well that, I could do. In the beginning anyway. It is the same thing as before. Deep, controlled breathing, clear mind, and focus. Call the vision to you. You are stronger than the images you receive. They do not control you, you are the source. The powerful one.

God, is it a lot harder than it sounds.

For the second time in the past few days, I find myself in my father's study. He is seated at the monstrous desk in front of the fireplace, shuffling papers with different dignitary seals plastered to the envelopes. The blood red seals are the only spots of color on the desk. His hands are deft and quick, but his eyes linger on each thing his fingers discard before going to the next. He sighs, frustrated. My father seems to be looking for one parchment in particular and doesn't seem like he is going to talk before he finds it. Rather than curl into my normal large chair by the hearth, I pace in front of the fireplace, wringing my hands in front of me. The repetitive rhythm of my footsteps help calm and soothe my nerves, but my father's silence nearly unravels it.

"Father, you told me if I ever needed to talk about what was going on that I could come to you. Is that still the case?" I pick at my fingernails, pausing my pacing long enough to watch him. He pauses in his shuffling, glancing up at me in the process.

"Of course. What happened?" He studies me, his eyes crinkling into a frown at my red and tearstained face. He puts the papers down on the desk, giving me his full attention.

I twist my hands, trying to figure out what to say. My eyes take in the room around me, and linger on the map table before glancing down at my hands while I nervously pick at my nails. It is a bad habit I picked up pretty soon after my mother died.

"Katerina?"

I continue to look at my hands, picking out the scars left there over the years. I hope I am not making a huge mistake in confessing the depth of my relationship with Peter. I breathe in deeply and glance once more at the map table. I know Peter's territory lies at the far end of the country within the dense forests and mountains to the north. Not that it matters now, unless the truth makes my father reconsider my engagement to Alaric, then it makes all the difference. I look away from the map table and looking beyond my father I study the tapestry. The giant flower in the middle is a rose surrounded by thorny vines. It reminds me of my mother, and I find comfort in it. I lose myself in thoughts of her. Her laugh, the feeling of her fingers in my hair, the softness of her voice. I don't want to abandon those memories when I leave because she is in everything that surrounds this place. The sea, the breeze, even the house. She, or at least the thought of the woman she was, gives me the courage to speak up.

"Call Peter back here. Send a rider after him, tell him you have reconsidered and that I will not be marrying Alaric." I finally focus on my father, whose eyes I have felt like a burn since I first spoke.

He shakes his head and begins to turn back to the papers on his desk. "Kat, you know that isn't possible. We have already had this conversation." I know he is tired of this being brought up time and again, so I decide now is not the time to beat around the bush. No matter what I say, I feel like it is futile. He has made his mind up, and there is very little I can do or say to sway that decision.

"Peter and I were intimate." My eyes bore into him, begging him to look at me, to do or say something, anything to indicate that this puts an end to Alaric and me. Rather than react in the way I had thought or hoped he would, his head dips and I hear nothing but the whooshing of him releasing a heavy sigh, and the slight flutter of the paper tickling the desk in response to the sudden wind.

"It is over, is it not?" He glances up, and when I don't respond he purses his lips and continues anyway, "He left. Indicating that it is. It does not matter. Nothing changes. You need to let Peter go." He looks pointedly at me, and my blood boils as my body grows warm. My breath comes faster and I clench my teeth in order to refrain from saying anything further. I spin on my heel, but he doesn't stop me or say anything further until the door creaks open and one foot crosses the threshold. "Oh, Katerina? You are expected to leave for Aurellia City tomorrow with the prince. Make sure you take anything you may want with you, as it is unlikely that you will return." I don't honor him with a response other than the door slamming shut behind me.

Thankfully the hallways are empty on my way into the garden. I stride through the property and down to the docks. I have no real reason to be here, but I go to the end of the middle tongue of the three pronged dock. It looks exactly the same as last night, except one essential component is missing. The one piece that will haunt me and own every part of me, regardless if I marry another. The fishing boat bobs wistfully beside me, and before I let what rage consumes me fade, I jump down into the boat, untie the lashings, and open the sails before pushing the small boat off of the old planks where it was tied.

The boat floats back and it doesn't take long to hear the wind catch on the sails, snapping them open. I stand at the tiller, waiting for the boat to start creeping forward. Living on the sea and at the port has its perks; Ian took it upon himself to teach both Andria and I to sail one of the times my father had gone to Aurellia City. Ian taught us a lot when my father wasn't around. He wanted us to be prepared in case something were to happen and we needed to fend for ourselves.

I am not sure if my father even knows that we know how to sail, but he made sure we at least knew how to swim. The small boat battles its way forward through the waves to the open sea, but not before I hear my name in a voice that I don't know well, but well enough that I groan inwardly and beg the boat to move faster. The waves that looked gentle from the dock try to push the boat back toward the shore and dock where Alaric waits, but the wind works in my favor and I manage to get maybe ten feet from the dock. I glance up, thanking my mother for helping push the boat along. She must know I need this, that I need to get away.

Knowing the layout of the country, I need to travel up the coast past Kilburn, and the rivers will eventually lead up to the pass between the Kingdom of Modiva and Lightspire, our northernmost territory, and Peter's home. I don't have any of my belongings, but I can make it there and figure out the rest. Plus, who knows what is in the room behind me. Hopefully there are clothes, supplies, food.

There is a faint splash, and I leave the tiller to peer over the side of the boat. No one is on the dock now, but Alaric's breast stroke is something to admire. He cuts through the waves with ease, and arrives at the boat in minutes. He grabs onto the rope net that hangs on the side of the boat, and hoists himself up and over the side of the boat with a grunt. He lies on the deck, sprawled out in a way that is like a star. He breathes deep, hard, like he pushed himself to the limit to reach me.

I stand with my hands on my hips, looking down on him. He meets my gaze, and I watch him take in my appearance. My hair is a disheveled mess, tendrils have long since fallen from the plait down my back, but my demeanor is far less disheveled— I am surefooted on the deck of the boat bobbing in the waves that are getting larger. We have moved a little farther out to sea than wanted in a boat this size so I dart across the small deck, sidestepping the man taking up half of it, and turn the tiller to the right in order to turn the boat.

I remain there, watching our progress, ducking under the sail as it turns with the tiller; sweeping over the boat to reach the other side. Once we are aimed for the mouth of the river and I see my home pass by on the shore to our right, I turn to face Alaric who has now at least risen to stand leaned against the starboard side. His pants cling to the muscles in his legs, and his tunic is like a second skin. He is powerfully built, his muscles demonstrate that much. As much as I wish I didn't, I can appreciate the view.

"Why are you here, Alaric?" I keep both feet firmly planted, but cross my arms over my chest. My hair floats around me in the wind, and I can't help but feel the most at home here in this moment that I have in my own house.

"You know how to sail?" He doesn't move, just continues to watch me with a small smile.

I roll my eyes. "Yes, I was taught a few years ago." We bob again with another wave, the gentle rocking soothing. "Why. Are. You.

Here?" My eyes burn holes into his tough exterior, and I start to see through the façade that he puts up to the world. He is truly just as lost as the rest of us.

"I don't know why, but you knowing how to sail surprises me. I wonder what other skills you have hiding up your sleeve." He glances back at me, taking in my crossed arms and unwavering glare, and releases a sigh, the smile falling from his face as he ducks his head and rubs the back of it with a hand. "Look, Katerina, I'm sorry. I shouldn't have stopped you. I was wrong, and I'm extremely sorry." I barely acknowledge his apology, and instead continue to glare at him. He clears his throat and continues, "He probably needed the goodbye and you probably did too. I was afraid that you were going to leave with him. I not only denied you the chance, but I also denied it to him too. I know you aren't thrilled with the idea of marrying me when you've basically been engaged to Peter your entire life. I know that, and I'm sorry for the way things are turning out."

He glances out at the open sea and the mouth of the river creeping closer. "I think that is why you are here on this boat. You want out. You want to leave." He looks back to me, and I see the vulnerability, the young man that he really is. I see someone that is just as terrified as I am, and just looking for a companion that they can trust and be themself around. "My father bade me to marry, told me it was well past time. That if I didn't marry within the next few months, or at least show I was engaged, I would have to abdicate my throne to my younger brother. I couldn't do that. I was raised for this. I knew all of the ladies at court would have loved to be my bride, but I didn't want any of them. I wanted someone that I knew would understand responsibility, or at least know the weight of bearing a title. You are one of the few daughters that my father's councilmen have. I decided it had to be you since your father is one of the more powerful members, and has the biggest territory. I truly am sorry that things panned out this way. I didn't have very many options."

He drops his gaze, and I understand now why he chose me. I reach my hand behind me and move the tiller further to the right, making the sails move once more, and the boat veers away from the river and back towards the harbor. I am still angry about this morning, and his lack of respect for my wishes, but I understand where he was coming from. He needs this marriage in order to keep his throne.

I stare out into the night, envious of the peace the sea air and the noise of the waves on the side of the boat provide. Although, it does help clear the mind enough to think. While this marriage isn't what I want, and doesn't seem to be what either of us want, it could hold an answer to the visions. Alaric doesn't need to know of the visions, at least not right away, if ever. He needs to gain my trust, and, so far, that isn't going well. It's quiet, aside from the usual sounds from the sea, the gentle lapping of the water on the sides of the boat, and the soft creaking of the wood underfoot. Alaric is quiet, and for that I am thankful. He must realize I needed a minute to adjust my perspective and wrap my head around everything that he has told me.

"I apologize for behaving as I have. I can't imagine how that may have made you feel." I watch him as he watches the water below us. He doesn't say anything, and for once, I wish he would. "I am sorry that this isn't exactly what you wanted either. But I am willing to aim towards friendship before we aim for more."

"I'm sorry as well. I didn't realize that you were engaged when I made my decision and notified my father of my intentions. I swear. I wouldn't have made that choice if I had known." He scratches his jaw, and I hear the faint noise of his fingers on his stubble. His eyes don't meet mine, and I wonder if he is telling the truth as he continues, "I know it doesn't help anything, but I am sorry, Katerina."

"You don't need to keep apologizing. I understand," I pause

before continuing, "call me Kat," I murmur, still watching him. His eyes meet mine finally, and we smile.

"Kat,"He grins widely, and pushes off of the side and takes the few steps over to me and reaches out his hand. I take it, and he firmly shakes it, adding, "Alaric, or Ric. And friends is a great place to start."

His fingers are warm on mine, and mine linger in his a moment longer before I gently pull away and rest the hand on the tiller beside me.

"So, tell me everything there is to know, everything that makes you 'Kat'."

"Ask away," I laugh, shaking my head. I didn't think we would end up here this soon, but we have nothing but time to kill until we reach the dock, and no better time to get acquainted.

"Favorite color?" He lowers himself to sit on the deck, one knee drawn up in front of him with his arm resting on it while his back rests against the side of the boat.

"Green, but not super bright green, more the deep green the sea turns during a storm. You?"

He thinks a moment before answering, "Probably a deep red, like a burgundy. Favorite time of day?"

Now this one is hard. There are many reasons to like all of them. Then it hits me. "Dusk, or early night. I always feel myself drawn to the sunset and the stars as they start to pop up in the sky, because no matter where I end up, it always is the same. I like to think that my mother is up there among the stars, watching over my sister and I."

His eyes watch the same sky I just mentioned above us, and he looks wistful, sad, as if remembering someone he too has lost.

"How old were you when your mother passed?" his voice is

quiet, full of emotion and empathy.

"Thirteen. She went to bed one night, and just never woke up." The practiced lie rolls off of my tongue, and I swallow hard against its acidity. My eyes flutter to the sky for a minute, but find his again when he tells me about his own mother.

"I was seven. She got sick, and never recovered."

We share a knowing glance and nod in understanding as we have experienced each other's pain in a way that no one who hasn't lost a parent could truly understand. It is the start of something between us, and while it is terrible that this is the thing that gives us a solid foundation, it is something that puts us on a level playing field. The waves work their magic alongside the wind. I turn the boat towards the middle dock where we originated, and Alaric helps tie it down once we arrive. His fingers brush mine and our eyes meet over the rope. I clear my throat and pull away, dropping my gaze to look at the wood of the dock at eye level. I rise to my feet, and climb out of the boat and stand on the dock where Peter left me.

Alaric climbs easily out of the boat, standing beside me and looking up at my family home. "It is very beautiful here," he turns to look at me, "very beautiful."

I bite my lip, not wanting to acknowledge the compliment, but feel that I should be open to giving whatever this is a chance. He is proving to not be what I expected, which makes this union more complicated than I anticipated. I glance up at Alaric, allowing a small smile before I extend a hand in front of me indicating we should head back to the house.

I start walking with him falling into step beside me. Our footsteps echo on wooden planks, and I watch the ships bob in the water as we pass. "I assume we are leaving pretty early tomorrow?"

"Your father mentioned that he had told you." He clears his

throat, and he swings his hands in front of him, clapping them slightly before swinging them back, he does this again and again. "We should leave as early as we can. It is a long journey, and the sooner we start, the better."

I nod, my thoughts racing as we climb the path winding up the steep bluffs. I know I need to go. It is harder than I care to admit aloud, especially not knowing anyone where we are going. I glance at Alaric, and find his eyes already on me. His hand grabs my elbow, pulling me to a stop at the top of the bluff overlooking the harbor. I search his face, and see that the façade he puts up around others is still down, and he shifts uneasily under my gaze. He is allowing himself to be vulnerable around me, and I appreciate that he is putting in the effort to not be the arrogant man that he showed himself to be this morning.

"I promise I will not only be your friend, but I will keep you safe, and I will be a faithful husband to you. I know we don't know each other yet, but I am not going to hurt you or betray you in any way. I trust you will extend the same courtesy." He looks at me almost as if expecting me to turn away from him. I dip my head, blinking a few times while focusing on my thoughts and words I want to say. I don't expect to see Peter again, and besides Alaric is to be my husband. I search his eyes, surprised by the glimmer of hope that I find there.

"Deal."

CHAPTER 5

I sit on my bed for a long time thinking about how this is the last time I will see my home in a while. I've already packed everything except for the simple gown I will be wearing while we travel, my nightgown, and an old lavender colored dress that I have long outgrown, but have kept stored in the back of my armoire. It's the dress I wore the day our mother died. I rise from my perch on the bed and cross the room to stand at the armoire. My fingers lightly trail along the buttery soft fabric of the dress, knowing it is well past time to let it go even though part of me screams in protest at the idea.

The memory is still fresh, almost like it happened yesterday. What was a great day, quickly turning into the worst day of my life. I was thirteen and Andria was nine. Peter had been visiting— we were actually down by the bay, holding our own rock skipping contest. The waves added a challenge to the contest, and I had been in the lead with the farthest distance. The guard's face and the sound of him clearing his throat lingers in my memory. We weren't supposed to be by the water alone, but I'm not sure if anyone ever did find out we were there. I don't remember exactly what they said to us, I just remember the numbness, and how the world around me went silent, muddled. Almost as if I were the only one in it. I couldn't believe that my mother was gone. That I would never feel her fingers in my hair or smell her perfume again.

Of course, we weren't told the truth of her death, not until recently anyway. We only knew the story that was told. Always the story. The dress bunches in my fist. The stupid story does such an inservice to us and to our mother. Sure, it is a half truth, but it is still a lie because my father would never let something like suicide stain his, or our, reputation, and simply told us and the world, that she had died in her sleep. Heaven forbid, he let anyone ruin his precious reputation. It's no wonder he kept us behind closed doors, hidden away. We are a liability, closer to breaking than the average person, closer to committing the same crime as our mother.

I suppose it is time to get rid of the dress, leave it and the memories tied to it behind me. I sigh, letting my chin rest on my chest as I breathe deeply, feeling the air build in my chest and slowly release it through my nose. *I'm sorry momma. I hope I am making you proud.* I send my thoughts upwards, to the sky where I like to think that my mother resides now. I blink hard, my eyes burning with sudden tears and release the dress.

I pull out the blue dress that I had put aside to wear, and place my nightgown in the bag that I have open at the foot of my bed. This bag will hold all necessities for the week long journey to Aurellia City, and will be in the carriage with us for easy access during the journey.

I turn back to the bed, and gather the blue dress in my hands, staring into the blue silk. I rarely wear this dress, let alone this color, even though it has always been my favorite. My mother chose to wear blue often enough that it was a staple, and I avoid it like the plague.

This dress in particular was the last thing that my mother had made. She never ended up being able to wear it, so it was given to me when I was able to fit it. The blue brings out the grey of my eyes, and makes my auburn hair brighter. The handful of times I've worn this, my father goes to a far off place in his mind, and over the years, he seems to find it more difficult to differentiate me from my mother. I pull the dress over my head and into place, reaching around to tighten the back, and glance up into the mirror.

The color is perfect on my skin, and I tame my curls enough to pull half of my hair up in a small bun. Other than the grey of my eyes, I am the spitting image of my mother. I know I can never escape the broken look in my father's eyes when he looks at me— not when a ghost stares back at me in the mirror. I turn away, and chew on my lower lip. I look put together enough that I am happy, but I can't help but be nervous for the journey, and for meeting the royal family.

I hear a timid knock on my door, and I walk over to open it. Andria greets me with tears in her eyes and open arms. She has avoided me since we talked about the visions, but I ignore the newfound distance between us as I walk into her outstretched arms, grateful for the comfort. We separate and I let her in. She sits on my bed, just like always. I have so many questions, but I bite my tongue and choke down every one of them knowing that the answers may not be what I want to know and won't really make a difference in the choices that I must make based on my own visions.

"What will I do without you, Kat?" she asks, the tears falling silently down her beautiful face, as she chews her lip and the small dusting of freckles across her nose makes me smile as they seem to dance with the movement. She looks so much like our father that sometimes I wonder if she has any of our mother in her aside from the family curse. My head tilts as I watch her with a small smile, and the burning in my eyes returns. I sniffle as I sit next to her and my fingers find hers, wrapping them within mine. I bump her shoulder with my own.

"Do what you do best. Just be you. Listen, be courteous, but don't be afraid to be heard. Father will be home with you." The curious part that wants to know something of what is coming wins out, and I blurt out before I can stop myself, "Andi, what did you mean by nothing will pan out the way I expect?" She starts to shake her head, her eyes squeezing shut. I squeeze her hand, plowing forward. "Please, tell me something. Anything. Please." I study her face, but she refuses to meet my gaze, and her body starts to shake as her head bows forward.

"Kat, I can't. Please don't ask me to tell you. Please?" Her voice is barely a whisper, and while I feel guilty for pushing, I *need* to know.

"Andi, please."

She glances up and into my eyes. She must sense the overwhelming panic rising within me— I need to know. She looks beyond me, but her eyes are hazy and don't seem to be focused on anything real. Her voice is small and the tone is broken, almost choppy when she speaks, "broken pieces, shattered in a field. Tied and unable to save him. But what lies dead is never truly buried. A girl runs from a castle, racing against a clock that only she can see," her eyes are still squeezed shut, and she shakes her head again, like she is in pain as she calls back what she has seen.

I almost stop her, but she likely wouldn't hear me even if I tried. "A boy with the same name tied to his, trying to live up to all of the expectations that are forced on him. Lies and more lies from everyone. It will destroy everything." Her hand is limp in mine, and she finally blinks as focus and life comes back into her eyes. Her face is pale as she turns to face me. I try to make sense of the fragments that she gave as I watch her features. What she is seeing…seems so much worse than what I have seen. She stands to leave, and stumbles forward. I grab her arm to steady her, and I worry if I pushed her too far.

"It's nothing, I promise. I'm okay. Promise you'll write?" She offers a smile, resting a hand on mine before she walks out of the room as strong and nimble footed as always; as if the stumble was a fluke and I wasn't meant to notice.

The servants take my luggage to the carriage and manage to neatly get everything in, and even left space for whatever belongings Alaric brought. There is a second carriage that will carry the two of us to Aurellia City that is waiting with an open door in front of the other. The driver waits patiently by the open door to offer his assistance. I nod in his direction, knowing that I am expected to climb inside and leave this all behind, but I can't without one last look at the house. My home.

The front of the house rises from the stonework that provides the base. The stone climbs up the rest of the house alongside the lattice on the sides. Morning Glory and other climbing flowers climb the lattice giving the house a homey feeling. The salt in the air has started to wear down the stone of the house making it look soft, but it gives the house character. It is a large house surrounded by lush grass and other plants and trees. The four chimneys rising from the roof let smoke out into the morning air and the mixture of smoke and brine is the smell of home— a smell I wish I could take with me. My heart longs to remain here, not knowing when the next time I will see it will be.

Looking at the house, I see the ghosts of my past running through the picturesque scene. My parents stand by the end of the house laughing as a young Peter chases me through the lawn with a lizard, then it changes to Andria and I playing hopscotch while our mother sits on a blanket in the shade under the trees that were much smaller then. The figures giggle and remind me of the life I had before everything imploded. I contemplate lingering to watch the reruns, but instead turn from the memories that haunt this place and face those who remain waiting by the door.

I stand there for a moment longer, my eyes fluttering closed as I lift my face slightly into the gentle breeze and fill my lungs one last time with the briny scent of home and the sea before opening my eyes once more and walking toward my family. Andria's silent tears stream steadily down her cheeks, and I can tell my father is struggling to keep it together. I watch his eyes dart around us, never settling on one thing for very long while he blinks rapidly as if to keep himself from crying. He shifts his weight from side to side, demonstrating his level of discomfort. I go to Andria first, knowing my departure will break my father and wishing to leave him some dignity for the time being.

"Hey you." I tug playfully at her braid and she gives me a sad smile.

"Hey," she whispers, her small voice breaking.

"Stop that. You're making *me* cry," I say quietly, wiping a few of the tears off of her cheeks. She giggles and throws her arms around me. Her scent of lavender and honey envelops me, and I breathe deep as we cling to each other.

"I love you, Kat," she whispers into my hair. A pang of regret fills me, and I wish I hadn't pressed her like I had this morning.

"I love you too," I whisper, trying to capture the faint flowery scent that lingers in her hair. She lets go and stands back slightly. "I promise I'll write, and we'll see each other soon." I watch her until she nods and wipes away her tears. I wish I could fix this distance between us, wish that I could take the visions away from her. She is too sweet, too good, for something as dark as this to plague her. I plant a kiss on her forehead and lean my forehead on hers murmuring an apology as she nods against me. I release her, and turn to my father.

"My gem."

"Father." He pulls me in tight, his stubble scratching against my cheek. He smells of cigars and salt.

"Be careful. Don't do anything stupid. Your every move will be watched and judged. Make sure your every step is taken carefully," he whispers in my ear then releases me. "I love you, Gem. I'll miss having you around all the time. We will visit when given the chance. I love you." He smiles, but his eyes continue to hold his warning. While I appreciate the gesture, I still feel such bitter rage that it is hard to reflect on what he says, so I simply nod. I know with time this anger will fade, but it is still consuming.

"I love you too. When you can't visit, please write. I want to know what is going on at home."

He nods. I wish I could talk to him about everything and feel heard. But as it stands, I don't, and won't, and I can't change that. The feeling flickers and I realize it is more disappointment than rage that burns through me, and I turn my eyes towards the empty skyline overlooking the sea to the left of the house. What I wouldn't give for one last walk on the beach, for one last rock skipping contest in the bay. I hug Andria and Father both one more time before I turn and head to the carriage. I want to linger, but I know that I am out of time.

"Ready?" Alaric asks as he comes up behind me from the stable. He must have been discussing the route with the driver and the men that will escort us to Aurellia City.

"Ready as I'll ever be." I release the breath I didn't realize I was holding and plaster a smile on my face, turn, and wave as I climb inside the carriage. I continue waving until the carriage picks up speed and the house disappears behind us.

CHAPTER 6

My mother, your grandmother, comes from a long line of seers. The family originated in Arrowhelm at Aouela, but my grandmother met a young soldier from Aurellia and moved here once they married and she found out she was pregnant with my mother. She was in love and made the jump. She knew that seers were treated differently here than in Arrowhelm. The people didn't understand having the sight, and didn't know how to cope with the visions they were being told. Seers were considered outcasts. The soldier left the military, and they settled in Eastbay. As far as I know, they are still there, and you have cousins in Aouela.

Eastbay is where I grew up. I had a whole life there: I was engaged to another before I started having visions, my friends were there, everything that I thought I wanted was in Eastbay. That is until I started having the visions of what was to come. It wasn't a random meeting with your father. Sure, the circumstances were different than I had originally foreseen; I never intended on my horse getting spooked and the chase through the woods, but I fully meant to meet Joel. I had seen that we would be happy together, and have two daughters that would change the outcome of our country and kingdom. I knew that I needed to take the steps necessary to ensure that they happened so I needed to meet Joel, marry, and have you and Andria. I knew that I...I knew what was to come and the steps I needed to take and when I needed to take them.

I saw it all happen, Kat. Everything that was to come, and I know I played my role to get you where you needed to be to succeed. I hope my interpretation of everything was accurate.

The days are long due to the relentless jostling of the carriage on the dirt roads, but the company is nice. Alaric and I take our time getting to know one another, firing off questions at each other, and making each other laugh until our stomachs hurt. We are four days into the week-long journey when we stop at a small inn at the crossroads. The road splits into five separate roads leading back to Stonebreach, or on to Springbay to the west, Ambertide to the south, Eastbay to the southeast, and Aurellia City north of us. Tomorrow we will take the road that borders the lake to Aurellia City. The lake spans the area to the north, its crystal waters reflecting the sun as it sets overhead. The inn sits peacefully just off of the road and to the right of the shore of the expansive lake. I can see the trees that line the opposite bank, but they are small and mere specks on the horizon.

The inn is covered in vines that crawl up the side facing the lake. There is a small stable attached to the right side, and we pull the carriage to a stop there. Alaric offers a hand as we climb out of the carriage, and he reaches in behind me once my feet hit the ground to grab the small pack that holds a couple of changes of clothes. The air is slightly warmer than it is at home, but there is still a chill to the breeze that comes off of the lake. Alaric takes my hand in his, his fingers wrapping around mine, squeezing gently before leading me toward the door to the inn. I want to linger on the shore of the lake and watch the sun set, but we should at least check in and order some food. We leave the carriage and the horses in the hands of the driver and stable hands.

I chew the inside of my cheek as we step through the creaking front door. The inn is sparsely decorated, just a few tables in a gathering room to the right of the entryway, and a tall desk directly in front of us. There are stairs that go up to the second and third floor of the establishment, and a long hallway behind the desk that likely leads to the kitchen and the innkeeper's room. There is a lone woman in colorful, layered clothing wiping down the tables, and an older gentleman whose skin resembles leather at the desk. He offers a bright smile that reaches his eyes, causing them to twinkle in the dim lighting.

"'Ello, lookin' for a room?" His voice is smooth, and thick with the typical accent I would hear on the fishing docks back home. He glances between the two of us, nodding to himself.

"Yes, thank you. If we could have one with two beds please, we would appreciate it." Alaric answers, his fingers placing a coin I didn't see him pull out on the counter. He slides it across to the innkeeper.

"Aye, I'll have Jan take ya to yer room. I can have some food delivered to ya, if ya'd like."

Alaric nods, but asks for us to grab it down here ourselves, before the woman straightens, slinging her rag through her belt, securing it in place before rubbing her hands together and leading us up the stairs. We stop on the second floor, and she leads us about halfway down the hall before coming to a stop in front of the third door down on the left. She takes a key from her pocket, and unlocks the door and passes the key to Alaric as we step past her and into the room.

"Dinner should be ready inna few minutes. Ye may want to come down earlier as the folk like to show up once the troubadour does. The ale flows freely around 'ere, and it can get noisy. This room should be far enough from the racket that you should be able to rest, but our apologies if its no'." she bows her head at us before she takes her leave.

Alaric softly closes the door, and turns to take everything in as I come to a stop across the room. It is larger than I expected- there are two full beds that sit in each corner of the room, a small room off of the right side of the room that leads to a small bathroom. There is a dresser beside the door, and a table in front of the large window that overlooks the lake. The view is spectacular. The sun glints on the water, sparkling like liquid glitter. I stand with my fingers resting on the table, watching the lake. Birds soar over the water, some dropping to the surface, their talons reaching beneath and breaking free with fish in their grasp. A pale pink shade is painted across the entire sky. It is breathtaking.

I feel Alaric's warmth as he comes to a stop just behind me, and can smell the smokiness that seems to linger on his skin. The smell reminds me of the cigars my father would smoke with his buddies from court when they would visit. It is a brief whiff of home, and it makes me bold. I turn to face him, and his eyes find mine. He goes to step back, but I tangle my fingers with his, keeping him in place. I search his face, trying to learn his features and read what lies behind his eyes. They are hooded and mysterious. I want to know this man. I can't deny the physical attraction that has been there all along, but I still heat in a touch of anger when I think of how this all started. I push all of that aside, and focus on the man in front of me. Focus on the here and now, since there is nowhere to go but forward.

I trace his face— my eyes dropping his to take him in. His nose, while seeming large from the side, fits the rest of his features. His cheekbones and jawline are sharply defined, almost chiseled as if from stone. His brows are lowered and there are creases in the space between them as he seems to try to decipher what I am doing. Then there are his eyes. They are beautifully clear, as blue as the lake appears under the glinting of the sun. His normally tidy hair has fallen more over his forehead and into his eyes, but he hasn't yet reached up to brush it to the side like I have noticed him do the past few days. He gets easily annoyed by the strands when they come out of place, but I prefer him like this— slightly unkempt and more at ease than I have seen him since he lounged against the side of the boat after he swam after me.

His lips are slightly parted, and I know if he were to smile, or even have a hint of one, the dimples that rest in those defined cheeks would appear. His lips are the perfect cupid's bow, and I am envious of that feature. They look soft, but I don't dare to test that theory. His eyes search mine, and I can't help but wonder what he sees. Can he tell my heart began to race the minute I noticed him step up behind me? Can he sense that my thoughts sometimes go fuzzy when he is around? I hate that I react this way to him, especially with the uncertainty of the visions and the time that we are fighting against. He has been open and honest with me, and I appreciate the vulnerability he has shown me. I know I owe him the same, and I will do better with this in time, but I can't let him in just yet.

"Do I have something on my face?" The quiet rasp of his voice shoots shivers down my spine. He runs his free hand against the dark stubble that lines his jaw, and onto the back of his neck. My lips tilt up and I shake my head. I watch as his face softens and he smiles crookedly as his winks at me. "Ah, I get it, you like what you see." He smirks and grins when I duck my head, hiding my own grin. He chuckles, and he tentatively lowers his free hand from the back of his neck and places it on my hip, drawing me a step closer until our chests brush against each other with each breath.

His touch scatters the butterflies that I have felt with no one other than Peter, and I freeze. It scares me. I don't know how to navigate these faint whispers luring me toward this man, or the way my heart stutters when his grin brightens his face. He truly becomes boyish and carefree and I want to see that light in his eyes at all times. He must have felt me stiffen because he steps back, releases my hip and rubs the back of his neck again.

"We should, uh, head down and grab a table and something to eat." He turns from me, crossing the room and pausing near the door. "Once the troubadour starts, it is truly something special down there. It is a great time. I wanted you to see it, and enjoy yourself." He clears his throat as he looks over his shoulder at me. I nod, push myself from the table behind me, and follow him as he steps through the door.

Music floats its way through the air, and we follow its call downstairs. The troubadour is set up in the middle of the room, and the tables are situated around him in a wide circle. The tables are starting to fill up as more people make their way inside the inn. I assume the people filling the room reside in the nearby farming villages we passed on our way here. I suppose this is really the only place for them to gather. We are lucky enough to snag a table near the center of the room, there aren't any behind us, but there also aren't any between us and the area in which the troubadour resides. The music is fun spirited, and I can't help but tap my foot to the beat as we sit and watch. Jan, the woman from before, comes up to the table with two tankards of ale, and two steaming plates of chicken, biscuits, and corn. She disappears into the growing crowd as quickly as she appears, and we are quiet as we eat, and the music morphs into a far-fetched tale.

Stacking our bone filled plates, our eyes glitter in happiness and laughter from the tale the troubadour spins, and we turn our attention to the center of the room watching as he gives a deep bow to the room. He takes a swig from his tankard, and picks up the fiddle that leans against his oversized pack at the edge of the makeshift stage. I empty my own tankard, feeling the bubbliness from the ale, and find Jan has dropped off more. I take another couple of mouthfuls, and set it down as my head feels light and carefree. The troubadour sets the fiddle to his chin and rests the bow on the strings. The room is silent in anticipation. He pulls the bow, releasing a long sustained note before his fingers start to fly on the fretboard and the bow bounces on the strings drawing several onlookers to the floor to dance. I watch with a grin, wanting to dance myself. Somehow the song gets faster, and Alaric rises from the table and holds a hand out to me. I look up, his eyes sparkle, and his face brightens with the grin that sends those butterflies off again.

My fingers find their way into his, and I let him pull me into the open area. He spins me, pulling me into him from our clasped hands. My bubbling laugh fills the air and his head tips back with a laugh that is just as contagious. With my hands now resting on his chest and his around my waist, we let the music move us as we spin and dance through the much larger crowd that lets the music consume them. A few others have taken to adding a drum beat to the fiddle, and I can feel the beat in my bones as I spin, laugh, and live in the moment. Alaric's body against mine, his hands on me ignite a fire that burns hotter with the ale that makes my head swim.

Pure bliss overwhelms me, and I can't help the laughter that bubbles to the surface again, and when the music slows, we linger in each other's arms. Alaric rests his forehead on mine, and when I glance up through my eyelashes, his eyes are closed, but a hint of a smile lingers on his lips. We sway gently to the now soft tune that shows the true artistry of the player. I keep my eyes on him, and linger in the moment. Still breathless from dancing, I find myself wondering if this is what life with him is going to look like. Will we have these carefree moments where we can be authentically ourselves and not feel like every move is being analyzed because of our roles at court? Or will we have to remain in control and not allow ourselves to simply be who we are? God, I don't want to put myself into a box or diminish myself based on some preconceived notion that I am supposed to act a certain way because of my rank. I can do it, I have played the role I've been placed in my entire life, but I long for something simpler, some place where I am free.

"Kat," his voice is soft, as his eyes open and meet mine. They flick down to my mouth, and my lips part slightly. Suddenly, I want him to kiss me. I thought about it before we even came downstairs, but froze. With the ale coursing through me, I have no hesitation. I wet my lips, drawing the bottom one in to bite it before releasing it again. He watches me, his eyes heating me as they linger a moment longer before the anticipation comes to a peak and his lips find mine. They are just as soft as I thought they would be.

The world around us disappears, and I am transported to another time— lips on mine, moving in harmony to mine. When we part, it isn't Alaric standing in front of me, but rather Peter as he turns from me and runs down a garden path. I hear laughter and music from behind me, and I turn to see a castle, with open ballroom doors. I am in a large red gown, and a woman rushes toward me with fire in her eyes. I blink and find myself back in Alaric's arms. His lips are still on mine, and I can't help but gasp against his mouth. He pulls back slightly and his eyes open to meet mine. I smooth my features into a smile, and hope that it meets my eyes. He smiles and his hands find mine. I squeeze them, and release them.

I turn and find our table, and sit as the troubadour plays one final note before putting the fiddle down and pulling up a stool. He sits, and everyone else follows suit. Alaric ignores the fact that almost everyone else in the room is seated, and stands in front of me. I ignore his gaze that sits like a weight on my chest. I swallow hard against the rising nausea, and try to stay seated when exhaustion hits me. The troubadour begins to weave a tale of mystery and wonder, and I finally glance up at Alaric.

"Are you okay?" His brows scrunch in between his eyes in concern. His right hand rests on the table beside us, his left on the back of my chair. His back is bowed as he leans closer to talk in my ear.

I nod, "I'm just exhausted. It hit me harder than I anticipated." I smile under now hooded eyes, and I know I probably look as exhausted as I claim to be. It is hard to keep my eyes open, and my body is heavy. I just want to lay down.

He continues to watch me, almost expecting something, but I can't tell what. He shakes his head slightly, his eyes blinking rapidly before he pushes himself to full height, and takes my hands in his, helping me to stand. I wobble on my feet, but his arm snakes around my waist and holds me securely against him. I feel safe, and we make our way through the room and to our room for the night. We move slowly on the stairs, taking them one at a time. My mind is hazy, and it is hard to focus on anything but the next stair as I lift my foot to meet it. His arm remains firmly planted around me, and as we reach the landing, it is all I can do to keep my legs from buckling under me. With iron will power, we make it to our room down the hall.

Alaric kicks the door shut behind us, and he helps me into one of the beds. The room is dim as there is only a single candle sitting on the table in front of the window to light the space. He gently removes my shoes, taking each into his lap to unlace my boots before sliding them off. I lay back on the pillows, and watch him through hooded eyes. Once the boots are removed, his thumbs push into the tender spots of the bottom of my feet. I groan as he works out the knots and my head falls back against the pillows and my eyes flutter closed. He repeats this same process on my other foot. Gently, he pulls the covers down and I curl up on my side under them as he tucks me in.

His fingers brush my hair to the side of my face as he kneels in front of me. I open my eyes, watching him. "You can tell me anything. I won't judge. Promise." He smiles, and his eyes soften as he looks at me. He places a kiss on the top of my head and rises.

"Thank you," I murmur. He walks across the room and sits on the edge of the other bed, and takes off his own boots before removing his tunic, leaving him in his billowy under shirt. The top is open, leaving a bare triangle of his chest to peek through. The hair peeking through is just as dark as that on his head, and the broad expanse of his muscled shoulders is impressive. His fingers run through his already disheveled hair from dancing, and he sits with his head in his hands. He seems to be struggling with something, something weighing on him, but he doesn't speak up. He remains there.

"The same goes for you, you know." My voice is deep with exhaustion, and I can feel the words slurring together slightly as they roll off of my tongue.

He lifts his head enough to look at me, and nods. "Thanks, Kat." He sighs, running one of his hands through his hair and scratching the back of his head. "I don't know how to navigate this with you. I don't want to push you in any way. I—" he breaks off, and shakes his head as he bites his lip. "You are important. I want your opinion on everything. I want a partner, a person working with me as a team. From what little I know, and based on the conversations and times we have shared the past few days, I know you can be everything that I am looking for."

He coughs, turning to face me. He opens his mouth to continue, but closes it quickly and shakes his head subtly, before settling his eyes on mine again. I push myself to a seated position, the weakness within me starting to subside. "You have to be willing to trust me. Completely, if this is going to work. And believe me, I want it to." He tilts his head back to look at the ceiling. The veins and tendons in his neck thrust out, and the contours of his bare neck are enticing. He is very nice to look at, and there is definitely intelligence behind those eyes. If I were any other person, I would be swooning, but I am still picking up the pieces from the wreckage Peter left behind.

"I can't just trust you like it is nothing. I barely know you. You swept in, and yes, I appreciate all of your candor and how upfront with everything you have been, but I need time. I need to know *you*— the man that you are beneath the crown that you will bear. The you that you are when no one else is around. I have seen glimpses of this man, but before I can trust you, I need you to show me *you*." I cross my arms over my chest, and pin my eyes on him. I avoid looking anywhere but his face, and he watches the floor.

"Deal." He glances up at me, and I watch his features settle a minute before he gets a wicked grin and a glint in his eye that I know only means one thing— "Honey, if you wanted to see me, all you had to do was ask." He winks, and I snort back the laughter that follows. I throw a pillow at him and he catches it before tossing it back and laying back on the pillows with a hand behind his head.

"You are ridiculous." I giggle softly, leaning back against the headboard and hugging the pillow to my chest. I can't help but grin.

"Just you wait, cupcake, just you wait."

"Cupcake? Of all the things you come up with, you choose cupcake?" I snort again, burying my face in the pillow before peeking back at him.

He grins and waves a hand. "Yeah, yeah, not all of us can be perfect." He chuckles, and crosses his ankles.

I shake my head, I don't think anyone is perfect, but sure, I can roll with that. "Yeah, I know. That is why I am superior. No use pretending to be anything less than what I am," I take on a haughty tone, but succumb to snickering. He chuckles in response before shaking his head and grinning.

"You really are something, aren't you," he states, still smiling at the ceiling.

"You are too." I murmur as I crawl forward to the end of the bed and lay on my stomach resting my cheek on my pillow. He glances at me and smiles before rolling to his side to face me more fully.

"Tell me something Ms. Perfect," he grins again, "what is something that you wish you could change?"

My heart stutters and freezes at what on the surface is a simple question. He is probably asking for a simple response like making sure that there are no droughts, or famine, or even conflict. What I really wish I could change? My ability. Of course, I can't say any of that. I struggle to find an answer. Instead, I deflect, "About myself, or about anything?"

"Both."

I linger on the question further, but the answer remains the same. "I guess I would like to learn some new skills, be more self-sufficient. Learn to hunt I guess." I roll onto my back and look at the low wood plank ceiling above me. "As for everything else, I would like to end pain, suffering, greed— there is too much that clings to all of these that it makes it impossible to be completely free."

He doesn't ask me to elaborate, and I am thankful. He is quiet, and I start to wonder if he has fallen asleep before his voice pipes up. "We have a training ground at the castle, I can teach you to use a bow if you like. Or throwing knives. I think you could be deadly should we put those blades in your hands." His voice, while soft, has a lilting tone to it that makes me smile.

He continues, his tone growing somber, "but, I agree. Those are good places to start when it comes to change, but are easier said than done, unfortunately. But I think with the right mindset and a solid idea, we can make steps to make it happen." The room is silent for a few minutes, and he speaks again. "Something is happening. There are whispers of unrest and a shadow of doubt that lingers in the emptiness of the castle. Something is brewing, and I have no clue how to find out what, or how to stop it when I'm at a loss for what is even lurking in the dark."

I wish I could reach out and touch him, but I don't move from the bed. Instead, I remain quiet. There isn't really anything to say to that, but I wish I had an answer.

"How do you chase a ghost? How do you decipher what is fact from what is rumor?" he muses.

"You listen. And you observe. There isn't a whole lot more you can do without stone-hard evidence."

His sigh fills the quiet, and I sigh right alongside him. It is impossible to do anything without having evidence or testimony to back up the information gathered. I can sympathize with his situation as I am in a similar one myself. I am at a loss of what advice to offer as I have been and likely will be asking the same questions. Can we go back to the moment we shared downstairs with the ale and music racing in our veins making us abandon all reason and just live in the moment? I roll back over, looking at Alaric. He lies on his back with his hands behind his head. His eyes are closed and the candle still burns on the table in front of the window.

"Alaric?"

"Mmm?" He keeps his eyes closed, but I know he is paying attention.

"We will figure it out. One day at a time, but we will."

CHAPTER 7

Katerina," He shakes my shoulder lightly as he whispers, "wake
up."

I wake blinking hard against the bright sunlight filtering
through the nearly sheer curtains in the carriage windows. It takes a
minute to reorient myself and shake the fogginess from my brain. I
shift in my seat, stretching as much as the small space will allow and
look out the window to see that we are passing through the palace
walls. Never being anywhere further than the edge of our territory
until now, I didn't think to expect the monstrosity of what lies in front
of me. I didn't think that the walls would be as big or as immaculate
as they are. They seem to stretch for miles, likely around the entire
castle and within the city walls itself. They are taller than I imagined
as well, almost reaching the height of the trees. The craftsmanship of
the wrought iron intermixed with the stone that makes up the walls is
incredible. The twists and images elegantly brought to life are amazing
and I wish there was enough time to take in every detail.

It doesn't seem like enough time has passed for us to have
arrived already, but the castle sits in front of me and my mouth opens
in surprise. The impressiveness of the walls dim in comparison to the
castle. It isn't just huge but massive. You could fit most, if not all, of

my father's fleet in the western end alone. The stonework is incredible. Larger stones make up the base and first few levels of the palace, but smaller ones quickly take their place. I'm forced to tilt my head against the window of the carriage in order to see the top. There are four sections that rise higher than the rest, towering over everything around, providing an overwhelming presence.

The carriage rolls to a stop, and my heart leaps into my throat, and the overwhelming flutter starts in the pit of my stomach. With my eyes wide and my face blanched in fear, I meet Alaric's gaze. I hear nothing but a roar in my ears, and I take a deep breath to try to settle the overwhelming desire to run. My legs shake with the need, and the world starts to have a dark tint around the edges. I need to calm down. Alaric's fingers find mine and squeeze gently. The pressure grounds me, and I fill my lungs to capacity before releasing in a slow stream.

He gives me a moment, guiding my breathing, and I eventually am able to breathe normally. I nod, a gentle dip of my chin, and he bobs his head and smiles as his fingers wind themselves around the handle of the door, and twists it to open the door to a wash of sunlight. He maintains contact as he steps out into the sun. The sun glints on his hair and it shines, still black as night, but almost with a bluish hue. I hesitate before stepping out of the carriage and into the sun. I know the direct light hits my hair turning it into a shade of copper, and I brush it behind my ear as I take a few small steps forward. I've left it down during the journey, and thankfully it has managed to not get too messy.

I glance around, spinning slowly as I take in my surroundings all the while gripping Alaric's hand like it's a lifeline. He is the only familiar thing and I cling to that in this foreign place full of vipers. I see that, thankfully, we are inside the inner gates hidden from the city. There is a back entrance to the castle that leads to the woods to the north, but since we came in from the south, we had to have passed through the city before entering the gates. The courtyard is empty save the servants who are already unloading the carriage and separating out our things and I can't help but wonder where everyone is. I expected Alaric's family to at least greet us when we arrived, but they are nowhere to be found. There is a giant door in front of us that have a pair of guards pacing, and a small door to what I assume is the barracks near the gate leading to the city. The stables lies to the left of us, and beyond that is open pasture; likely for the horses and other animals that reside within the walls. The castle wall connects with the wall to the right of us, giving the space a tight, enclosed feeling.

"Are you ready to head inside?" Alaric asks quietly. He has been watching me since we climbed down from the carriage, and I feel his gaze like a weight. I barely dip my head, biting my lip and trying to wrap my head around why I'm here and what that really means. I knew that we would end up here, and that I would be marrying the man that my hand desperately clings to to ground me and keep me from spiraling. When did he turn from stranger to acquaintance, then to friend? Was it the night he swam after me and we connected over our losses, or was it somewhere else along the road that brought us here?

I came into this arrangement angry and broken, and while I still am all of these things, I am starting to pick up the pieces, and Alaric has been there every step of the way. Every night as we traveled, he would respect my boundaries and needs. He ensured my safety, and there were nights we talked until the sun came peeking up over the horizon. He is funny, leaving me breathless with giggles. He is obsessively kind, and ultimately wants to be a good person. He is brilliantly intelligent, and I'm surprised with each new discovery I make. He has become real to me, and much more than the villain I made him in my mind for stealing me away from the things I wanted in life. There may not be resentment towards him anymore, but the thought of what started this tumultuous relationship stings on the wounds that are still fresh.

With my hand still interlocked with his, Alaric leads me through the castle— turning left once we step inside to bypass the giant entryway and grand staircase that starts as one before reaching a landing and branching off into two staircases that curl around the sides of the room leading to other parts of the castle, past servants that dip into shallow curtsies or bows as we pass, and dozens of rooms before stopping in front of two huge immaculately carved, mahogany doors. I feel his eyes on me and I suddenly wish he had given us time to freshen up before meeting his family, given me a moment to make sure I am not as disheveled as I feel before we enter the room that lies beyond the doors that dwarf us. I swallow hard and take a deep breath and release it slowly as Alaric opens them. As they swing inwards, I note the curling vines and floral design in the engraving. I straighten my chin, holding it high, and put on a façade of confidence that I hope will convince Alaric's family as well as myself.

The room is easily as big as half of my house. The stone walls are decorated with colorful tapestries of far-away places, and things in fairytales. The one about halfway down the wall on the left side of the room catches my eye; it is a vibrant gold color and depicts a red dragon facing down a knight. The size of the tapestry is significantly larger than the rest as it runs a large portion of the wall. The golden color of the border pops against the grey of the stone. It's breath-taking. I wish I could study each and every one of these tapestries, but the royals wait at the end of the room.

There are two large, intricately carved wooden thrones that take up the majority of the stage-like area at the opposite end of the room. One throne is larger than the other, likely meant for the king, and that is where I find the king seated. The curving design carved on the throne makes the king seem even larger. He emanates power- the room is full of it. Alaric's brother stands to his father's left, and Alaric's sister sits on the steps below them. They are engaged in conversation and must not have heard us enter.

We continue to close the distance, taking long strides down the long carpet leading the way from the door to the thrones. My vision tunnels, and I feel like no matter how many steps forward I take, no progress is made. My vision fades in and out as I see Alaric as a child, sick in bed with a mousey haired woman with kind eyes wiping his brow and holding a cup up to his mouth. She must be his mother. A smaller boy plays with a wooden carriage beside the bed, but he keeps his eyes on Alaric. I hear their mother say something to the younger boy, she calls him Lucas, and they exit the room. The room fades, and returns, this time Alaric is older, maybe just entering his teenaged years. Lucas hovers over the small table across the room, and I watch as he takes a small vial out of his pocket, and he tips some of the contents into a teacup before stopping the bottle and sliding it back into his pocket. He then adds a sugarcube to the cup before plastering a smile on his face and bringing the cup to Alaric who rests in the same bed as before.

Everything shivers in my mind, and I find myself back in the throne room, and I pinch my leg in an attempt to focus, and I blink hard, forcing myself to take in everyone's appearance now that we are closer. I remember Alaric telling me about them both on our journey here, and I quickly recall their names. Lucas has darker, more tanned skin and is stockier than Alaric, but he could be his darker twin. I immediately recognize him as the other man in my visions, and a heavy weight settles in the pit of my stomach. He radiates darkness, and I wonder if the others even notice. Where the boys take after their father with their dark hair and his tall muscular build, Alaric's sister must take after their mother. She is slender in frame, with lighter brown hair. She is still tall like her siblings, but she seems almost petite seated like she is. The king is laden down with jewels and his clothing is of the finest quality. He has dark hair like his sons and is broad in the shoulders, and even though he is dwarfed by the throne, I can tell that he is massive in stature.

Alaric's brother is the first to notice us. His lips move as he nods his head in our general direction, and the others turn to us and stop the conversation. The room is completely silent, no one says a word as we reach the steps where Alaric's sister now stands.

Alaric bows slightly, and rather than the shallow bow that he does, I sink into a deep curtsy, keeping my eyes downcast. Even when Alaric rises and stands tall, I remain in place, waiting for the signal to release the curtsy. Alaric greets his father and his father's voice is deeper than any I have heard before; its booming quality is hard not to shrink away from. My breath catches in my throat, and I can feel the king's eyes on the top of my head.

"Father, may I introduce Lady Katerina Smith, of Stonebreach, Daughter of Counselman and High Lord Joel Smith, and sister to Lady Andria Smith." Alaric's voice has taken on that undertone of authority that he had when he first came to Stonebreach. I wonder why he feels the need to put up this persona, and hide the person I have spent the past week acquainting myself with. I wonder if this is the role he has been raised to play, much like the one that I have myself. Knowing this is finally my cue to rise, I plaster a smile on my face as I face the king. I hope the smile looks more authentic than it feels. I soften the edges of my mouth since it feels fake and a little crazy.

"You convinced her father to let her out of her prior engagement for you?" His father looks between the two of us, and I know he noticed our hands intertwined when we first got to the steps. We have since released each other, and while the support was needed when we arrived, a large part of me wishes I hadn't needed that support. Alaric simply nods. "Very well," his eyes meet mine as he continues, "I am pleased to welcome you to your new home." His gaze lingers and he seems to notice things about me that I can only guess at.

"Thank you." I curtsy again, out of respect, but refuse to break eye contact. I know appearances are everything, and I don't want to give the wrong impression. I am from a noble family, and my father owns the King's fleet. We hold power, and it is important that I demonstrate an ounce of that power now. Even when I feel completely powerless. My father has always said that being at court is like a game of cat and mouse. You have to be the cat in order to survive. I am aware that I am walking on eggshells, and that every move I make is going to be watched and analyzed. It is a high stakes game, and one I can't afford to lose.

With a brief nod, and a wave of his hand, the king dismisses us. He and Alaric's younger brother walk to the back of the room to a small door, waiting there for Alaric. He glances toward them, but before following, he turns to me. "I'll meet up with you later. Annine can accompany you to your rooms." He pauses, but before he can think further or talk himself out of it, he takes my face in his hands. His hands are warm, and his stubble scratches me slightly as he leans forward and leaves a quick kiss on my forehead. His lips are soft. He bites the inside of his cheek, as he steps back and his eyes meet mine, as his hands fall to his side before he dips his head and jogs over to meet his father and brother. They all duck into the room on the other side of the door. Annine waits a few paces away, not much farther than where she sat before. I hide my shiver. I don't know what to make of the kiss. In a lot of ways, I am still not comfortable with that level of intimacy from him, and to be completely honest, I don't know when I will be. Anna takes the few strides between us, her dress whispering against the ground as she approaches.

"Hi! I'm Annine, but everyone calls me Anna," she says with a bright smile. Her bubbly personality is instantly captivating. She seems to bounce when she walks, her long hair waving against the small of her back as she tilts her head with a smile. She rubs her hands up and down my upper arms, before sliding down to take my hands in hers.

"You can either call me Katerina or Kat, and you can drop the title, it isn't necessary." I grimace, my nose scrunching up with the thought of hearing Lady Katerina all day everyday. I rarely heard it growing up, and while I know the power that lies in a title, especially the one I will be gaining, I don't necessarily want it. I allow her to pull me back the way I came, back through the room to the double doors. She walks backwards, pulling me forward with both hands and a wide grin. I stumble slightly, but return her grin. She releases my hands, but doesn't release me, instead she places her arm in mine.

"Yeah, my brother is great with the formalities." She rolls her eyes. "Always has been. Me, I could care less. I hate having a title." She glances at me, and I nod my agreement with a grin. "I take it you don't like the formalities either," she laughs.

"Not particularly, no." I grin. Her happiness is contagious, and I allow myself to be swept up in her. Her light brown hair reaches the small of her back, and it hangs in loose curls. Her light eyes tilt slightly up in the corner, but it suits her. Her cheekbones are defined, but they give her an edge, and I find her breathtaking. She is beautiful, and I know her confidence and bubbly personality add to it. She outshines anyone in her proximity, myself included. Her lavender gown glitters and brings out the blue of her eyes. She has dimples that pop out with every movement of her mouth. She is a wonder, and I hope that we become friends. I want to know her, have someone that I can confide in and grow close to here that isn't Alaric.

She suddenly stops in front of a door that looks like every other one we have passed, and I look around and realize I have no idea where I am or how we got here. I should have tried to pay better attention. She opens the door to reveal a sitting room. I step inside at her small reassurance, and take in the pale blue walls, the beautiful brick fireplace that accents the room perfectly. A two person couch faces the fireplace with a small table in front of it and two oversized chairs sit across from the couch, but beside the fireplace. There is a lounge chair along the back wall, and a small writing desk to my right against the wall behind the couch in the center of the room. There is a rust colored rug on the hardwood that takes up the space from the couch to the fireplace, and about a foot past the chairs. It brings the space together, and each piece is a part of one cohesive whole. There is a door in the right corner of the room, which I am assuming leads to the bedroom. The walls are left bare, likely left for me to decorate, but I assume once Alaric and I are wed, we will share chambers, so I don't see a point in hanging anything. If these chambers are mine, I can only imagine the grandeur of his.

"These are your rooms. You have a sitting room, bedroom, and a bathroom. You even have a balcony." She leads me into the bedroom, and I follow without a word. I've never lived in anything as nice as this. Yes, we had everything we ever wanted growing up, but the splendor that surrounds me? Nothing even compares. The bedroom walls are a dark red, a toss up between ruby and burgundy. Either way, it gives a sensual feel to the room. The light beaming in from the double balcony doors makes the room brighter, and chases the shadows from the room. The bed is on the wall opposite of us, centered on the wall with another door that is directly across from us that must lead to the bathroom.

The coverlet on the bed is black and there are big red pillows at the head of the bed. The headboard is a dark cherry, as is all of the rest of the furniture in the room. There is a wardrobe on the wall opposite of the bed with a large vanity beside it, and the door leading onto the balcony is on the wall to our left. It is centered on the wall, and takes up a majority of the space. There is a trunk at the foot of the bed, and the wall to the right is empty aside from a small bookshelf. The chambers are beautiful, I feel like the colors are a good representation of me, and I know that is nothing more than coincidence. I can see myself feeling at home here once the dust settles and I grow used to all of the changes. I turn to Anna and realize that while I have been absorbed in my own thoughts and the room, she has continued talking. I feel my ears grow hot, and I know the tips of them are probably the same shade as the walls around me. I know my cheeks have turned pink as well.

"You'll find that the wardrobe holds gowns made for you by our seamstresses, and shoes to match. They were on a rush order as soon as we heard you were coming, which was only a couple of days before you arrived. They will continue to arrive throughout the week, since some of them aren't ready yet. I made sure to keep room for your clothes from home." I nod my understanding and she continues, turning to her appearance in the vanity mirror. I watch as she ruffles her hair, adjusts her dress, and wipes under her eyes. She speaks so quickly, and I struggle to keep up. She seems to ramble quite a bit, and I don't know her well enough to know if it is just because she likes the sound of her own voice, or because she is simply lonely. She finally takes a breath and watches me slowly spin in place, taking in everything. "I could stay and help you unpack and get ready for dinner, the servants should have brought your belongings up already." I glance toward the wardrobe and sure enough, there is a small pile of things on the far side. "Besides, I want to get to know my brother's fiancée." She beams, and practically skips to the wardrobe, and opens it to peer inside.

"I'd like that. Thank you." I stay quiet, studying her further. She is taller than me, but the height suits her. There is something about her personality that reminds me of Andria. She is captivating, and I wonder if everyone that meets her falls entranced.

"Of course. I definitely want to help you get ready for the ball tomorrow." She must see something on my face, because she shakes her head and rolls her eyes. "You didn't know about it, did you?" My wide eyes must answer the question for her, and she looks at the ceiling. With a huff, she continues, "figures. That's Alaric for you. He sometimes assumes people know things so he doesn't bother saying anything. Although, it is possible that he didn't know since you have only just arrived…but either way, our father thought it would be a good way to welcome you by hosting a ball for the both of you in celebration of your engagement."

As I take time to freshen up for dinner, she continues to talk about the ball tomorrow evening, but I find myself not paying attention. My thoughts drift to my mother and how she would feel seeing me like this; grown up and engaged. I glance in the mirror before we leave the room, and my lips part in pleasant surprise— with my grey eyes twinkling almost blue with refracted light and my auburn hair in ringlets, I'm the exact replica of my mother.

CHAPTER 8

The next morning, I'm one of the last people to show up in the dining hall.

"Ah good. You're here. Now we can begin," Lucas says, his tone sarcastic. His impatience is evident in the way that he fills his plate before I can fully sit down. I lower my gaze, embarrassed, and quickly sit.

"Don't worry, Katerina. We are still trying to teach Lucas some manners." Anna glances at her brother, sticking her tongue out at him.

Lucas ignores her, and instead rolls his eyes. "Katerina, Alaric and my father can't make it this morning. They have some important business to take care of. Alaric told me to tell you that he will see you later today." He watches me from across the table.

"Thank you, Lucas." I dip my head down toward the table, quickly glance between the two siblings, and fill my plate.

"Would you like a tour?" he asks, and knowing what little I do from the visions, I can't help but wonder at an ulterior motive, but I decide to give him the benefit of the doubt.

"Yes, please. I'd rather not continue getting lost." I am grateful for the offer, but can't help but wish it were someone else offering. A flash of an earlier vision comes to mind along with the memory of sounds and ominous feeling— Lucas stands in front of me bringing along an overwhelming sense of helplessness and the clanging of swords, and I'm left more uneasy and with more questions than answers. I take a few deep breaths to steady myself and stop my hands from shaking. I move my food around my plate rather than eat any of it, my appetite suddenly gone. I glance up at Anna and return her smile. I'm tempted to ask her to come with us because I don't trust Lucas, but I don't, knowing I will see her later before the ball. Silence lingers and before I can bring myself to really eat, Lucas rises from his chair, wiping a napkin over his mouth before tossing it carelessly onto the table.

"Well, Katerina, if you will follow me, we shall begin the tour," Lucas says, barely hesitating by the door for me. I quickly stand, bid Anna farewell, and follow. If this hastiness is any indication of how the tour is going to be, I am never going to learn my way around. I sigh and follow his retreating footsteps into the hallway outside of the dining hall.

The tour goes by quickly. Lucas rushes through the wings where the royal family resides as well as the wings where the councilmen and other nobles that live at court reside. We pass by rooms where visiting dignitaries from neighboring kingdoms stay, and pass through the lower wings where a giant library, ballroom, music room, and what once was the Queen's Court are. While we walk, Lucas gruffly spouts off different facts: when the castle was built and by whom, listing the visiting dignitaries as well as the councilmen, when different areas of the castle were added to the original structure, and lesser known facts about the library and the Queen's Court. He is very stand-offish and gets snappy when I ask questions, although he is kind enough to pause every now and again to allow me to take a closer look at some of the tapestries and other things around the castle. The place is massive, which I was fully aware of before the tour, but I guess I didn't realize just how big the castle truly is.

We end up in the garden to take a small break. Lucas guides me to a bench and the sweet scent of the roses and the gentle bubbling of the fountain fills the air around me. The visions overwhelm my thoughts, but the garden is peaceful around me. Perhaps this could become a place that I could feel comfortable and almost at home. We sit quietly for a moment, Lucas on the bench beside me. I try to enjoy the quiet, but Lucas shatters the picturesque scene that reminds me of home, and twists it into something else entirely.

"You don't belong here. And I'm fairly certain that you are well aware of that. I don't want you here. You are not one of us and never will be. I don't like you, and I don't trust you."

I sit up a little straighter, facing him. "Excuse me?" I blink rapidly, frowning. What the hell? I stare at him, and he looks back, until I'm forced to drop my gaze. This was some sort of battle, and I just lost.

He stands, pacing directly in front of me, and each word feels like a nail in the coffin solidifying everything that I have come to understand. "Alaric was sickly for years. He was never supposed to survive to adulthood. You can even ask our father if you wish. I was told to prepare myself to take over in his place, but he survived. It was deemed a miracle. My father believed it was a sign that he would be a strong, capable leader, but I think it makes him weak. When I turned fifteen my father said Alaric would still get his throne, and I would be stuck as a dignitary in some country no one has even heard of. I will not be doing this, rather, I am setting my own path. Alaric needs to be wed, and soon, if he wishes to keep his hold on the throne. That is why he is marrying you." He snarls pointing at me. "You are no one. You will be nothing more than a figurehead. You will never be my queen. I will do whatever I can to ensure that you won't be."

He turns on his heel and walks off, leaving me to stare after him. I try to understand why he would tell me any of this, and what his possible motivations may be. I already knew Alaric's reasons for marrying me— did Lucas think his brother would keep that to himself? Every word Lucas spit at me solidified my realization of who the danger is that I have come to stop. I need to figure out how Lucas will start this war, if he truly believes he should get the throne, and who I can even tell about all of these theories. I'd like to eventually trust Alaric with all of this and more, but I know we are not there yet. With the weight of what feels like the world resting on my small shoulders, I realize that I can't tell anyone. It is as my mother wrote; seers in Aurellia aren't trusted by the people. We are outsiders, and it is hard to find those who believe and will heed advice given. But there are some areas of the kingdom where seers are honored members of the territory in which they reside. My mother was one of these. Our dignitaries were made aware of my mother's condition, Ian being one of them. Maybe if it comes down to it, I can talk to him about everything once I have more concrete evidence. Besides, who would even believe me without it? I know I have to do something; I am the only one who can.

Anna and I arrive at the ballroom together, but Anna pushes through the closed doors, leaving me with a wink. The doors close with a soft clunk, solidifying that I am on my own, and have been since I arrived here at the castle. I linger in the hall, hesitant to face all of the nobles and people who live here. I was never a part of society like this, and I know I'm going to say the wrong thing, do the wrong thing, or generally stand out among those who have been in court for years. I'm not sure I'm ready for the judging eyes or the jealousy from the other young women that may feel jaded that their prince didn't select one of them to marry, and instead chose me, who in their eyes, is some nobody from the coast. I wipe my sweaty palms on my silver gown. The skirt is full, and has a shimmery overlay over the full skirt. The dress is tight where it needs to be; hugging my waist. There are full sleeves, but they are made of a sheer, shimmery fabric that matches the skirt overlay, and the neckline plunges but has a bit of this same shimmery fabric to give the illusion of modesty. The corset is a little tight, making it difficult to breathe deeply, but somehow, I manage to take a deep breath and slowly walk into the ballroom and into the middle of the ball.

When I enter, the people nearest to the door go quiet and stare. Instead of dropping my gaze like I want to, I stand my ground. I face them all with my chin held high, ignoring the whispers that float in the air around me; *Is that her?* and *Who is she?* I hear a few snide remarks but choose to ignore them. I feel my cheeks flush. I know I should move forward, head towards Alaric and the royal family, but I am frozen. I don't know how to be this person. I rarely had the opportunity to interact with people within my rank, the only opportunities were when dignitaries or other council members came to the house and brought their families, but even that was rare. My chest grows tight and it becomes even harder to breathe. I search the room for a familiar face, but each face blurs into the next. I feel the surge of a desperate need to run consume me, and before I can bolt, Alaric's face swims into focus directly in front of me.

His eyes meet mine, and he bows his head to me. He takes a deep breath, and I imitate. After a couple of breaths, Alaric takes my hand and gently pulls me through the crowd of guests and up to the thrones where the rest of the royal family is standing. Once we reach the rest of the family, I take a little time to take in the ballroom and the guests. I scan the room from this higher vantage point, and find each face turned toward us, but not one stands out among the sea of them. There have to be at least a hundred people here, and I feel my pulse thundering in my veins as the weight of every gaze falls on me. I quickly turn my gaze back to Alaric, my eyes frantic in the search of something even vaguely familiar as the loose tendrils of my hair swing and catch in my lip gloss. I reach a hand up to free the tendrils and lower it quickly. Alaric seems to sense my panic because he places a reassuring hand on my shoulder and stands slightly behind me, allowing me to borrow his strength.

King Henry rises from the throne to my right and raises his hands to put a hold on the festivities. Once everything is quiet, he speaks; "Welcome. As you all know, this ball is for my eldest son and heir, Prince Alaric. He is to be wed in three short months to this beautiful young woman, Lady Katerina Smith. Congratulations, son, and welcome to the family, My Lady."

"Thank you, Father," Alaric responds. He then looks at me and nods, encouraging me to speak.

I shake my head, opting out of speaking for the time being. It's hard enough being the newcomer let alone the Prince's chosen bride. Hopefully with time, the people will come to approve of my presence, but I don't want to test my luck. Alaric quickly smiles and turns back to the guests.

"Please. Let's begin." Alaric lifts his hands, and the musicians begin playing again. I glance toward Lucas who stands on his father's other side, and quickly regret it. If looks could kill, Alaric would be dead. There is so much hate in his face that I wonder how no one sees it or has done anything. It makes me even more uneasy. The world around me begins to focus in on Lucas and I jump when Alaric whispers in my ear, breaking me out of the trance, out of the vision before it can begin. What would it have told me this time?

Alaric leads me from the thrones and into the crowd. This image is familiar; my arm outstretched, hand in his as he smiles and leads me onto the dancefloor where a waltz has begun. Some of the ladies shoot me curious glances, while others shoot daggers. We find a spot in the middle of the dance floor and he spins me into him. His hand remains in mine, with the other on the small of my back. He takes the lead, and we slowly waltz among the others.

He leans forward slightly, his lips brush against my ear as he whispers, "You look stunning,"

I shiver slightly and smile, still trying to calm myself and ignore everyone around me besides him. "Thank you. You're not so bad yourself, you know."

He chuckles and kisses me on the cheek, quick but sweet. Suddenly the waltz becomes a fast-paced dance. I begin to grin as we dance, quickly becoming breathless and losing myself in the music and steps. My sister and I would make sure that we were up to date with all of the dances, practicing with each other— taking turns on who would lead the dance and play the male counterpart. I grin at the memory and from the freeness that comes with dancing; the lighthearted joy that I feel every time I let music take over. The partners switch, and I spin until I come face-to-face with Peter, and the music slows once again. My breath catches and my eyes burn. I completely forgot that he was staying here. With the visions and the move, it completely slipped my mind that he mentioned living at the castle as a correspondent for his father in the council.

"Peter." I stare up into his beautiful green eyes, losing myself in them like I have a thousand times before. The world around me melts away, and I forget about Alaric, and the castle, the visions, and the destruction I'm trying to avoid.

"Kat," his voice breaks, and his eyes close briefly at the heartbreak in his voice. The music swells, and so does the storm of emotions raging inside of me.

"I'm so sorry," I whisper, tears welling up in my eyes.

"I wish we had run when we had the chance." He gestures to the luxury and the ball around us; "I could have given you this. I would give you the world and more," he pauses, his grip on my waist tightening for a moment. "Why didn't we run? We could have left the day he got there; boarded a ship and never looked back."

"Meet me in the garden outside at midnight," I whisper. He nods and walks away, leaving me alone on the dance floor. I watch his retreating figure, each step sending another crack through my still shattered heart and wish things could be different. I sigh, glancing at the vaulted and carved ceiling ignoring the burning in my eyes and turn to leave the dance floor, but Lucas sweeps in to take Peter's place and I am stuck.

"How rude of Lord Gold to leave a lady alone on the dance floor." He smiles as he gracefully leads me across the floor in the dance. Growing up in the court gave him some perks, he is a brilliant dancer. He makes it look easy.

"It's not a problem." I avoid his gaze, and instead watch the other dancers. My skin crawls everywhere he touches me, but I remain civil even though I want nothing more than to shove him away and go anywhere else.

"You are handling this very well," he looks down at me, the same smirk on his face. "I'm surprised. I would have thought you'd be more distraught at running into your ex-fiancée. Rumor has it you've known one another for a very long time."

What is he trying to gain with this? "Peter and I grew up together and my father has known Mr. Gold's family for a while. We are friends, nothing more." The lie, while necessary, is bitter on my tongue. There is no point in admitting my or Peter's feelings, especially when they don't, and can't, matter now.

"It's obvious he is more than a childhood friend. I think a lover, perhaps?" He must see something in my face because he grins. My body goes cold before the fire ignites and it takes a lot of effort to keep my cool. What is he trying to do? What is the point of this? Why draw this out? I wish he would just leave me alone. How has no one seen the monster that lurks in their midsts?

"You don't deserve your title, let alone the throne," I hiss as I turn on my heel and stalk off into the crowd of dancers.

"Katerina!" Alaric calls, noticing me as I stalk off the dance floor. "Where are you going?" he asks once he reaches my side by the refreshment table.

"I needed a drink. It is stuffy in here." I avoid eye contact, but he comes closer anyway. I wish I could tell him everything, who his brother truly is, but I don't even know where to start, or how to convince him there is something evil lurking beneath the surface. I need proof before I can bring this to him, or anyone else. I turn to face him, my eyes watching the dancers, but ask low enough that the other bystanders can't hear me, "what is wrong with your brother? He is… not who you think he is."

He laughs softly, shrugging. "He can definitely be an ass, and he never knows when to shut his mouth, but he wouldn't intentionally cause an issue. What did he say to you anyway?"

"Please," I scoff, rolling my eyes and taking a drink of the wine in my hand.

"You don't understand what he is like. I've dealt with him my whole life. You met him yesterday. You don't know him. You can't judge." Alaric smirks, and looks back at the crowd of his people, nodding his head at a few of them as they bow in his direction as they pass. He plays the role perfectly, but clearly isn't interested in anything I have to say about Lucas. I continue watching him as I shake my head. I shouldn't be surprised, I am the outsider in this situation, but sometimes that is the position that sees things the most. I blink rapidly, clenching my jaw. I refuse to bow to Alaric or any of these royals or give in to Alaric's attitude. He has no idea who his brother really is; the monster I have glimpsed these months in my visions, and the man he confessed himself to be. I open my mouth but decide the fight isn't worth it, not until I have evidence to back myself up. I clench my teeth, causing the muscle in my cheek to tick while I shake my head again, turn on my heel, and walk away alone.

I manage to find my way to the gardens near my chambers, even after the unfinished tour I received earlier. The moon is starting to break through the clouds, offering enough light to see the path in front of me and my eyes immediately find Peter over near a fountain surrounded by tall hedges. The cobblestone path leads through the hedges and circles the fountain before disappearing down another path lined with hedges. Peter stands with his back to me, staring into the water of the fountain. The small train of my dress whispers along the stone under my feet, and my small heeled slippers are somehow quiet on the stone. I pause behind him and it takes everything in me to refrain from touching him, no matter how much I long to.

"Peter," He jumps at the sound of my voice, but he doesn't look at me and rather continues looking into the water. He picks at a light pink flower in his hands, the stem and leaves shredding in his fingers while the petals remain whole and untouched.

"I wondered if you would show." His reflection stares back at him, and that is the version of him I watch. He twists the flower in his fingers before dropping it into the water. His reflection ripples and distorts itself. I look up, longing for his eyes to meet mine.

"I am so sorry. I truly am," I whisper, wanting nothing more than to rush into his arms and cry into his chest. The pieces that I have barely begun to pick up still lie at his feet. I gave him everything, every part of me, and he left me abandoned on the dock trying to stay afloat among the tears that threatened to drown me. I am shattered, and I don't know how to move on; to move forward.

"I know you are. I'm sorry, too."

"The day you left I boarded a boat and tried to sail up the river to Lightspire. I was leaving. I should have tried to run away with you. You are everything I've ever wanted," my voice breaks, and I let the floodgates open. My breath is shaky, as tears run down my face.

"You are mine," he whispers as his long strides close the distance between us. His fingers wipe away my tears before they can fully fall, and I smile through the tears and breathlessly meet his eyes as his hands fall to my back, pulling me into a hug. He smells like wine and fresh air, but somehow, even with all of this space and distance, he smells of pine. My forehead rests on his chest and I breathe deeply, making sure that he is all I will smell for the days to come.

"I just want to run, and never look back," my voice is muffled as I speak into his chest.

He holds me closer, as he breathes, "then come with me. Run away with me. We can leave this all behind." He pulls back slightly to look at my face. I study him, wishing I could say yes and go. But I can't. I have to stay. I have to fight. I trace his features with my eyes forcing them into my memory. I don't want to be the one to leave him this time, but I can't keep going back. I need to let go, even if every ounce of me belongs to him, and probably always will. I stand on the tips of my toes and lean forward to kiss him on the cheek.

He turns his head at the last second and catches my mouth with his. His hands on my back pull me closer as my fingers curl themselves into his hair, and the kiss deepens. There is no space between our bodies, but I still somehow want him closer. I pull his head down and kiss him more forcefully, more urgently. I need him now like I need air. We cling to one another as if the other is the only thing keeping us from drowning. He bites my lip, making me gasp, and I recapture his mouth almost immediately. Our mouths move together in perfect harmony. When we separate, he leans his forehead against mine. I close my eyes, breathing deeply to steady the racing beat in my veins.

"Run away with me," he breathes, and my heart plummets, my world crashing down around me again as I barely breathe.

"I can't."

He freezes against me, then abruptly pulls away and goes back to the fountain. Looking down into the water, he asks "Why are you here, Katerina?"

"To explain." I wait for some sort of acknowledgement, but he simply remains where he is, which is the push I need to move forward. I think about the vision from this morning— Lucas bore the crown that currently rests on his father's brow, and he was lounged in the throne as if he were invincible. He was ordering the deaths of an entire town simply because they couldn't pay the increase of tax that he had forced on them. The castle had lost its vibrancy, its life. It was hollow and destitute. I shiver at the thought of what could happen if he were to succeed in his ploy for the throne. Then there is the strange moment when I arrived that I have yet to understand. "Lucas wants Alaric's throne, and he will do anything in his power to get it. If I leave now, with you, he will have it. I know you have said that you favor Lucas to

Alaric, but I promise you, Lucas is not the guy he claims to be.

He would destroy everything that we stand for. He has basically admitted as much to me." I wave my hands frantically, but still speak in hushed tones as Peter turns to face me. He looks baffled, but for some reason doesn't question my judgment or how I know. I reach for his hand and take it in both mine. "He would not rule the kingdom fairly. I don't have concrete evidence yet, and I can't really explain it, but trust me. He cannot get the throne. Alaric will be a good king. Lucas would be the end of us all." I shake my head, clutching his hand like a lifeline.

"You stay to make the kingdom a better place?" he asks, turning back to the water, but I have eyes only for him. Anytime he is in the same vicinity, I notice him. I don't have to see him to know he is nearby, it is like my body can simply tell that he is there; my skin tingles and it is like a wave of peace washes over me. I know he prefers Lucas to Alaric, but I hope that the words I say hold some sort of weight. I wish I could tell him about the visions, but I know that now isn't the time. I'll find a way to tell him everything in time; he has been one of the only people I trust. But now? After everything that we have gone through? I'm not sure. For the time being, he seems to be content with my reasoning, but I'm still not sure it is enough.

"Yes, I stay to help my country. I can't see the throne go to Lucas— I would rather die than see that happen."

"If you could, you would come with me?" He turns back towards me, his eyes searching mine. I know what he sees there, but I don't say anything and continue to watch his face. "Katerina?"

"Yes, I would. You know I would," I whisper, watching as he quickly and roughly wipes away a tear before it can fall. He nods and walks off into the night.

CHAPTER 9

There is already a fire going in the fireplace when I blindly stumble through my balcony door. I am not sure how I remembered which was mine, but somehow I managed to make it through my tears. I leave the balcony door open, letting the light breeze in to help alleviate the stuffiness of the room. I hear a soft sound, like someone setting something down and I whip my head around. There isn't anyone in my bedroom, but when I walk over to the sitting room door and glance inside, I see Lucas with the portrait of my sister and I in his hand. I stifle a gasp, watching as he trails his fingers along the side of the portrait where my sister resides. His fingers linger on her, almost possessively and I breathe deeply, trying to calm the boiling anger that threatens death at the way he looks at my sister. I settle my breathing, and clear my face of anything that would tell him anything. The tears are gone, and I hope the evidence of them is gone as well.

I try to slow my pulse and make it seem like he doesn't scare the hell out of me as I cross the threshold and cross my arms over my chest. His eyes flick up to me, and he smirks.

"Get out. Now," I order, pointing toward the door, anger making my words sharp as daggers. He snickers, shaking his head in response as he dangles the portrait between his forefinger and thumb.

"I don't think so. You aren't my queen yet. You can't order me around. By the way, that was a beautiful show of affection down in the garden not too long ago. I wonder what Alaric would say about it."

I don't give him the satisfaction of a response, or give any indication that I even know what he is talking about. My arms remain crossed across my chest, and I feel my eyes shrink in a glare that I can't stop. This man is a monster.

He laughs. "Are you ready to play nice?" he asks, looking at me like I'm a piece of meat. He places the portrait down carefully on the mantle before circling me, studying me as if I were an animal at the managerie, or something on display. I stand completely still not wanting to give him a reason to hurt me. I don't trust him, and so far, he has not given me a reason to. "You're actually quite pretty. A nice figure," I watch his eyes dip down to my exposed cleavage and his tongue darts out to moisten his lips. "Those perky little…" his smirk widens to a grin and he chuckles softly. "Your red hair becomes you; you've got quite a temper. Full of spirit and fight. A woman by any right. So I can still see why he is drawn to you, why out of all of the women here at court, he came for you. Is there some sort of magic that sings in your blood, that draws those around you to your side? That captivates them?" He taps his chin, stopping his predatory circling to stand mere inches from me. I feel the warmth radiating off of his body, and my body trembles. I have to tilt my head back to meet his gaze, and the plain desire there sends a shudder through me. He chuckles softly again, raising a hand to brush my hair behind my ear. I hold back my flinch. "You're naïve. Young. Fresh blood. Not one of the silly, shallow women we've had to deal with here at court." He smirks as I glare at him. He reaches his fingers out to brush my cheek, and I pull my head away wanting nothing more than to snap his fingers from his hand. He reaches his hand out again. This time, he runs his fingers along my jaw and grips my chin, turning my face to look at him. "You can try, but you will never be my queen." He roughly releases my face and stalks out of my room, leaving me staring after him, my mouth slightly agape.

I shake my hands, pacing the room for a few min. My mind races and thoughts are dark and I again wish I had someone here to talk to about all of this. I draw in a deep breath and slowly release it as I head into my bedroom, change quickly, and sit on the edge of my bed. I pull my mother's journal off of the shelf built into my headboard, and pull back the covers on my bed. I'm about to crawl into it when I hear a timid knock on my balcony door. The door is still slightly ajar, but whoever is out there stands outside of the light. I place the journal on the pillow, groan, and take the few steps to the door and push open the door lightly, shedding light on Alaric. I roll my eyes. Of course, it would be Alaric. I'm not sure who else I was expecting. Peter? I've hurt him enough for one night. Since the door is open, I know Alaric will enter whenever he is ready. I walk back over to the bed, and sit on the edge, my arms crossed over my chest, my foot tapping rapidly on the floor. I know I am wound tightly, and I could use the distraction he can provide with his jokes and the carefree man that I met on the journey here. Although, I know this will likely be an argument more than anything else. I have a short temper, and one thing I've noticed is Alaric's patience. I hope he shows that tonight. So I stare at the door waiting for it to open and soon enough, it does.

"Katerina?" Alaric peeks his head in the door looking for me. I'm not sure what took him so long. He finally steps through the door and stands with a sheepish look. It is a glimpse of the man from the road this past week. It makes me wonder even more if he even realizes the façade he puts up for others. Why not let himself just be who he showed me he really is? It would do nothing but serve him and help establish needed relationships with his people, his councilman, foreign dignitaries. Because the man he acts to be, is not always a good one.

"You found me, now what?"

"Katerina." He subtly shakes his head, biting his lip and running a hand through his hair.

"You know what? No," I break in, holding a hand up to stop any rebuttal he may have. "I want this to work. Truly. But you have to work with me, not against me. I need you to trust me, and believe me when I say something. Can you do that?"I start out with my voice raised with fire still burning in my veins, but quickly I deflate; the embers cooling to ash. I realize I'm tired— tired of fighting, tired of crying. I'm tired of lying and hiding everything from everyone. I don't know what I need, but I know I need something more than this. My life is completely in shambles, and I can't tell up from down, let alone who I can trust. My hands fall to the bed beside me as I tilt my head back maintaining Alaric's gaze as he kneels in front of me.

"I swear to you, I will. We are partners. Here on out," he whispers, his voice breaking as his hands find mine. "Please don't leave."

He is acting like he knows what Peter and I shared together in the garden earlier, but I don't think Lucas has had the time to get to him yet, and I'm not sure he will actually tell Alaric anything since I neither confirmed or denied what Lucas claims he saw. Regardless, Alaric seems to have this idea that I will leave, and I am not sure where that came from. I think back to our argument in the ballroom, the moments that we shared on the journey here, the various conversations, and I can't fathom where he possibly could have gotten this idea unless he knows about Peter and my rendezvous. I study Alaric as he looks up in my face from his knees. His hands in mine are warm, a little rough from the calluses at the base of each finger, but still soft against mine. I lace my fingers with his. His eyes are bright, apologetic, and from what I can tell, he is sincere, but I'm still not sure I trust it. My visions have led me here, and I need to make the most of it even if it isn't what I've wanted or dreamed of my life becoming. Besides, it's not like I have much of a choice. I couldn't really leave if I wanted to.

I continue watching his eyes. They are a captivating shade of blue, seeming to change hues every time I see him. His eyes have every ability to destroy me and bring me to my knees. They glisten in the warm lighting the candles and fireplace provide, and I beg and plead with myself to feel something more than friendship for this man. I know it's going to take time. I rise, pulling him up with me refusing to release his fingers until we stand with our chests pressed together. I wrap my arms around his waist, and bury my face in his chest. His arms circle me, holding me close and he rests his cheek on the top of my head.

"I'm not going anywhere. Okay?" My voice is muffled, but I feel him nod in response. I lift my head to look into his face. His face tilts down as he looks into my eyes, his shoulders sag slowly as he sinks into me.

"Okay." He leans his forehead on mine. I'm not ready to move on from Peter, or ready to fully give in to the idea of a wedding or life with Alaric. I just need time, and we are running out. There is too much at stake to risk taking too much time to be ready. I need to give this, give Alaric a chance. I sigh and look into his eyes. The look I see there leaves me breathless and butterflies erupt in my core. I can sense he wants to kiss me, but I think he hesitates due to the incident at the inn. His eyes flutter closed as he breathes deeply and nozzles my nose with his. Our breath mingles and I feel the pitter-pattering of my heart skipping in my chest. I know I shouldn't feel guilty for feeling this way, but it settles like a weight in my stomach. I barely know this man, aside from the week we have spent talking and learning what makes the other tick. It has only been a week since my life got turned upside down, and I don't know how to do this. How to maneuver my way through these feelings that creep in and the brokenness I feel over the loss of my relationship with Peter. I don't know how to move forward from here. Alaric pulls away with a sigh, his hands sliding down my arms to squeeze my hands before releasing me completely.

"Night, Kat." He leaves with a smile, and I have more questions than I do answers.

CHAPTER 10

My mother told me stories of Aouela while I was growing up.

The city is so full of life, color, and wonder. The buildings were close enough together you could travel the city on rooftop if you wanted. Each roof is a different color, a kaleidoscope under the sun. The people were or are just as colorful. The clothing is loose and ranges the rainbow, beading and fringed hemlines are rampant. The people are carefree and lively. Art and creativity are in abundance, and the seers, they are treated almost like royalty. The people are kind, and open to new ideas, and follow the directives of the seers. Our people are listened to, and we are trusted. I am not sure where things became so different here in Aurellia.

The late morning sun blinds me before I can even try to open my eyes. With the angle of the rays, I know I must have slept through breakfast. I heave a sigh and groan as I rise out of bed, stretching. Stumbling to the balcony door, I pull the sheer curtain aside. There isn't a cloud in the sky. I let the curtain fall and scan the room as I turn and take the few steps to the sturdy wardrobe to get dressed, trying to keep my thoughts away from Peter and my visions. While I've only been here a couple of days now, it feels like years. My fingers catch in my hair as they run through it, taming the worst of the tangles and smoothing the curls down as I pull it into a low knot at the nape of my neck and slip some shoes on my feet on my way out of the door.

Once I'm out in the hallway, I am at a loss of what direction to even head in, so I decide to go left. I start to wander aimlessly, hoping to find something that could point me in the direction of the kitchen.

I wander past twenty doors before a groan of frustration escapes and I stop to lean against the wall, and stare at the ceiling. I try to recall my steps and figure out my surroundings, but it is to no avail.

I wish Andria were here, she would have found the kitchen by now. She has this innate ability of immediately knowing where she is and how to get somewhere. It has helped us out of sticky situations in the past. I grin to myself, remembering the time we went to the shipyard to explore one of our father's ships. We didn't have permission to be there, but we snuck around thinking we were being sly. At the time, we didn't know that everyone around knew what we were up to and were turning a blind eye. We also didn't know that someone had told our father of our whereabouts. We eventually got lost on the docks until we heard one of the commanding officers shout a welcome to our father. I remember our wide eyed glances before Andria managed to sneak us back to the house before father was able to find us on the docks. We heard about it later, of course. But at the time, we thought we were invincible and could do anything.

I grin, shaking my head and looking away from the ceiling and down the hall. I really miss her. I wish I could see her rather than just communicate through letters. There was already one waiting for me when we arrived. I didn't expect one so soon, but with the week-long journey here, I shouldn't be surprised. The ravens can send a message within a day or two. I make a mental note to write back to Andria today. I sigh and walk over to the window across the hallway from me, and glance at the clear blue sky. The blue of the sky seems to jolt something awake in me.

My vision blurs momentarily before I see Peter in the gardens outside of the ballroom. He seems to be waiting for someone. I can only assume it is me. His eyes glitter in the fairy lights that light up the area, and his beaming grin ignites a fire in me that is hard to put out. He is haloed in white. Peter holds his hands out to me, and I rush into them. As soon as I feel his arms close around me and the faintest brush of his lips on mine, I jolt back to the present. I catch myself on the windowsill, pressing my palms into the cold stone to keep myself from fainting. Somehow it works. I take a few deep breaths, grounding myself.

As I linger to catch my breath and hold back the dizziness, I hear two sets of footsteps around the corner. They pause there, and their hushed whispers cause my heart to leap to my throat, and my eyes widen in fear.

"We can't help him. It is insane!"

"We have no choice. You saw what he did to John. He is ruthless."

"But kill our King? Come-on, man. Not only is it treason, it goes against everything I was raised to believe."

"Do you want to end up like John? I'd rather take my chances with his brother's need for vengeance afterwards. You do what you want, but I'm not going to stand against him."

I hear one set of footsteps come closer as they turn the corner, and I quickly look out of the window and try to look like I didn't just hear everything they said. A tall blonde soldier walks past me without even a second glance. The other soldier must walk off in the opposite direction because his footsteps fade into nothingness. I sag against the wall, mulling over everything I just heard. Who is the 'he' that they are so afraid of? It can't be Lucas, he wouldn't kill his own father, would he?

Sharp, short footsteps fill the hall, and I turn my face from the window glancing down the hall just as Alaric comes striding around the corner followed by a young curly brown-haired guard. He must have alerted him to my presence. They nod to each other and the guard walks off down the hall. I know I've wandered farther than I should have, but if my tour hadn't been cut short, I might not have gotten lost. Rather than find my way, I ended up even more lost than before and for some reason Alaric is striding in like I did something wrong.

"Kat? What are you doing?"

"Exploring." I shrug before chancing a glance at his reaction, and quickly jump to a different answer when he doesn't look amused. "I got lost trying to find the kitchen."

Alaric studies me for a moment then dismisses the guard. "Did my brother show you around at all?" he asks, looking in front of him rather than at me. I watch him, he stands tall, but his fingers tap against his leg and a muscle ticks in his jaw. He doesn't seem angry, but rather uncomfortable or threatened. I take a step toward him, slowly.

"He left halfway through. I gathered that something happened that he had to take care of." I contemplate telling him what I overheard, but decide not to because I feel I need to get more information and evidence before I do tell him or anyone. He nods, still avoiding my gaze. "Did I do something wrong?" I ask, trying to catch his gaze. He finally looks at me, rolling his eyes at the question. "If not, then why won't you look at me?"

"The guests and my father's advisors and councilmen reside in this wing. Peter lives here. I can't help but think that was why you are here, rather than getting lost. I'd like to believe you," he pauses, rubbing the back of his neck as he dips his head before continuing, "but I'm not sure I do." He has the courtesy to look sheepish, but his eyes dart around and his fingers still tap against his leg, and I can imagine the wheels turning in his mind are still unsure. It appears trust doesn't come easy for either of us.

"I promise you I was unaware. I woke up late and left in search of the kitchen, but I got lost. Your brother left me stranded in the garden without showing me much of the palace. You can trust me."

"Okay." He rubs the back of his neck again before he shrugs off the moment, looking at me with a grin. "Let's get you some food."

"Thank you," he murmurs as he grabs a handled basket from one of the kitchen staff. She bobs her head in response and backs away to get back to whatever task she was doing before we arrived. Her brown hair is pulled into a small bun at the nape of her neck, and is covered in a white bandana. She is wearing a brown dress with a white apron to prevent her dress from getting covered in food. I watch her as she wanders to the back of the kitchen and disappears. She didn't say much, but made sure that Alaric's every request was met. The basket is of fine quality, a dark brown weave that is large enough to hold a decent sized picnic lunch. I don't ask what is inside, and instead follow him silently as he weaves his way through the busy kitchen to a small door that leads outside.

He seems completely at home and comfortable, which is expected. The basket swings slightly with his movement, and the outside sun is bright from the dim light of the kitchen. I blink and squint until my eyes readjust. There is a small shed with firewood to the left of the door we just exited, with a chopping block and axe jutting out of the wood, the handle at a ninety degree angle. Just beyond that lay pastures where I spot a couple of cows and a fenced off area where a small hen house resides. I hear the faint crooning of the chickens and wonder what other animals they have back here. Looking to the other side of the wood shed, there is a path that winds around the side of the building and out of view.

Alaric sets down that path, and I wordlessly follow. He is just as quiet, just watching the world around him as he walks. The air is warm, but it feels nice. The sun is bright and there isn't a cloud in sight. I want to bask in the sun; let it soak into my bones and add some color to my pale skin. As we round the building, the area becomes slightly more familiar. The path diverts into two, and we take the left path. There is a small creek that bubbles through the garden, and I notice the fountain where I met Peter a little ways off down the path to my right. That way must lead back toward my chambers. I have not been down the left side of the gardens yet. The gardens and property surrounding the castle are sprawling, and a lot larger than they appear. I can see even farther off to my left is another path that branches from this one, and leads to what looks like training grounds. We stay on our current path for some time, and I take in my surroundings and Alaric. He is content: whistling softly to himself as he leads the way, and he has a slight bounce to his step. He is so hot and cold, I don't know what to make of him. One minute he is threatened and angry, the next, gentle, funny, and sweet. It is confusing and I never know which version I will meet the next time.

The path winds past a white gazebo that is engulfed by hydrangeas and other flowers. It is picturesque, and looks like something out of the fairy tales that my mother would tell Andria and me as children. My lips perk up in the corners into a small smile. I turn from the gazebo and watch as Alaric ducks under a weeping willow to the left, and disappears. I tilt my head as I carefully step through the soft branches dangling overhead, brushing them aside as I step through after him. There is no real path, but there is a small wishing well sitting just on the other side of the branches. There must have been a path here at some point in the past, but now, it has disappeared over time. The area is hidden from view, and is blocked off on all other sides by hedges, hydrangea bushes, and the stonework of the castle walls. I can see through the branches to the garden on the other side, but unless a passer-by knew to look, they would not know we were here.

Alaric places the basket on the ground and sits beside it. He draws one leg up and the other is bent under him. He opens the basket as I kneel on the grass beside him before sitting completely, leaning on my right arm as I watch him. He carefully removes a sandwich and hands it to me. I take it, our fingers brushing with a jolt and our eyes lock over the sandwich. I draw in a breath, pulling my hand and sandwich away from his. We look at each other a moment longer, trying to read the other. He looks away first, glancing into the basket as he reaches in again to withdraw a second sandwich. We eat in silence, listening to the wind whistle through the trees and birds chirping as they ride that same wind.

The quiet is refreshing, and not feeling the need to fill it with mindless chatter is nice. He reaches back inside the basket, and pulls out a small bundle of cookies. He unties the ribbon holding them together, and hands me one. I murmur my thanks, and lay down in the grass watching the sky above. The cookie melts on my tongue. The sweetness of the chocolate pieces mixed in with the sugar and butter of the cookie makes my jaw ache. They are amazing, and the cookie is gone before I really notice. My fingers dig into the grass at my sides and I continue to watch the sky. Some clouds have wandered into the area, and laying here, watching the clouds roam reminds me of times spent as a child with Peter, imagining shapes among them. Alaric is lying beside me, but instead of looking at the sky, he looks at me. I get a sense of déjà vu and I realize that I have seen this moment before.

"I can feel you looking at me." I turn my head slightly to look at him but quickly look away, wishing he hadn't found me where he did. I can tell that he still thinks I was trying to find Peter. He tries to catch my gaze. I avoid it and sit up slowly. "Alaric," I sigh, meeting his gaze. We remain locked in each other's gaze.

"I want you to be happy, Kat."

"Alaric, I'm okay." I look out into the garden, watching the bees zip from flower to flower. "All of this is going to take some getting used to. Just give me some time."

"I understand. Please let me know if there is any way I can make you feel more at home. I will do anything that I can."

"I will. Thank you." I smile and reach for his hand. He takes it as he sits up beside me.

"Let's dance." Alaric declares suddenly, pulling me to my feet after he leaps to his own. I laugh as he pulls me close into a slow waltz. He dips me low, and a giggle bursts out of my throat, causing him to laugh as well. He pulls me back up and we trip over each other's feet, falling onto the grass, with Alaric buffering my fall. We look at each other, laughter dancing its own dance in our eyes. Before I can even realize what is happening, his lips brush against mine. They are soft, and I kiss him back with all the pent-up desire I have for the man I'm starting to know, but still long for Peter to be the one in my arms instead.

Alaric's grip tightens and I sink into him, trying to forget about Peter and the way his kiss lit my body on fire. I try to open myself up to who is to be my husband in a few short months. My pulse starts to quicken and I feel the glimmer I've felt growing in my core. This man, he can make me laugh so hard I cry, he aggravates me in ways that make me see red, but at the end of the day, he is trying to find happiness too. He is trying to show me the person he wants to be but doesn't know how to be. And that is the person that may slowly start to put all the pieces that shattered when Peter left me on that boat back together. He just might be the glue that holds me together again.

He rolls us over so he rests on his elbows above me. We pull apart, breathless. He chuckles, trailing his nose along my jawline and down my neck. I shiver. He starts to pull back and looks at me with mixed emotion. I lay there, my eyes trying to understand the emotions flitting across his face. My eyes flutter closed. I know I should tell him everything, but I can't. I open my eyes again momentarily and watch Alaric shake his head as if to clear it.

He smiles and rolls off of me and rises to his feet, offering me a hand. "You have grass in your hair." He laughs as he starts plucking strands of grass from my tangled locks. Once he is done, I motion for him to turn so I can wipe the grass off of his tunic. I pat his shoulders, letting him know I'm done. He turns, making sure my hands are still on his shoulders. He pulls me close and kisses me once again, taking his time. He pulls back, and I sigh as I open my eyes to look at him. He takes my hand, grabs the picnic basket, and leads me back to the castle.

CHAPTER 11

Alaric!" I call as I chase him down the hall toward the throne room. He pauses, turning to look at me with a smile. "Do you mind if I come with you to today's meeting with the council? It's about time I join you since I will be leading with you soon enough." This could be my way of hearing everything that is going on, and possibly get more intel on Lucas and things he might be planning. I don't hold out a lot of hope, but it could be a start.

When I catch up, we continue walking to the throne room and through the door. "I don't mind, but I'm not sure how others will react since we aren't officially married yet." He leads me through the room and pauses at the door at the back of the room. It is the same room he went into with his father when we first arrived. His hand rests on the handle. "Peter will be here." He refuses to meet my eyes, but I can see that his face is drawn and his shoulders are tense.

"I'm aware Peter will be here, but that is not why I want to come. I need to learn the procedure and get to know our advisors." Still, he hesitates. I can't help but roll my eyes and heave a sigh. "Alaric, I promise you. I couldn't care less that he will be here." The moment the words leave my mouth, I wish I could take them back because they aren't entirely true. The chance to see Peter again is something I have been longing for. Even in passing, the sight of him is enough to get me through the day. The pang of guilt races through me, and I wince as my teeth sink into my lip a little too hard.

Thankfully Alaric doesn't look at me, and instead nods, seemingly content with my answer. He opens the door, and ushers me inside. I step through the doorway, and my breath catches in my throat. The small chamber is brightly lit, and the ceilings are high and magnificent. There are golden wood arches that add to the height of the room, and are carved with immaculate detail that I wish I had time to study. The stonework of the wall is well done, and it is obvious that the mason that accomplished this took his time and consideration when choosing where to place the stones.

I take in the rest of the room. A tapestry depicting a ship at sea during a storm adorns the wall to my left. To the right of the doorway is a large fireplace that takes up a majority of the wall. The long wooden table in the center of the room is occupied by men from all of the seven territories that make up the council. The table itself is a large map that is subset into the table itself depicting everything: the mountains to the East and North, the marshlands to the east, the pass between Aurellia and Arrowhelm, and the bridges that cross into Modiva.

Each of the territories are shown with little markers for each city and the men that each contain. The map is impressive, and shows exactly the army's numbers, as well as where each group is located. The edges of the table are higher than the map, and this is where everyone's hands rest. King Henry sits at the far end of the table and there is an empty chair to his left for Alaric. His eyes meet mine, and his face lifts in surprise. Behind him on the wall is a painting of the royal family. The queen was beautiful, and Alaric and Anna have a good bit of her in them.

The King clears his throat, bringing the room to attention. "Everyone, this is Lady Katerina Smith, my son's fiancée." The men stand, turn to me, and nod their heads in a small bow. The representative from Stonebreach, Lord Ian Whitfield, stands beside Peter. Ian shoots me a grin across the table, and I give a nod of my head in response, knowing that my eyes smile back. His light brown locks are cropped short and he has the beginnings of a beard along his jawline. His dark eyes are bright and he appears happy to see me. It has been awhile since I have seen him, and seeing him now is like a breath of home. It has been too long since we have seen each other— my father decided to stay home with Andria and I about two years ago, but would make the journey here four times a year to stand beside his King. That is the last time Ian has been home.

I let Alaric lead me to the chair by his father and he encourages me to take it. I sit, but I feel bad that he has to stand. "Now that everyone is here, let's go ahead and get started."

The men hesitate for a moment, looking at me, but since the King is allowing my presence they quickly jump to discussing issues going on in their territories that require attention. I look around the table, easily recognizing several of the men. I avoid looking directly across the table. Since Lightspire is the largest territory, they occupy the seat beside the King. I know Peter is there, I can feel his gaze like a weight on my chest. I glance up and catch his eye. I steel myself against the flood of emotions that rush through me. This is foolish. The way he still ignites a fire that rages through me, even after everything is all consuming. I hate it. He smiles, but I quickly glance down, ignoring the smile and try to dampen the fire. Maybe I shouldn't have come. I force my attention away from him and towards the conversation.

Lord Tyrin from the territory that borders my father's is currently discussing some things that he has heard regarding his fishing villages. "My King, I implore you to send help. I'm unsure of who is attacking my villages, but my people are terrified. Their homes are being burned, their food and anything of value, stolen. I have tried to send my own men, but they return either dead, or on the verge of death. Whoever is doing this is cunning and creative. The men who have returned cannot name who it was that attacked them. They attack under a banner that no one can name; they fight under a falling star. We need assistance, my lord. I don't know what else I can do. Please," Tyrin looks around, his eyes pleading as he stands there helpless and desperate, "send some men."

I watch the King for his response. He remains emotionless, his face betraying nothing. He searches Lord Tyrin's desperate face before he turns to Peter, "Lord Gold, do you have any men that you can spare to send to Lord Tyrin's aid? When is the earliest that he can expect them?"

Peter clears his throat before responding. "I can send a hundred men, and they can be there within two weeks on foot, or we can send them down the river and they can be there within the week's end." He turns to Lord Tyrin. "Will this suffice? I am sorry that it can't be sooner."

Lord Tyrin nods. "Thank you. That should be enough." He lowers himself into his seat, and glances around the room at the other men.

"Are there any other concerns that need to be discussed?" The King looks around the room.

"Sir, should we look into these men? Those that travel under the falling star insignia?" A raspy voice utters from further down the table. I glance at Lord Melvin Sharp. He leans forward across the table in order to see King Henry, and I try to recall what little I know of the man. He owns the area to the east of Aurellia City: Tradesport. It is a hub of people at the far end of the country with the Bloodstone

Mountains across the river, and Riverstrand across the bridge in the marshlands that make up the area. They are a hearty people, used to the muggy atmosphere. They are the major city that makes up the eastern side, and provide a lot of different medicines and art.

From what I have heard, they are a strange people, but are good people. I don't know much about the man himself, so I take in his appearance. He is short, and has these eyes that bug out of his head slightly. They have a slight upward tilt, and his mouth is tiny. His chin is pointed, and the cleft in it cracks it almost in two. His hair is a reddish blonde, and pulled back in a low tail at the nape of his neck. He is skinny, almost too thin and has a greyish pallor to his skin. He is on the older side, maybe in his forties, or close to my father's age.

King Henry nods, and I watch him scan the room, waiting to see if anyone else voices an opinion. I watch the men shift in their seats, and I almost speak up, but Lord Samuel Fairvein lifts his hand. He derives from Riverstrand, the territory on the other side of the bridge from Tradesport. He is young, and around my age. He must be new to his station, because when he speaks his voice has a slight waver, as if he is unsure and nervous to speak up.

"I think we should look further into this group. I believe there is something larger at play here than what we are seeing right now, but I feel it is something that we shouldn't take lightly." His voice has a sweet timbre to it, something almost musical. He is raven haired, with dark eyes, and freckles dusting his nose and cheeks. He is stocky, and fills his chair with his size. He is darker in complexion, tan skinned. He has a solid presence, but clearly lacks confidence. But that will come with time.

"I second that." Ian Whitfield's deep gruff adds. He nods at me, and I dip my head slowly. He is aware of my mother's visions and knows that it is a possibility that both my sister and I could have them too. He is privy to a lot of information and worked alongside my father to make sure that information went to the right people. I may be able to get his help with what is going on. I will have to seek him out sometime soon. "In fact, I can offer up a small team to search to find out more. See where they stem from, what they know, and what the intentions are. I can send a raven to have them dispatch within the next couple of days."

King Henry flutters his eyes as he looks to think about this. "Very well. Send the raven. Let's see what we can find out. The best place to start may be in Springbay or Kilburn. See what further information Becker can provide you, and start there." He holds his hands up and looks around the room at each councilman before placing his hands back on the table and pushing himself to his feet. "If there is nothing else?"

No one voices anything else, so he dismisses the meeting. As the men leave the room, Peter and I share one last look. The way he looks at me seems to warn me of something. But he looks away before I can figure out what. I watch Ian leave as well, and I want to run after him, see if we can talk, but King Henry pulls my attention back into the room. Everyone has gone except for the three of us; Alaric, King Henry, and me.

"Lady Katerina, I'm surprised you came today. I wasn't expecting you to take an interest in this sort of thing. My wife never joined in on the council meetings." King Henry lingers at the head of the table beside me. His fingers still rest on the table, and he stands about a foot taller than me, but mere inches taller than Alaric.

I meet King Henry's gaze. "I thought that I should know what is going on in our kingdom. I will eventually be Queen, and I figured I should be a part of it. When Alaric rules, we will be ruling alongside each other, a partnership. It is how my father ran his territory with my mother, and it is how I believe it should be everywhere." I continue to hold his gaze, standing my ground. I know my father might argue against this, but I do feel that it is a partnership, and should be treated as such. I will not simply be a figurehead, some bumbling idiot that is present to look pretty and hold court over the other women. I want to make a difference, and actually have a voice. Henry holds my gaze. I stand there, feeling bare beneath his critical eye, but feel the tension ease when his face breaks with a smile that reaches his eyes. I must have passed some sort of test, one I wasn't aware that I was taking.

"Very well said, my lady. You will make a very fine match for my son." King Henry dips his head toward us before circling around the table and heading out of the room. The door closes with a soft click and I look up at Alaric from my stance in front of the chair. I'm not sure what his father meant by that. I thought for sure I was overstepping, but maybe that was exactly what he wants for his kingdom. Someone to shake things up and change things for the better.

Alaric leads me from the council room, his fingers warm in mine, and through the winding halls until we are in the gardens. We take the path that heads toward the hidden wishing well we went to previously, and where the path separates from the path toward the well, we follow the new path. I watch the area around us, I haven't ventured down this way yet, but I know it heads to the training grounds. We pass several different groups; guards, nobles, and townsfolk heading back to the castle from their sessions. The path is wide, cutting through fields and areas that could be used for different sorts of combat lessons on a grander scale than what we will see on the actual training grounds, and a wooden fence lines one side of the path.

Eventually I see a large square area roped off where three men are engaged in hand-to-hand combat. It seems an unfair fight, with it being two on one, but the one working against the two is massive. He towers over the two others, and is wide with bulging muscles in his arms. He lets out a yell, and charges one of the men, who lowers himself into a crouch, and right before the bigger man can touch him, he rolls out of the way. My breath catches in my throat as I watch the fight. Alaric chuckles beside me, his fingers still in mine. My free hand rests on the fence, and my anxiety spikes as the larger man swings a fist out toward the second one that darts in behind him.

The swing misses, as the second smaller man spins out of reach while landing two quick jabs on the big one; one on his side, the other on the flank of his back. I hear him grunt, but he kicks out behind him, and connects with the man who landed the hits. He stumbles backward, clutching his stomach, but manages to keep his feet. The first man spins and kicks out at the same time, and the head of the big man flings back, and he stumbles back a step as well, but the assault continues and it is mere moments before he is on the ground with the two smaller men standing over him. It is impressive, I was genuinely concerned that the larger man would still come out on top, but the smaller men were able to defeat the larger opponent.

"That is the captain of the guard, and the two smaller guys are the trainers. They spar every once in a while to keep each other on their toes and ready for combat." Alarc nods at the group and tilts his head back to the dirt path towards the rest of the training grounds.

"That was…" I shake my head, but follow along as he takes us past the sparring ring and towards an area that has straw targets about twenty-five feet from a row of wooden tables. There is a group of three nobles at the first table throwing stars at the first two targets. One hits the target each time, while one of the other men's throws are short of the target or miss entirely.

Alaric chuckles, and stops at the stand just inside the opening in the fence that has another path that leads to the tables. Within the stand, a burly looking older gentleman sits just in front of a wall of rows and rows of daggers. Each is intricately made, and absolutely beautiful.

"Afternoon sir, I have the bundle you requested. Will you be using those today?" The old man's voice is surprisingly warm, but has a huskyness to it that reminds me of the accent Peter has. I wonder if he came from the north originally, but push the thought to the side as Alaric nods and takes a leather bundle from him. He waves and leads me to the table in the middle. The bundle rings slightly as he sets it on the worn wood in front of us.

"You had mentioned before that you wanted to learn how to be self-sufficient. I had these made for you," he says as his fingers deftly untie the twine that holds the bundle closed. The leather unravels, revealing a set of six small daggers sheathed within. Each one is adorned with dark silver vines wrapped around colorful gemstones that glint in the sunlight. The weapons are beautifully wrought, and I am touched by the gift. I look up into Alaric's face, and am greeted with the smile that I love so much- the one that lights up his face. "You like them?" His voice is quiet, and I simply nod.

"Thank you…I don't know what to say. They are beautiful."

"I'm going to teach you the proper way to place your feet, and how you need to hold them before we move into the correct movement in your wrist." His face is bright, and the smile on his face broadens. I can feel my eyes widen and I nod meekly. He chuckles at me, and I shoot him a glare from under my eyelashes. I watch him make a motion over his lips like he is going to be quiet, before he continues. "Go ahead and face the target and place your feet shoulder-width apart. Like this," he demonstrates and I imitate the position. "Good. Now place the foot that is on your dominant side slightly forward a step. When you throw the knife, you will shift your weight forward into the motion, so it needs to be the foot on the side with which you throw."

He moves his left foot forward and shows the movement by swaying in his step. I guess I never realized that he was left handed.

I move my right foot forward, and practice the motion. It feels awkward and strange, but will likely feel more natural as I practice and add the knife to it. "Like this?"

"Perfect. You can go ahead and pick one of the daggers," he murmurs as he moves to stand directly behind me. I trail my fingers over the knives until I find one that feels right. It has a ruby on the hilt, and I pull it free from the sheath. It is lighter than I thought it would be, but still has enough heft in my palm that I notice it there. I feel Alaric against me and his breath tickles the back of my neck and cheek. "Now for the hard part. Hold the knife by the blade, pinching it between your thumb and first two fingers. Feel the weight settle in your fingers." I feel his fingers slide down my arm to my right hand, and he lifts it until it is directly beside my head. I try to control my breathing as his touch electrifies me and I struggle to concentrate. I swallow and breathe out through my mouth. *Come on, Kat. Get it together.*

"Just like that."

He pinches the knife over my own fingers, and moves our hands angling them backwards and moves them forward in a flicking motion. He picks up the pace, flicking forward faster. "Release the blade right before your hand comes to a stop. You'll feel when it is time. Let go when you feel it." He demonstrates the flicking motion again, and says, "now," as he hits a specific spot in the flick forward. He is right, it is exactly where I felt I needed to let go. His voice is a caress, and I suppress a shiver and lick my lower lip as I concentrate. He releases my hand, but does not step back. He lingers against me, and I swallow again as I keep my hand raised, release my wrist back and snap it forward letting the blade fly when it feels right. The dagger flies true, and lands in the outer rim of the target. His hand rests on my hip, and I throw my hands up in a silent cheer. I can't believe it actually hit the target.

He chuckles, the sound vibrating against my neck as he leans forward to whisper in my ear, "Absolutely perfect. Beautifully executed." His words send a shiver through me as the butterflies erupt in my stomach. I don't suppress the shiver, and instead lean into Alaric's touch. I feel his breath on the back of my neck and shoulder as he leans forward and his breath becomes a whisper of his lips on the top of my shoulder. My breath hitches, and I melt. He nips at my shoulder, and the bite of his teeth on my flesh shoots sparks through me and I can barely stifle the soft moan. His hand grips my waist harder and spins me to face him. His lips find mine, as his other hand cups my cheek and I give in to every pent up feeling that I have harbored, and simply, let go.

That evening, I pace my balcony, my thoughts running a million miles a minute. I try to catch one fleeting thought before it morphs into another, but all I get are fleeting images. I can't pinpoint what exactly stirred up this rapid fire of things, but I want to scream in frustration. I had another vision today, shortly after returning from the training grounds. It lingers in my mind on replay. There is a young girl with eyes exactly like Peter's that stood in the forests to what I assume to be the north, screaming as the banner of the falling star flies in the background. She was involved in hand to hand combat with men dressed in solid black, her face bleeding from a cut on her cheekbone.

Her strawberry blonde hair twirling around her as she spins away from the blade coming toward her and she undercuts the man and lodges her knife in the side of his neck. She rises and wipes the blood dripping down her face as she stands over the man, watching the blood bubble out of his neck. She looks up, and it is almost as if she can see me because for a moment our eyes lock. The vision focuses in on her face; the strong jaw, dimple in her left cheek, and freckles that dust along her cheekbones and nose. Her hair is more blonde than mine, but I would recognize her anywhere. That girl? She is my daughter.

I place my hands on the railing of my balcony, and lift my face to the sky. My daughter. This must be how it felt for my mother when she saw visions about Andria and I. I wonder if she had the same gut wrenching fear and the bitter tang of metal on her tongue when imagining the world that is to come based on the visions that arise. What even is there to do to change something this far in the future? She had to have been the same age I am now. What difference can I make that will change her from ever having to fight? To ever have to wield a blade.

I groan, and I again wish that I had someone to talk to about all of this. My father might be able to help, but not extremely likely. Andria went silent since I forced more information from her before I left. I can't go to her. I toss up the idea of talking with Alaric and Anna, but I don't know how the royal family views seers. I wish I knew someone from Arrowhelm, or that general area of the world. I have so many questions, but no one to provide answers. I rest my forehead on my clasped hands on the railing and breathe deeply. I hear the rustling of the wind in the branches of the trees down below, and the squawk of a bird in the distance. I remember Ian's face from earlier.

I wonder if my father asked him to keep an eye on me while here at court. Maybe I should pay him a visit, and see if he can tell me anything. With the light lingering in the sky above, I descend the stairs into the garden and set off towards the main garden that parallels the Great Hall in hopes of stumbling into him.

I pass a few nobles that reside here, but none that are familiar. The air is warm, but comfortable. The walk is relaxing to the muscles that had bunched and tensed with my relentless pacing. There has to be something that I can do to change the course of fate, to change what is coming. I thought I was already on that path, but seeing her fighting against the same enemy proves otherwise.

The garden is relatively busy, but it isn't until I enter the castle through the double doors leading into the Great Hall that I find Ian leaning against a section of wall in a small alcove behind the grand staircase that leads up to the different wings of the castle. He is with a couple of other men that I recognize from the meeting earlier, but can't place their names.

I believe the younger athletic man with curly dirty blonde hair and hazel eyes to be Lord Hayden Conway. His father runs Frewich, the waypoint between the pass to the capitol city. It is a rich city that has had a huge influx of artisans and music. It is a beautiful city that Alaric and I had stopped at on our journey to the city. I longed to linger and explore the cultural district that had the most colorful buildings and life held within. Ian must notice me, because he excuses himself from his comrades and makes his way over to me.

"My lady," he bows slightly, but his face scrunches up into a grin. His eyes crinkle in the corners, and his beard becomes him. It makes him appear older, more sophisticated.

"Can we talk?" My eyes dart around the room, and I can't help but feel exposed here in the open surrounded by other nobles.

He dips his head, and leads the way out of the room full of prying eyes to a quiet alcove further down the hall. The area is empty, and thankfully quiet. I know that I will still need to choose my words carefully, but at least there is a familiar face here at court that knows my family history.

"Your father warned me that once you realized that I was here, that you may come to me. I hoped it wouldn't be so quick, but I am at your disposal." His eyes meet mine, but he leans against the wall of the alcove, facing me, and partially blocking off the opening in an attempt to conceal me inside. I am grateful for the coverage. It makes me feel more secure and like I can actually speak.

"What do you know about Lucas?" I peer up at him. He stands a few inches above me, and I press my back into the wall.

He looks surprised, but lowers his voice as he speaks, "I'm not entirely sure what you mean, but he is cocky. He is arrogant, and he wants everything that he can't have. He likes to push buttons and test boundaries. I don't trust him." He looks over his shoulder as a servant passes by in the hall. He waits until the sound of her footsteps are gone before he continues. "But not every person on the council or here at court feel this way. Why? What have you seen?"

"He all but confessed to me that he wants Alaric's throne. He seems willing to do whatever it takes to make it happen." I peer around him, ensuring that there is no one nearby, "I overheard a couple of guards talking about a plot to kill the king. They mentioned something about facing someone's brother's wrath afterwards. They sounded terrified, and didn't want to go through with the plan, but were so they wouldn't end up like a man named John. I don't know if it is necessarily Lucas's doing, but something is going on, and I need to figure out a way to stop it. I've seen flashes of war for months now, and it is only getting more prominent. Even today, there was a flash of the banner of the falling star, and someone fighting against them. It is still occurring years down the line. I need to put a stop to it. I need your help." I shake my head, biting my lip, then plowing forward. "Please, I don't know what to do anymore. I don't know what steps to take, or if I should tell Alaric everything."

Ian runs his hand over the top of his head, and releases a big breath. I don't think he anticipated this conversation happening. I chew the inside of my cheek, needing to know what to do next. I am lost, and I don't know which way is up let alone forward.

"Don't mention anything to Alaric yet. We will get there, but for now, let me try to talk to the king. See if I can relay the message about there being a plot against him, and see if he will take it seriously. I will work on this. I need you to continue gathering whatever intel you can, and come find me if there are any changes, or if you see anything more. You aren't alone in this, Kat. Whatever you need, I am available to you." He dips his head, and meets my gaze. His eyes are unwavering, and I know he means every word he says. He will be a partner in this, helping me get messages to those who need it- the same way he was for my mother. He reaches a hand out to me and I take it. His calloused palm squeezes mine. He nods again, and turns out of the alcove and stride off down the hall. I linger a moment longer, release a deep breath and head down the hall to the staircase and path that leads to my chambers.

CHAPTER 12

I peek both ways down the hall before exiting my room. I shouldn't be so paranoid, but I can't help but feel eyes somewhere watching me. I know it is my imagination, but the palace is full of people, and I have no idea if any of them are reporting back to anyone. I know Lucas has his fill of spies flitting through the castle, just begging for something interesting to happen so they have something to report. I hope no one catches me today. I know Peter is somewhere in this castle, and I can't not find a way to see him. I set off at a brisk walk through the halls. My long skirt annoyingly twists around my ankles to the point that I yank it up, the soft fabric bunched in both fists, and begin to walk faster, while my eyes dart around me every few minutes. Surprisingly, the halls remain empty. There is not a single servant or guard to be seen anywhere. Rather than put me at ease, this serves to make me even more paranoid than I was before. Where is everyone? Even in the West Hall where all of the royal guests and council members reside, there is not a soul to be seen.

I received a discreet note a few days ago, in Peter's handwriting. He had somehow convinced my maid to pass it off to me, and I'm surprised he thought that was a good idea. I release my skirt and open my hand to reread the note to double check the correct room. Of course, I already have the note memorized and my hand drops to my side as I stare at the wooden door in front of me. My breath catches in my chest and I pause, unsure whether I should continue. There's no telling what Alaric will do if he finds out. I am engaged, and it will only do more harm than good for both Peter and I. But I have to see him. I need to…there is so much I need, but know I can't and shouldn't have. I hesitantly knock on the door, and as it swings open and the light from within pours out, he appears, standing in front of me with hope in his eyes. I don't have the strength to keep from entering the room as he peers around the hall to make sure no one has seen before closing the door behind me.

Before either of us can say anything, we are wrapped in each other and I find that I can finally breathe properly again. The weight of the visions, Alaric, and everything else seems to disappear. He buries his nose in my shoulder, and I cling tighter to him. He smells like home, and I long to linger in his arms, but that isn't why I've come. With a sigh I pull away, but he keeps a hold of my hands. He leads me to the bed. I sit on the edge with him beside me, and I look around the room. His wardrobe is slightly open, and I can see that he shoved his clothes that were likely on the floor or the chair in there at the last minute. I try to fight back a grin as I take in the rest of the room. The bed is made, and the floor is free of anything out of the ordinary. My eyes linger in the corner, noticing the small pile of discarded shoes and his sword balanced haphazardly on top of them. It is nice to know that at least these little things haven't changed. He is still the Peter that I've always known.

I smile and turn to face the man beside me. His eyes have lingered on me this whole time, and rather than make me uncomfortable they have the opposite effect. I blush, and open my mouth to begin, but I am at a loss for words as his hands softly trace random patterns on the back of my hand. I shiver involuntarily and my eyes slide closed as I briefly imagine the life we could have shared, could still have, if I left with him. I remember what it felt like to have those same fingers trail over every inch of my being. I feel the bed dip as he slides closer to me. His fingers wind themselves in my hair as he turns my face. His lips slowly caress mine, and I allow myself to get swept away and give in to the desire between us even though it feels wrong to do so. He gently lays me back on the bed, following me down. I move to the center and gaze into his deep green eyes. They take me home. In his eyes, I see the green of the pasture, and the eerie green the ocean turns before a storm. I see the trees in bloom, and I see him chasing me through the gardens as children. It is safe and warm here in his arms.

In an effort to distance myself, I sit curled into the chair on the other side of the room with a small blanket wrapped around my shoulders, although I'm not cold. In a way, it is to separate myself even more from him, a small barrier to protect me. While I know that what just happened, and what we are to each other, can't happen again, I don't fully trust myself to remain beside him. I need to let him go, for my own sanity, my own well-being. If Alaric were to ever find out about this, about us, it isn't just him or me that would be killed. He would feel the betrayal like a physical wound, one that affects me as well. I blink hard against the sudden burning in my eyes. If I am being honest with myself, and with Alaric, I need to finally tell him about the visions. I need to be honest with everyone, including myself.

Peter remains comfortably lounged in his bed, the sheets

draped lazily over his lower half, his chest bare. He has an arm raised over his head, resting on his head while the other lays across the bed beside him. He looks comfortable, and I envy him the ease in which he carries himself. I force myself to look away and try to think of how to start. I came with one goal in mind; to tell him everything. My mind stumbles. How do I even start? I guess it is best to start at the beginning.

"Do you remember the day my mother died? We were by the bay, and the guards came to get us? We thought we were going to get in trouble for being by the water without supervision, and to this day, I'm not even sure our parents even knew we were down there," I pause, smiling at the memory before continuing, "but remember how when we got back to the house everyone was shocked and silent? It was strange," I shake my head, looking off into the distance, almost as if watching the memory. "I remember being scared. Then my father was there, his eyes dead, and we had no idea what was going on. I remember your mom taking you away, and I thought they were separating us to keep us out of trouble, but rather it was because my father wanted to talk to me about my mother. At the time he told me that she died in her sleep, that she never woke up. That is what he told everyone. The servants, the other noble families, even the royal family." I stare at my hands before wrapping them around my knees. I feel bare, in all ways, and the blanket cocooned around me does little to help with the feeling.

"Did something else happen to your mother?" he murmurs softly as he raises himself to more of a sitting position.

I stare at a spot on the headboard, avoiding his eyes. "I found out a few years ago that she committed suicide. She had gone to the local apothecary and had them make something that would help her sleep. She must have taken the whole bottle before she went to bed that night, since she wasn't found until late the next morning. I remember her occasionally sleeping through breakfast, so I didn't think it was odd that she wasn't around that morning. None of us did. My father had stayed in his study the night before working on something for the King, so he wasn't around either. Sometimes I wonder if he had been there, been with her, if she would have still done it." I sometimes wonder if my father blames himself, and if that is why he was so protective over Andria and I, and if that is why there are times he can't even look at me. I shake off the thought and gaze around the room. His windows are open, and his curtains flutter in the breeze. I watch the fluttering fabric for a moment. Peter waits and gives me the space I need, until I feel ready to continue.

"She had visions. She could see, hear, and feel things that were going to happen in the future. It wasn't always a definite thing, sometimes just a feeling rather than true knowledge of something. It was something that she was born with and passed on to her own children. It doesn't seem to happen until young adulthood. The visions killed her, and they may end up killing me." I clear my throat and try to swallow past the dryness that makes it impossible. "Believe me, I know this whole thing sounds crazy. If I weren't experiencing it, I would think the whole thing was made up, but it's all happening. I swear to you; it is all true. I see things like she could. I don't know what I'm doing, or how to interpret anything, and I keep trying to do this all on my own, but I can't anymore. You are the one person I trust completely, and I needed you to know. I understand if you want me to go."

I continue to watch the curtains, refusing to meet his gaze. I begin to cry, whether about the visions or my mother I'm unsure, and I raise my hand to wipe the tears away, but Peter grabs my hand before I can, and instead he kisses them away. I didn't notice him get out of the bed and come to me. His gentleness causes more tears to fall, and I completely lose it. Peter wraps his arms around me, lifting me until he sits on the chair with me curled on his lap.

With his lips against my hair, he speaks, "I believe you, Kat. I believe you. I've heard of other people with a similar gift. I've actually heard of a city in Arrowhelm that houses a whole sector of seers. From what little I know, they are revered, sought after." His thumb runs up and down on my arm as he continues, "Maybe I can help you work things out?" All I can manage is a nod until I get myself under control. The tears fall, but it is a mixture of all of my emotions and stress breaking free, and it is hard to stop. I take a few deep breaths to try to settle myself, and the shaky release eases. "Now, why don't you tell me a little more about the things you have seen?"

"You really believe me?"

"Of course." He shrugs. "I have no reason not to." His face is free of judgement, his eyes clear, and full of gentleness.

What do I have to lose? I already told him everything else, so why not this too? I clear my throat. "Mostly war. Lucas is involved, that much I know. But before you say anything, just listen." My voice starts out shaky, but finds strength as I continue. I hold my hand up, holding off his speech. "I know you have always preferred Lucas to Alaric, but remember what I told you the night of the ball? It still stands true. He is a cunning liar who is planning to take over everything. I'm not sure when, but I know that it is going to be soon. I don't know what to do. I thought agreeing to marry Alaric and going through with the wedding would be enough to stop him, but I'm starting to think it might not be. The visions haven't changed, and things have been strange. A couple of weeks ago, I overheard a conversation between two of the knights here. One, if not both, of them were terrified of someone and the things they were making them do. I'm fairly certain they were talking about Lucas, but I'm not sure he would go far enough to kill his own father to get what he wants. Since then, I've noticed the guards' numbers dwindling. Have you noticed— I can't be the only one. I didn't pass a single one on my way here, and usually this place is crawling with them."

"And you are sure that Lucas is involved?"

"Definitely. I know what I heard, not only from him, but from the guards too. It's as if he truly believes he should have the throne over his brother." I shake my head and rise from Peter's lap, the blanket still loosely wrapped around myself. My fingers clutch the fabric as I pace in front of him.

"Kat, I know you don't trust Lucas, and for good reason, but you have to try to see things from the public eye. A lot of people would rather see Lucas on the throne. Alaric was sickly for a long time, and he hasn't been the strongest leader. Yes, he is growing into the leadership role, but he still has a lot further to go. He can be arrogant, and, frankly, an ass. He doesn't seem to know, or care, to hold his tongue, and he ends up saying things he shouldn't to people he shouldn't say them to. Lucas may be younger, and not the heir, but a lot of people think he should be. He knows when to keep quiet, and when he needs to step in. I personally can't stand Alaric, but I tolerate him because he is my future King and I am one of his advisors. But I stand for the largest territory in his country, and he has yet to realize that I send him men for his army and I have more influence in this world than he does. He may be higher in rank, but the nobles on the council are the ones who truly run things."

I turn to glare at him. I'm already aware of the hierarchy here at court, as I've seen it first-hand. But he doesn't seem to know the Alaric that I have seen and come to know. He only knows the façade that he has put forth. I do think Alaric is starting to change this image he put forth of himself, but he has a lot of ground to cover and make up if he is going to forge the relationships he needs to with his people. "I understand that Lucas seems like the better choice, but I am telling you that he is behind the war and the evil that lurks here. I have to figure out a way to stop it, but I just don't know how. I think my mother knew this was going to happen too. She kept a journal, and I've been reading it at night before I go to bed. There are a few things she wrote that I swear are about this, about us, but I'm not sure. I can't quite decipher the meaning behind them," I pause. "Would you help me? I know I'm asking a lot of you, but I don't know who else to trust besides Ian, and he is already helping in the ways he can. I'm drowning in it all."

He leans forward in the chair, grasping my hands in his. "Of course. When can you come again? It is too risky for me to come to you. I think we should either meet here, or the gardens. No one should suspect anything if they see us in public together. To the public, we are just old family friends. We will have to be careful with our meetings, but this should work. We will make this work."

I wish I could tell him that this is truly the assumption that others will make, but the one person that could do a lot of damage already is aware of our relationship. I decide it is better to tell him the truth about our meeting in the garden a couple of weeks ago, and that Lucas threatened me afterwards. His body tenses and his expression goes dark: his brows furrow together in a frown and his eyes are hooded. His mouth tightens and his voice is icy as he asks, "what do you mean, he threatened you?"

I shrug. "He threatened to tell Alaric about the night in the gardens, but as far as I can tell, he hasn't. There were a couple of days where it seemed like maybe he had, although. Alaric has been acting jealous toward you, and our relationship. He has accused me of secret rendezvous with you anytime we are in certain areas or there are places that you are going to be. Hell, he asked me if the reason I wanted to attend the council meeting was because you were going to be there. His insecurity; I seriously wondered if it is related back to this threat from Lucas. I just know that we need to be careful, but we also have bigger things to worry about."

Peter rises out of the chair. My eyes trail the man in front of me, and despite the seriousness of the conversation and knowing that nothing further can happen between us, tingles rise through me. "When can you come again?"

I stare at him for a moment, soaking in the heat coming off of his chest, and I swallow the sudden knot in my throat. "I can get away in two days."

He comes closer, his hands finding their way into the blanket and curl around my waist. "Two days? Okay." He rests his forehead on mine, and I struggle to keep my breathing even. "Kat?"

"Mhmm?" I close my eyes, refusing to speak. I don't trust my voice not to shake. His nose bumps into mine before our lips meet. I melt into him as his hands on my waist pull me close again. I feel his skin on mine from my toes to my chest, and the heat of him makes me burn hotter. Whatever this is? It is addicting.

CHAPTER 13

Feigned illness
poisoned lies
misplaced trust
all for the sake of a planned demise

I walk through the gardens, thinking about Peter. The sun on my skin warms me, but the thought of the way Peter touched me yesterday warms me more. I can feel my face flush, and I lift my face toward the sky, my eyes closing. I don't notice Alaric come up behind me until I feel his hand on the small of my back. I jump, my eyes opening as I turn to face him. He grins.

"Sorry, I didn't mean to scare you."

"It's fine." I smile, swallowing the guilt that rises like a ball in my throat. "I wasn't expecting to see you until later."

He offers me his arm, and we continue to stroll through the gardens. I watch the bees buzz through the air, zipping from one flower to another as we walk. "I thought it was too beautiful a day to spend inside." I look at him, my eyebrow raised. He laughs, bobbing his head slightly as he continues, "and I wanted to see you."

I chuckle, "There it is. Well you found me." I smile and shrug, before looking back out into the garden. The flowers are full and fragrant. The sweet smell of honeysuckle and roses surround us, and I spy a bench not too far away. I lead us to it and take a seat, with Alaric next to me. I bite my lower lip, and try to forget the events of yesterday, before my face gives something away. Guilt washes over me again, and I feel my eyes burn. I never thought I would be the type of person that I am becoming. I vow that yesterday will have been the last time with Peter. I can't be unfaithful, I won't be able to live with myself or be able to look Alaric in the eyes. I look away and watch a hummingbird flit between flowers until my eyes dry and the feeling passes. I glance at Alaric, and notice that he has been talking this whole time. I focus on his words.

"My father is worried about this force that keeps attacking the coast. He is thinking of taking Lucas and I to settle the issue. I think it is a bad idea. If Peter's men didn't help stop the issue, then what good are we going to do? It is more likely that we wind up dead too. I've voiced my concerns to him, but he brushes them off, just like he always has." Alaric shakes his head, he picks at the skin by his thumb nail. I reach out to take his hand gently in mine to stop him. He will make himself bleed if he continues.

"I'm sure he is taking your concern into account. Just because he didn't say anything at the time, doesn't mean he disregards it, or you, completely. He may try other options first. Maybe my father can send a ship or two, to scope out the situation?"

He ponders that for a moment. "I suppose that could work. I'll mention that to my father later today. Try to see if that is an option we can try before we go ourselves. I want us all to be safe, I don't know what would happen if we all were to die. I suppose Annine would take over, but she was never primed to lead. I don't know if she could do it."

I roll my eyes and pat the back of his hand. "I'm sure she would figure it out. We women are pretty resourceful, you know." I bump my shoulder into his with a grin. "Don't forget that I will be ruling alongside you."

He chuckles and looks sheepish- ducking his head with a grin.

"You're right. I'm sorry. I didn't think. I'm probably worrying about nothing."

I squeeze his hand in mine. I watch his face. He chews his lip in worry, and his eyes are darker than normal. I murmur as I lean my head on his shoulder, "I wouldn't say it is nothing. Your heart is in the right place. You care. That's a good thing." I smile, watching the garden around me as I feel him breathe against me. I feel strange, sitting here like this with him after the afternoon I shared with Peter. The guilt worms its way into my chest and I bite my lower lip to refrain from saying anything more. What am I even doing?

Alaric wraps his arm around my shoulder and rests his cheek on my head. "Thank you." He turns his head slightly to kiss the top of my head. We sit there like this for a while, and enjoy the warmth of the sun and each other's presence.

I knock on the wooden door in front of me, and anxiously glance around me, waiting for someone to walk up to me and demand to know what I am doing. I wore one of my dresses from home today, hoping to remain inconspicuous, but the little red leather-bound book resting in the crook of my arm screams for attention. To anyone else, it is simply a book, and nothing that would raise suspicion, but to me, it is everything. I tap my foot, anxiety making my mouth cotton, and my body feels like it wants to take flight while waiting for Peter to answer the door. I know he should be here, we agreed to meet today. Just as I'm about to leave and run back to my rooms, the door opens and Peter steps out of the way, allowing me to enter, but the letter in his hand holds his attention. I sit on the edge of the bed and watch as he slowly closes the door, while continuing to read the page in front of him. I wait patiently for him to finish. I bring my mother's journal to my lap, and absentmindedly run my fingers on the cool leather. His hand drops to his side, and he stares at the ground.

"Peter?"

His eyes find mine, and I watch as his face contorts in agony and the letter shakes in his trembling fingers.

"Peter, what's happened?" I rush to him, leaving the journal on the bed. I cup his face, as his body shakes.

"My sister, she's been ill, very ill," he pauses, his body still shaking, and his voice doing the same. "I should've been there, my family needed me, but I thought," His tears finally fall, and his voice grows thick with emotion. "I thought she would be okay. That she would get better." He reaches a hand out to his bed, using it to slowly lower himself to the ground. He sits there, legs outstretched with his head in his hands.

"Oh, Peter," I sigh, crouching down with him and pulling him against me. My arms wrap around him. "Please don't blame yourself for this. Even if you were there, there wasn't anything that you could have done. I know your parents would have employed the best doctors. They would have done everything they could. It is no one's fault."

Peter shakes his head and sobs harder. I wish there was something I could do. I understand how he feels, but I don't know how to comfort him. I don't know what to say. I may have lost my mother, but if I ever lost my sister I would be devastated. The two are completely different. My heart breaks for him, and I long to do something to ease his pain, but I know that there isn't anything that can be said or done to ease his suffering. I sigh and rub his back and arms.

"Peter, if there is anything that you need, anything at all, please let me know."

He nods and clears his throat. "I think I just want to be alone."

I nod against him and rise to my feet. I rub his shoulder one last time, before stepping out of the door and gently closing it behind me. I slowly make my way back to my chambers, the halls barren of anyone else. My mind races. I wander over to the window facing the front gate of the palace. I notice that I'm close to my own chambers, and in an area of the palace that wouldn't be questionable for me to be in, but at this point I don't care. I rest my cheek on the cool stone of the wall around the window and stare out, trying to gather my thoughts and feelings and control them.

For a moment, I feel as if I have everything under control, and my mind is finally clear, but it is quickly filled with images. A carriage pulls through the gate with both Alaric and Lucas running around giving orders. Then I see inside of the carriage. The king is lying in a pool of blood, a large wound crossing most of his chest. He is dying. The scene changes, and I watch Lucas giving orders to some of his guards. I can't hear his words, but I can tell his intent isn't good. When he is alone, a grin crosses his face. He looks up as if he sees me watching through the glass. I gasp, and the scene disappears. The gate in front of me is empty, as is the courtyard.

I rub my forehead, trying to rub away the beginnings of a migraine. I have to think of a way to warn the king, but I don't see a way to do it without seeming crazy. Perhaps if I talked to Peter, we could come up with a way to tell him, but I can't go to him now. It'll have to wait. I quickly stride to my chambers and enter the room. I search the bedside table for my mother's journal, but when I come up empty handed, I realize I left it in Peter's room. I sit on the edge of my bed, thinking about the vision and my mother. How did she get people to believe her? She helped numerous people, but I still don't know how. I could write to my father, but it may take too long. It is already the start of summer, and this will clearly take place mid-summer. There isn't much time, I need to figure out what to do and how to do it quickly. I sigh and lie back on the bed, staring at the ceiling. Ian offered his help, but clearly what conversations he had with the king held little weight and nothing came of them.

Maybe I could write an anonymous letter stating what I know, and maybe just maybe, the King will believe it. I jump from the bed, and rush to my desk in the corner of the room. I pull a piece of paper out of the drawer and set it on the hard surface, grab the quill from the ink well and hesitate before setting the words to paper. I briefly describe what I've seen and heard from people here at the palace, and try to convey the urgency of the message. I leave the note unsigned. I place the quill back in the inkwell and blow gently on the paper to dry the ink. I lean back in my chair and wonder about the method of delivery. I can't just give it to a servant to have delivered; I would be found out and with the way seers are seen by a lot of people here, I could be thought a witch. I could have a raven deliver the message; it would likely work better than any other alternatives. This will work, it has to.

I decide to also write to my father. I quickly write the letter, asking how my mother got around the stigma of our gift. How she told people what she saw and how she made them believe her. I tell him a little more about things going on around the palace and wish him well before signing the letter and rolling it up. I rise out of the chair, slip on some shoes, and head towards the roost near the gates of the palace, both letters clenched in my fist.

I hope this works, and that the King takes care and listens to my advice. I find the two ravens, one for my household, and the palace raven, and tie the letters to their feet before taking them to the window. Somehow, the place remains empty, and for that I'm grateful. I send the ravens off, and slowly make my way back to my rooms. The halls remain eerily empty, and at this point it is starting to concern me. Where is everyone? It is mid-afternoon, there should be people and guards everywhere. I shake my head, trying to ignore the silence, and continue to my rooms. There must be some explanation as to where everyone is. Perhaps there is a meeting in the barracks, and that is what is keeping the guards busy. I decide it is too strange to continue to ignore. I turn on my heel and head back the way I've come, down the hall toward the barracks and the throne room in search of answers.

I glance around me as I walk across the cobblestones of the front gate to the barracks on either side of the gate. I enter the door to the left of the gate, and no one is in the room. There are flyers and papers scattered on the table in the center of the room. I peruse through them, trying to see if anything jumps out at me. Nothing does, so I continue through the room, my eyes moving through the room faster than me. There are pieces of armor and swords scattered through the room. It is almost as if they left in a hurry. I note a wardrobe in the corner of the room, likely where the banners are stored. I keep that in my mind in case anyone comes back into the room, so I have somewhere to hide. I have no business being here, but I have to know what is going on.

Beside the wardrobe is a small table with more papers. I head over to investigate. The first few papers give nothing away, but underneath them is a small book. Inside, there are several written down instructions. I read them over quickly. From what I can tell, they have been meeting to discuss some event that is coming up. The leader remains unnamed, but I can guess I know who it is. The instructions are vague, just meeting times and places. No specifics on the content that will be discussed. I consider sneaking my way into the meeting place, but I think better of it. I would be found out almost immediately. I would stick out against the men.

I carefully put the book back and shuffle the papers on top of it, trying to replicate how they were before I messed with them. Before I can get it perfect, I hear voices on the other side of the door. I look around the room, but hurry inside of the wardrobe, pulling the door closed behind me. I hear the outside door open and the voices enter the room. My heart pounds in my chest, and I barely breathe to remain as quiet as possible. My hands cover my mouth, and my eyes are wide and I watch through the very thin crack between the two doors. The voices come closer, but stop once they reach the middle of the room. One voice I recognize immediately. The second takes me a moment to place. The second belongs to the guard from the hallway a few weeks ago, the one that wanted to stand against whoever is leading these meetings. The first voice is exactly who I thought it would be; Lucas. He is plotting something, and I now may find out exactly what.

From the crack I watch as Lucas takes the guard by the throat as he sneers in his face, "do you want to end up like the others? I have no problem replacing you. And yet, you still continue to try and defy me. I *will* be King, and you will be within my control soon enough. It is better for you to get on board now." Lucas's voice is full of venom as a little bit of spit flies out and lands in the guard's face that is starting to go purple with the increased pressure at his throat.

"My Lord, I understand what you are saying, but to do what you are asking me…I would be forsaking the vows I took and the things I believe in. I'm sorry, but it is not so easy for me to forget and betray."

There is a loud crash as Lucas throws the guard to the table and pins him there face down with his arm behind his back. There is a sickening popping sound and a sharp grunt of pain before Lucas's harsh whisper, "you will obey me, or you will suffer the consequences."

"…Yes…sir." The guard's voice is dejected and laced with pain. I watch as Lucas gives one last shove as he releases the guard and his footsteps echo as he crosses the room and enters the barracks.

The guard lingers, his arm hanging limply and unnaturally at his side. I hear a grunt as he gingerly pushes himself up from the table, papers crinkling in protest. He slowly stumbles from the room after the first set of footsteps. I hear the door creak a second time, and I am alone once more.

I let out a deep breath and quickly exit the wardrobe and the barracks, glancing around me. I've heard enough for one day. I know it is Lucas behind the plot, and that there are still soldiers that are against what is going on. I know I should tell someone, but I still feel like I need more evidence. I retreat to my room before I can run into anyone. As soon as my family arrives for the wedding, I will confide in my father. He will know what to do. I just hope that by the time he gets here, that it won't be too late.

CHAPTER 14

Letters are the easiest way to pass along information gained from the visions. Anonymous is better, but it is still not easy. Most will take everything with a grain of salt, and resist the idea of someone knowing better than they do.

Trust Ian. He is a good man, and someone that has been a huge help over the years. He is as much your brother as he would be had he come from me himself. He will do anything to keep you and your sister safe.

lmost a month passes, and while uneasy about missing my mother's journal, I know Peter is not going to let anything happen to it. He has been excusing himself from council meetings since the news of his sister's death, which is to be expected. I haven't had a chance to sneak away to see him, what with all of the upcoming wedding and Alaric stealing as much of my time as he can. When I'm not with him, Anna is a constant shadow trailing me everywhere. As much as I appreciate and love her company, it is exhausting not having a moment to myself. Today is no exception— Anna and I walk through the gardens, discussing my upcoming wedding, and the gown that the seamstress is making. The seamstress has met with me a couple of times to go over the details of the gown and the different elements that I would like included.

We have another meeting this afternoon, this time to be fitted since the wedding is coming faster than I imagined. The gown we have drawn up has an intricate lace detail on the skirt of honeysuckle blossoms, and it even has the touch of the golden hue of the flowers. There are beaded embellishments within the flowers, adding a slight sparkle to the lace florals. The bodice has a corset and will be fitted, with sleeves that come directly out of the bodice and to drape over my arms. It is gorgeous, and the sort of dress that I dreamed of getting married in.

Things with Alaric have improved over the last month; we meet up at least once a day and I do truly enjoy his presence. He is funny, charismatic, charming, and sweet— but he still has an arrogant streak that annoys me like nothing else, and I loathe how easily he gets under my skin. He is quickly becoming the person at the forefront of my mind. I catch myself wondering what he is doing, or when the next time we can go to the training grounds is.

Anna is quickly becoming my best friend. Walking arm-in-arm along the cobbled path through the garden, the sun warms my skin deliciously. She giggles softly at my side as we gossip about the eligible councilmen that will be at the wedding festivities, and rank those she might be able to flirt with. Her blue eyes sparkle when Ian comes up in conversation. She has met up with him a couple of times, and they have flirted on more than one occasion, and she has been shameless when it comes to her pursuit. She is eager to find her match, and hopes that she will find the right man to make her happy. With her fierce personality, and even fiercer love for her family, she isn't hard to love. I have discovered her lack of a filter, and whether that be because she simply doesn't care what others think, or because she is a royal and can get away with it, I'm not entirely sure. Either way, she is constantly making me laugh with her witty remarks and blush with her boldness. Whenever I'm not planning my wedding, or meeting with the council, my time is spent with her.

Her bouncing laughter fits right in with the summer flowers and the sun that beats down on us as we venture further through the garden. I have finally come to know the castle and the attached gardens, and recognize that we are headed back toward the castle. The gazebo is ahead, partially hidden within two giant hydrangea bushes and a couple of dogwood trees. Anna's long hair hangs down her back, swaying gently with each step. She releases my arm and walks backward through the garden, facing me as we walk. She is not paying any attention to the path around her and I start to call out for her to turn when I recognize Peter's loping gait headed our way and she walks directly into him. She whirls around, one hand over her mouth as she takes a hurried step backwards out of the way.

"I am so sorry—"

My pulse skitters at Peter's soft chuckle. "Good morning, ladies," Peter says with a small bow and a smile in my direction. He seems to be in better spirits today than he was when I left him the day before.

"Peter, I am so sorry, I wasn't paying attention," when Peter waves off her apology, she continues, "It is a beautiful day, isn't it?" Anna grins, and based on the devious look in her eye, I wonder how many times she has tried to make him her latest conquest. I decide I don't want to know, and I cough, trying to mask my discomfort. My chest tightens, and I refuse to meet either of their curious glances. The way she is sizing him up makes my nails dig into my palms. If I clench any harder, I may draw blood, but the small sting settles my racing heart and I glance up to meet Peter's eye. His brows scrunch slightly in confusion, but he hides it easily as he grins at Anna in response to her flirtatious demeanour.

"Yes, it is quite a beautiful day, but nowhere as beautiful as either of you. Your Highness, do you mind if I borrow Katerina for a little while? I have a question for her, and it is rather important. I promise to return her to you later on." I notice the emphasis on using the title. It creates a certain distance and removes any inkling of a pursuit on his end. I hide a smirk with a slight duck of my head. I'm not sure why I was even remotely concerned.

Anna studies him for a moment, before heaving a sigh. "I suppose," She rolls her eyes, "that would be alright. There are some things I need to do back at the castle anyway." She turns toward me, pointing in emphasis, "don't forget, you have a fitting at three with the seamstress." She nods her head at us and turns toward the castle, leaving us standing in the stone path between the hydrangeas.

The bushes are in full bloom, the pink and blue blossoms bright against the green that surrounds them. I look away from the flowers and turn to Peter. "What did you need?" I watch him. His happy façade fades and is replaced by a sad smile. He is still mourning his sister but is able to keep up the impression of contentment for everyone else. "How are you?"

He shrugs, rubbing a hand on the back of his neck. He brushes past the question and jumps into why he sought me out. "I apologize for how I acted the day I received the news." I try to interrupt, but he holds a hand up, keeping me from doing so. "You came to work on your mother's journal and sort through it and your own visions. So," he pulls the small red leather-bound book out of his pocket, "I brought it with me today." He smiles, but it doesn't quite meet his eyes. I didn't even notice he had it with him, but when I see the book I grin.

Peter leads me over to the small gazebo across the lawn. It is as nicely hidden between blooming dogwood trees and more hydrangeas as I remember. It is unlikely that anyone will see us unless they come to the gazebo itself. A small surge of excitement races through me as I sit on one of the two chairs in the gazebo. The gazebo itself is clear of people or other furniture aside from the wrought iron chairs and matching table between them at the far end of the gazebo. Peter claims the other chair and sets the book on the small wrought iron table. My eyes linger on the small red book that holds what is left of my mother.

I gather all of my own thoughts and personal feelings and shove them into a box in my mind and lock them up tight. I need to focus, and that is hard enough to do when I know exactly what the man across from me is capable of making me feel.

Peter clears his throat and his voice is gentle. "There was this one poem in here that got me thinking about things going on currently. Let me see if I can find it again." He flips through the pages, mumbling under his breath, then stops on a page about half-way through the book. "Ah. Here it is." He pauses looking up at me with concern. "It was okay that I took a look through it right? I didn't mean to intrude…"

I shake my head with a smile. "Don't worry about it."

He smiles with relief. "Okay, good. But this poem, like most of the entries, talks about war. Or a sense of it anyway. There is one image in particular that stands out to me. It's of a little girl, standing alone holding a stuffed animal crying. You mentioned a similar image, right?"

I pull the journal closer to me, so I can read the poem for myself.

> *War. It reaches and grasps*
> *anything it can. The young,*
> *the innocent standing alone. Afraid,*
> *a small child, nothing more than a girl*
> *alone in the world except for a small toy*
> *crying in the road longing for an end,*
> *for a new beginning, with no fear.*

I hold the table so tightly my fingers cramp up and go white. "Yes. I've had this vision, or a similar one anyway. It came with other sounds and feelings, but I never knew how to really interpret them. I heard the sounds of war; the screaming, and crying, the sound of swords clashing…and then there was the girl. Standing alone in the road crying for her mother. I hadn't noticed this poem before," I whisper, pushing the journal away. It's difficult to look through and read, and more painful than I thought it would be. My mother knew about this threat for years, and never did or said anything to fix it? To prevent it? How could she lay this all on me?

"I almost didn't notice it either, until I saw the date on the page. She wrote this just days before she died. Maybe she knew more than she let on, and couldn't handle it? It isn't an excuse, but it could be some sort of explanation." He looks at me, his gaze steady.

I rise, unable to sit still. A soft breeze picks up, washing us with the sweet scent of the hydrangeas. A hummingbird flits from flower to flower, and I can almost hear the strange humming noise from its wings. I pace in front of the chairs, thinking, trying to ignore everything else around me. If this is some explanation, it is a weak one. "Maybe," I pause, sitting back down and looking at Peter. "I wrote an anonymous letter to the King regarding a vision I had about his death. It confirmed everything I heard from the guards in the hall. I tried to warn him, and I hope it works. Hopefully Ian got through to the king. If Ian wasn't successful and the letter doesn't work, I'll just have to try harder." I reach my hand across the table, towards him.

Peter nods and looks back to the book, leafing through the last few pages. He doesn't seem to find anything else extremely pressing to discuss right now, so he closes the book softly and rests his hand on mine. "Maybe you should go to Aouela. Train with the best Seers in the world. Learn about your gift, meet your family."

"Alaric will never let me go. It is too late. Had my father sent Andria and I when my mother wanted to, this would likely be an entirely different conversation. But as it is right now, there is no way that I can go. No matter if I want to or not."

He nods, as if he already knew the answer. The silence falls between us, and it grows uncomfortable, completely different than what it always has been. My feelings are shifting, and I can't keep pretending that Alaric doesn't mean anything to me. I need to end whatever remains between Peter and me. I can't keep pursuing an idea when I have something in stone set up for me. I glance up at Peter; his face is somber, as he stares at the journal on the table between us, and I can tell that we are both haunted by our losses. I shouldn't react the way that I have been to my mother's words, but I get more confused and hurt every time I read something new. I know it has only been a month since the news of Peter's little sister, so the pain he is feeling is much fresher.

"I'm sorry about Rose. She was a sweet little girl. She deserved so much more than what she was given." I turn my hand, so my palm is against his and twine my fingers with his. "I'm surprised you're still here, shouldn't you be in Lightspire?"

"My father told me I was needed here more than I am at home. I will mourn her loss here, in my own way." He squeezes my hand but looks away toward the dogwood tree. He watches the breeze flutter the leaves of the tree, and he sighs. "When we were younger, Rose and I, I would show her how to make little people out of different flowers. I used to call them her fairies."

He rises, releasing my hand as he walks over to the hydrangea, then to the dogwood, picking two flowers of each before heading back to the table. "You take the smaller flower, and that becomes the head of the fairy. The bigger, fuller flower is the body. You take the stem of the bigger flower and put it through the bud or the center of the flower, like this," he demonstrates with the purple dogwood flowers, "and it becomes a fairy. It's simple, and silly, but she loved it. For the longest time she would ask me to make them for her, at least until she got the hang of it herself. Then she would create herself a swarm of these flower fairies and would play with them until they either fell apart or were too wilted to be of use," he pauses for a moment, a smile creeping across his face, "it would drive my mother crazy to come outside and see her garden ransacked and half of her flowers missing, but it was worth seeing the life and laughter in my sister's face. I like to imagine that she is doing the same thing now, wherever she is." He lets the small fairy fall from his fingers to the table in front of him. His gaze lingers on the flowers, and I can see that he is trying his hardest not to cry.

"Andria and I used to do the same thing. My mother was the one that taught us how to do it. I remember one summer when we were children, she taught you to make them too. She said it was an important skill to have for when you had kids." I laugh, tearing up slightly. "I hope Rose is out there somewhere making these fairies and is happy. She deserves to be happy." I reach for his hand again, but before I can feel his skin on mine, there are muffled footfalls headed this way. I pull my hand back and pull the journal towards me. And just like that, the moment is broken.

"Katerina! I told you that you had your appointment with the seamstress at three! She came to find me when you never showed. Come on, you have to get fitted so she knows the proper measurements for your gown." Anna storms her way onto the gazebo, and practically pulls me from my chair. She completely ignores Peter, and I shrug at him. He waves his hand at me, indicating that it is fine.

"Take care." I smile and allow Anna to grab my elbow and pull me towards the castle. My mind lingers on those little flower fairies, and the day that my mother taught us how to make them.

CHAPTER 15

I'm pregnant. I know it will be a girl, and I know she will be a fighter. A survivor. My little Katerina. My darling girl. She won't know what is coming for her in life, but I will be there every step of the way. I can't wait to see how Joel takes the news. I know he will worry that she will inherit my gift, and I know that she will. But she will prove to be stronger than either of us.

I gaze out across the castle grounds to the city just outside of the gates, my chin resting on my palm as I lean against the railing of my balcony. I can just make out the people on the other side of the wall at the end of the garden. I get lost in the abruptness of life here. Out within the city, the people are always busy, involving themselves in the hustle bustle of the city life around them. I can occasionally hear the shouts and laughter of the city from here, but the stark difference of life at the castle is shocking.

It is nearly silent here a majority of the time. There are the occasional shouts and laughter of the court in the garden, and the dining hall is always busy with the nobles and other families that reside here at court. There is almost always a cacophony of voices to be found somewhere, but overall, life is quiet. The castle grounds are cut off from the city with thick walls that dampen the noise, and while I am used to the quiet, I miss the sounds of the naval fleet in the harbor back home. I miss the camaraderie that could be heard over the sound of the sea crashing into shore in the distance. I miss the creaking of the ships against the dock when I would wander among them. I long for some semblance of life before I came, and I wish I could spend a day among the people rushing and living life to the fullest in the city.

I've been here for almost two months, but it hasn't gotten any easier. I know the reason I don't easily fit into this city life is because of the closeness, the intimacy required. I'm not used to the mindless chatter among the court ladies, and I stick out like a sore thumb. I hope that it comes more easily as time passes, but I fear I will always be the outsider. I don't know how to do this. I've held some semblance of court at home, but nothing to this extreme. There are always people around, no matter where you go. There is even a guard that has started following me as of late. I am aware of his presence even if he lingers in the shadows and tries to meld into the background and go unnoticed. I am not sure of his allegiance and whether he stands on Alaric's side, or has been manipulated to follow Lucas, but I know I have been unable to meet with Peter for the past couple of weeks since we met in the gazebo.

I long for home, the sea, and the forest. I miss the expanse of land, and the beautiful emptiness that enveloped the house. Ever since the ball, the people have been beside themselves with excitement or jealousy. Due to the jealousy, I haven't been able to get close to any of the other ladies here at court. Most of them seem to inherently hate me for being here, and for my connection to Alaric. Anna has tried to bring me into the fold of ladies that she surrounds herself with, but they have made it abundantly clear that they believe they would be better brides than I seem to be. They would all be ecstatic to be planning a wedding, let alone marrying Alaric.

They ask all of the questions regarding the wedding: what sort of flowers, what will the dress look like, what will you do with your hair, the jewelry— they want to know all of the little details. They are fickle, and I give in to the idle conversation, but I want *more*. They want to gossip about the men and the eligible bachelors that will be in attendance since almost all of them are currently unattached and are hopeful they can swoop in and catch the attention of one of the eligible men and potentially raise their station. They all believe that I should be over the moon about the whole situation. The friendship that Alaric and I have created has started to grow; there is definitely a connection, I feel the draw toward him, and while it eats at me daily, it is hard to resist. The pieces of me that are still broken, are slowly starting to mend when I am around him. But these women, they haven't even tried to get to know me, and frankly, I don't think I really want to know them, even knowing that I will need to form some sort of relationship if I will successfully lead them at Alaric's side.

I sigh and push off from the balcony railing. I lift my gaze to the horizon to my right. The sun is about halfway up the sky, almost to full height. The sky is a beautiful blue that stretches as far as I can see. There isn't a cloud to be found. The air is warm on my skin, and I am glad for the billowy, sheer short sleeves of my gown. It is a deep green, and the color complements my skin and eyes well. My hair seems even more copper today, and lies in its normal curls against the bare skin of my back, with the upper portion of my hair pinned back so my hair is out of my face. My gown is open to about my mid back, where the dress gathers in a low v shaped cut. The skirt hangs loosely until it barely touches the floor. My feet are covered, and I can hear the slight whisper of the fabric on the ground. My fingers grip the warm stone railing in front of me. I blink against the brightness and turn back toward the city view.

Time has sped by since my arrival. As far as I know, my letters have made their way to the king, but he has taken no heed to my words. The council meetings have been ramping up and occurring with increased frequency. The skirmishes along the south-western border are happening more frequently. My father has sent some men to help as well, but to no avail. There seems to be no end in sight to the attacks. No matter how many men are sent, there seems to be more in this opposing force that remain undetected. They have not been able to find where this unknown militia are being dispatched from, and there is not much left that we can do outside of what we are already doing. I believe the king has even sent off a few spies to look into Modiva to see if they have any involvement.

Lord Tyrin is growing desperate, as are the Lords of Kilburn and Ambertide. For some reason, while these attacks are starting to hit more of the southern cities, my home in Stonebreach has remained untouched. My father and Andria have been in frequent communication with me, and while Andria's letters are vague on the details regarding the state of things at home, my father is starting to share more of that with me. He is aware that I have been in attendance at each council meeting, and while he has stated his approval, he warns me to be careful. He is aware of how the visions have picked up in frequency. Even so, they aren't bringing to light too many new details and instead show more of the same. I have grown restless and have tried the tactics my mother has mentioned in the journal, but the visions still come when they want to, and I have no more control over them than I did when they started. I just wish they would show me something new, something that I can work with, or something I can change.

The wedding is in one week, and my family should be arriving later today. While I am eager to see Andria again, I can't help the uneasiness that grows in my stomach. There is something I am missing, and I know the potential for something happening is at an all time high. Especially with the recent lack of guards on patrol within the castle. It has been eerily quieter than normal, which continues to spread the longer time stretches on. Other than the guard who has tailed me the past week or so, I rarely see one unless I am around the King. He still has three or four guards around him at all times. The rest are nowhere to be found. I sigh as I turn away from the world around me and head back into my room to exit into the rest of the castle. The fireplace is cold, but the room is still warm from the summer air. While there is currently no breeze, I leave my balcony door open in hopes that there will be one later and it will work to cool the room. Striding across the room, my gaze lingers on the red journal on the table by the fireplace, but I leave it there as I open the door to the hall. I close it behind me with a soft click and slowly start to make my way down the hall towards the dining hall for lunch.

I never heard back from my father regarding my latest letter. I know he has been busy, and I know there is only so much that he can do when not here. I'm so involved in my worries of the future and when Lucas is going to strike that I don't even notice when I reach the dining hall. Even through the closed door, I can hear the low hum of voices. It is a little louder than it is first thing in the morning, and at this point I have been here long enough that my arrival will go unnoticed. I clear my face of any worries, knowing that Alaric will see through any façade that I put on, as will the rest of his family. I draw in a deep breath, and slowly let it out, before forcing a smile and opening the door to enter the room.

Anna grins from her seat at the raised table at the front of the room and beckons me towards her. I weave my way through the tables closest to the door, nodding at the people there as they murmur a hello as I pass. Ian sits with Hayden Conway and Peter, and he raises an eyebrow as I pass. He is aware that my father is due to arrive back at court today, and he is supposed to meet with him once he arrives. He has been my eyes and ears on things revolving around the king. He has his ear and his trust, and he has tried talking with him on my behalf on several occasions. Unfortunately, his warnings fall on deaf ears. I smirk as I pass Ian and the two others while brushing a hand along Ian's back and squeezing his shoulder. He pats my hand, his fingers tapping four times in quick succession and I squeeze again before I release his shoulder and continue to the table where Anna and Alaric wait. Ian will be meeting with me after he talks with my father, and he will relay all information that they discuss. His single pat on the back of my hand signals that we will meet in the alcove where we met each time, while the four smaller taps indicate to meet at four. I ignore the weight of Peter's gaze and instead focus my attention on the family on the dais. Anna and Alaric are laughing at something Alaric said, and I watch as Anna throws her head back slightly with a hand on her upper belly. Her laughter is contagious, and I can see Lucas even crack a smile. Alaric glances my way with a grin, and I can't help but smile as I climb the two steps to the raised platform where the table sits.

"Hello Anna. How was your night?" I ask as I take the empty chair to her immediate right. Her hair is tied back in a high ponytail that swings with her every movement and her tiara is carefully placed on her brow. She is in a pale pink gown that makes her blue eyes brighter. Laughter still dances in her gaze, and her joy is evident in all she does. I wish I had the same carefree demeanor that she encapsulates, and a part of me wishes my father hadn't hidden me away until I was twenty, and had let me come with him to the castle when I was younger.

"Ugh." She heaves a dramatic sigh and tilts her head at me. "There was more talk of marrying me off to the future king of Arrowhelm." She rolls her eyes and scoffs. "Arranged marriage is so archaic. What happened to meeting someone and falling in love?" She tilts her head and leans closer to whisper in my ear, causing my hair to tickle my cheek. "I know you get what I am saying. This political shit is getting old. I know I am of royal birth, but come on, I'm not going to inherit. Why can't I have a little freedom to choose?" She sighs as she leans back in her chair and sticks her tongue out at Alaric who sits across the table. He watches her closely, and I wonder how he feels about the idea of arranged marriage. While I agree with Anna, I know our own relationship was forced on me, and I know he at times feels similarly. She reaches out and touches my arm, recapturing my attention. "Anyway, how was your night?"

Her eyes reflect her frustration of her own situation and my mouth twitches into a sympathetic smile. I reach out and take a napkin, and unfold it slowly before placing it on my lap. I take a minute to respond as I peer along the table. There are small sandwiches, pasta, potatoes, salad, and chicken scattered on platters along the center of the large table. There is also a bowl of fruit in the very center. I start to fill my plate with chicken and salad, before I finally speak, "Slow. I decided to walk in the moonlight through the gardens and read by the fire when I returned." I wish more than anything for a *real* conversation. I've been considering telling her about the visions, or at least everything else that I have heard and seen. She has proven over the past couple of months that she has an open mind, and a quick wit.

"Kat," Her tone makes me turn. She studies me, her eyes seem to search my soul and she must to find what she is looking for. It is almost as if she knows how lately I want to run and never look back. Her voice is quiet, and her eyes grow sad, although I'm not sure why. "Will you go into the city with me?"

"That would be fantastic." The corners of my mouth tilt up and I dare to begin to hope that she will be receptive to the news I decide she has the right to know. Both she and Alaric deserve the truth. I've been biding my time, keeping quiet in hopes that everything would sort itself out, but it has become clear that I need to share the information I have gathered about their younger brother, soon, before it is too late.

"You will be back in plenty of time to greet your family when they arrive later this afternoon. I promise." She grins, and I can't help but to relax further. I nod and grin myself, my mind racing at the possibilities of what waits for us in the city. "I've been needing some girl time." She lightly elbows me. I couldn't agree more.

Alaric comes around the table and lowers himself into the seat to my right. "Katerina," his voice is gentle, soft. It is the voice he uses when he is with me and is free of the persona he puts out for others. I turn to face my fiancé and have to smile. His smile is sweet, and I feel my heart stutter. He is breaking free of the person he led his peers to believe he is at my encouragement, and I am glad he is doing so. "How is my wife-to-be this morning?"

I smile, feeling the dark cloud that has followed me around today fade and instead find that I am starting to lose myself in his eyes. For the first time, the idea of giving into these new feelings scare me. I allowed myself to feel this way for Peter, and that got ripped away from me. I may have been making mistake after mistake when it comes to him, and while a large part of me still clings to the idea that if Lucas is taken care of and the threat no longer remains, that I may be free to leave. I know it is nothing more than wishful thinking, but these feelings that I am starting to have for Alaric, put me in a vulnerable position that I don't like. He watches me, like he can see the wheels turning in my head and the thoughts that I have been grappling with and trying to understand. I open my mouth, and feel suddenly shy. "I'm okay. How are you?"

"I'm better now that I am with you." He whispers the last part softly in my ear. I sigh, wishing I could roll my eyes at the cheesiness, but instead smile and try to ignore the skipping of my heart over the comment. *When did things shift in our relationship? How long have I been falling through the broken pieces that are no longer broken, but are now whole? Has he started to feel the same?*

"Will you be there to greet my family with me this afternoon?" The excitement of seeing my sister again makes me giddy, and I bet he can feel the giddiness within me, wanting to burst out like bubbles spilling from champagne.

Alaric's face falls slightly, and shakes his head. His father must need him for something, but I know I will see him for dinner. He has been here these past two months, exactly when I need him to be. He is a breath of fresh air and stability in a world where I find none. He is slowly becoming one of my best friends and I find that I am starting to care more deeply for him. He is healing parts of me that I didn't know needed mending. I didn't even notice that with each laugh and shared moment, I started to heal. Who knew he would be the person that I needed to help pick up the pieces that my mother left behind, the same pieces that Peter discarded like they were nothing.

I glance over at Peter. He laughs with Ian and Hayden. Ian and Peter had grown close when Peter would visit when we were younger, and I'm not surprised that they still are. Hayden is new to his appointment on the council, but even with Ian and Hayden being almost ten years older than Peter, it makes sense that he fell right into place with the two of them. The three of them are always together—I've seen them wandering in the garden and heading to the armory and training grounds on several occasions. I've seen the antics that they get into together, and know that they frequent the tavern in the city. My gaze lingers on Peter, and I realize again that despite my feelings for him, I need to let him go. The stolen moments, the kisses and sighs of release we shared, can't happen. I swore to Alaric that I would be all in, be a faithful and true member in our union. I can't let Peter be anything to me anymore. A sharp pang of grief fills my chest, but I push it aside to deal with later. My eyes flit back to Alaric, and notice the small crease of concern in between his brows.

"Would I be able to steal some of your time while you wait for them to arrive?" Alaric asks, and while I would enjoy his company, I know I need the escape the city provides. At least for a couple of hours.

"Anna and I are going into the city. I've been wanting to check out some of the shops, explore the city and meet our people. Maybe

I'll have one of the artisans make something for the wedding." I nudge his shoulder with mine and continue, "besides, I need a little girl time." I glance at Anna and smile. Alaric tries to hide his disappointment, but I see through it. We will have some time later today, and while a part of me would like to invite him along, I would also like to spend some one-on-one time with Anna. I stab some salad and a bite of chicken with my fork, and force the bite down.

Alaric looks past me to his sister, and raises his voice slightly so she can hear, "Anna, take a few guards. I don't want anything to happen to you two."

"Alaric. When has anything bad happened to any of us in the city? We are good to our people, so they are good to us." Anna interrupts, looking at her brother, bemused. Is she not aware of what has been happening and how it has been creeping up toward the capital city? I glance toward the other end of the table. Lucas appears to be paying little attention to us, but I know he is listening to every word. He watches the nobles throughout the room, and pushes food around on his plate.

Alaric looks sheepishly at Anna, he starts to say something, but seems to think better of it. He heaves a sigh, and I watch him glance at the ceiling before looking back at his sister. "True, but Anna, be careful. Please? You never know what could happen. Don't let anything happen to her."

"I'm sitting right here," I raise my eyebrows at him as Anna talks over me.

"Whatever, Alaric. Everything is going to be fine. Plus, I'm fairly sure she can handle anything thrown her way," she says, smiling at me. Alaric nods, and keeps his mouth shut. He knows that I am capable, as is his sister, to watch out for ourselves. He knows that I know some basic self defense. Ian taught me when I was younger, back before he became my father's dignitary, and Alaric himself showed me some basic moves when the attacks started becoming more frequent. I've even seen his sister take down Hayden on a bet one of the times we ventured to the training grounds. She is wickedly fast and surprisingly strong despite her small frame. Alaric holds his tongue, but I can tell he is worried about the uptick in attacks, and how much closer they have become as of late. His leg jumps under the table, as if he can't quite sit still due to the nervous energy that seems to be buzzing through him. The muscle ticks in his jaw, and I rest my hand on his on the table. I squeeze his hand, and I feel some of the tension leave him. He sinks back in his chair, letting out a sigh. I push my plate back and rise to stand. Alaric does the same beside me, keeping my hand in his.

"Katerina? May I speak to you for a moment?" Alaric asks, his fingers interlocking themselves with mine. I nod and let him lead me a short distance away from the table, near the windows that overlook the garden. There are no other tables nearby, and it is as alone as we can get in a crowded room. Anna waits patiently at the table, but based on the flutter of her eyes and the set of her jaw, I can tell she is annoyed with his objections to us going to the city unprotected. I buzz my lips as Alaric turns to face me and takes my other hand in his. I look out into the room, and avoid his gaze. He knows something is up. He has known since I walked into the room.

"Is something wrong?" I briefly meet his eyes, note the furrow of his brow as he searches my face, and quickly turn my gaze to the garden on the other side of the window, thinking of what to say. He dips his head toward mine trying to read my face. "Kat?"

"It's just nerves. It'll pass. I'm fine." I purse my lips, biting the inside of my cheek to keep from telling him absolutely everything. Now is definitely not the time, or place to have that conversation. Honestly, I'm not sure this feeling is going to pass, and I don't know if I will be okay. If anything will be okay again.

He seems to read my mind, or he has just learned how to read me. "No, you aren't okay. Look at me." He places a palm on my cheek, and I sigh before turning to face him. My eyes drag along the window panes, catching the glare of the sun through one of them as I finally meet his gaze. I want to look away, but I don't. Even though I've come to care for the man in front of me, I can't stop thinking about how it was supposed to be Peter. It was always supposed to be Peter. No matter how hard I try, I can't seem to let go. I can't help but linger in his smile and his eyes that remind me so much of home that I want to cry. I want to feel this way for the man standing here with his hands on my face. I want to know that I am safe with him, and while that feeling is there, I want it to be enough to drown out everything else. I beg and plead with whoever decided this cruel game fate is playing, to release me. I don't want to play anymore. I am desperate for an end, and I desperately hope this doesn't show on my face.

My voice wavers in the quiet space between us. I blink against the burning in my eyes and try to breathe through the thick knot that has formed in my chest. "I'm scared. Nervous. I can't wait until this is all over, but at the same time, I don't think I'm ready. This may be new and exciting, but I'm terrified." I swallow hard, choking on the words as I force them out, "Alaric, there is so much I want to tell you. That I need to tell you. I—"

"Oh sweetheart, why didn't you tell me?" He pulls me close. I bury my face in his shoulder and try to remind myself why I'm marrying him and why this is so important. I try to shove any thought of Peter from my mind and focus on the man in front of me. The beautiful man that holds me close regardless of who may be watching from the depths of the room. Guilt creeps its way in, but is chased away immediately by shame. Alaric runs his fingers through my hair, and I feel him rest his cheek on the top of my head.

"I didn't want to worry you." I whisper, keeping my face

buried in his warm shoulder. He smells amazing; like cedar, smoke, and something slightly like citrus. He tilts his head to look at me, and takes my cheeks in his hands. His palms scratch against my skin slightly as they cup my face as he tilts my face up to look at him. His touch is gentle, his thumbs rub back and forth on the side of my cheek. My mouth falls open slightly as I gaze at him. His dark hair has gotten long on the top and it falls into his sapphire eyes. His sharp features seem almost soft today, as his eyes crinkle slightly in the corners as his lips tilt up in a smile.

"You don't need to worry about me." His voice is like velvet as it runs over me, causing a fluttering in my belly. I am mesmerized by the way his mouth forms the words. My breath is shallow, and my heart thuds in my chest as I stare in awe of this man. "You go have fun. You *will* have fun. The city, the people, embrace it all. It can be a wonderful place full of distractions. I will see you later this afternoon, when you get back." He leans his forehead against mine, before leaning back and kissing my forehead. His lips are soft, and the kiss is quick, and leaves me wondering if it really happened before he pulls away and his hands fall to his side. I nod, the words I want to say stuck in my throat. I need to tell him everything, and soon.

The city is more exciting when you're inside of it, rather than just looking in. The artisans stop us in the middle of the street trying to sell their wares, while others call out their goods. The noise is a welcome change to the near silence that lingers at the castle. It is exactly as Alaric said, a glorious distraction. It is hard to even hear myself think, let alone hear one individual vendor in the raucousness here in the streets. A young girl selling roses in a wicker basket walks through the throng of vendors smiling broadly and nodding in my direction when she passes. I spin, taking in everything. The sounds, smells, the sights; everything is exactly as I imagined. The road is grooved from the many wagons and carts that mill about slowly since the crowd is too thick to move faster than a snail's pace. Almost every stand on each side of the road is decorated with brightly colored cloth that ranges the rainbow, with some decorated with more than one color. There are signs and wares set up on the tables, or hanging from the tapestries that act as a temporary roof to the different stands. The skin of a lot of vendors are tanned from their time spent in the sun, and their clothing is demonstrative of their work. The smell of roasted nuts and fresh rolls cause my mouth to water, and even though we have just eaten, I feel my stomach growl. The sweet aroma surrounds us as we carefully pick our way through the throng of the people.

When vendors and their stands stick out to me, I drag Anna over to look at them. I feel as if I am floating, and nothing can wipe the smile from my face. The third stand that I stop at, I decide to order a jeweled headpiece to wear at the wedding. It is made of gold with jeweled flowers that match the lace ones that adorn my dress. As soon as I saw it in the display case, I knew I needed it. I thank the vendor graciously, and they assure me that they will have it delivered to the castle before the end of the week. Anna and I move on, not having as much time as I wish we did to see everything. I will have to make another trip into the city before long. There is so much here, and we have barely made it down one of the busier streets.

One stand near the end of the line of artisans draws my attention. When we approach, I notice a young woman around my age and a little girl whom I assume is her daughter, selling hand-sewn gowns, hand-crafted jewelry, and other beautiful hand-made items. Momentarily forgetting about Anna, as I leave her at the stand adjacent to this one, I tune out the noise around me and lose myself among the fabric of the gowns hanging around me. Out of the corner of my eye, I notice the little girl tug on her mama's skirts and point in my direction. Before long, I find my way to the table itself from among the fabric and finger the garments laid there. I linger on a pale blue gown with hand-stitched flowers on the hem of the skirt and along the bodice, and instantly fall in love with it.

The little girl peers over the table at me, curiosity igniting her eyes. Her head is angled slightly to the side as her eyes watch my every move. She is barely tall enough to see over the table, and I smile as I study her from under my lashes. I keep my face turned to the dress, but glance up when I see her peek at me from behind the table directly in front of me.

"Hello, sweetie." My face softens, and I smile before crinkling my nose at her. She giggles and ducks back under the table. She pops back up a couple of seconds later with a grin. Her long, black hair lies flat on her back, nearly reaching the skirt of her dress. Her light blue eyes are a little unsettling, but they suit her angelic features. She is a beauty, and I wonder briefly what she will look like as an adult. Her mother shares her dark hair and angelic features, but her eyes are dark and I can't help but notice how striking the woman is, even if it is in a slightly more subtle way than her daughter. She watches the entire interaction, and welcomes me warmly. "Hello, miss. Anything I can help you with?" she asks softly, gesturing to the items laying out on the stand. Her accent is odd, and I can't quite place it. It lilts and dances, almost like the way a stream flows over the rocks beneath it. It is strange, but suits her angelic features. I gently run my fingers over the blue gown that I know will be coming home with me today.

"These are absolutely beautiful. You made these?"

She nods. "Yes, ma'am."

"How much for this one?" I ask, my fingers still slowly tracing the flowers stitched into the soft fabric. With how soft it is simply sitting here, I can only imagine how comfortable the gown will be on my skin.

"It differs per item, but that particular one is 50 silvers." She leans closer over the table, "That is one of my favorites. The blue would look amazing on you." She looks past me as someone approaches. "Good afternoon, Princess." She dips down into a curtsy.

"Good afternoon, Miss Sasha." I turn to see her grin. " I see you've met Katerina, my sister-to-be. She and Alaric are to be married on Saturday." She lays a hand on my shoulder and turns to me. "I have a lot of my gowns made by Sasha. Her work stands out from the other artisans. If you like anything, I would recommend getting it, and I can give you her information if you would like to order something in the future. We are lucky that she decided to make the journey here from Aouela!" She scratches her fingertips against my shoulder lightly before she wanders off to look at the different things that Sasha has available.

Aouela? I turn back to Sasha and her daughter. She dips into a low curtsy before I can finish the transaction, but she doesn't seem surprised by my name, but the title and my position is what causes her voice to shake. Her words are quick, almost panicked as if I would be angry at the lack of formal introductions. "Oh, I didn't recognize you. My apologies, my lady."

I raise my hands, waving them frantically as I look around us, then back to her. I try to catch her eye as I lower my hands back to the table. "Please, don't do that. There is no need to, I beg you. Treat me as you would treat any other customer."

"But you will be our Queen?" Her face scrunches up in confusion, and she raises her shoulders as she searches my face. She still seems unsure, as if I am playing some sort of cruel joke on her. She is still making herself as small as possible, and is not portraying herself as she had mere minutes before. Who in the royal family treats her in such a regard to cause this sort of reaction? I know it isn't Anna, and I can almost guarantee that it isn't Alaric making her fear for her life. That leaves Lucas. She cowers back, and the little girl hides behind her legs, but peers around to still watch me curiously. Her eyes draw my attention. They are the same icy blue as the royal family, and while her features favor her mother, they are sharp, angular, much like a certain dark individual that haunts my visions everyday. My mouth opens as I realize her daughter's lineage, and wonder how Sasha knows Lucas. I push the question from my mind, and instead focus on the transaction we were doing before Anna came over and disclosed my identity that shifted the entire interaction.

"I will be Queen," I laugh. "but not for another week. I may have the benefit of my lineage, but I am one of you." I can't meet her eyes, so I look back at the gown still in my fingers and flip it over, checking the stitching on the back. "My father was the lord's son, yes, but he took an interest in my mother, and they ended up falling in love. She came from a smaller town nearby, but wasn't of noble birth. Please don't worry about formalities with me." I glance up, and meet her eyes. She must sense something in me, because she smiles and offers me a nod.

"The gown is yours if you truly want it. No charge."

"I can't just take it. I insist on paying for it; I will pay every penny." I glance back at her daughter. She has been watching the whole conversation with vivid curiosity, her head turning toward each of us when we speak. The resemblance is there, and I can't believe I didn't notice it when I first came over here.

"But…" Sasha trails off, glancing at her daughter quickly. I can tell that she needs the money the purchase would provide but is torn about making me pay. While their clothing is fine, and they are well-kempt, I can't help but wonder if she needs the money to get away. Does Lucas even know about the little girl, about his daughter? Does he even care?

I drop one of the straps of the pack I wear on my back, and let the small bag swing forward. I pull my coin purse from the main pocket, and count out seventy-five silvers rather than the fifty that she told me a few minutes ago. I palm the money, and place it in her hand. "The gown is worth every penny." I glance down at her daughter, and I smile and try to ignore the pang of sadness that threatens to cloud over everything. I glance back up at Sasha as she tries to give me the extra back in protest. "Keep the extra. Treat your little girl." My eyes fall back onto her daughter, and they linger there. As much as a part of me longs for one of my own, I find it difficult to wrap my head around the idea. Especially knowing the war that is to come if I don't find a way to stop it.

"Miss!" she gasps. The little girl steps out from behind her mother's skirt and pulls the gown off of the table, places it into a cloth bag, and tries to hand it to me over the table.

I grin, and reach over the table to take it from her small hands. How old is she? Four? "Thank you, sweetie." I tweak her nose with my other hand and receive a grin.

"Thank you, Lady Katerina," Sasha says as I turn to go. I only make it a few steps before I feel a hand on my elbow. I turn to find Sasha there and watch as she looks around to see if there is anyone listening. "Please be careful. There are people in the castle…people that will hurt you. Please, watch yourself." Her voice is low and trembles. Her eyes are pleading, and I place my hand over hers.

"Who?" I murmur, my eyes searching her face. Her eyes dart around us as she leans closer to murmur urgently in my ear.

"I think you know who." She meets my eyes, her eyes dark with a deep hatred toward our common enemy. She leans forward to whisper in my ear again, her breath tickling my cheek. "You aren't safe. None of you are. He has men based out of Modiva, they have been sending men across the river. They are everywhere now— every city, even here. Hidden in plain sight."

"How—"

She shakes her head, cutting off my question as she murmurs, "It doesn't matter how I know. You don't have much time. None of us do." She takes a step back looking around again. "I need to save my little girl, but where can we go that will be safe from his reach?" Her eyes glaze over with tears, and her voice starts to waver in fear for her.

"Go north, to Lightspire, or take her back to Aouela. You both will be safe there. I can promise you that." I take her hand in mine, noticing the bruises that are starting to fade into non-existence and are a strange yellowish color circling her wrist and forearm. I feel terribly for the woman standing before me, and I gently squeeze her hand in mine with a small smile. "Leave today, but do whatever it takes to keep your little girl safe. Does he…?" I trail off, and I know she knows what I am asking.

She subtly shakes her head, and I sigh in relief. At least he doesn't know the girl exists. Sasha glances down at her daughter and back up at me before giving a curt nod, and backing away to stand right in front of her table. Her urgency in her warning…it is familiar, much like my own urgency in relaying my own. *Could she be like me?*

I want to crouch down and hold the little girl close, but instead I wave as I start to turn and step back. The little girl waves enthusiastically and in the blur of her waving hands, I see a face. I blink rapidly and lose myself in the flurry of movement. Lucas's face swims into focus. His laughing face fills me with unease, and I see a light-colored tent in the background. A hand squeezes mine. Alaric's or someone else's?

"Katerina? Is everything okay?" Anna grabs my elbow, turning me towards her, effectively breaking me out of the moment. "Kat?"

I shake my head, clearing my eyes and mind. I look back at the little girl. Her mother has turned to her other customers and didn't notice my moment of confused staring. Her daughter, on the other hand, did notice. Her eyes are confused as she watches us. I grimace and turn away, not wanting to give her a reason to get her mother involved. I meet Anna's concerned face, and I look towards the castle. While the feeling of wanting to run had faded significantly, it floods back through me now; crashing in waves that threaten to pull me under.

"Are you okay? You disappeared for a minute there." Anna's eyes dart around my face, studying me, and I try to keep it clear. I smile, nodding trying to ease her confusion and concern even though I fight back exhaustion. I'm not sure she believes me.

CHAPTER 16

My sister races towards me as soon as she steps out of the carriage, her blonde hair billowing behind her. Her green eyes sparkle with excitement as she breaks from protocol and runs to me. My feet move on their own accord and I run toward her, leaving Anna to close the gap between us and the carriage. Andria and I crash into one another giggling and holding the other close. My arms wrap around her shoulders, and I feel her arms tight around my ribs. My breath comes out in gasps that move her hair. She smells of home.

"I've missed you so much," I whisper.

"Can't. Breathe," she chokes out as she releases me and starts to back up a couple of steps.

I laugh and let go. The giddiness returns and settles in my core as I step back to get a good look at my sister. She looks the same, but seems taller and her hair has grown significantly; it stops at the middle of her back now rather than reaching just beyond her shoulders. The excitement and happiness radiates on her face, making her glow. She may have been on the road for the past week, but she looks refreshed and eager to experience everything around her. I turn to beckon Anna forward from the position she lingers in near the door to the castle. She takes the few steps toward us, and bows her head at my father who has come up behind Andria, and then bows her head to my sister. She stays poised and formal, and I know it is simply her reflecting back to her roots and the role she has been forced into her entire life. She remains a semblance of decorum around the older councilmen, while showing her fierce and captivating nature to the younger men. She comes to a stop beside me, and smiles in welcome.

"Andria, this is Anna, Alaric's older sister. She has been a great friend to me during my time here. I've written to you about her." I squeeze Andria's hand in mine, and grin.

"It is a pleasure to finally meet you," Andria says with a slight bow and her lips tilt up and her eyes crinkle in the corners slightly as she smiles.

"The pleasure is all mine. Welcome to the palace. I hope you find everything to your liking." She smiles and nods at all of us before excusing herself, "If you'll excuse me, I must get back inside. My father is expecting me. I will see you for dinner." She dips her head in our direction before turning on her heel.

My father steps closer and rests a hand on Andria's shoulder briefly. His eyes sparkle as he turns to me. "My beautiful shining gem," he holds his arms out to me. I reluctantly release Andria's hand and rush into my father's arms as they close around me. While brief, the embrace is warm and tight.

"How was your journey?" I ask, stepping back.

His face is drawn, which makes it so I'm not entirely sure I believe his response. "Everything went smoothly." I shoot him a look, wanting him to tell me, but his next question distracts me from following that further. I am sure Ian will update me when we meet later this afternoon anyway. "How are things here? Are you ready for the wedding?"

"Everything is fine," I pause, trying to push down the discomfort. I'm tempted to discuss the letter or my visions, but know it is better to do so elsewhere. Somewhere not as open as the entry gate, to avoid the chance of someone overhearing. I turn as quick footsteps hesitate behind us. A servant lingers just outside of the entryway, and glances between us before his gaze falls to his feet.

"My Lord and Ladies. May I show you to your rooms?" He keeps his head down, waiting for a response. I look to my father, even though I now hold more power than he does. My father holds his head high, squaring his shoulders and straightening his spine. This stance emits power, and his presence screams his title: Duke of Stonebreach. His voice bears the weight of this title as he agrees to follow, even though he knows the way from his years spent here.

We follow the servant through the twisting, curving halls of the palace. They have rooms in the west wing of the palace. In fact, Peter's rooms lie about four doors down from Andria's, which is directly across the hall from my father's. My father nods as he enters his room, his fingers tapping on the doorframe as he enters. I assume these are the same quarters he has each time he resides at court, since he is here quite often. I know he is going to be meeting with Ian here shortly, and is likely just biding his time until then.

Watching until his door closes with a soft click, I turn to follow Andria into her room. Her room is a deep red, and the furniture is a beautiful dark ebony. The room is comfortable, but not quite as large as mine. Where mine has a sitting room, hers does not. She also doesn't have her own balcony or window. I am assuming my father's is similar to Peter's since his is on the exterior wall. I linger near the door of Andria's room. She wanders the room, taking everything in. Her fingers run the length of the foot of her bed which sits at the center of the room. The headboard rests against the wall to my right. Directly in front of the bed is a fireplace, and a couple of chairs sit with a small table in between them. The door to the bathroom is in the far right corner of the room, and there is an armoire in the left corner. There is a desk directly to my left, and a chest to my right. She stays quiet, and I long for the easy conversation that we used to have.

"How is everything? How was the trip here?"

She stills, her fingers falling from the bed frame to her side. Her eyes flick up to mine over her shoulder as she slowly turns to face me. "It has gotten scary beyond the castle walls. It is fine in the general vicinity of home, and the closer we get to Aurellia City, but the distance between? Kat, we need to stop this. I don't know how, but we need to stop this. Farming villages were burned to the ground, crops destroyed, animals roaming the countryside alone," her voice hitches as she takes a breath and shakes her head. "Who is destroying our home?"

"I'm doing everything I can. I promise." I dip my head, take my lower lip into my mouth and bite down hard. I don't know what else I can do.

Her voice is small, defeated as she turns away from me again to stare into the empty, cold fireplace. "I know, Kat. I know."

Ian is already in the alcove hidden just outside of the grand foyer. I glance both ways down the hall before I duck inside the small compartment hidden unless you know where to look. Ian presses himself into the wall to give me space to duck further inside. He then turns to stand more in the mouth of the alcove, blocking us further from view. He leans against the wall, one hand dangling, while the other rests on his hip. His ankles are crossed, and his face is dark. He rests his chin on his chest for a moment, breathing deeply before he glances up to meet my gaze.

"It is worse than we imagined." His voice is gruff, and he clears his throat running his free hand through his hair. "They are everywhere. Skirmishes are happening across the kingdom. Most heavily along the coast line to the southwest, but are starting to encroach on the northern territories and to the east. The king plans to take a group to investigate in Redden. He is meeting with a spy there. Our messages, however, are not being heard. Have you seen anything further that can help us?" His eyes bore into mine, and I clench my jaw before responding.

"Lucas is the one leading the rebel militia. There is a woman in the city, Sasha. She gave me a warning— she said that we all need to get out while we can." I lower my voice to barely a whisper. "She has a daughter. *His* daughter, Ian. She had bruises that she tried to hide, but she is *terrified*. I believe her warning to be true. I can feel it in my gut. I have gathered enough intel, enough to make them see the truth in my words. We need to tell them. All of them." I blink hard, ducking my head. "We don't have much of a choice anymore."

"Your father said just about the same thing. We don't have much of a choice. We need to come clean about everything that you have learned, and your visions."

I whip my eyes and face to peer at him. He is on board with confessing about the visions?

He sighs, a heavy breath that manages to reach me to ruffle my hair. "I've known Alaric for years. He is a good man— a better man since you have arrived. We can trust him. Anna," I can't help but notice the blush that pinkens his cheeks and tips of his ears. "can also be trusted. She would kill for those she cares about, and I believe you to be one of those few." He reaches up to rub the back of his head before letting his hand fall. I nod. Now to find the right time to tell them, and gain the courage. Ian rests a hand on my shoulder before he turns and ducks out of the alcove and walks away. I stay, listening to his footsteps fade into silence.

CHAPTER 17

The people from Aouela are beautiful. Their fair skin, dark hair, and crystal eyes make them stand out among those from Aurellia. Luckily, I took after my father with my red hair. But my eyes and fair skin came from my mother. The accent of Aouela is close enough to the southern cities in Aurellia, that it was easy for my mother to acclimate. But imagine a bubbling stream— that is the sing-song lilt that she always had to her voice. I wish you had been able to meet her.

As Andria and I walk into the dining hall, I watch as Alaric perks up and sends a warm smile in our direction. He is the first to be seated at the table. I lead my sister across the room, saying hellos to the court people as we pass. It is almost second nature at this point.

"Katerina, how was the city?" Alaric asks as I take the seat beside him, and indicate for Andria to take the empty one beside me. Once I am seated and comfortable, Alaric takes my hand under the table. His fingers are warm against mine as they lace themselves with mine. I draw our hands into my lap, holding them there with my free hand. While I'm surprised he doesn't hold my hand on the table, I think he must sense that my mind is elsewhere, and am not really in the place for visible affection. I push aside any dark cloud that lingers, and focus on the good parts of the day.

"The city was everything I thought it would be. It was amazing. The colors, the sounds, the smells…" I grin and rub my thumb on his hand. "I found this headpiece that I plan on wearing for the wedding, and a dress from the nicest woman." I give his hand a slight squeeze that he returns.

"I'm glad you enjoyed yourself," he turns to my sister, leaning forward enough to see her beside me. "Andria, how was your journey?"

"Everything is so different here than it is at home. It made for a very interesting trip." She smiles at him, then looks back down at the table. While polite, her tone is cold, and I can't fathom why. I can tell that she is lost in her thoughts, and I know she has the weight of what is coming on her mind. She wants to help stop what is coming, and I wonder what else her own visions have shared with her.

The room is quiet enough to hear footsteps come up behind us and up the couple of stairs that lead to the table. A darkness settles over the table, one that I know is only in my mind, as Alaric smiles, and Andria looks up curiously. Lucas settles into a chair across from his brother.

"Good evening, brother. Katerina," He nods his head at us, then turns to my sister. "And who are you?" His voice lilts up in clear fascination of my sister. It is hard not to notice her beauty, and I can see by the look on his face that he notices. I keep my breathing slow and controlled, even though the way he looks at her like she is some sort of prey, makes me want to end him here and now. He is four years older than she is, and a monster at that.

"I am Lady Andria Smith. I am Katerina's younger sister." She rises and offers him her hand from across the table.

Lucas studies her for a moment, his head tilted to the side like a viper deciding whether to strike, then reaches out and shakes her hand. I watch as his face shifts to a broad grin that causes his eyes to darken rather than brighten. His whole demeanour shifts as he puts on this new façade of a charming young man. This must be how he wins everyone to his side before he turns to brute force. He is truly a viper, and I don't understand how no one else sees it. "I am Prince Lucas. A pleasure to meet you."

"The pleasure is all mine." Her smile actually reaches her eyes as she lets her hand linger in his. I watch her cheeks grow pink along her cheekbones and she slowly lowers herself back into her seat. Her eyes sparkle, and he smirks across the table. I watch this whole exchange, praying that Lucas doesn't try anything with her. Then again, I know Andria can hold her own, and she would bite his hand off if he tried anything that she didn't want.

Father struts into the room, actually looking the part of Duke of Stonebreach, in his more formal attire and demanding presence. He settles in across from Andria, with Anna sneaking in to sit in between him and Lucas. Both are soon followed by King Henry. We all stand, and he quickly nods his head in each of our directions as he strides to his seat at the head of the table. The noise in the dining hall has risen to a dull hum, and I watch as servants start to bring platters out to each table, each platter layered high with food.

"Welcome, Lord Smith, Lady Andria. I hope you had a safe journey?"

"We did. Thank you, Your Majesty," my father says, bowing his head at the king. My sister bows her head exactly like our father. The king spreads his hands and we all sit once more. We settle in, filling our plates as the conversation continues around us. There is roast duck, which happens to be one of my favorite meals here at the castle, and what we will be serving at the wedding.

"Thank you for allowing us to come and stay in your home. It is lovely." Andria's soft voice breaks the quiet.

The king smiles. "It is my pleasure. You are always welcome here, my lady. In fact— you can stay here at the palace for as long as you like. We have plenty of room, and I think Lady Katerina would like for you to stay."

"Your Majesty, if I may speak," my father begins, and the King nods his agreement. "my daughter is sixteen. She is not ready, nor prepared to live within the court."

"She seems like a capable young woman, and has her sister to guide her in the ways of court. She will be fine, Joel." The king seems exasperated, and I wonder if this is an argument they have had before. "Plus, how is she supposed to find a good suitor if she hides away in your home?" The king turns back to my sister.

My sister is silent and I can see the wheels turning. I know her decision will have something to do with the visions and her trying to combat them to help in whatever way she believes she can. I watch as her head begins to dip up and down as she blinks rapidly. "I think I would like to stay. Thank you."

Andria and I sit silently as the men discuss matters of state. Anna looks bored and moves the food around on her plate as she flirts with her eyes with Hayden across the room. I smile and shake my head as I turn my attention to the conversation happening beside me. The King mentions some skirmish in an outer region town to the west, but he has a meeting that he and his sons must leave to take care of in the morning. He claims they will be back in plenty of time for the wedding.

I pause, listening intently. Could this be what I foresaw, and tried to warn him against? Is this what Ian confirmed just this afternoon? There is no indication that the king has received my letters, which is unfortunate. He seems as sure of himself as he always has. I really hope he is careful; it is too soon to lose him- neither Alaric or myself are ready to take over. The topic shifts, and questions regarding the wedding start popping up.

"What sort of flowers would you like? And what sort of gown? I'm aware the seamstress is already working on the gown, but I am wondering the design you chose." The King turns to me, smiling over his wine. I swallow and look around at everyone at the table.

"I prefer lilies and honeysuckle for the flowers. As for my gown, there will be lace, and a little color— I don't want a pure white gown. I don't want to share too much; I'm not overly superstitious, but they say it is bad luck to see the gown, and I feel that giving too much away may lead to the same outcome." I glance at Alaric, before glancing back at the king. "I'm not overly picky when it comes to the wedding, whatever happens, I am sure it will be beautiful." I hope Alaric doesn't take this as I don't care about the wedding, I just simply want the moment and the magic of it between him and I more so than all the fine details.

The king chuckles, "I suppose you are right, we will just have to wait until the wedding then!" He turns his attention away from me and the wedding and starts talking to my father about something of little importance or relevance to me.

I push my plate away, finished, but watch the room. The light from outside is waning and the shadows grow longer on the walls, which play tricks on the mind. They seem to stretch and move, almost as if alive. It is a little unnerving, and I have to glance away in an effort to keep from getting dizzy. The room is a little more crowded than normal, likely due to the increase of nobles and dignitaries that have been arriving for the wedding. I easily find Peter sitting with his normal group of Ian and Hayden. There are a couple of noblewomen at the table, and one makes herself friendly with Peter. His eyes glitter in the torchlight and based on his mannerisms, I can tell the ale that was served with dinner has hit him. The woman laughs and touches his arm, and I watch as he ducks his head with a lopsided grin and his cheeks turn crimson. I feel my body flush, and I focus on the woman. I have seen her in the women's court— she is a wonderful pianist, and is on the quieter side. I can't recall her name, however, and even knowing all of these things, I can't help but feel the hatred that seeps into me at the sight of that blush creeping up Peter's cheeks at her doing. Why does this affect me this way? I am engaged, and the way I feel toward Alaric is shifting— I should *want* Peter to find another and be happy. Why can't I let him?

I blink against the burn and turn back to those who surround me. Anna is arguing quietly with Lucas, Andria sits quietly beside me, watching Lucas. Alaric is involved in the conversation between his father and mine, and no one seems to have noticed the way my own skin has flushed in frustration. My fingers reach out and find the handle of my goblet of ale. I grip it, bringing it to my lips. The cool ale that tastes faintly of apples and cider fills my mouth and I gulp it down to quench the burning in my core. It does little more than fan the flames that I tried to diminish. I sigh, and lean back in my chair. Lucas slides his gaze from Anna's lecturing face to mine. His lips twist up in a smirk, and he winks. I keep my face devoid of any emotion and my gaze blank as I lift a single brow. He barely shrugs his shoulders, and his eyes look past me to Andria. His eyes seem to change from cold, to lukewarm and I watch as he smiles and winks. Out of the corner of my eye, I see Andria return the smile. I roll my eyes, and rest my head on the back of my chair.

Finally, the King clears his throat, and announces that he is going to retire. He bids us all goodnight then exits the room. Prince Lucas quickly takes his leave, leaving Anna seemingly frustrated as she glares after him. What is that all about? I shake my head, and bid my father goodnight as he leaves as well. Anna stands, her eyes on the door that her brother had exited, and murmurs a goodnight to us as well before walking out of the room. I stand, and Andria does the same.

Alaric turns to face the two of us, a slow smile softening his eyes as they meet mine. "May I walk you lovely ladies to your rooms?" Alaric asks, offering up an arm to both Andria and me. I take his left arm while Andria takes his right.

"You may," I flirt, fluttering my eyes at him playfully. The ale must have loosened me a little more than I originally thought. The edges of my vision is hazy, and I am thankful for the support of Alaric's arm in mine.

His voice is playful as he leads the way out of the dining hall and turns left out of the door. "Right this way M'Ladies." The walk back to Andria's room doesn't take us very long, and while it is a quiet walk, it is comfortable. We pass a few nobles in the halls near her room. It will be a lot harder to sneak anywhere with the influx of people that will continue to grow over the next few days, not that I have any plans to sneak anywhere anyway. Andria's room creeps up on us and we pause just outside as she unlinks her arm from Alaric's and rests her fingers on the handle to her door.

"I will see you in the morning. If you want, I can come before breakfast and help you get ready," I say to Andria as I give her a hug.

"I would like that. I'll see you in the morning. Good night, Kitty Kat." The name reminds me of our mother, and I blink the sudden tears from my eyes.

"Night, Andi."

She smiles and ducks into her room. We wait until we hear the door close with a light click. Alaric pats my hand on his arm, keeping it there as he starts to lead me away toward my room. I follow, drawing myself close enough to rest my head against his arm as we walk. I sigh, content in the moment with him. I want to linger here, slightly tipsy, with his warm presence beside me. What I wouldn't give to spend more time getting to know him, learning the way his mind works, what makes him who he is.

"You're glad she is here, but do you really want her to stay?" he asks quietly. I know he means my sister, and I ponder the question before answering.

"Yes and no. I'd love for her to stay, but at the same time I don't want her here within the clutches of politics. There is so much more at play here than you know." I lift my head from his arm and look at the ground in front of us. It isn't necessarily the clutches of politics, but more so the clutches of Lucas. I want her safe, and until we figure out how to stop this war, to stop Lucas, there is unfortunately nowhere safe.

"She has you," I feel him shrug. "I know you won't let anything happen to her, and neither will I. Anna won't either." He keeps his voice low, his tone comforting. Light flickers around us from the torches and candelabras on the walls, and the shadows lengthen as night settles in around the castle. I lift my head from his shoulder to look up into his face. The open vulnerability I've come to expect from him is there, but so is something else. His eyes seem lit by a spark that has started to burn. My heart thunders in my chest, and maybe the ale makes me bold, but I let myself simply *feel*.

His blue eyes capture mine and I almost tell him everything, right there in the hallway. I clear my throat and turn my gaze back to the hall in front of us before I can speak up. I bite my lip. Hard. We still have a little ways to go before we reach my room. We walk in silent companionship, simply enjoying each other's presence before we reach the final curve leading to my quarters in the royal hall. I wonder where Alaric's room is in comparison to mine, and I mentally shake the thought from my mind. I will find out soon enough, I'm sure. I see my door, and my pulse races in anticipation. Will he kiss me again? Will he admit to his growing feelings, and will I admit to mine? Or will I finally break my silence and trust him completely?

"What do you mean there is more at play?"

I was waiting for him to ask. I bite down harder, and sigh through my nose. My neck prickles under his gaze, and I look up at the vaulted ceiling lined with carved arches outside of my room. The shadows sink into each crevice that the light doesn't reach. It is almost ominous. I glance at him, and etch the lines of worry on his face. I wish I could erase them, but I know as soon as I tell him everything, they will remain forever. And suddenly, I just can't tell him. Not yet. As we reach my door, I turn, my hands resting on his chest and I let my fingers grip his tunic. His hands slide around my waist, and I bite my lip as I look up and meet his eyes. His face is tilted down toward mine, and his dimples seem more prominent today than normal. His tall, broad frame leaves me feeling small in his arms, and while that should make me nervous, it doesn't. He has been nothing but gentle. Kind. There is a crease between his brows that shows his concern and confusion, and I get the urge to kiss it away. His eyes are the same icy blue, but they are warm and I can see the desire mixed with hesitation in them as they search my own. I wonder what he sees.

"You will be a great king," I whisper, and I have no doubts that what I say is true, even if the statement started as a way to avoid the question.

He seems taken aback, his eyebrows lifting slightly but he doesn't miss a beat as he says, "and you will be a fantastic queen."

He leans close, pressing his forehead against mine as he slowly closes the distance between our lips. I count the seconds, as my breath comes faster and my pulse races under my skin. While the kiss starts slowly, it grows. His hands splay across my hips and lower back as his mouth presses more firmly on mine. My lips give in to his, and I melt into him; my body pressing into his as I venture into the feelings that have started to grow over these past few months. It feels new and a little unsure, but exactly what I didn't know I wanted. Slowly we pull away, our foreheads resting together, our hands entwined.

"Can you believe that in six days we will be married?" he

whispers.

"I know, it's all happening so fast." My mind races. I wish I could slow time down or stop it completely for a multitude of reasons, but mostly to figure out how to tell him everything without breaking this newfound bond between us. He leaves a brief kiss on my forehead before squeezing my hands in his and walking away down the hall past my quarters and toward what I assume are his own. I wish I knew what he was thinking. I watch him disappear into the shadows of the dimly lit hallway before I open my door and into the comfort of my space.

I glide through the sitting room and into my bedroom, before floating over to my vanity to take off my tiara. I set it into the holding case built into the vanity. The vanity has space for several tiaras in a column along the mirror, as if it were specifically designed for someone of royal lineage. I look into the mirror, and run my fingers through my hair, causing the pins holding it in place to fall out. My hair cascades down around my face, warming my nearly bare shoulders. My cheeks are flushed either from the ale, the moment with Alaric in the hallway, or a mixture of the two. I turn from the mirror, not wanting to linger in the girl that is the replica of my mom staring back at me, and instead head to my bed where a nightgown is laid out. I untie my gown, and let it slide to the floor before I pull the nightgown on before turning the dials on the bigger lights in the sconces along the wall dimming them to a very low glow.

The small lamp on my bedside table flickers as the flame licks at the oil keeping it lit. I tuck myself into bed, my fingers grazing the supple leather of my mother's journal from the shelf on the headboard as I reach for it once I've settled in among the pillows. I dive into the poems and lose myself in the things she saw, as well as the things that she wanted me to know. A soft knock jumps me from the words that have started to blur together, and I lurch into a seated position. My heart pounds as I listen, and sure enough a second knock sounds. My fingers grab my satin robe from the chair in front of my vanity as I pass, and I pull it on as I make my way through my sitting room to the door. I just get it tied as I open the door and my father makes his way into the room, without asking my permission. I close the door behind him, crossing my arms as I turn to face him.

"Father? What are you doing here? It's late…"

"We need to discuss a few things." I gesture for him to take a seat, as I walk to the armchair near the fireplace. I lift a foot under me as I sit, and draw the other knee up once I am seated. My father remains standing, and begins pacing in the space between the chairs and the table in between my chair and the others. "You must convince Andria to return home after the wedding. She cannot stay here."

"It isn't your decision. Trust me, I don't like the idea either, but she is a year away from being able to marry. She should be out finding a suitor." I sigh, running my fingers through the ends of my hair in my lap. "I will be with her. I will not let anything happen to her. With everything happening, maybe here is the safest place for her."

I watch his pacing pause as he looks at me, his face incredulous. "Even you can't keep an eye on her at all times. You will be queen. Your time will be filled. When will you have time to make sure she is safe? She will be alone." He shakes his head and continues pacing. "You and I both know that nowhere is truly safe right now, is it?"

"She won't be alone. I've met my fair share of young maidens. She won't be alone. There are many young ladies for her to interact with when I am unavailable. Believe me, I want her to be safe as much as you do."

My father shakes his head again, but realizes that I am on his side regarding Andria remaining at court, but knowing that we can't sway her mind since she is more stubborn than both of us combined. He sighs, and finally settles into one of the chairs across from me. "We also should discuss your mother and ways you can get around your gift."

My eyes widen, and my brows lift slightly. "How did she get them to believe her?"

My father runs his fingers through his hair, pausing at the back to scratch before his hand falls back to his lap as he sits back in the chair. "She tried her best, but not everyone believed her. I urge you to use caution. She never dealt with anyone with as much power as those you are dealing with. It didn't matter as much if those she told believed her. Her reputation remained untarnished because they weren't higher in rank. You need to use caution. You have to try to remain anonymous." He coughs, and takes a minute before continuing with his eyes boring into mine, his face drawn and mouth tight.

"I will not see you fall from grace. I will not lose you. While there are places where seers are honorable members of society, it isn't necessarily here. I've been trying to work the idea into the king's mind, and while he is more open to the idea, it is going to take some time before you may speak freely of what you see. I don't know Alaric well enough to tell you one way or another with him yet, but just be careful. Your raven idea was clever." He nods, and continues, "I hope Henry takes heed from the warning and doesn't go on the expedition. Who wants him gone?" He leans forward with his hands hanging between his knees. "Gem, there is unrest everywhere. Nothing is right. People are homeless, and starving. Whoever is behind this, it is working. Things will continue to get worse until we stop him."

My hands still in my lap, releasing the hair that I had been twirling around my fingers. My mouth goes dry and my teeth sink into the lip I've drawn into my mouth before I tell him everything that I know. "It's Lucas. It is all Lucas. He is behind the attacks, and has somehow turned some of the guards in his favor. I had a resource tell me he is working with Modiva and has several bases across the river that he is launching these attacks from. I know he wants his father's throne, and I believe that he will do whatever he can to get it. I don't know how to stop it without exposing myself. I've tried talking with Ian, he believes that I should tell Alaric and Anna."

"I'm of a mind to agree with him; Ian knows them better than I do. If he believes that you can trust them, then I would. In the meantime, we will figure something out. I will try talking to Henry and see if I can get him to postpone any plans he may have. I will do what I can," he rises, and I do the same, coming to stand beside the table between us. "Please come to me if anything changes." He rests a hand on my cheek and kisses the top of my head before crossing the room. I watch the door click shut behind him.

I linger there, beside the table for some time. He was as honest as he could be, and I wonder what more he knows that he did not share. He trusts Ian's judgement, and if he thinks that I need to tell Alaric, then that is what I will do. I chew on my lip, half tempted to wander the castle in search of his rooms, but know it would likely just get me into trouble. I shiver, not from the cold, but rather from the stress of the situation hitting me. More than anything I just wish I could talk this out with my best friend, but he is the one person that I can't trust myself to be around for fear of failing to follow through on the deal that I made with Alaric when we entered this engagement. I can't allow myself another moment of weakness, no matter how much I feel I need his words of encouragement. This person I am becoming is not who I wanted to be. I sigh, running my fingers through my hair as I turn and head back into my bedroom, blowing out any candles I pass in the process.

CHAPTER 18

You will have to choose.

My mother told me the same thing. You will have to choose.

I asked her what I would need to choose between, and she never would elaborate. She would simply leave it at "you will have to choose." And while I hate to do the same to you, I have to.

You will have to choose.

The next few days pass in a blur, and King Henry decides that he needs to investigate what is going on himself, regardless of the numerous warnings and rebuttals from his councilmen. He has proven to be extremely stubborn and nothing anyone has said to him has given him any sense of hesitancy. He left the morning after my father and Andria arrived at the castle, taking Alaric and Lucas with him. They swore to be back in time for the wedding, and the date is quickly arriving in three days.

The castle has been eerily quiet, guards are still missing and even the nobles are quiet and keep to themselves. Peter has kept his distance, likely due to my father hovering nearly everywhere I go. It has been exhausting. I roll my shoulders as I head down to the dining hall for breakfast, knowing it is going to be my family, Anna, and I since everyone else went with the king. My hair is pulled up in a high pony with small tendrils that hang loose, framing my face. My dress is a pale blue satin that flares at the hips until it hits the floor. The sleeves are short, thankfully, because if they were any longer I would sweat uncomfortably in this heat.

The walk to the dining hall has already caused sweat to trickle down my back, and I wipe the back of my hand across my forehead to clear the beads there. I enter the room, ignoring everyone and take a seat. Anna is in a similar mood, it appears the heat doesn't sit right with anyone. The windows are all open, as are the doors to the rear courtyard to the right and to the gardens on the left side of the room, to try to circulate some airflow. It helps some, but there isn't much of a breeze yet this morning. I lean back in my chair, using my napkin to fan myself as I try to cool off. Who knew it could be so hot this far from the coast? At least at home, we had the breeze coming off of the sea to cool us down, but here? There isn't much here to help fight the heat.

Andria slinks into the room and collapses into the chair beside me. I glance over and see her using a small hand fan to fan herself. At least she was smart enough to bring one. My father must have decided not to make it to breakfast this morning, and I can't say I blame him. I groan, and sit up as the servants start to make their way out of the kitchen doors at the far end of the room. Before the servants can even make it to the table, there is a commotion in the courtyard by the back gate. The gate flies open, and men shout from the top of the gate to the men rushing inside. The royal carriage pulls into the gate; soldiers leap off of the horses, and the princes jump out of the carriage and begin shouting orders at anyone within earshot. No, please, don't let this be what I think it is.

"Anna?" my voice quivers as I continue to stare out the window, standing. I don't notice my feet moving me forward, closer to the window. My fingers cover my lips lightly, as my other hugs around my middle.

"Oh, no." Anna's face goes white, and her hand flies to her mouth. Based on her reaction, and the scene unfolding before us, I dash toward the already open door to the courtyard, and find myself quickly within the middle of everything.

The commotion outside is even more intense than it was from inside. Both Alaric and Lucas are shouting orders to soldiers to gather men to search the outskirts of the city and shouting for the royal doctor. The soldiers are running from the gates to the barracks, gathering a team to find who attacked them. I stand just inside the courtyard, taking everything in. I panic, getting a strange sense of deja-vu that makes my stomach churn. Alaric sees me and waves me over. I run to him, careful not to get in anyone's way, which isn't an easy feat. The carriage is only a few feet away, and I know what I will find inside. Everything is happening exactly as I saw it.

"I need you to get into the carriage and help my father until the doctor can get here. He is on his way, but he needs someone with him now. Can you do that?" His hand finds mine as he looks at me briefly, but his eyes flit everywhere, unable to focus on anything for long. In the brief moment our eyes connect, I know he needs me to do this for him. He is terrified, and he doesn't know what to do. His mouth is tight with either worry or fear, and his skin is pale and clammy. His hand holds mine tight, and I squeeze back, nodding and I decide to keep my questions to myself for the time being. I've studied the healing arts, but I've never really been good at it. I will do what I can, but I know it isn't going to help what lies in the carriage. I step forward, but Alaric doesn't release my hand. I turn back, and he quickly pulls me against him as he buries his face in the crook of my neck. "Thank you. Please, just please." He squeezes tight and releases me, his eyes feverish with fear. I nod and move toward the carriage and start to climb in, feeling as if everything is happening in slow motion. I brace myself against the blood I know I'll find inside.

I open the door and step in. The King is laid down on the right side of the carriage. His skin is starting to turn very, very white and cold to the touch, and there is a constant stream of blood flowing from a wound spread across his chest. I rip one of the curtains down from the small window and kneel beside him to apply pressure to the wound.

"I'm so sorry. I'm sorry..." I whisper as I slowly start to apply more and more pressure. I shut out the rising sense of panic and try to focus on keeping the pressure steady. The curtain isn't helping much; it doesn't seem to want to soak up any of the blood that keeps coming. It isn't the right type of material. I scan the carriage looking for something, anything else that could help. I come up empty. There isn't anything. There can't be much time either, not with how much blood he has lost already. I may not know much when it comes to medicine, but this much I do. My meager skills are of no use here, and I choke down the bile that threatens to rise. Unless the Doctor can work some sort of miracle, there isn't much that he can do other than provide some comfort for him to pass on into the next life. Tears start to run down my cheeks and land on the King's chest. I lift one blood covered hand to roughly wipe away the next tear before it can fall. *I will not break.*

"Don't worry about me, Katerina. I'll be just...fine..." he coughs a few times, and blood rises to his lips. He manages to raise a hand up to wipe it away. "Now, listen to me. Do whatever it takes... to take...Lucas down. I know what he wants, it's what he's always... wanted. You can't let him succeed. I didn't...want to believe..." he gasps and coughs again. I maintain pressure on the wound, and try to tell him it's okay, that he doesn't need to worry about it, but he continues speaking despite my weak protests. "I wasn't strong... enough to stop him. I fear I may have made him worse. But you... will stop him. I see the fire you hide. Promise me...you will stop him. Promise me..." he pauses, and I nod, as everything blurs. He coughs and continues, "Promise me that you will treat Alaric and my kingdom with the respect…it deserves. Help Alaric…understand. He won't…" his words become garbled from the blood and his diminishing control. "why Lucas…do what he is…going to do. Take care…of him. Love him…he loves you. Promise…me. Promise…" he coughs again, and his eyes flutter closed. I feel the breath leave his body, and I break. The tears escape with a choked sob that turns into a cry of pain.

"No, no, no! No, you can't just leave! I'm not ready for this. I can't do this. You can't die on me, I won't let you!" I shake him, but nothing more than more blood seeping out happens. I start sobbing. Nothing seems to work. Nothing I do makes any difference. I don't even notice when the Doctor climbs into the carriage.

"My Lady, you can stop now. There's nothing anyone can do. He's gone." He places a gentle hand on my shoulder, and I lean back on my heels. Tears stream down my face, and blood drips off of my fingers. I turn my gaze to the ceiling before I rise to my feet slowly, wiping my hands on my skirt before covering my face with my trembling hands. I exit the carriage in what feels like slow motion. I hear nothing but the rush of my blood in my ears and while everyone is still running around me, I stand still. Alaric rushes over when he sees me stumble off of the last step of the carriage, catching me in his arms as I collapse to my knees. He sinks to the cobblestone with me knowing from my appearance that his father is gone. His head rests on my shoulder with one arm holding my front, the other around my back. I feel his body shake against mine, his tears soaking my dress that is already destroyed. I know from the rawness in my throat that I either scream or cry out hard enough that salt and iron coats my tongue. The blood on my hands is too much. And this is just the beginning.

CHAPTER 19

Two days. That is all the council has allowed to mourn the death of the King. Two days to collect ourselves and act like nothing happened. The wedding is set to happen regardless of the missing parent and patriarch. Alaric has been silent since the courtyard. He has been a ghost, a shell of the man I have come to know, and I wish he would simply speak. But there has been nothing but silence. My balcony and the garden below have been my sanctuary, my refuge in the storm of emotions that still threaten to drown me.

I glance around the garden surrounding me; it is pretty magnificent, more so than the one we have back home. I can't help but wonder whether I will ever see home again, or if I will be stuck here for eternity. I suppose I could get used to the grandeur, but I don't necessarily want to get used to it. I want to run and never look back, more so now, than ever before but I know that if I were to do what I want, there wouldn't be a home to go back to. The stone of the fountain beneath me is cool in the warming air, and the bubbling of the water does wonders to calm my nerves.

I'm glad we decided to have the wedding out in the main garden. I know the preparations have been underway since dawn. We lucked out; it is absolutely gorgeous out. The sun shines, with the rare cloud in the perfect azure sky. The temperature is warm, but not too hot: a perfect day for a wedding. Thoughts of postponing have been brought forth a few times over the past two days, but Alaric didn't want to seem weak, and with the circumstances of his father's murder, we can't afford to. It feels like the world is watching, especially with all of the dignitaries here for the wedding. Personally, I don't think they would have done or said anything if we had postponed the wedding. We did just lose our king. At least Alaric agreed to postpone the coronation a couple of weeks to give his father the respect he deserves.

"Hi you." Anna puts on a smile as she walks up to my perch on the edge of the fountain.

"Hi yourself. How are you holding up?" I study her, and notice that she looks better. Not as pale and a little closer to her normal. She has a little color back in her cheeks, and the dark circles she has had under her eyes have faded. She looks like she's finding the ground under her feet again.

"I'm okay, but it is still hard. How are you doing? Is he talking to you yet?" She looks over at me, already guessing the answer.

"Eh, I'm okay. Making it through." I let out a small laugh, shake my head, and turn to watch the fountain. "He barely even looks at me, let alone speaks to me. I don't even know if he's going to go through with saying 'I do'. Has he talked to anyone?" I stare into the fountain, watching the water bubble out of the spout. I know he is mourning, but to completely hide himself away?

"He will. He loves you. You know that."

Love? I know he cares for me, but love? No. I fight back the laugh that bubbles inside of me and instead, shake my head again. I roughly wipe under my eyes, catching any hint of moisture before it can form into a tear and fall. I shove the white hot anger into a box, and lock it tight. I can't let it out. Not yet. It isn't Alaric that I am angry with.

"It's time to head in and get you looking the part of the royal bride," she says with a smile. She takes my hand in hers and I let her lead me back up the stairs that lead to my balcony and my room. Andria is waiting for us inside.

Everywhere I look is something white; my dress, my shoes, the veil, everything. My body is numb, and my legs have turned to lead. I am deposited in the chair in front of my vanity, and I look at my dress while Anna gathers the makeup she plans on using. It's gorgeous and is certainly fit for the future Queen of Aurellia. The bodice is a sweetheart cut with sleeves that will rest on my upper arms only. The cut is designed to bring attention to my collarbones and the lines of my neck. The bodice has the golden lace in the honeysuckle floral pattern, scattered along the bodice and into the skirt. There are gold and pearl crystals that accent the floral pattern, adding to the color and beauty of the gown. The skirt is full and has enough body that it could probably stand on its own without me in it. My headpiece was delivered yesterday, and waits on the vanity for Anna to work her magic. The veil I chose is simple; the fabric is tulle that matches the skirt, with the same golden honeysuckle lace along the edges.

"Let's get started, shall we?" Anna smiles, seeming to sense what is going on in my mind. I nod, swallowing the rising panic, and watch her in the mirror, prepared to become the royal bride every girl wishes to be. Every girl but me. She pulls half of my hair up, leaving the smaller face framing pieces in the front. The rest she configures into a twisted bun that she pins the veil into at the back of my head. The headpiece rests on my brow, and twists into the small braids she has leading to the bun. The image is starting to come together. As for my face, she keeps it simple, gold for my lids, a very light pink rouge for my cheeks and lips, and that is about it. She shoos me from the chair, and starts on my sister and herself.

I take a minute to sit and breathe. I can do this, I have to. Whether Alaric talks to me or not, I need to do my part. I have made it this far. I snap to attention when Anna shoves my dress into my hands and points to the bathroom for me to get dressed. I roll my eyes, and do as I'm told. I step into the dress, doing it up myself the best I can. I have Anna finish the corset as I step out into the bedroom. When the dress is tight, and I am cinched in, I turn to face Anna and Andria and am met by awed looks and stunned silence.

"You look stunning."

"Like a real queen. Momma would be so proud."

The words sound empty. I feel like a puppet; like someone else is pulling the strings and making all my decisions for me. I walk over to the full-length mirror to take a look for myself. I see some young beauty, in a huge dress. The bodice is form fitting, accenting her tiny waist, and the full skirts add a little sugar to the spice the bodice provides. It's a very mature gown, and definitely something a queen would wear. I gather some of the fabric of the skirt into my fists, just to smooth it out again. The dress is everything I wanted and more. It is just the wrong man that will be waiting for me at the end of the aisle, or at least I used to feel that way. Now? All my emotions swirl and cause more conflict than answer. I don't know what I am doing anymore. I turn away from the stranger in the mirror and take in my sister and Anna. Anna looks regal. The gown she chose for herself fits her every curve perfectly. She looks elegant and like the sister of the future King. My sister on the other hand, her dress is a little bit more modest due to her age. The skirt is fuller, and the gown doesn't fit her form as much as Anna's does, but she still looks stunning. Our mother would be so proud of the young lady she is becoming.

"Come here you two." I hold out my arms, and they squeeze

me tight, and surprisingly, Andria is the first to let go.

Anna pulls away with a smile. I smile and nod, with tears in my eyes. I wonder if she can tell how my legs itch to run. They ache with the effort to remain where I am.

"Thank you," my mouth forms the words before I turn to Andria. "Are you ready for this?"

"I should be the one asking you that." She sticks out her tongue, but nods nonetheless. Before we can say much more, there is a timid knock on the door. I stay back as Anna goes to open it. She stands at the door for a few moments, talking to the person on the other side. She holds the door open and calls, "It's your father. It's show time." She winks at me, and I feel nothing.

My father enters the room, taking both of us in. He first turns to Andria, "You look beautiful, my dear." He gives her a brief hug, then turns to me. "Come here you." He holds his arms open, and I quickly enter them and cling to him the way I did when I was young. My arms go up under his, and I take a few deep breaths before I smile and pull away. "Well, let's get this started then." I gesture for my father to lead the way. He takes me through the garden connected to my balcony, which eventually leads to the main garden outside of the ballroom and dining hall. As we turn the final curve in the path leading to the area they have prepared for the ceremony, I gasp at the sight before me.

The garden is stunning. There are fairy lights streamed up along all of the trees and above the walkways. The flowers and the trees are in full bloom, filling the place with life, color, and their sweet aroma. It is as if someone had plucked this place out of a childhood dream. I half expect a fairy to come flitting out of the butterfly bush or a unicorn to come trotting down the aisle. It is everything, everything I ever dreamed. I never told anyone that this is what I wanted, so how did they know? How did Alaric know?

I finally notice all of the people, and I only know a few out of the hundreds in attendance. How does anyone know this many people? My head spins at the thought of everyone watching me walk down the aisle, and again the thought that Alaric might not go through with it leaves me breathless. Alaric waits at the end of the aisle, dressed in a dark green tunic, so dark it is almost black, and white trousers. The outfit is embellished with gold; a gold chain that hangs from one of the buttons and disappears into a small pocket, likely holding a small pocketwatch. He is the direct image from one of the visions. The ones leading me to this exact moment. My mouth opens slightly as he takes in my appearance. His eyes widen slightly and his lips part slightly before the corners lift in a small smile. His eyes soften, and his dimple deepens in his cheek. I blink and glance at the ground in front of me before looking up again.

That's when I see him, Peter. He stands near the front of the aisle and drinks me in. I stop in my tracks and look around to see if anyone notices the way my heart stops, or the way I can't seem to get my feet to move again. I open my mouth, my heart pounding and screaming inside at the thought of who waits at the end of the aisle. I'm not sure I can do this. It isn't fair to Alaric, to Peter, to me. I'm frozen. I glance at my father, and he seems to sense that I need a firm push to be able to continue my way down the aisle. "Together," he murmurs, and I just barely nod my head and we step forward again, as one. I stare straight ahead, meeting Alaric's crystal eyes. He looks amazing, the green of his tunic bringing out the blue of his eyes, and the gold looks good on his tanned skin. He looks like he finally got some sleep, but there is still a sadness that lingers over him, and likely will for some time. Anna and Andria are already beside him, waiting alongside the priest.

The aisle seems to get longer and longer, and that's when everything disappears. All I see is a mousey haired little girl holding a cloth doll by the hand sobbing uncontrollably in the middle of a country road calling out for her mommy, then it flashes to an image of a burning village somewhere south of here, then it flashes to huddles of people trying to hide from the rain under a patched tarp in a ransacked fishing village.

I'm left breathless by what I've seen. I hardly notice that I've made it to Alaric and the Priest.

"Who gives this young maiden away?"

"I do. Her father, Lord Joel Smith of Stonebreach."

"Welcome, Lady Katerina Smith. Join your betrothed up here beside me please." The Priest opens his arms wide making his white cloak flare around him as his face breaks into a big smile. My father places a small kiss on my brow and steps back into the crowd behind us, and I step forward and do as I'm told. All the while, I can't help but feel like I'm making the biggest mistake of my life. I glance behind me and catch Peter's eye. He must sense what I'm feeling because he whispers, "It's okay," and nods his head at me with a small, sad smile. I turn back to the Priest and force myself to take a few deep breaths to attempt to calm myself down. It doesn't work.

"We are gathered here today to bring together Prince Alaric Lyle and Lady Katerina Smith in holy matrimony. I'd like to start out by saying that marriage and love aren't easy. It is going to be hard; it will ultimately be one of the hardest things you two have ever done. But I can guarantee that by the time you are old and gray and have had a long and wonderful life together, it will have been well worth it. I hope you two find that out for yourselves," he then turns to Alaric, "Alaric, will you take this woman to be your wedded wife, to hold and to cherish, to love and protect for the rest of your life?"

Alaric turns to me and I watch him swallow. He stares at me for a moment, studying me. He must've seen what he was looking for because he continues with, "I will from this day forward, for better, for worse, for richer or poorer, in sickness and in health. Until death do us part."

The Priest nods, satisfied, and then turns to me. "Katerina, will you take this man to be your wedded husband, to hold and to cherish, to love and protect for the rest of your life?"

I turn to Alaric, and really look at him. I look into his blue eyes and see the worry that I won't go through with this, the feelings he has for me, and the desire to fight for justice for his father and his country. I see the same fight I have in me. I see a companion, a friend. Someone I have come to like and trust, someone who I care for, and could someday grow to love. I owe it to him to try, but I still feel like something inside me is breaking. I take a deep breath to begin to say my part of the vow, and I feel a tear escape the tight hold I have had on my emotions.

"I will from this day forward for better, for worse, for richer or poorer, in sickness and in health. Until death do us part." My voice cracks on the last bit, but I make it through. I hold myself together, I don't cry, I don't scream. I'm going to be okay.

"I now pronounce you husband and wife. You may kiss the bride." The congregation is cheering, and before I can even grasp what is going on, I'm in Alaric's arms. He dips me low and gently places his lips on mine, a feather light caress. An apology, without actually saying anything. He straightens us back out, and we turn to face everyone, smiles on our faces, hands clasped together. Playing the perfect couple.

As we make our way through the throng of cheering people towards the feast awaiting us in the dining hall, I can't help but feel thankful that we decided to wait two weeks to have the coronation ceremony. I don't think I'd be able to handle losing all of my freedom in one day. I can sense everyone following us into the hall and filing into the tables in the lower half of the room. We make our way to the main table on the raised section overlooking the rest of the room. We take the two seats at the head of the table, facing each other with our families filling in the rest of the table.

"That was truly a beautiful ceremony," Anna remarks as she takes the seat to my left. I nod in agreement and give her a small smile. My father takes the seat to my right, with Andria sitting down beside him. Lucas ends up beside his sister and across from Andria. They make small talk with one another, which leads to Lucas using his "charming" demeanor to flirt with her. At least she holds her own, but I can't help the seething anger from seeping out of the locked box within me.

"Lucas, what did you think of the ceremony? Was it to your liking, or are you just here for the alcohol at the party in a little while?" I jab, a snarky smile on my face. "I do wish that your father were able to be here, he was so excited for this. He would have been so happy." I hope this comes off as innocent and kind, but I hope Lucas shows some sort of discomfort regarding his father. I know what he did, and, in a way, I want him to know that I know. I want him to know that I will be a thorn in his side until the day he dies.

"Yes, my father would have loved the ceremony. I know the rest of us thought it was quite lovely and full of emotion. I swear there probably wasn't a dry eye in the place." He chuckles, "and I do like a nice party. My father was known to love a party too." He winks and turns to talk to one of the servants. I roll my eyes, giving up for the time being and decide to people-watch. Everyone seems to be enjoying themselves. There is laughter and merriment everywhere around me. It makes me wish I was a normal girl. Someone who got to marry the love of her life and live out her days the way she wanted to, rather than how she is being told to. I just wish I could go back to before I got these stupid visions. Back to when I was happy.

"Dinner is served, M'Lady." A servant bows as she places a plate piled high with food in front of me.

"Thank you." I murmur, before I start eating. No one speaks for a while, and I'm left to my thoughts for the time being. I look at my husband, at Alaric, and I feel trapped. All of my anger comes to a peak, and it is hard to shove back down. I don't want to feel this anger, this resentment for the man in front of me. Over the last several months, we have grown closer, and there are even times where he is all I think about. Alaric must have sensed my gaze because he glances up with a small smile. I smile back, but quickly glance away before he can read too much into my expression. When I turn away, my eyes meet Peter's from across the room. He is seated with the other High Lords of the court and a few of the young maidens I've seen roaming the palace. The same one from earlier this week sits beside him, leaning into him and basically throwing herself at him. He seems to be enjoying himself, for the most part anyway. But I can still sense the same longing I have in his gaze, and I can tell that this bothers him as much as it does me. It is hard to abandon what you thought was your future for so long, but I am trying. I break my eyes away from Peter's and look down at the table.

"Katerina, are you ready to be named Queen?" Lucas asks, noticing what had captured my gaze. I look at Lucas and wish I could wipe that smug smirk off of his face.

"I suppose so." I shrug, and glance back at Peter, but he has already turned back to his friends and doesn't return my gaze. I look back at the table and wonder if Lucas has some other reason to be smug about the coronation. Soon enough everyone is done eating, and it's time to head to the ballroom for the party. All of the guests take their leave, and I can hear the excitement in their voices. It isn't everyday that there is a massive party thrown.

By the time that we arrive in the ballroom, the small orchestra is already playing, and the guests are laughing and dancing. Everyone goes quiet when we first enter, then the room erupts into cheers. Alaric raises his hands, and everything goes quiet again.

"I want to thank you all for coming out to celebrate our union today. It means a great deal to both of us. I hope all of you enjoy your time here in the palace." He gestures to the orchestra and they strike up a lively tune. Alaric turns to me, his hand outstretched. "May I have this dance?" I give him a smile and place my hand in his before he leads me to the dance floor. Our guests smile and watch us walk hand in hand to the center of the floor and begin to dance. Soon, the guests join us on the dance floor. The next dance calls for quite a bit of skipping, hopping, and twirling, and I'm out of breath by the time the dance is complete. After the song ends, and the dancing partners bow to one another, I leave Alaric's side and head to the refreshment table. Alaric lets me leave and goes to strike up conversations with some of his nobles.

I select a wine glass from the table and turn to see Peter standing maybe fifteen feet away. He motions for me to follow him to what I can assume are the gardens outside. I glance around to make sure no one is watching me, and when I see the coast is clear, I quickly follow. He leads me to a secluded portion of the garden, well away from prying eyes, and far enough from the party that we won't be stumbled upon. As soon as he turns and sees that I followed him, he pulls me close and ever so slowly lowers his lips to mine.

At first the kiss is so gentle and light, but our need for one another quickly changes that. He pulls me flush against him and kisses me more fiercely. *No, I can't do this. Not anymore.* I push my hands against Peter's chest, and he stumbles back from the force. His face is incredulous, and still flushed from kissing me. I shake my head, lifting a hand to my mouth.

"We can't, I can't….Not anymore."

He doesn't respond, simply stares; his eyes lose all warmth and turn ice cold.

"I'm sorry—" my voice breaks as I back up several steps and head back into the ballroom.

I notice that nothing has changed as I reenter the party. Alaric is still talking to his nobles, my father being one of them. Anna is talking and laughing with some of the ladies and sips on the wine in her hand. It seems like no one has noticed my absence, so I go to the refreshment table for another glass of wine. I down it, trying to drown my guilt before grabbing a third glass and turning to find Andria. When I find her, she is waltzing with Lucas. For a moment, everything around me disappears, and I want nothing more than to make the musicians stop, so I can gouge Lucas's eyes from their sockets for how he is looking at her. As my hands clench themselves into fists, Anna comes up to me.

"Where have you been? I've been looking for you."

I snap out of imagining the worst possible deaths for my brother-in-law and turn to look at Anna. "I needed some fresh air, so I went for a walk in the gardens. I lost track of time." I glance back at my sister, my skin crawling at the thought of Lucas's hands on her.

"Lucas seems to be enchanted by Andria. She is a lovely girl and will make any man happy. She's a lot like you." She smiles, watching them.

"Lucas can have anyone he wants. Just not my sister. He will never have her if I can help it." I spit out, making Anna look at me in shock. I may have spoken harsher than what was necessary, but I don't care anymore. I'm done playing nice. It is time to come clean.

"Are you okay?" she asks, studying me. I nod and continue to stare daggers in Lucas's direction. "You would tell me if something was going on with you, wouldn't you?" Again, I just nod. She nods and walks away. But she must still be concerned, because she comes back a short time later with Alaric. "If you won't talk to me, at least talk to him," she says before she walks away, shaking her head.

"Katerina?" Alaric studies me, trying to figure out what's wrong. I turn to look at my husband, and what I see in his eyes makes me feel ashamed. The guilt I tried to drown comes flooding back, and I bite my lip. His eyes are full of wonder and amazement. They hold the care he has for me, and his dreams of our future together. I glance away, and my eyes find Peter. He is talking to other nobles, laughing and carrying on and completely ignoring me. "Katerina, talk to me."

"Why? This is the first time you've talked to me since your father died. You haven't bothered to check in on me after the whole thing. Seeing as he died when I was with him and all. Now if you'll excuse me, I am going to go dance with my sister." I storm off into the crowd of dancers, leaving Alaric behind. I begin to realize that maybe I have had just a little too much to drink.

When I reach my sister and Lucas, I tap him on the shoulder. "May I cut in?" he turns to look at me annoyed, but he nods and bows before taking his leave. I step in to take his place. "Remember when we used to practice all the dances together when we were children, taking turns leading? I miss those days. They were so much simpler than things are today." I smile, and Andria grins.

"You were an awful man. You would always step on my toes." She giggles, and I laugh too, but I quickly turn serious.

"Andria, stay away from Lucas. He is not the good person he pretends to be. He has evil plans for us and our country."

"I'm afraid I can't do that."

"What do you mean you can't? Andria, you need to listen to

me. I'm serious. You've known him all of what? A week? He is not the person he seems to be. I don't want you to be wrapped up in this. Please."

"You can't tell me what to do Katerina. I am my own person, and I will make my own choices."

"I can tell you what to do. As your Queen, I forbid you from forming a relationship with Lucas."

"Now you tell me what I can and cannot do?" she scoffs, "I have them too you know. I am well aware of the man that he is. I am playing my part in this. Every piece has to come together. I cannot, and will not, abandon this to you alone."

"Andria, I'm begging you. Don't continue with Lucas. Please."

She stares at me for a moment. "Fine. But only because of the visions. But I can't do this," she gestures between us, "right now." She turns on her heel and leaves me standing alone on the dance floor. I slowly walk to the refreshments and grab another glass of wine, and down it quickly. I put the glass down, grabbing another and quickly down that one as well. This evening, no, this past year has just been one thing after another. I just want it all to end. I finally understand why my mother killed herself. Why did I ever stop dreaming of boarding a ship to take me far away from here?

I'm standing near the refreshment bar, holding my sixth glass of wine when my father finds me. I refuse to look at him, knowing that if I do he will see everything on my face.

"Gem, look at me."

I shake my head and take a swallow of my wine. "You can say what you came here to say, but I will not look at you." My words slur slightly. I've never been one to drink, and I think I may have over done it.

Father chuckles. "And why not? You think that just because you aren't looking at me, I can't see what you are trying to hide?"

"Okay?" I scoff, shaking my head again and watch the dancers.

"I know you still love him, and you are headed down a very dangerous path if you continue to play both sides. I will not see you hang for him. I will not see you die too. I will not lose you both."

I turn to face him, my eyes wide. "How did you…?"

"I saw you follow him out and how you froze when you saw him earlier. Trust me when I say this. You must end it."

I nod. "I already did. But thank you for your concern." My eyes slide back to the dance floor, my mind fuzzy.

I hear him sigh, but his voice comes out warm. "Now, are you planning to dance with your dear old man, or am I going to have to beg?"

I grin and take his offered hand, placing my wine on a servants tray when we pass as he leads me onto the dancefloor. We get a song or two in before Alaric steps in. "May I cut in?"

"Of course, Your Majesty." My father bows and winks at me before taking his leave. Alaric sweeps me into his arms, and we begin to dance.

"I am sorry about my behavior lately. I'm sorry I didn't come to you. I didn't know what to say, or how to approach you." He meets my eye and I notice him bite the inside of his cheek. I remind myself that I was never truly angry with him, and was lashing out in my own pain.

"There wasn't anything I could do. You do know that, right?"

"I know it wasn't your fault, and I'm sorry if I ever gave you that impression. I would like you to help me find my father's murderer and help me end all of this. You will be beside me, ruling our country so it's only fitting." His lips twitch up into a grin, and I can't help but smile back. He dips me low and kisses me. I let him.

CHAPTER 20

Death, there is too much of it. Way too much. You will see even more than I have, and for that I am sorry. I never wanted this life for you. I never wanted this trait to pass to you. I hoped to take you to train, but you needed me in other ways before I had the chance to take you.

You are going to be a wonderful mother, Katerina. You may not know it yet, but you are everything your children will need. You will make things right. They will never wonder if they are enough.

I stumble on the way to my quarters, but Alaric keeps me upright. The copious amounts of wine I've consumed throughout the night turns my stomach, and it is hard to imagine consummating the marriage when I feel like this. The way to my room remains clear, the halls are quiet as most everyone is still at the party downstairs, or wandering the gardens reveling in the joy of our union. Peter left the ball long before we did, and for that I am grateful. I don't know what would have happened if I had seen him in this state. As it is, the moment we shared in the garden, before I shoved him away, was one final moment of weakness in this tumultuous sea of uncertainty.

I hiccup as our footsteps echo in the empty hallway as we approach the familiar area of the castle where my rooms are. Rather than stopping at my door like normal, Alaric's strong arms lead me past it to areas that I have left unexplored. The hall curves to the left, and we follow it for a few minutes, passing statues and busts of marble on pedestals that are as immaculately carved as the art pieces themselves. The hall is otherwise the same as mine, and we come to a stop outside of a set of double doors. There are three other sets of them; one directly across the hall, another about 50 feet further to the end of the hall, and a larger more ornate set at the end of the hall. I know without a doubt that the king's chambers lie through those doors. Alaric glances at me, his eyes unsure but he pushes open one of the doors in front of us, and holds it open for me to enter before him. My heels click on the stone floor before the sound dissipates as a soft carpet that lies on the other side of the entryway cushions each footfall as I enter the room. I hold my breath, my head spinning slightly as I take in my surroundings. If I thought my rooms were nice, I was sorely mistaken.

There is a crackling to my left, where a fire burns in the fireplace and sheds light into the large sitting room. The chairs and lounge circle the small table in front of the fire, and there is a small writing desk in the far left corner. There are three doors off of the room; one immediately to my left and right, and one at the back of the room to the right. From what I can see to my left, the room is occupied with a large desk that sits in the center of the room. I can't see much since it is dark, and I can only see what is within the light cast by the fire and the light sconces. I spin in a circle, taking in the art on the walls as I turn to peer through the door to my right.

My breath catches in my throat as I see the painting of the sea near my home on the wall between the two doorways to my right. There is a ship at sea, but a storm churns up the waves in a haunting green color that is nearly impossible to capture, yet this artist has managed it. The fingers of my right hand graze my lips, and the other hugs my ribs. The painting is a shocking reminder of home, and a pang of sadness works its way through me. I blink rapidly and turn my gaze from the painting, and tilt my head to peer into the room to my right. I again can't see much, but it looks like there is a long table with chairs set up around it. Is that his own personal dining room? Why ever bother eating downstairs when he has this available to him?

I hear the soft click of the door closing, and hear Alaric chuckle as I linger just inside of the doorway. I turn my head, my eyes sliding from the barely seen contents in the other room and focus on Alaric who has stepped closer to me in the process of closing and locking the door behind us. I feel the heat coming off of him in waves, and he smells amazing. He smells of smoke, mint, and something slightly citrusy. He stands close enough that I can feel him breathe against my shoulder. I turn to face him, and notice the breath of space that lies between us. His tunic has been partially unbuttoned for awhile now, but I really take notice of the way the sharp vee of the top of his tunic opens to his chest. That chest is just as chiseled as his face, and I swallow. Hard. His hands rest in his pockets as he watches me. His mouth is slightly parted, and the tip of his tongue darts out to moisten his lips. His hair has fallen from its usual manicured swoop that rests along his temples, and falls into his eyes. Blue eyes that have grown dark find mine, and the air becomes hard to breathe. My lips part as I stare. He lifts a hand from his pocket and rubs the back of his head at the nape of his neck, his head ducking slightly as his mouth twitches. That smile tells me everything that I need to know.

Suddenly, all the space that lies between us is too much. His lips are sealed to mine, and I give him everything I have to give. A gasp passes my lips as his trail down my neck, exploring the uncharted territory there. My breathing grows haggard as my fingers grip his hair and his face swims into view again before his lips are back on mine. His hands find the corset on the back of my dress, and make quick work of the ties. I feel the dress loosen around me, and I shiver with the flash of memory of what moments of passion I have shared with another. I slam the thoughts down, my eyes grazing over the dark haired man in front of me. This is my husband. Alaric is my husband. The feelings that I have shoved and kept at bay these months flood forth. We started this as strangers, but now, he has helped me heal. I want this, even though I have clung with such ferocity to something that was no longer mine. This man, Alaric, is what I want.

His fingers slide up my back from the undone corset, and my skin tingles under his trailing touch. I sigh his name as he leaves kisses down my neck and to the top of my shoulder. With his name on my lips, his fingers dig into my hair, and I hear as well as feel him groan against my neck. I shiver again, this time in anticipation. His hands release my hair, and slide to my shoulders where he slowly pushes my gown down, leaving me trembling before him when the warm night air hits my bare skin. I take a step back, stepping out of the gown and meet his gaze. His lids are heavy, and his chest rises and falls with each breath. He takes the few steps that lie between us, brushing my dress to the side of the room as his hands are on my skin again. My fingers grip his tunic, and they waver on the buttons. I fight with them as my fingers betray the amount of alcohol in my system. They are clumsy and damn-near useless. I finally get them done as we stumble toward the door at the back of the room. His bedroom must lie through the doorway. I am too focused on his shirt buttons to notice the room change around me as we make it through the doorway. Soft bedding hits the back of my legs, and I fall backward. I land among the grey cushioned blanket and lush pillows while Alaric stands at my feet with his shirt unbuttoned and his eyes glazed over. He runs a hand through the hair that falls in his eyes, but the hair falls right back where it was. He blows out a sigh, the hair fluttering with his breath. His eyes graze over me, and I find it hard to sit still. I press my thighs together, attempting to pause the heat that spreads through me with his eyes on me like that. And that chest is as chiseled as the day I remember on the boat where his soaked shirt clung to him much like I do now.

"Alaric, please," I gasp, my fingers gripping the blanket at my sides. His eyes continue to devour me, but his fingers quickly take care of his pants before he leans down over me, his hand holding him above me by my head. He lowers his lips to mine as his body covers mine.

His skin is warm on mine and he keeps control of the weight of him pushing into me. I can feel him against every inch of me, and I simply want more. Our tongues battle for control, as he slides further onto me, and we move into the center of the bed. My body is on fire, and he solely controls the flames. His fingers trail along my body, flaring new trembles and sending tingles through me. Each touch elicits a new spark, and we burn together as one.

I wake with the sun as it comes through the open double doors leading to a large balcony that isn't mine. Memories from last night come flooding in alongside the pounding in my head. My fingers search the bed beside me, and find the firm ridge of Alaric's back. I turn my head on the pillow, rolling over to face him. He sleeps on his stomach with an arm under his head. His face is peaceful, there isn't a worry to be found. The blanket settles around his waist, leaving his muscled back and shoulders bare. I lie on my back, and turn to stare at the ceiling. One hand lies under my head, and I play with my hair with the other on my chest. I relish the silence, and for once my mind is at ease.

I hear Alaric sigh beside me as he rolls over. I smile at the serenity on his face, and carefully climb out of the bed, avoiding moving too quickly so I don't wake him. I find his shirt on the floor, and pull it on buttoning it as I quietly make my way out of the room. The shirt is huge on me, and hangs to my mid thigh. I wander through the sitting room, taking a moment to fully take in the seascape painting before wandering to the two other rooms. A twinge of nausea settles in my stomach, and I pin it on the headache still pounding away under my temples. A sharper stab of nausea brings my hand to my mouth, and with how quickly it comes and passes, my mind starts to race, quickly counting days, double counting, triple counting. How did I not realize how late I was? It's been a couple of weeks since I was supposed to have my cycle. My eyes fill with tears and everything inside me shatters. I try to pick up the pieces, but hard as I try, they keep falling just out of reach. I take a few deep, steadying breaths. No one has to know. No one *can* know.

I breathe in deeply, feeling the air fill my lungs and slowly release it to settle my still churning stomach as I continue my exploration of Alaric's quarters. The office to the left of the door that I saw last night is small with the large desk dwarfing the room, but it is cozy with a leather couch in the corner facing the desk. The desk is bare, and looks mostly untouched. There is a thin coating of dust on the desk and bookshelves lining the walls behind it. He must not come in here often. I trail my fingers over the books on the shelf, reading the titles. There are history collections, as well as books of fairytales that I grew up reading. A smile tugs at my lips as I move on further down the shelf. There is a small book on Seers and their importance to society. My fingers freeze, and my hand falls to my side. My eyes linger on the spine of the book, and itch to pull it from the shelf. Why would he have a book on seers?

"Damn, you look great in my shirt," Alaric's voice is husky as I turn from the shelf to find him leaning on the door jam with his arms crossed over his bare chest. His mouth is drawn up in a lazy grin and his hair is still mussed from sleep. His ankles cross slightly where he leans, at least he pulled on a pair of trousers that hang loosely around his hips. He looks completely relaxed and at ease. I moisten my lips but decide that I need to know more than I need to have his hands on me.

"What is your opinion of Seers?"

His eyes flutter closed as his brows scrunch together before his features smooth out slightly with a sigh. He is taken aback by the question, but I don't offer any explanation. Instead, I watch his face, his reaction. He glances down, his mouth pursed, before he meets my eyes.

"I wondered when we were going to have this conversation."

My eyes lock on his, bewildered. "How?"

"How do I know? You hinted at things a couple of times now." He pushes off from the door jam, striding barefoot across the room. He leans against me, his mouth next to my ear as he reaches just past me onto the shelf at my back, "Give me some credit here, hun. I'd like to think that I know you by now. I know you're hiding something." He steps back, the book on seers in his hand, which he hands to me as he half sits on the desk behind him. He nods his head at the book, looking at it pointedly.

I gently lift the cover, and my eyes widen briefly and I blink a couple of times to make sure that I am reading what I think I am. I suck in a breath and try to calm the dizziness that threatens unconsciousness. My mother's handwriting fills the front cover. I glance at him and he nods again, so I turn back to the words.

Alaric,

This book tells you everything that you need to know about Seers and how they can relate to society. Read it, let it sit with you, then read it again. There are those of us who have this power, but are still terrified of the consequences of our gift. The consequences of coming forward with what we see, what we know. Make the changes necessary for our survival, as your own depends on it.

You will find yourself looking for a bride— Katerina Smith is of age, and holds the highest rank you can have without being royalty. She is a good match for what I know of you.

My daughter, Katerina, is a force to be reckoned with. She will test you in ways you don't expect, and she will push every boundary, but she will be the one that needs you the most. She will push and fight against this union with everything in her until she realizes that you are everything that she needs and wants, and while you may question your reasons for pursuing this relationship, it will be worth it. She is everything that you need and more. She will be like coming up for air.

I hope this book speaks to you and makes you understand; she will need you to understand. Give her time to come to you. She will tell you of her gift in time, but please don't push her. She will need to do this in her own way and on her own timeline. She will trust you, just give her time. Please.

She needs you as much as you will need her. Trust her,

and she will save us all.

Clara Smith

He has known this whole time. My eyes find his over the book, and his eyes are crystal clear. Not a drop of doubt or hate to be seen. He has held this secret, my secret.

"How long?" my voice comes out strangled as I let the book close and I gently place it on its side on the lowest spot on the shelf.

"Your father gave that to me a little over a year ago."

CHAPTER 21

A year? But that's impossible; I didn't know of our engagement until five months ago when he came to Stonebreach. My mind whirls, and I sink to the ground, one hand lingering on the shelf behind me, the other is a fist against my lips. My eyes stare blankly ahead, and I press my knuckles into my mouth, making my teeth dig into the inside of my lips. They have been planning this. Planning this engagement for quite some time behind all of our backs. Peter and I were simply pawns in this twisted game of chess. A year?

"I didn't plan on pursuing you until I did. I swear to you Kat, I didn't know of your engagement, and I didn't know I was going to go through with it until a week before I showed up on your doorstep." I blink hard and see him kneeling on one knee in front of me, his hands resting on the ground beside him. He gently takes my cheek in one of his hands, tilting my face to look at him. "Please, Kat, I swear I didn't know. I have never lied to you."

His face is sad, and his eyes dart back and forth between mine. He is just as scared as I am. I feel myself nod and he releases the breath he must have been holding. He rests his forehead on mine and closes his eyes as he breathes me in. I breathe deep, attempting to calm my racing heart, but it doesn't soothe the ache that settles in my chest. A fresh kind of heartbreak that I am not sure what direction to move forward to fix. I decide to pick the path laid out in front of me, the one that my mother took the effort to cement into permanence for me.

"Lucas killed your father, and plans to steal your throne."

I tell him everything.

His eyes stay on me as I unload eight months worth of visions, and how I have struggled and searched for answers I never thought I would find. His face is haunted throughout it all, but he doesn't stop my flood of words, and instead listens intently, only interrupting to ask questions to gain further understanding. We pause long enough for him to answer the quiet knock at the door, where he orders breakfast to be delivered to the room. We move to the dining room, continuing to talk through everything that has transpired since my first vision over the trays loaded with pastries. He believes every word.

"Why didn't you tell me sooner? Why wait until now?"

"Why didn't you?" I look at him pointedly. The same question applies to him. He has the decency to look sheepish, as he ducks his head and purses his lips. I sigh as I tear my croissant into bite size pieces. "I think I needed time to know whether I could trust you. You hinted at everything in the very beginning, didn't you?" I watch him from across the table. He nods, his eyes fluttering slightly. "At the inn, you said something about talking to you and being able to trust you with everything. You were implying I could come to you and you would be my safe space. I just didn't know it yet."

I watch as Alaric stands and rounds the table to kneel beside my chair.

"I was always on your side. Always looking out for you. Hoping that you would come to be the same for me." His voice is soft, and my hand finds his on my knee.

I curl my fingers into his as my other brushes his bangs to his temples and rests on his cheek. I search his eyes, and I know what he says is true. He has always been here, exactly where I have needed him. I wish I had realized it sooner, than maybe things wouldn't be headed the way that they are. Maybe his father would still be here.

"I tried everything I could think of to save your father. Once I had enough evidence, I warned him through a letter, I had Ian talk to him, I tried everything. I am so sorry." I shake my head, and lean my forehead against his. My breath shudders through me, and I look into his eyes. They are clouded, but he meets my gaze. His hand squeezes mine on my knee.

"I know."

The rest of the morning following the very difficult conversation that tore open the ground beneath both Alaric's and my feet, passes smoothly. He takes his leave to meet with Ian and my father to discuss moving forward when it comes to the visions and what we have been doing to relay information thus far. I wander back to my own quarters, but linger just inside the door. My eyes scan the room, taking it in for what I assume will be the last time as we have decided to move my things to Alaric's quarters. A lot of my things have already started the transfer— the portrait of Andria and I is missing from its usual perch on the mantel.

I slowly step through the room, my fingers trailing on the furniture as I pass. I hear a soft knock on my balcony door, and hesitate in the sitting room. Who would even be coming for me here? Knowing I don't have the door locked, I freeze when I hear the soft click of the door latching as it closes. I scan the room around me for something to use as a weapon should I need it, but come up empty. There is very little left aside from the furniture itself, and the fireplace tools to the immediate right of the stone. I reach behind me, and as silently as possible, wrap my fingers around the poker and slide it free of the hanger. I bring it in front of me, raising it, ready to strike.

Familiar blonde hair flutters as Peter steps into the room.

"Peter!" I gasp, dropping the firepoker to my side, and releasing it from my grasp. My heart beats frantically, and I try to catch my breath as I rest my hand against my diaphragm.

"Kat?" he scans me and sees the discarded poker. "Going to stab me with a firepoker?" he smirks and shakes his head.

"I should." I murmur, crossing my arms. "What are you doing here?"

"That is a good question, honestly. I've been asking myself that already."

"You shouldn't be here." I shake my head. "You can't be here." I chew my lip, my eyes searching the room behind him and avoiding looking at him directly.

He ducks his head, running his fingers through the mess that his hair always is. "Believe me, I am aware." His tone is sharp, and I flick my eyes to meet his.

Bad idea. Very bad idea. The pregnancy news rises to my lips, there is no doubt that it is his, but it isn't fair to give him false hope. He can't know. My mouth opens slightly, and my tongue darts out to moisten my lips before I clamp my mouth tight, clenching my jaw.

"Kat, I…" he trails off as he reaches out to me.

I take a step back, and my head whips to the door as Alaric's voice cuts through the air; "What the hell is going on here?"

Peter drops his hand, but raises them in defence and in protest.

"Alaric, nothing is going on. I swear to you." My voice rises in terror as Alaric strides across the room and his fist cracks against Peter's jaw. I flinch at the sound of the impact, but Alaric doesn't slow, and Peter doesn't fight back.

"That is my *wife*. You stay away from her." Alaric's voice is ice, and his fists are relentless as he knocks Peter to the ground. "Do you understand me?" He towers over him, and he reaches down, pulling Peter up by his tunic before shoving him into the wall, his forearm pinning him there. "She is not yours. She is *mine*. You touch her and you are *dead*."

Peter barely nods and Alaric drops him to the ground. Alaric turns to me, his eyes scanning me— taking in the tears and fear etched into my face. Betrayal makes his gaze feel like ice, and I don't know how to fix this. He turns on his heel and walks out of the room, leaving the door to the hall wide open. I watch him go, before I glance at Peter. He leans on the wall, staring at the ceiling. He wipes the corner of his mouth with the back of his hand, wincing as he brushes against the cut on his lower lip.

"Go. Don't let me stop you." He doesn't look at me. His tone leaves no room for argument, and while I have never heard that tone from him before, I don't linger. Instead, I race out of the room after Alaric.

What the hell just happened? My feet fly along the carpeted hall that leads to Alaric and my quarters. I don't know how, but I need to fix this. I quietly close the door behind me, and I scan the room for Alaric's familiar frame. I don't have to search long since he lingers beside the window overlooking the gardens below. He tenses, but doesn't turn to face me. I breathe against the battle of nerves trembling through my core. The nerves remind me of the feelings that I finally released yesterday— *I love him.*

"There is absolutely nothing going on between Peter and I. I promise you."

I hear him scoff, and watch as he shakes his head. His hands clench into fists. "Say I believe you. How *long* has there been nothing between you." His voice is cold, and he spits every word. He does not look at me, simply continues to look out of the window.

My eyes flutter closed as I breathe deeply, hold it, then slowly release as I open my eyes. I step forward, coming to a stop behind him and lean against the wall. I decide to come clean about everything, well, almost everything. "We would meet to review my mother's journal and my own visions. He was there, the day my mother committed suicide. He knew her and could offer another perspective. I didn't know yet that I could trust you." I pause, my voice going quiet, and the lie tastes bitter on my tongue. "We shared a night together— once a- a million years ago. The night before he left…he abandoned me on the same dock you swam to me. I—" My voice trembles, but I come clean. He deserves to know. My eyes burn with tears that I refuse to let fall.

I did this to myself by playing this fatal game. "I let myself be swept up by the lingering depth of feeling I still harbored and a moment of weakness lead me to him when I first came here, and we shared one final moment, but I swear…I abandoned him and those feelings for him there. I shattered when he left. I tried to find any way I could think to stop the dissolution of Peter and my engagement in the beginning because I thought he was everything I wanted, but then everything changed. Alaric, he is no longer what I want. You healed those broken shards that cut every time I felt his presence. You picked me up from the heap he left me in. He tried to kiss me last night, but I stopped it. But I swear to you, there has been nothing for some time now. When I told you I was all in, that I would give this, give us a chance, I meant it."

I reach out to lay a hand on his shoulder, but he spins to face me, and I back into the wall. He towers over me, leaving very little space between us— leaving me pinned to the wall. His fist punches the wall to the left of my head, and I flinch, holding my breath and squeezing my eyes closed.

"Fuck, Kat." He takes a deep shuddering breath, and sinks into me. "I'm sorry. I'm sorry. Please…"

I swallow hard, opening my eyes and see the terror in his. I reach a hand up to cup his cheek. I keep my touch soft, a whisper along his skin.

"You swear there is nothing going on now? It is over?"

I nod, my eyes not leaving his. His forehead comes to rest on my shoulder, and I run my fingers through his hair. He shivers but says nothing further, simply breathes me in and shudders against me. Breathing him in, he smells of home. I confess my feelings, knowing that he needs to hear the words now, more than ever.

"I hope you know that it is you, Alaric, *you*. You have healed the broken pieces that I didn't know how to put back together, and you have become the one person I don't want to be without."

He lifts his head to meet my eyes. "What are you saying?"

My eyes flit between his, and I lick my lips, biting the lower before admitting aloud to both myself and him: "I love you."

His eyes widen, and he crushes his mouth to mine. We twist up within each other's embrace, each fighting for control, but relinquishing it to the other. His fingers dig into my back as he clings to me tighter. I cling to him just as tightly. He lifts me, and I wrap my legs around his waist. He pulls away enough to lean his forehead on mine. I gasp, each breath of him.

"You are everything. Everything I never knew I needed, but everything that I want for the rest of my life. How you have managed to capture every ounce of my being, I don't know, but you have. I am yours. For the rest of my life." His words are music to my ears, and I pull him back in, tightening my legs around him and kissing him fiercely.

He lets go of what control he still had over himself, and presses my back into the wall as his hands shift to my ass. He lifts my skirts further, and one of his hands disappears before I feel him guiding himself into me. He moves slowly, and I gasp against his neck, but he ducks his head and recaptures my mouth. "You are *mine*," he breathes against my lips and I can't help his name forming on mine as he moves, emphasizing his words. We burn together, adding fuel to the feelings that we have decided to nurture.

CHAPTER 22

Wide blue eyes, curious,
innocent.
A replica of me,
my daughter.
Too young to let go,
too young to know why.
Before my eyes,
she grows like waves
kicked up by a storm,
furious, deadly. A hero
to all.

Two weeks pass in a blur— I move into Alaric's quarters, my things taking space in his wardrobe and in his life, and he encourages me to make the space mine and make myself comfortable. Somehow I've managed to hide the sickness that comes and goes without warning. Thankfully I am not showing, and hopefully won't for some time.

Finally, it's coronation day. The constant buzz of the people of the court in my ears reminds me over and over— it is coronation day. My gown is a deep red with gold accents and has a full skirt and train. It is similar in style to my wedding gown, at least in the silhouette. It's gorgeous, regal. Anna tells me to wait outside of the throne room, so she can make sure they are ready for us. I'm sitting in the small window seat staring at the garden below, my train tracing the edge of the seat and wall beside me. My reflection stares back at me, and I'm so absorbed in my thoughts that I don't notice when Alaric walks up to me until his finger brushes along my cheek. I smile, and my gaze slides to him. He is in gold, and it works wonders on his eyes. The tunic and doublet combination is striking, and his entire being screams of power. His tunic is custom made, and it hugs his form. His dark hair is perfectly styled , and his eyes are warm as they meet mine. His lips tilt up into a smile as takes my hand in his and takes a seat beside me on the bench. Even though we just saw each other as we were getting ready, my heart skips a beat.

"They should be calling us in soon. Are you ready?"

I laugh, wondering why everyone keeps asking me that. Have I been that difficult? Before I realize what's happening, my vision starts to go in and out. Instead of the garden, I see the after party. I'm standing talking to Andria and Father when Lucas bursts into the room, sword drawn. Guards follow him into the room, and they start their attack. They take down anyone in their way, and I know exactly who their target is. Alaric. And me.

Just as quickly as I slipped into the vision, I slip out of it. My free hand grips the edge of the seat beneath me and the one that holds his squeezes in response to the vision. I struggle to prevent the gasp that escapes, and I feel Alaric tense beside me. His eyes search my face, and his tone is urgent as he asks if I'm okay. It's all I can do to nod my head. I hear our names being called, although the voice is distant and I struggle to catch my breath. The roaring returns in my ears, and I close my eyes, breathing deeply and controlled. Our names are called again, and I realize it must be time for us to head inside. Alaric is supposed to enter the room first, seeing as he will be king, and I'm supposed to enter shortly behind him. He hesitates, staring at me. He knows I just had a vision, and won't leave my side unless I force him.

"Go. I'm okay. I'll see you in there." I force myself to smile, but inside I really want to get everyone I love out of here and to safety. I need to find Peter, Ian, someone that might know what to do. Someone who would be able to help me get everyone away from the castle before it is too late. Alaric should know what is coming, and his name is on my lips, and the concern deepens the creases between his brows. "Meet me in the ballroom after this, okay?"

He needs to at least be crowned as the rightful king so if all else fails, his people might still stand behind him. Alaric nods but his eyes never leave mine as he heads into the throne room. I stand and take another deep breath, wringing my hands and counting to five before I make my way into the room as well.

The entire room is filled. Most of the faces are familiar from my time here at court. The council stands at the front of the room, as do my father and Andria, and Anna. I scan the room, and don't see Lucas. He couldn't be bothered to show up. The rest of the crowd fills the room. The sea of faces blur together as I walk at an even pace. I maintain my composure, if not for myself, then for Alaric. My shoulders are straight, and I hold my head high as my heels click against the floor with each step, a growing knell that keeps time for the death that awaits us before the day is done.

The curtains in the windows lining the room are wide open, showering the room with sunlight. I watch the dust motes dance in the beams that break through the window near the thrones. It shines on the spot where I will stand once I reach the dais. It seems to take forever to reach the priest standing at the top of the steps in the front of the room. The deep breaths come almost naturally at this point, but they do little to ease the rising panic. Will I be able to save everyone in this room? Who will die because I am too late? My breaths quicken and I turn my gaze to the floor in front of me, trying to ground myself. I count to five, listing five things that I know as a fact to ground me in the moment. *One. My mother died because of the things that she saw.* One foot after another. *Two. I have the same gift she did, I am a Seer.* Alaric waits with his back to me at the end of the aisle. *Three. Alaric is my husband and will be king of Aurellia.* I swallow, and blink against the burn in my eyes. *Four. I am from Stonebreach. Five. I am the eldest daughter of Lord Joel Smith and Clara Smith.* Finally, I reach the steps where Alaric waits. Alaric ascends first, and I wait at the bottom, allowing him to embrace his title alone.

"All hail King Alaric Lyle." Alaric kneels, and the Priest places the crown on his head, then he waits for Alaric to rise. Once back on his feet, he takes the scepter into his hand, then turns towards his people gathered in the room. I climb the stairs, turning toward my people once I reach my place beside Alaric. My train twists beside me, but remains open on the stairs in front of me. The royal crest of Aurellia is detailed into the train. The dress weighs on my shoulders, and I refuse to give in to the desire to roll my shoulders back in an attempt to even the weight distribution. Instead I ignore the discomfort and face my people. Each face I store in my mind, swearing to remember each and every one of them if I am unsuccessful in providing their survival.

"All hail Queen Katerina Smith," I kneel and wait for the Priest to put the crown on my head. When he does, I take a small step backward to stand slightly behind Alaric.

"Long live the King! Long live the Queen!" The crowd cheers, and while it should be a cause for celebration, my blood runs cold. I shiver, and force a smile, trying to appear exactly as they expect me to when really I want to get as far away from here as possible.

After the crowning ceremony, everyone is herded to the ballroom for the party. I glide along after them, but not until Anna helps detach the train from the dress, which helps lessen the weight of the gown, but does nothing to ease the weight of what is to come. Panic races through my veins as each minute ticks by. How much time do I have left? How do I get everyone out in the quickest way possible without seeming out of my mind? How much can I give away to convince everyone of the danger looming over us? I'm lost and I desperately need to find Peter. Lightspire may be our only hope right now. There have been too many attacks to the south and west to venture in those directions, which leaves North to Lightspire or East to Tradesport. But knowing Lucas has conned several council members to his side, who's to say Lord Sharp isn't in league with him. That leaves Lightspire as the only option. I need to secure our journey there— I need to find Peter and hope that he will take us there.

I pause by the door, and Alaric turns to face me. "We need to leave. Tell the people you trust to leave. We are in danger. I have a plan, but we need to be gone before the next bell." He freezes, and I take his hand in mine. "Do you trust me?" He nods. "Then do this. We don't have much time." He squeezes my hand and we enter the ballroom.

We are surrounded by smiling people who have no idea of the terror that will be taking place at some point this evening, and for them, I'm terrified. I don't know what to do to help them get to safety. Alaric kisses me on the cheek, before taking his leave to get those he cares about out. I frantically search the room for my father, sister, and Peter. I find Peter over by the glass doors to the gardens, and his eyes meet mine from across the room. I nod to him and hope he understands to go wait for me in the garden and I release a sigh of relief when he nods in response and heads outside. I take a deep breath before heading toward the double doors leading to the garden. My father stops me before I can get there.

"What's wrong?" He studies my face as he pulls me off to the side, glancing around us.

"Lucas is bringing an army here tonight. We need to get out of here. Now. I need you to get Andria to go somewhere safe. I know the first place he comes for me if we make it out will be back home, so you can't go there. I can't lose either of you." I whisper, glancing around the room, just waiting for the vision to come true. I need to get to Peter, so I can warn him, and so I can try to get all of us safe passage to his home.

"I know of a place. Get yourself out of here before it is too late. I love you, Katerina." He quickly hugs me close, then takes off to find Andria.

I hope she listens and does exactly as our father tells her. I quickly head to the double doors that lead to the garden. I take one last look around the room. Alaric is dancing with his sister, and I hope they will still be there when I get back inside. He must have decided to warn her first, and was being discreet by doing so while dancing. I head outside, and Peter waits at the bench just outside the doors. His bruises have faded and the cut on his lip is mostly gone.

I stop in front of him, wringing my hands as I rock onto the balls of my feet. Biting the side of my cheek, I glance at him before I blurt everything out;"We need to leave. Lucas has an army and they are coming tonight. They will kill everyone until they get to Alaric and I." I pause, searching his eyes. The coldness that lingers chills me, but he can hate us all he wants as long as he agrees to get us out of here. "I need you to provide us safe passage to Lightspire. We will hide there until we gather our men and figure out what to do. Can you do that?" I chew my lip and search his face. Fear that he will refuse to help my husband, refuse to help me, makes me jittery.

He nods before responding. "I told you we were in this together, didn't I?" I can't help but heave a sigh of relief. He continues, "Of course. Tell whomever else you need to, and I'll go ready the horses. Try to get as many out as you can." He pauses, looking at me and gently brushes a stray piece of hair behind my ear. "I love you." He turns on his heel, and takes off toward the stables.

I quickly head back inside the glass bay doors and run right into Anna.

"Anna! There you are. I was just coming to look for you."

"Were you? To me it looked like you were enjoying the company of an old friend." She stares blankly at me, obviously upset by what she saw. It isn't what she thinks, not anymore, and hasn't been for some time now.

"Please. I need you to trust me." She starts to turn from me, but I grab her shoulders, forcing her to look at me. "Please!" She reluctantly nods and I slide my hands down to hold hers. "I know what I'm going to say is going to sound crazy, but I need you to trust me." I pause a moment, taking a deep breath before continuing, "I have visions and feelings about things that are going to happen in the future. I inherited the gift from my mother. But that is a conversation we can have later." She looks skeptical, but I plow forward.

"Believe me, I know this sounds crazy. Anyway, right before the crowning ceremony, I had a vision of Lucas coming through those doors," I gesture to the hall doors, "with the beginnings of an army. He took down every last person in here until he got to Alaric and me. He killed us, Anna." I squeeze her hands tightly. Tighter than intended. I release the tension in my hands and let her go. She shakes her hands a little. "We need to get out of here. Now. Before he gets here." The urgency in my voice must have scared her because all she does is nod her head. But she still doesn't seem convinced so I push further.

"Don't you think it's odd Lucas couldn't be bothered to show up to his own brother's coronation or party? Where is he? Look around. There aren't many guards either. Why aren't they at their post? Something is wrong here. It's going to happen, and it is going to happen soon." I study her, waiting for it to fully sink in. She searches the room, then fearfully meets my gaze and nods quickly. I gently push her toward the path in front of us. "Peter is going to help us get out of here. He is in the stables readying the horses. Go straight there. We will get whatever we need on the road. Go." She nods again, her eyes wide and her breathing fast as she steps back.

"Get my brother out of here. Be careful." She brushes past before running through the gardens toward the stables. I quickly turn from the path and back toward the open patio doors.

That just leaves Alaric. I glance around, and thankfully I notice that Ian is gone too. My father must have told him when he got Andria out of her. I frantically search the rest of the room and I find Alaric almost immediately, leaning against the wall talking to some of the nobles that live here at court. I recognize their faces, but can't recall their names. I know this fact will haunt me in the years to come. As I start to make my way over to him, the ballroom doors fly open, and soldiers storm into the room, with Lucas leading the attack. Alaric stares at his brother, shock and pain shadow his face.

Lucas pulls his sword from his belt. Time seems to freeze. I whip my head towards Alaric, my hair hitting my face, getting stuck to my lips that part to cry out to Alaric. I lift a hand to cover my mouth as the sounds of swords ringing and people screaming fills the air. I can't understand why he would do this. Violence for the sake of violence isn't going to help him win the throne. He has to be thinking to get rid of us and any that support us as a way to cut down any threat to his reign. The soldiers plow through our people, cutting them down one by one. I try to make my way through the chaos to Alaric, but he must've seen or heard me cry out, because before I can push through the throng of people headed toward the door, he is by my side.

"We need to get out of here." His voice is gruff and strained.

"Peter is meeting us in the stables with Anna to lead us to his territory. He will give us refuge until we can gather our forces and figure out what to do next." I watch him, hoping that he realizes what is at stake. He hesitates. I can tell he wants to fight, to protect his people, but he seems to realize that if he stays, he will not survive, and his kingdom will fall into Lucas's hands anyway.

"Let's go." He quickly turns, grabbing my hand and pulling me out of the door which is thankfully only a few feet away since I didn't make it far into the room before chaos ensued. Tears stream down my cheeks as we race from the horror inside. Terrified screams chase us the whole way.

Peter and Anna are waiting for us when we arrive at the stables.

"Oh, thank god." Anna rushes to her brother, and Peter wraps me in a quick hug before letting me go.

"I have a horse for each of us. Pick one and let's go. We don't have much time before he realizes we are gone." Peter waves us all towards the 4 waiting horses. We mount up quickly but once seated on his horse, Alaric pauses, looking torn. I can tell he wants to go back and save his people, but he knows he needs men to do so. I know this is going to haunt him as much as it will haunt me. We are abandoning our people to a massacre. He clears his face of all expression and nudges his horse forward, causing us all to do the same. As we nudge our horses into a gallop, we all hear the screams of the people at our backs. I shiver and feel my chest tighten. The tears still flow, silently grieving all we have lost already. I wish I could have gotten everyone out. There had to have been something else I could have done.

If only I had had more time.

CHAPTER 23

The man that is there in the end, he is the one. The one that you need to show you the way, the one that will pick up the pieces when you shatter and fall apart. He will be the one to heal you and make you feel alive. I promise you will love him, but it will sneak up on you, and you will push against it before you finally give in. I've tried to give you all of the resources, you just need to see what is right in front of you.

We ride hard for hours; leaving the royal city and several neighboring towns behind before we come to a small village. If my timing is right, this must be Redden. The stars are already in the sky, and we have had to slow our pace once dusk made it difficult to see the road in front of us. "We should stop here for the night," Peter says, pulling his horse to a stop in front of an old tavern as if familiar with the place.

Peter motions for us to remove our crowns, in an effort to make ourselves less recognizable, but I'm not sure it will work, especially dressed as we are. But we try to disguise ourselves regardless. He dismounts, and we all follow suit, leading the horses to the attached stables. We leave the horses to be cared for by the stable hands, throwing them a couple of silvers for each horse. I guess Peter managed to grab some money in the few minutes he had before we arrived. Peter leads the way into the tavern and approaches the man at the counter.

"Hello, sir, I was wondering if you had any rooms available for the night and any food to order? We would need two rooms." The old man looks us over, silently noting our fine clothes, but not commenting on them. I wonder if he recognizes Peter from the times he has likely traveled through here on his way back home.

"Aye. I do have a coupla' rooms. And I'll have my cooks roast a coupla' chickens for ye." His voice is gruff, and his eyes tell how tired this man truly is. I instantly feel for the man and speak up.

"Will this be sufficient?" I ask, handing him a small drawstring purse with 10 gold coins in it.

"Miss, I do not know who ye are, but this is too much for my simple rooms and decent food. The rooms are yours for less than half of that." He takes 3 of the coins from the purse and hands it back to me. "There ye go Miss. I'll take ye to your rooms." He leads the way up the stairs and stops about halfway down the hall. "This is one'a the rooms," he says indicating the one to the right, "along with the one across the hall. I'll have the servants bring up the chicken along with some mulled ale as soon as possible." He nods at us, before heading back downstairs with a slight limp.

Peter gazes at all of us before deciding that the boys should take one room, and the girls the other. "We will talk in the morning." We all nod, too tired to argue and are all well aware of the threat looming over our heads. Anna and I head into the room on the right, and Alaric and Peter head into the one on the left.

There are two small beds in the room, and I fall backwards into one before my feet can give out from under me. I stare at the ceiling, numb from the high emotion of the events of the day, waiting for Anna to break the silence. I know there are at least two things she will want to discuss. The wood planks of the ceiling remind me of the roof of the stables back home. I think of the times Andria and I would lay in the hay staring at a similar ceiling. I've almost dozed off thinking of simpler times when Anna speaks.

"Did you really see it happen?" Anna asks quietly.

I open my eyes, blinking back the exhaustion that has washed over me and stare at the ceiling. "Yes. Somehow, we managed to slip away before he saw us. The terror on all of their faces, and their screams…" I shiver and I hardly recognize my own voice. "I wish there was something I could have done, some way I could have saved them all. But I was too late."

"There is something you can do now. Stay alive and fight back. Save us."

I choke on a laugh and shake my head, rubbing my forehead and temples as I answer. "Easier said than done. I just hope that my father, Andria, and Ian got out before this all happened. I know they left before us, but still, I worry. I don't know what I would do if they didn't make it out."

"They got out, Kat. They were racing out of the stables when I got there. I saw them. They got out."

With that, I finally break. The thick wall I put in place around the emotions breaks and the tears come forth, and I sob. The stress of everything starts to leave my body. "But nothing is going to be okay. War is here, Anna, and I could have done something to stop it the moment the visions started. It's been months. I hoped it wouldn't come to this. Something like this was going to happen, and I thought if I married your brother and went through with everything the visions would change. But it didn't work." I pause, "I will fix this. I will fight back. I will be who my country needs me to be. That, I can promise."

I wipe my eyes, and sit up, pulling my hair free from the loose knot held at the nape of my neck. Anna avoids my gaze, and I can tell that she regrets not seeing the person her brother was. Before Anna can help me take off the majority of my dress so I can lay comfortably, there is a knock on the door. Our eyes meet, but I rise and head towards the door before she can say a word. I hesitate before opening the door, calling out, "Who's there?"

"Miss, I am one of the kitchen maids. I have your chicken and ale." My stomach rumbles as I quickly open the door and take the load from her. I didn't realize how hungry I was, and I can only assume Anna is just as hungry.

"Thank you so much. Here is a coin for your trouble." I hand her a bronze coin, and she grins.

"Thank you, Ma'am!" She gives a small curtsy then retreats back down the hall and down the stairs. I close the door with my hip since my hands are full. A bronze coin is a small price to pay, especially knowing the wreckage that is likely to follow in our wake. I place the food and drinks down on the small table on the far side of the room, and Anna and I each take one of the chairs placed around it. I grab a plate and start to dig in. We both eat in silence and it isn't long before my portion of the chicken and ale is gone. I leave the table and try to unlace my gown before giving up with a sigh. Anna sighs, but comes over to help before she goes to her own bed. I curl up facing the wall. When Anna makes herself comfortable, she finally speaks.

"How long has something been going on between you and Peter?"

I lie there in the broken silence listening to the crickets sing outside. I let the question hang in the air, hoping it can just be forgotten.

"Kat?"

I sigh and contemplate exactly what to say. I know I can't lie to her, and I shouldn't. "I want to be honest with you, and to do that you need to know everything." I turn my head to look at her. She stares at the ceiling above her. I wish I knew what she was thinking. "We grew up together and were arranged to be married when we were both young, although this was unbeknown to us until years later. He's my best friend and the one person in this world that made me feel normal; he believed me when I thought I was crazy. He understands me. I had been in love with him for years, and I know it has been the same for him. I broke off my engagement to him for your brother because of the visions I had been having and because I wasn't given much of a choice. Due to what I've seen, I knew that I needed to marry your brother if there was to be any sort of hope of saving our country. I felt that saving everything and everyone was more important than my own happiness. I was piecing together what was going to happen, and I thought I could help everyone have a fighting chance."

I finally roll over fully to meet Anna's gaze which has turned from the ceiling to me and watch her tears fall as I guiltily continue. "I am doing everything I can to leave my feelings for Peter behind and give this marriage a chance. I have strong feelings for Alaric that have grown significantly, and I know he is the man that I want. I'm not making an excuse, but Peter was so deeply ingrained in my life for so long that he, and what I thought my future was going to be, has been extremely hard to let go of. I love your brother. But I can promise you this," I pause, realizing that no matter what I say, I will still be the woman that cheated on her brother, the king. Somehow, I convince myself to continue despite the betrayal in her accusing eyes. "I promise you I will save our country. I will bring peace back to our people and to our nation. I will end this terror and get us back to where we are meant to be. That, I can promise you. Once we are home, I promise to give Alaric everything. I will provide an heir, and I will make him happy."

Anna angrily wipes her face, making sure there are no tears left. She has come to her own conclusion about everything, and will do and feel how she sees fit, and I just have to accept it. I've hurt her enough. I can tell by the set of her jaw that she is ready to speak.

"If you somehow don't save us, I will kill you myself."

I rise to my elbow. "I will save us, Anna. Or I will die trying. I understand your anger, but I've tried to do the right thing to save our country. I won't deny that I have made mistakes. I know I have, but I am trying to make it right."

The speed Anna possesses when she sits up is terrifying. Her eyes meet mine, and her tone is just as piercing as if she had physically stabbed me. "If cheating on my brother is trying to do the right thing, you seriously need to rethink what is the 'right' thing."

I also rise to a sitting position. I hold my hands up, palms facing her trying to slow things down. Surrendering myself to her wrath, because I know I deserve all of it. "Look. I am sorry. Your brother is aware of Peter and my history, and anything involving Peter is done and over with. It is all in the past. I know that means nothing to you, but I want you to know that I ended it weeks ago. Long before the wedding. I know I messed up. I know it is going to take time to trust me, and I know you don't believe me. I swear it is over. It will not happen again. You are all I have outside of your brother, and I can't lose either of you." At this point, we are staring at each other, breathing heavily. I tear up, but fiercely blink to keep them from falling. Crying now will be a slap to her face, and I feel as if I have no right to be upset since I did do this to myself. I got caught, and it blew up in my face. This was likely going to happen eventually, and I'm not sure what else I expected.

"I believe what you say regarding your visions and your promise to truly be with my brother," she pauses, and holds up a hand. "but only because you are the only thing that saved us today. I won't tell my brother what I heard in the garden; but that's only because I know it will break his heart, and it should be you who tells him. It is going to take me some time to forgive you for this, so I hope you don't think things are going to go back to how they were before." She rearranges her skirts around her before continuing, "now, I'm getting some sleep. God knows we are going to need it. Goodnight." She lies back down and rolls over, blowing out the candle as she goes, leaving us in darkness.

With the light out, the tears I spent the last few minutes fighting back, fall freely. Silently, thankfully. I have to end what is between Peter and I, I can't keep holding on to him after this is done. Peter needs to let me go, and we somehow have to go our separate ways. My hand rests on my lower stomach. How do I save Peter from Alaric's wrath if he finds out the truth? There is no happy ending here. No way out of the mess that we created by starting this affair in the first place. I bring my other hand to rest on my forehead. I blink away the tears, taking a few breaths before I turn to my side and curl into a ball. There is nothing more to do, and we need all the sleep we can get. I breathe deeply, closing my eyes and wait for sleep to take me.

The awkwardness lingers between Anna and I the following morning. We hardly speak, and when we do, it is only two or three words at most. We quickly put our dresses back on and are both ready by the time Peter knocks on the door to let us know it is time to go. We follow him to the stables with Alaric taking up the rear. Alaric watches the world around us, probably wondering if anyone recognizes their new king and queen, or if Lucas will strike here next. I know that is what runs through my own mind as I watch the townsfolk mill about, oblivious to us and what may be coming their way. We are in Redden, a village whose people don't travel to the castle or anywhere very often. The most they know of us is probably our names, although, I wonder if Alaric and his father had made it here before the attack— if so, I would think a few may recognize him. Looking back towards the horses, I notice that their once empty bags are now full— food, clothes, medical supplies— anything that we could possibly need on our journey north.

"Peter, did you get all this?" I ask.

"Actually no, when I came down earlier this morning, I found the innkeeper adding these bags to the few we already had. I asked him how much he wanted for everything, but he said he used some of the gold we gave him for the rooms. He had noticed we didn't have much with us and assumed we could use some supplies, so put these together," his voice trails off, and we all nod.

A part of me wonders if the innkeeper knew who we are. It is likely he knows Peter from previous transactions, and possibly knew Alaric's father. He does share a heavy resemblance to him. Either way, I'm grateful. Once all of this is over, I will have to come and thank him. We mount up and Peter guides us out of the stables and onto the road going north. We ride hard in an attempt to put as much space between us and the castle as possible. We continue to ride for what seems like hours, until the sun is high in the sky. Peter slows his horse to a stop near a small clearing. We all do the same. He dismounts first and encourages us to follow suit. We lead the horses over to a small patch of trees on the outer rim of the clearing and tie the reins to the trees to keep them from running.

"I don't know about you, but I'm starving."

I stretch with a grin as Peter pulls the food from the pack on his horse. Everyone scatters in the grass, laying down or sprawled out in various positions and stretches to help release the tension and ache from riding. Peter hands the food to Alaric, then turns to sit down. We exchange glances, but no one says a word. We all have reasons for our silence, but right now, they don't matter all that much. I know Alaric is concerned for his country and his people and I'm pretty sure he and Anna are mourning the loss of the brother and man he thought he knew. I know this isn't easy and is extremely hard. He takes things personally, and I know this is hitting him hard especially after the loss of his father. Even having the past couple of weeks to come to terms with Lucas's betrayal, but seeing it first hand…I know it is eating at him. Alaric passes out food to everyone else, and comes to me last. He lowers himself onto the grass beside me. He hands me an apple and some dried jerky. I offer him a smile, and his fingers linger on mine.

"You okay?" I murmur, meeting his gaze. I tear off a piece of the jerky.

"Not really. When he stormed in— that is what you saw before we went into the ceremony, isn't it?"

I look past Alaric and into the forest as I nod. I pause, looking around the loose circle, noticing everyone's attention is on us. My eyes linger on Anna since she is the only one who isn't up to speed on everything.

"The visions started three months before you came to Stonebreach. They've always revolved around events, and would come in flashes, sometimes nothing more than a feeling, but nothing like what I saw before the ceremony and it was too late to do anything. I have tried everything that I could think of to prevent all of this from happening, but clearly," I hug my knees to my chest and rest my chin on my knees as I stare at nothing. "I failed. I didn't see the attack until it was too late to make the biggest difference. I knew right before the crowning ceremony that he was going to attack. I should have said something then, got everyone out or stopped the ceremony, but I knew you needed the crown and title or we would be the uprising against Lucas. I needed you, Alaric, to be the rightful king— in name and decree."

I take a moment to recapture my thoughts and watch the hawks circle overhead. Alaric doesn't speak, and keeps his head bowed, staring at his hands. Anna listens intensely, her fingers pulling at the grass beside her. Peter is quiet and rests on his back watching the clouds and hawks above. "I wanted to warn you, all of you. I didn't know how to go about it the right way. But I promise, I will save us. I will do what I couldn't before, I will figure out the visions and get our country back. I will save the peace and take down Lucas, or I will die trying." *It is the least I can do after everything.*

Anna quickly wipes away a tear before it can fall, and sets her jaw. Peter pushes up to rest on his palms, waiting for Alaric's response. Alaric remains frozen. The minutes seem to take years, and I anxiously pick at my food, my stomach doing nervous flips. Peter shakes his head and rises to his feet, stalking to the horses. He may have taken all of this in stride, but it wasn't his brother that started cutting through everyone like it was nothing. He doesn't have to deal with the consequences of abandoning his people to a monster. Peter has no right to be frustrated with how Alaric copes with his world deteriorating around him. I sigh and shake my head as I turn back to find Anna's eyes on me. She wipes her eyes almost angrily, as she nods her head and rises to help Peter with the horses. I watch them, ensuring Alaric and I are alone before I break the silence.

"I will do what it takes to fix this Alaric. I swear to you."

"I know." His voice is broken, as lifeless as his body. He remains bent over his hands, staring blankly. I rest a hand on his shoulder, kiss his cheek, and rise. With one last glance at my husband, I walk to the horses and rest my forehead against my mare's and feed her my untouched apple.

We are all just fractured pieces that somehow fit together to create the Aurellia we all know and love. We just need to cut down the one who broke it.

CHAPTER 24

Blue eyes or green, unsure until they open—
a babe born, following in the mother's steps
and similarities to him are easily explained away.

Growing up protected, cherished by everyone.
Sneaking back to see her, a mere glimpse is all that's asked.
She is clever, connecting pieces that were well hidden.

Flashes pointing to the past
a journey to save the person she didn't know she missed.
Castles crumbling as old foes return.

The terrain from Aurellia City to Lightspire is heavily wooded and the altitude climbs drastically, which makes the journey take more time than the two weeks we estimated. Peter says we are about three days' ride from Lightspire, and thankfully, there hasn't been any sign of Lucas. We have avoided the main road as well as the villages on our journey, which is likely why we haven't run into any trouble.

The sky brightens with the setting sun in shades of pink, purple, and a greyish blue, when Peter leads us just off of the path into a small clearing in the woods. The ground looks soft enough with plenty of grass and soft needles from the hemlock trees surrounding the clearing to be able to sleep. The deep green of the needles stand stark against the reddish amber of the bark, and in the dimming light, gives an ominous vibe to the area. We don't have much to sleep with, but at least we have our cloaks to keep us warm.

My feet throb on the landing as I try to slowly slide off of my horse. Wincing, I limp a couple of paces away and twist, cracking my back then lift my hands toward the sky. I feel the gentle burn in the muscles of my upper back and shoulders, and groan with the release of tension from spending the day in the saddle. I fold over my legs, my fingertips gently brushing the grass at my feet. I rise slowly, feeling the movement all the way through my spine. It feels incredible to be on my own two feet again. There aren't enough words to express how exhausted I have become. It is a struggle to stay upright on the horse most days, and the relentless fatigue and growing nausea are getting harder to hide. I swing my arms at a ninety degree angle, loosening my shoulders. I scrunch my nose, and limp back to my horse. Every joint hurts. Opening the small pack on the side of the saddle, I rummage around until I find the small brush that I use on her hide everytime we stop. I gently run the brush through her coat, and her head bobs in appreciation. Her soft knicker brings a smile to my face and after I remove the saddle, I brush her again before leading her to a tree at the edge of the clearing. I loosely tie her lead to one of the branches, and pat her nose. She nips at my fingers, and I wish I had a sugar cube to give her. She has been a solid companion and has been extremely patient with me these past two weeks.

Stepping back, I gaze around my surroundings. The grass is the prettiest green color, bright and vibrant, almost glowing in the strange light cast through the branches overhead. The light is almost a golden color, but will slowly darken as the sun sets and night rises. The trees circle the clearing, providing a nice barrier to the outside world. It is almost as if we are in some sort of bubble of safety and serenity. I sigh and head towards the center of the clearing where the rest of our small group is standing. While the burn in my bones remains, I have loosened up enough to no longer be limping. At least I've got that going for me.

"We should start a fire, it should keep us warm and we can warm up some of the chicken we picked up a few days ago," Peter suggests, glancing in my direction as I stop on the other side of Alaric. Distance is necessary between us, for my own sanity, and for everyone else's.

"But the smoke from a fire will give our position away. What if Lucas is out there somewhere?" Alaric argues. While his reasons are sound, I think all of us would like a warm dinner. With us being on the road for as long as we have been, warm food has been sparse, and civilization even more so. It has been berries, nuts, bread, and dried meat that the innkeeper provided, until it was gone. The past couple of days we have had little more than some fruit and bread.

"I'm not completely convinced that Lucas has started looking for us yet," I glance around the small circle with a shrug of my right shoulder. Everyone is as ragged and run down as I am, and we could all use the small comfort a fire can provide. "He has gained control over the castle and guards. We don't know who else has been involved, but I don't think he knows exactly where we have gone. I haven't seen anything new either." I pause, looking at the darkening sky before meeting Peter's green eyes briefly on their way to Alaric's. "I agree with Peter. We should build a fire, but keep it small and don't use anything that will put out a lot of smoke just in case." I shrug my shoulders again, feigning nonchalance.

Anna nods, her arms crossed over her chest before she shivers and fights a yawn as she rubs her upper arms. Her feet thud softly against the grass as she stomps her feet. "I agree. I'm starved, and there hasn't been any sign of Lucas or a pursuit of any kind."

Alaric throws his hands in the air, turning and strides to his horse, muttering under his breath. I watch the muscles in his back ripple as he takes the brush from his saddle bag and starts rubbing down and brushing his mare before he reaches up to take the saddle off. His shirt lifts enough to show a strip of bare skin just above his hemline, and I quickly glance away feeling heat creeping up my neck and into my face. I close my eyes, breathing deep enough to feel it in my stomach. We haven't had a moment to talk about everything; at least not for longer than a few murmured questions when we've lain down under the stars. I understand his hesitance, I would be in the same boat if I weren't letting the desire for comfort rule my thinking. We all are. He is right to be concerned, to be fearful of the shadows that surround us. We have no idea what is lurking beyond our clearing and I can't stop the shiver that rolls down my spine.

"Why don't you two start gathering firewood, and I'll get out the supplies we need. Don't wander too far into the woods though."

Anna crosses the clearing and enters the treeline on the opposite side of where I stand. Things are still uncomfortable— we glide around each other and talk in stilted sentences that demonstrate to anyone who pays attention just how broken things still are between us. I turn from her and to the treeline behind me. I crouch, rooting through the leaves, bushes, and underbrush looking for anything viable to feed the fire that won't put out too much smoke. Soon, I have an armload of wood that I think will suffice, and head back into the clearing.

Peter has set up a small ring of stones in the center and has the chicken we picked up from a small farm we passed a couple of days ago ready to go, and beside it lies a rabbit that still needs skinned. I watch as Peter takes a small knife from his saddle bag at the tree by the horses. He turns on his heel and heads back to the circle of stones he has set up. I didn't think we were gathering wood long enough for him to find and kill a rabbit, but he must be familiar with the area in order to know where a burrow might be. His long legs cross the clearing faster than my own slow pace from the treeline. Peter crouches beside the circle of stones and takes the rabbit by the ears, bringing it to the ground in front of him.

Movement at the edge of the clearing where Anna had disappeared captures my attention and she carefully picks her way out of the trees and makes it to the fire ring the same time I do. She drops her arms, effectively throwing the firewood down beside the ring. I do the same and back up a few paces. Peter murmurs his thanks and makes quick work of skinning the rabbit before inspecting the pile of sticks and wood for something that will work as a cooking spear.

Anna and I lower ourselves to the ground. I am too sore and tired to offer to help and I sigh as I sprawl out on my back, staring at the first stars breaking through the small opening in the branches. My fingers play with the soft grass at my sides— it slips easily through my fingers. The temperature difference of the grass in comparison to the air around it provides a nice chill on my neck that works to cool me down significantly. It may be early August, but it is still pretty temperate.

I close my eyes for a moment, enjoying the buttery soft grass and the fresh scent of pine before I open my eyes and jump. Alaric stands directly above me, blocking my view of the stars through the branches. His eyes crinkle as he smiles. He ducks his head and I hear the soft sound of him sitting on the grass beside me. I study him without turning my head. He watches Peter start the fire with a smirk tugging at his mouth. He seems in better spirits than he has been, but the haunted look still lingers in every line of his face masked behind the smile and playful demeanor that he currently displays.

Alaric looks down at me, a smile tugging at his lips. "You see what you wanted to see?" His voice is quiet as he glances away quickly. His fingers are in the grass near mine, and I take them, wrapping my own around them. He twists his hand so he holds mine completely. He rubs his thumb over mine as he continues, "we need to come up with a game plan. Sooner rather than later. You are just as big a part in this as I am, so I want your input. We are a partnership, remember?" He looks at me sideways with a grin that reminds me of the conversation we had when I first asked to attend a council meeting.

I grin in response, and see some of the tension leave Alaric's shoulders. I must not have been as good at hiding my own grief and turmoil as I thought. A sigh escapes as I force myself to sit beside him. I really hope no one asks me to move for the rest of the night, it is highly probable that I will sleep right here. I shift slightly, rolling my head on my shoulders and wince when a muscle pulls weirdly. I rub the back of my neck and down onto my right shoulder. There is a twinge of pain and a dull ache that echoes with any movement. I can't wait until I can sleep in a bed again.

I glance around the clearing, my eyes burning slightly from the smoke of the fire now burning, and hear the sizzle of grease and blood hitting the wood beneath the meat cooking on sticks above. Peter sits near the fire, one arm wrapped around a knee and the other resting on his lap. His eyes reflect the flames licking the logs, but he must sense my eyes on him because his gaze flicks to mine. His face softens and the corners of his mouth tug up slightly before he looks back at the fire.

My stomach churns, and I fight back the rising nausea. I wondered when it would hit— it has been regularly striking at about this time every day. It is getting harder to hide and push aside. I have to be at least two months along. I'm going to start showing soon and it won't be long until they notice, especially if the nausea continues and comes in full force. Hidden away is still an ember of the fire that burns for Peter. How can I still feel the way I do after everything that has happened between us and between Alaric and me? Ignoring the pull of him is almost impossible, but I've been managing. He is my best friend.

Has been long before anything further happened. I miss my best friend but how can I even entertain the idea anymore when Alaric needs me to be that for him, and I desperately need him to be as well?

Alaric clears his throat, and I jump before turning my head to look at him. "What is our next step? Once we reach Lightspire that is."

"I will gather any able-bodied man within my territory and have them meet in the forest near my home. There, we will get them to fight for us." Peter's voice cracks and he clears his throat before continuing, "some of my people aren't completely convinced you are the better ruler and brother, unfortunately." He grimaces as he glances away from Alaric and back to the fire. "Once we determine our numbers are significant enough to go against Lucas, that is what we will do." Peter rotates the sticks over the fire, then faces Alaric once more. His face is devoid of his own thoughts. Has his own opinion changed since my wedding? My eyes linger on him as Alaric responds.

"I know you have the biggest territory in the country; however, I believe we are going to need more support from the other territories, if possible. Once word gets out of my brother's betrayal, I feel we are going to have more men running to our side than not." Alaric continues speaking, but Peter shrugs and he lifts a brow slightly before settling his features into smooth nonchalance again. He doesn't agree. I wonder if he knows more than he has been saying about Lucas's reach within the people. I slowly turn to face Alaric. "However, I have no idea how many men my brother has gathered— I don't know how large his reach is. He was able to murder our father, so I can only imagine what else he is capable of. We must be careful." Alaric continues to speak, but I lose focus on the words.

Alaric gestures with his hands while speaking and I lose myself in the flurry of movement. Instead of seeing his hands, I see Alaric and myself surrounded by men in solid black uniforms. Their uniforms are form-fitted and their leather armor straps around their torsos in an intricate pattern that makes them look deadly and intimidating. I know they aren't on our side, none that we would call on have armor made in this fashion, and once the banner adorned with a falling star is shown, it becomes clear.

Dread and terror grip me as I look around the scene and notice that they have us held at sword point. Lucas strides into view and chills run down my spine with each lilting note of the laugh spewing out of his mouth. His laugh is the only thing I hear. I hear nothing from the soldiers surrounding us, or anything from Alaric. The laugh lingers with me as the clearing comes flooding back. All of the noise here is louder, but still doesn't drown out the echo of his laugh. I can't gauge how much time has passed and I don't think I've been gone all that long, but with a quick glance around me, I find everyone's eyes on me.

"Katerina, are you okay? What did you see?" Alaric grabs ahold of my shoulder as I sway, helping me stay upright as the exhaustion from the weeks of travel, the pregnancy, and the stress of the situation hit me. The visions take every ounce of strength out of me as it is, but in combination with everything else, I'm a shell of nothing but exhaustion.

I nod, and slowly begin to speak. My voice is strained, as if speaking is an incredibly difficult task. "We were surrounded by soldiers. I'm not sure when, but they were Lucas's men. They wore the symbol of the falling star," I pause, taking a few deep breaths. All of the pieces are coming together, but there are still pieces that are missing. Peter and Alaric share a look before Alaric meets my eyes. His face is drawn, his mouth tight with worry. I open my mouth to continue, glancing away briefly towards Peter before my gaze finds Alaric's again. My voice trembles, "It was just the two of us, I'm not sure where you were," I raise a hand towards Peter and Anna then let it fall back into my lap, "but the last thing I saw was Lucas. And he was laughing."

CHAPTER 25

The pounding in my head wakes me with a groan. I rub the heel of my palm into my eyes, wanting to avoid the sunlight as long as possible, but know I have no choice. I flinch, blinking against the light as I push myself onto my elbows and see that someone has left me a little bit of rabbit and bread with some water to wash it down. I push myself up into a sitting position and hungrily dig into the food but the food goes sour in my mouth, and it takes a lot out of me to keep what little I ate down.

The water does little to settle my stomach. I need to be careful, I need to keep everything down to preserve my strength. We don't know when Lucas will show up. I wish I could tell someone, but I don't know how anyone will react and there is already so much at stake. I watch everyone around me. Alaric is over by the horses putting the saddles back on our mounts and checking our bags to make sure everything is ready to go. Anna leans against a tree beside him talking in hushed tones. I don't see Peter, and his voice behind me makes me jump.

"How are you feeling?" He sits down beside me, his legs outstretched in front of him, as he leans back on his hands.

I shrug. I could really live without the headache that tends to chase the visions, but I don't mention it. "I'm sorry if I kept us here longer than intended. The visions usually don't affect me this hard." I lift my hand, the small piece of bread bobbing with the movement. "Thank you for leaving me the food though." I tear small pieces off of the bread and pop them in my mouth. The headache and nausea is thankfully starting to subside with the food and water entering my system.

He bobs his head with a grin. "I figured you would be hungry when you woke. It was nice having a longer break from riding. We knew you needed the rest, so don't worry about the late start. We just want you to be okay." He bumps his shoulder with mine, grinning. "I can't wait for you to see Lightspire. I just wish it were under better circumstances." We had always talked about when I would come to Lightspire. It would have been after the wedding, and he would have shown me all of his childhood haunts before we would have found a spot of our own. We would have eventually had to move to Aurellia City since he serves on the council, but things would have been different. My hand rests on my stomach, and a part of me still wishes that things could have happened the way we had planned. I miss the easy pace and simplicity the two of us had. Now things are complicated and I am married to another, and things can never go back to how they were before— friendship included. Too much has happened between us to go back.

He sighs and rises to his feet, extending a hand to me. I smile and take the offer. He pulls me to my feet, catching me when I stumble forward. His hands linger on my waist, and my gaze meets his. I can feel the tension and longing between us like an echo, but I pull away before either of us can act on it. I run my fingers through my hair, shaking my head trying to clear it as I head over to my horse. The saddle is already on her, so I run my fingers through her dark mane gently untangling some of the snarls. I press my forehead against hers, and she nuzzles into me, almost as if she is aware of the turmoil of emotions that have taken up residence in my core.

"Are you okay?" Anna asks when she approaches. I keep my head pressed against the horse's and my fingers continue to run through her mane.

I nod. "We should get going though. If my vision was any indication, Lucas is on his way."

"Are you sure you're okay? I couldn't imagine seeing the things you do." She rests her hand on my shoulder. This is the first real moment we have shared since she saw me with Peter and heard his words. I turn to look at her, my eyes burning with unshed tears.

I dip my head again, but confess; "No, I'm not okay, but I will be. Thank you for your concern though." I smile and begin to turn away to mount my horse.

"Wait," she sighs, and I pause, looking back at her. She ruffles her hair as she continues. "I'm sorry, and I forgive you. I understand that this isn't exactly what you wanted or asked for at first. I understand now, why you found solace in him." She watches Peter across the clearing. He is packing up the rest of our things into his saddle bags. Alaric is helping him, and they are laughing together. My heart warms watching the two of them together. Especially knowing how things went down following the wedding. I suppress a shiver that trails down my spine at the memory of Alaric's fist connecting with Peter's face. I look away, and find Anna watching me. I shift uncomfortably as she clears her throat and continues. "I just want you to know that I understand, and I don't blame you."

I nod in response, and she drifts off to her own horse. I watch her go before glancing back towards Peter and Alaric. They are an odd pair, not one you would expect to be friends, but it seems like they are trying. Whether it is for my sake, or because of the circumstances that threw us here, it doesn't seem to matter. Alaric leans against a tree, one foot on the ground with the other behind him. His arms are crossed against his chest, and his carefree demeanor is captivating, considering everything he has been through this past month. His dark hair flutters on his forehead in the slight breeze.

He must feel my gaze because his eyes find mine. He offers a smile and a small wave before turning his attention back to Peter. I raise my hand, but slowly lower it when I realize he is no longer looking. Peter is just as carefree as Alaric, perhaps more so. He must have finished putting our belongings away because he is sprawled in the grass, leaning on one hand with his legs outstretched in front of him. His sandy hair sticks up in the back, still mussed from lying down. His laugh gets carried to me on the breeze, and I want to lose myself in the musicality of it. Instead, I sigh and take the reins in my hand, leading my horse over to theirs.

"Hey Kat. Are you ready to go?" Peter looks up at me, grinning. I nod and smile down at him. I wonder how he can be so nonchalant.

"You two look relaxed."

Peter manages to look sheepish but grins all the same. "We probably should be going. It is still another three days ride to Lightspire, and that's if we don't come across any problems." Peter turns toward Alaric. "Give me a hand up?" Alaric reaches out a hand and pulls Peter to his feet. "Thanks." Alaric nods in our direction before heading off to mount his horse. I start to turn towards my horse as well, but Peter stops me. "Everything okay? Things have been strained with you and Anna. You could cut the tension with a blade."

I look around, making sure no one is near enough to hear. "Everything is fine. But Peter," I pause, licking my lips. He steps a little closer and I continue. "I'm pregnant." I should have told him when I realized rather than now, but after the incident with Alaric, Peter wouldn't look at me let alone listen if I tried to talk to him. I can't keep it to myself anymore.

He stills, his eyes wide as they search mine. "Are you sure?"

I nod, biting my lower lip. Tears well in my eyes, making everything blurry, but a smile grows on my face. "Once he has his throne back and Lucas is taken care of…I love you, and this baby…" I shake my head, and my voice simply stops. I don't even know what I am offering him. How can I forget everything that has happened that has led us here? How can I forget the way my heart races in nervous anticipation from Alaric's presence or how I rarely feel safe unless he is there beside me? Peter is not the man that I need by my side, and hasn't been for some time. It is stupid, and I'm stupid for even telling Peter about the baby. A moment of weakness, that's all this is. How am I supposed to leave the king, and not live in exile or in fear for my life, Peter's life, or my baby's life? I won't risk them. I can't.

His face lights up. He reaches his hands out to either hug me or touch my stomach, but he lowers them and looks across the clearing. The others are by their horses having their own conversation, and aren't paying any attention to us. He quickly steps forward, takes my head in his hands, his thumbs rubbing my cheek and along my jaw, and leaves a soft kiss on my cheek, so close to my mouth I feel the zing of electricity I always do from his touch.

"I will do my best to get us out of this alive. I love you."

He releases me, kissing me one more time on the forehead before backing away and heading to his horse. I watch him leave. Get us out alive, and then what? I can't shake the feeling that I just made the biggest mistake of my life by telling him about the baby. I exhale slowly before I climb on my horse. I look up to the sky and see a bright flash of light arc its way through the break in the limbs overhead, in what appears to be a shooting star. That is until I notice it starting to fall through the trees.

"Run! We need to go. Now!" I scream as I mount my horse. The flaming arrows fall through the trees, slowly starting to fill the clearing. I don't see anyone yet, but that doesn't matter. I duck low on my horse and start to ride toward the trees. My breath comes out in spurts, and my chest aches with the clench of pure terror that drives me forward.

Alaric whips his head toward me, ushering Anna into the woods. "Peter, take my sister and get out of here. I will get Katerina. We will meet up with you when we can. Go!"

Peter nods briefly, his eyes meeting mine for a brief moment before he tears into the woods after Anna. Alaric waits for me at the edge of the clearing, but before I can get my horse to move more than halfway across, she balks at the flames of an arrow whizzing past inches from her nose which causes her to rear up on her hind legs effectively dumping me on the ground before she takes off in the opposite direction. The ground meets my back forcing the air from my already aching lungs. I lay there stunned, gasping for air. My eyes widen as I choke on nothing until finally the sharp inhale jolts my chest. I cough and sputter as I sit and turn onto all fours. I barely notice Alaric's horse come up beside me through the thickening smoke as the clearing catches fire from the arrows.

"Katerina! Give me your hand!" He reaches down to me, and I grab hold. He forcefully lifts me from the ground and across the horse in front of him. I manage to swing a leg around and sit straight up before Alaric steers the horse into the woods and away from the fire. We tear through the woods, trying to find a way to the road so we can figure out which direction we need to go. I can barely see the road in the distance through a break in the trees, but before we can break through to the other side, armed men in solid black uniforms with intricately patterned black leather armor close in on us from all sides, closing off our only getaway.

"No, no, no, no, NO!" Alaric screams as the horse balks and he notices that we are completely surrounded. I grip tighter, my fingers locking with the mane tangled in them and realize with sinking dread that this is it. This is almost exactly what I saw last night, except we are on horseback rather than facing them head on.

The horse begins to balk, rising slightly to her hind legs, but Alaric manages to keep her on all fours and us seated instead of allowing her to dump us to the ground. One of the bigger men stride forward and tear the reins from Alaric's grasp with a snarl. The soldier stands with the reins in hand, and it appears the snarl is permanently hewn onto his face. His dark hair is cropped short, almost nonexistent on his tanned skin. My mind should be racing, but instead it focuses on the little things— the shooting star symbol on the cloaks of the men, the way their swords glint in the sun, and the sinister laugh that slices the air. Even knowing the laugh would shatter what remained of the peace in the air, it still catches me off guard and I fight against the shiver that rakes down my spine.

I allow my eyes to trail around the circle of men, searching for him. Directly in front of us, the men part and he strides forward. Lucas appraises us on the horse, taking in our ragged appearance, as well as the angry defiance on our faces. He lifts his hand as if to dismiss us and his voice cuts through the trees.

"Take them."

He turns on his heel, not even watching his men, and walks out of the woods. Before I fully realize what is happening, I feel rough hands on my waist, hair, and legs forcefully pulling me from the horse. I flail my arms and legs, trying to break free, but their grip tightens. I scream and pull harder. Nothing works. I look around for Alaric, and I see him knocked unconscious and being tied to a nearby tree. I yell out to him, to anyone really, but the sound cuts short when an armored fist crashes into the side of my head and I taste blood.

CHAPTER 26

As I sit here, pen in hand, I am at a loss of words. First, you are everything I ever needed, and everything I didn't know I wanted. I didn't think I wanted kids. I didn't want to pass along the trait to any female child, but I also knew that I didn't have much of a choice. Unfortunately that is how it is for most women. But thankfully, you and your sister are the best things I ever did. I am so sorry that I couldn't be there for you in the way that you needed me to be. I put everything in motion— I laid out all of the pieces, I just hope it turns out the way it is supposed to.

The metallic tang of dried blood coats my lips and there is a pounding behind my eyes as I open them. My body is stiffer than it has been and the burning in my shoulder has gotten worse. I move to stretch and quickly realize that a rope around my middle ties me to the tree. I wiggle against the rope, but it is no use. Alaric sits with his legs out in front of him and his head tilted back against the tree. His eyes stare blankly at the sky, which is covered from view by leaves and limbs from the different types of trees around us, although the bulk of them are coniferous. I know that he has given up, and somehow I need to convince him we still need to fight back. We still have a chance.

Alaric is just as stuck as I am, but at least they kept us together rather than splitting us up. I feel a slight pressure in my left hand, and I look down and see Alaric's hand in mine. He keeps his head in the same position, but I can feel his eyes on me. I meet his gaze, and I can tell by the look in his eye that he is in pain and is defeated. I will not let this be the end for us. I know Peter isn't going to leave us here, he is a better man than that. He will do whatever it takes to make sure that I am safe, that our baby is safe. I know he will get himself killed trying to save us, but I know we also can't rely on these possibilities. We need to do something for ourselves. We need to come up with a plan.

I look around me trying to figure out where we are, and if they moved us at all. The break in the trees displays the road and I realize that we are exactly where we were when we were captured. The clearing we stayed in is only a few hundred feet behind us, and it is likely that is where Lucas set up camp. Alaric's dark horse is tied to a tree near the road with the soldiers' horses. There are more than a dozen horses scattered along the tree line, and twice as many men wandering through the trees calling out to one another. They are paying no attention to us, which is surprising seeing as there are so many of them.

They wander the trees, clapping each other on the back as they pass, grinning ear to ear and poking fun at each other. Some have accents I can't quite place, and I assume they come from parts of Modiva. I don't see Lucas anywhere, but I know that he must be here somewhere. I wish I could force the visions, my mother wrote that it could be possible. I just need to breathe and focus. But what use is it if she couldn't even make it work? I rest my head on the tree, staring up at the leaves and towering pines overhead. If only I could see something that could help us, but nothing is forthcoming. What good are the visions if I can't even control when they happen, or change anything before it comes to pass? I groan inwardly. I stare up through the leaves to the sky beyond. Alaric squeezes my hand, silently asking if I am okay. I squeeze back in response.

I close my eyes, ignoring the pain in my head, and try to come up with a plan. I try to relax, breathe deeply, and focus *so damn hard*, but I get nothing but the blankness of my eyelids. *Dammit.* I hit the back of my head against the tree a couple of times, before settling. I inhale through my nose, exhale through my mouth, trying to calm down. I need to remain calm and collected, if not for myself, my own sanity and Alaric, then for my baby. I want nothing more than to let my rage burn this place to the ground, but I am stuck. Stuck against this tree, stuck in the mental roadblock that apparently keeps me from being able to control the visions, stuck in the trauma my mother caused when she died, and stuck in the conflicting emotions that circulate the two men in my life. I am stuck, and I don't know how to break free.

I open my eyes and turn to look at my husband. My heart sinks. The man beside me, surprises me, betters me, and somehow completes me in a way I didn't know I needed. Yes, he kept the book from my mother secret, and waited for me to confide in him, but he has picked up the pieces that were left ragged and bruised, and brushed them off before putting them back together. He has made me whole, all while I wasn't paying attention. I study him, taking in every inch of him as he stares off into the distance, seemingly not paying any attention to what is going on around us.

His clothes are covered in dirt, and he has a deep looking cut on his cheek. There is also a gash where he was hit over the head and his dark hair is stiff with the blood that has long since dried. I wish there were some way to maneuver around the rope that binds us, his wounds need attention, and I'm sure I have some of my own as well that could use tending. I know I have some sort of head wound which is the source of the throbbing in my head, and I hope that wound is the extent of what I have gained. I can only imagine that Alaric will likely succumb to more wounds before we are finished here. But in order to do anything, we need to come up with a way out of this. Since the soldiers are otherwise occupied with each other, I lean as close as I can toward Alaric, turning my face to rest my cheek on the rough bark of the tree.

"Alaric," I whisper. When he looks at me, his eyes are void of anything. No emotion, no fear, nothing found in the icy blue. It is chilling. "We need a plan."

He nods briefly. "Well, let me know when you think of something. I've got nothing." He turns away again to watch a few of the soldiers playing a knife game. I ignore the soldiers and stare at my husband. He has completely given up. This isn't a side of him I have ever seen— the helplessness, the vast emptiness that is starting to consume him. If I don't find a way to break him out of it, I think I might just lose him.

"Alaric, don't give up on us. We can still beat him, we can still get through this." He refuses to look at me, and stares blankly at the leaves. That is all he has really done the entire time I have been conscious, and I need him to get angry, I need him to fight back. I need the arrogance that I know he has, and I need the Alaric I know him to be. I need him to just *look* at me.

His voice is just as desolate as his eyes, "I don't see how, Katerina. Look around us. We are done. Finished. There is no coming back from this. You saw what happened with my father, it is just a matter of time."

"Look at me." He ignores me, but I snap his name in a tone I rarely use. "Alaric." He sighs and turns to look at me. He raises his eyebrows, waiting for me to continue. "We aren't finished yet. No one is paying any attention to us. I'm sure we can slip our bonds. We have to at least try. If you think we are going to die anyway, then what's to lose?"

"You. You are what there is to lose." He finally lets a little portion of the gate holding everything he is feeling open to me, and I watch as he sags under the weight of what he allows to seep back into him. He is broken, and it is going to take some time to bring him back. His spirit has been crushed from the minute the blades started to cut down his people and I can't deny that I feel the weight of their deaths on my chest, suffocating me every minute since we left. I can't help but wonder what councilmen have survived, and the sort of wreckage we will go home to when this is over. Alaric blinks rapidly a few times, clearing his eyes of the crushing sadness and continues. "I just got you, and I am not ready to let you go."

"We will survive this. I know we will. Just trust me okay?" He searches my eyes, and seems to find what he is looking for because he nods, his hair falling into his bleak eyes. I long to reach out and brush the tendrils to the side. He still isn't ready to fight, and as difficult as I know it will be to stand up when we have been taken so low, there is one final thing I know will work to get the rise out of him that is necessary for survival— the baby. Telling him I am pregnant is a dangerous game, especially knowing who the father truly is, but I know I won't leave Alaric once this is all over, regardless of what feelings may remain suppressed beneath the surface for Peter. And this baby? The baby will be his in every way except biological, which is all that really matters.

"I see your point, but I still don't think anything is going to come from it," he pauses, looking around, his eyes are still empty, and his shoulders are slumped against the rope that binds us. My eyes start to burn, as does my throat from the tears that gather there. I will help him through this, there is no other option.

I lower my voice even further, and I can barely hear my own voice over the games and shouts happening around us. His eyes find me and he freezes as the words fall from my lips; "I'm pregnant."

His eyes widen and his mouth falls open. His hand squeezes mine, and I squeeze it back just as hard. His eyes dart downwards, glancing at my stomach, before finding mine again. He leans closer, resting his forehead on mine. "Truly?" his voice breaks, and is so soft I barely hear it. I simply nod against his forehead. He rubs his nose against mine, and his lips find mine. He kisses me softly, and I know we both wish we could live in this moment, but we need to get out of here. He pulls back, and I watch as determination sets into his face and he straightens his spine and cranes his neck to look around us. The Alaric I have come to know and care for is back. He continues to watch around us as he states, "I don't think he would notice your disappearance; it is me he truly cares about. I'll get you out. Perhaps you can get help and get back here in time." His eyes find mine, and I can see how desperate he is to get me free. He will fight until he dies if it comes down to it. I know he is a force to be reckoned with— I have seen him on the practice field. He is quick, and lethal with a blade.

"When do we start?"

"Now."

He watches the soldiers again, and one of them cries out as he stabs a knife through his hand, effectively losing the game. He is on his feet and jumping around like a fool in mere seconds after the knife embeds in his hand, clutching it to his chest as he turns a strange tinge of green. He looks like he might be sick. His cohorts are doubled over in laughter, paying no attention to anything else, and doing nothing to help stop the blood or pain of their comrade. Alaric's hand leaves mine and searches the base of the tree within his reach for some sort of rock to cut us free. I do the same. While he comes up empty, my fingers find a rock to my right. It is small enough to fit in the palm of my hand, but has an edge that should be ragged enough to cut through the rope. I grasp it in my right hand, and slowly pull it in front of me to begin scraping at the rope there. I push hard enough to begin to fray the rope, but not hard enough to scratch myself.

Alaric notices my movements and smiles briefly before watching the area around us. His hand takes mine again, and I know he will squeeze when he sees someone approaching. I work quickly, but efficiently— the rope is fraying, and starting to separate. I only get through half of the rope before two men approach the group of soldiers from the road. The soldiers lean in towards each other, putting their heads together before glancing towards us. I drop the rock, my hand falling to my lap as I glance at Alaric. His eyes dart between me and the men. They don't come closer right away, and continue their conversation with the soldiers that were playing the game. I notice the one that stabbed himself is no longer with them. I wonder if he went to find a healer to wrap and stitch the wound. The soldiers that joined the group don't seem to know what I was doing, and for the time being I forget about trying to escape. I need to give it a little time, especially with them keeping a closer eye on us than what was previously on us.

Watching the men, overwhelming sadness contorts everything around me and my mind goes blank before I see myself on my balcony at the castle with the wind in my hair and a very pregnant belly. As quickly as the image appears, it dissipates and I'm staring at the soldiers once more. My breath comes easier knowing that I will survive this, but I worry about Alaric, even though I have this feeling that because I was at the castle, he survives as well. I wouldn't be there without him. Regardless, I need to save him, or all of this will have been for nothing. The soldiers begin to come closer, and one calls out to Alaric. The closer they get, the more familiar they become. They were guards stationed at the castle.

"Your majesty! How are you faring?" The bigger guard calls out, laughing. The others laugh too, but the second guard at least has the right idea to look uncomfortable. "Your brother would like to see you. Both of you actually."

The bigger guard digs his fingers into Alaric's shoulder, I watch Alaric fight back a wince, and waits for the smaller one to grab me. His fingers knot in my hair and I cry out as the one holding me cuts through the rope and pulls me to my feet by my hair. I scramble up as quickly as possible, tears springing to my eyes with the strain on my scalp. The man holding Alaric leads the way, with us following behind. My hands go to my head as the tears fall from my eyes. There is no stopping it, my scalp burns with the pressure, and I wonder how long it can hold on to the strands before they pull free. The man pulls harder, before letting my hair go and grabbing my wrist. I try to yank away, feeling the tug in my shoulder, but he stops walking and pulls me against him. His arms lock me in place, one hand still holding my wrist which is twisted up behind me, and the other encases my head in a headlock. I gasp for breath as I freeze against him.

"I wouldn't do that if I were you." His breath is foul, and I go limp, trying anything to get away from him, but it does nothing against the hold, except make it worse around my neck. "That's what I thought."

He releases me enough to begin walking again, but maintains his hold on my wrist as he pulls me behind him. This time, I let him. I try to stay on my feet on the uneven terrain, stumbling as he roughly yanks me along the path to the clearing. My breath comes in sharp spurts as I try to regain what breath I lost when in the hold. My chest burns and I fight the rising panic. *We survive. We survive. We survive*; plays on repeat, becoming my mantra as we break through the trees and into the clearing we stayed in the night before. It may be the same place, but it has become completely different. There is a large red tent with gold adornments in the center, with the fire ring we had set up directly in front of it. Around the fire are armed generals, some of which are supposed to be in Alaric's control.

Obviously, Lucas's reach is much farther than we thought. One of the generals calls out to Lucas, who emerges from the tent. The flaps that serve as a door flick closed behind Lucas as he strides out to greet us a few paces away. His eyes are pure ice as his face twists into a wicked grin. The generals at the fire all pause in their own conversations to tune in to Lucas. The area buzzes with expectation, and I do not like the tingling that coats me as the electricity stemming from the charged environment crackles in the air around us. I stand as tall as I can with the guard at my back, pinning me in place with a heavy hand on my shoulder. Alaric is doing the same at my side, but attempts to shrug off the hand that holds him, which causes the guard to dig his fingers in further, and I watch Alaric struggle to remain standing. His knees nearly give out under the pressure on the sensitive spot in his shoulder being aggravated by the guard. The guard notices and smirks behind him as digs his thumb in a little more, and I hear Alaric grunt as his legs give out and he hits his knees on the ground.

Lucas's smile widens as he watches his brother get taken to his knees, and his voice is laced with sarcasm as he holds his arms out wide in invitation, "my dear brother and his," he sneers in my direction, his eyes grazing over me. I shift uncomfortably and he spits, "*wife*. I am *so* glad you could make it. Please, come in." He turns on his heel and heads back into his tent. The man holding me releases his grip, Alaric is pulled roughly to his feet before he is shoved toward the door of the tent, and I fly forward with the rough shove against my back. I trip on my way in but manage to stay on my feet by taking a few extra small steps. I look around the interior of the tent. Lucas is already seated to our left at a small table that holds a pitcher of water with lemon and a few glasses. The table has three unoccupied chairs around it, and it is clear we are meant to join him. Lucas sits with one ankle rested on his knee with his hands folded and resting casually in his lap. In front of us is a cot, and to the right is a wash basin and lamp. Lucas extends his hands toward the chairs. "Please, sit."

I find myself moving forward to take a seat, and Alaric does the same beside me. I glare at Lucas, but glance at Alaric as my fingers grasp the chair and pull it out. The chair is sturdy, and warm under my fingers. Alaric nods his head to reassure me as we sit. I turn back to Lucas, crossing my arms as I sit back in the chair. Alaric imitates my position, and I long to know what is going through his mind as he stares at his brother.

"I'm very disappointed in you, brother. You ran from your own castle, surrendering your own people to my blade, rather than facing it yourself." His voice sends an icy shiver down my spine, and if I weren't already looking at him, I would have whipped my head to face him. How *dare* he? He has the audacity to spin this on Alaric, when we all know this was all a part of his scheme to get the throne. Unfortunately Alaric bites at the bit.

"You speak of disappointment? How dare you! You killed our father and tricked me into believing you a better person than you are. I don't know you— I never did. You, brother, are the disappointment." My hand in Alaric's is the only thing keeping him seated. The venom in his voice is terrifying. I've never heard hate in his voice before, and I hope it is never directed at me. I squeeze his hand in mine, and he settles back into the chair again, but his knee bounces with the pent up anger, tension, and malice that emanates from him.

"You are weak. You are nothing! All of this," Lucas gestures around himself, "is supposed to be mine. You were never supposed to survive! Father promised me all of this years ago, but you— you are nothing more than a disgrace to us all." Lucas rises out of his chair and slams his hands down on the table. "Then *you* had to enter the picture," he says, looking at me, "always seeming to be one step ahead of me." He spins then quickly turns back to point at me. "I had to change my plans on more than one occasion because you interfered. That letter you wrote? I had to convince my father to go on that trip like we were supposed to. You messed with the whole thing. I don't know how you knew, but I. Will. End. You."

He points with each word, getting closer and closer over the table. "I will dispose of you, both of you," He turns back to Alaric, "once and for all. I will not be displaced again just because you have the gall to survive yet another attempt on your life. Dear brother, didn't you ever wonder why you were always ill?" he lowers his voice, sneering at us and raising both hands up as if asking why. "I did that. No one knew."

"You *poisoned* your own brother?" My outrage breaks loose, and my own hands slam on the table. The vision from when I first arrived at the castle resurfaces, and I finally put the pieces together.

"But yet you survived. And here we are," he continues as if my outburst didn't even happen. "I never wanted the armies, or the glory that comes with being a soldier prince. I wanted *everything*. I was second in line, and I refused to let the lineage of my own birth interfere with the throne." He laughs as he sits back in his chair, leaning back casually as if without a single care in the world. "You are pathetic. Both of you. Brother, you are too soft, to…comfortable in your own role and place that you forget the *power* at your fingertips. The things you can accomplish, the lengths you can go…why would I let *you* have it, when it could have just as easily been mine?"

"You will never get my throne," Alaric spits. "You can try, but you will *never* rule."

"Look around you!" Again, he gestures around himself as his voice drops to a whisper. "I have already won! Your men? They don't follow you. Whatever hope you had of recapturing your throne," he waves his words away, "disappeared the moment I caught you. You have no moves left." He begins to laugh. "You have nothing left. Nothing." Lucas rises to his feet once more, and goes to the mouth of the tent, gently lifting the flap and allowing the sunlight to filter into the small area. "You will both remain here until I need you. Enjoy each other's company while you can." Lucas's laughter lingers in the room long after he is gone.

Alaric's eyes meet mine, and I know they mirror my own. We linger in the silence that resonates within the small tent. I don't even know what to think about everything that Lucas confessed. I guess he no longer sees us as a threat, if he ever did, now that he has us exactly where he wants us. Looking at the situation as it stands, it does appear we have very little chance of getting out of here alive, but still I fight against it. We have to.

Hours pass, how many, I am not sure. We haven't even tried to lift the tent flap to see the path of the sun, or to see what is even happening beyond the tent and in the clearing. Alaric is restless, pacing back and forth, over and over as I remain seated in the chair at the table. We have been bouncing ideas back and forth, but it is pointless. There is very little we can do for the time being. His voice splits the quiet, "perhaps we can make a break for it?" He pauses, waiting for my opinion. We have already shot this option down. Twice.

"We wouldn't get more than ten feet before they caught us. This place is swarming with men. However, maybe when Lucas finally decides to get rid of us we can escape. You and I both know he is going to make it a public affair. He is going to want everyone with any kind of power there to witness your death. Maybe we can get away then. It will be crazy enough as it is." My fingers dig into my forehead and in my temples, rubbing circles into my flesh trying to ease the headache that still pounds away like a hammer in my skull. My body is heavy, aching with every movement as I reposition myself in the chair, trying to find some ounce of comfort that evades me to the point that I want to groan in pain. I am mentally and physically exhausted. I am almost entirely out of energy to keep this up.

Alaric nods, his hand rubbing his jaw. "True. I would also want it to be a public affair. I'd want no one to second guess the truth of his death. There will be supporters there that are on my side. Maybe they can help us escape." His eyes take in my ragged appearance, and he softens. He walks to the far side of the tent, stopping in front of the small mirror behind the wash basin.

His fingers dip into the water in the basin, and I watch as he takes a washcloth from the basket beside it, wets it, and seconds later he is kneeled in front of me. His fingers are gentle as he starts to dab the cloth at the cut on my lip and forehead, cleaning any remnant of dirt or sap from the wounds so they can heal. He pays no mind to his own injuries, and focuses on mine. His touch reminds me of different times in a different place, and the cloth is cool on my skin. It does wonders to make me feel human again, and I perk up slightly as I gaze into Alaric's crystal eyes. He places the cloth on the table beside me and cups my cheek in his hand, his thumb rubbing my cheek bone as his forehead comes to rest on mine. His breath causes my hair to tickle my cheek, but I don't pull back, rather I embrace his touch. My own hands grip his shirt.

"I hope you know, I never wanted this for us. For you. I imagined so much more."

"I know," I whisper. I release his shirt and lift my hands to cup his face, and my fingers are greeted with tears. I look up into his face. "Hey, don't do that. Ric, please. We will survive this. We will make it home, we will have time, and be happy. Please don't cry. I have you. I love you." My voice cracks as my own tears choke me. He saved me. When I was stumbling and drowning in the visions and in myself, he found me and taught me to swim. I hate to see him breaking when he has been so strong for me this whole time. His blue eyes are as tumultuous as the sea back home, and the color would bring anyone to their knees. Grief, sadness, loss, and fear have made themselves at home in his eyes, and I wish I could erase just one of them. I kiss each cheek, salt from his tears coating my tongue.

He nods, and takes a deep, rattling breath. The fingers of my left hand find the washcloth on the table, as I lean back. My eyes graze over him to inspect the wounds on his face. His eyes are steady on my face as I begin to clean his wounds. I ignore his gaze, focusing on cleaning what I can, and checking for anything worse. He is quiet and allows me to work. My fingers are gentle on his skin as I prod at the gash on his forehead. It could use a stitch or two, but for now, just having it clean will have to suffice. I gently brush his hair to the side and out of the wound in order to press the washcloth to his forehead. He winces and lets out a hiss of pain.

"Sorry, sorry." I murmur, but before I can continue, he grabs my hand and lowers it and the washcloth. With a gentle tug on the washcloth, I release it as he rises to his feet with it in his grasp.

"I'm fine. Don't worry about me." He smiles softly, as he turns and tosses the cloth into the wash basin.

"Alaric? I always worry."

His large hands run through his hair, and I remember how it feels to have those fingers run through mine. My gaze lingers on the strands of his hair as it flutters back to its normal position at the side of his face. The same face that started as a haunt but has turned into the one that brightens my day. The water in the basin just behind him still ripples from the entrance of the cloth. The ripples catch my attention, and grow to fill my vision, until that is all I see. I sense a vision coming, and I grasp the arm of the chair I'm in to ground myself.

The tent around me disappears. We are still near the camp, but this time we are tied to tall pedestals that are erected at the top of a hill. People swarm the bottom of the hill; their faces upturned to the pedestals and everything happening on the hillside. Their mouths are open, screaming and shouting, but there is no sound. It is eerily silent outside of the beat of my own heart and the whisper of my feet on the grass. I am overwhelmed with pain and despair that nearly bring me to my knees.

I fight to stay standing as I watch a second copy of myself step away from the pedestal. My body is still tied to the pedestal, but hangs limply from the bonds. The ghost of myself steps forward until she stands directly behind a laughing Lucas who raises a fist in victory. There is a figure at his feet, slumped in a way I can't make out their face. I can't move, so I watch the ghost of me shove a hand forward with a blood curdling scream. No one at the foot of the hill takes any notice.

"Katerina?"

I hear Alaric in the distance. I shake my head, trying to shake off the voice, and pushing to see what happens next; but the hillside disappears as Alaric's face swims back into view— his voice effectively breaking me out of the vision. I lean forward with my elbows on my knees as I hold my head in my hands, my face tilted to the ground. I take a few shaky breaths before my breathing returns to normal. Alaric waits patiently as he rubs comforting circles on my back; he gives me time to wrap my mind around everything I saw and figure out how to put it in words.

It doesn't take long to tell him of the vision outlined in my mother's journal, and compare it to the one I just saw; "I don't understand what it is or what it means either. But my mother had a similar vision before she died. But I don't know what it means."

"Do we survive this?" He tries to catch my eyes, but I avoid them. I nod slowly, as far as I can tell, we do. "Are you okay?" His fingers, while gentle on my chin, force me to look at him. His eyes search mine, and I don't know what he sees. I am terrified of this vision, of what comes next. He didn't feel the utter destruction that I did. Whatever happens, is enough to bring out a version of me that I didn't know was even possible. I am absolutely terrified. Whether that is conveyed through my eyes or not, he takes me gently in his arms as he lifts me as if I weigh nothing and sits with me cradled in his lap on the cot. His arms are tight around me, and his lips rest on the crown of my head. It is everything I need, and I tremble in his arms until I fall asleep.

CHAPTER 27

My darling,

I am so sorry for what I have to do. You see, I knew you would be better off without me. I saw what this world would have become had I been there to watch you grow. Not only would the man you love and the one you will come to love die, but so would you. You needed me to go for you to live. And this is a sacrifice that I was willing to make. I couldn't imagine living in a world that you were no longer in, so I made a call, and I hope that it was the right one. I love you. Please forgive me.

Clara

The light filters in through the canvas of the tent walls, and my neck *aches* from the odd position we must have fallen asleep in. My head rests on Alaric's chest, and he has me tucked into his side in order to not topple to the floor. I tilt my head enough to look into Alaric's face. His face is drawn, and he has dark circles under his eyes— he looks like he didn't bother to try to sleep.

I'm surprised Lucas hasn't come for us yet, but based on the crowd that filled the base of the hill in the vision, he is waiting for arrivals. It is noisier beyond the tent this morning than it was the day prior. The people he was waiting on must have arrived. I'm tempted to lift the flap that serves as the door to peer outside, but I don't want to leave the comfort and safety I feel in Alaric's arms. I nestle in closer to his side, breathing deeply.

The air smells faintly of rain, mixed with the smokiness from the militia's fires from the night before. How long has it even been since we were captured? How long were we tied to the tree before we were brought here? I leave a kiss on Alaric's shoulder as I push myself to sit at the edge of the cot before rising to my feet and walking to the wash basin. The water has long since turned lukewarm from being left out for who knows how long, but I splash it on my face regardless. The water is refreshing, and I long to submerge my entire being to clean off the past two weeks. I take my wet hands and clean the back of my neck before wetting them again and running them through my hair. I sit back on the edge of the cot, re-plaiting my hair in an attempt to feel normal. Alaric sits up beside me on the cot, resting a hand on the small of my back before he speaks.

"I think today is the day. It has to be. There is no reason for Lucas to put it off any longer. Especially since we haven't moved from this spot."

Before I have the chance to respond, the tent flap flies open, and two guards enter the tent.

"Get up. Let's go," the taller, heavier set man with dark hair demands. The smaller of the two takes a threatening stance, as if he were about to tackle Alaric and force him to obey. I look at Alaric and take his hand as we stand to follow the guards out of the tent. Before I can stop Alaric, he murmurs, "How could you, Brian?" The young guard's eyes flash, and pain causes him to flinch.

"How could *you*? You allowed so many of us to die when you left. I wasn't left with a choice. You abandoned us. My brother died because you left rather than fight for what is yours. My faith in you is gone."

"Brian, I…"

"Shut up. Both of you. Now let's go," the bigger guard yells, roughly pulling us along. The bigger man leads the way, with the smaller taking up the rear. They lead us through the clearing, past the jabbing, laughing, demeaning guards in the camp, and towards the road. I can see a handful of soldiers lingering towards the back with somber looks on their faces. It is clear that Lucas doesn't have everyone on his side. We reach the road and continue for about 500 feet until a big opening breaks through the trees. The opening is full of people, guards, noblemen and women, peasants, anyone that could come on such short notice. I notice Peter's family standing in the back near the trees, they avoid eye contact and study the ground at their feet. I shake my head, trying to force the tears back. I manage to keep a hold of myself until I notice the stage-like area at the top of a small hill at the back of the opening.

There are two large pedestals erected in the back, and I know that they are going to be tying us to them. I want to run, but there is nothing but a massive sea of people surrounding us. They call out, either taunting us or crying. There is more taunting and laughter than anything, and for some reason that surprises me. The smaller guard behind us pushes us toward the top of the hill, and I balk, my eyes widening, nostrils flaring, and my whole body freezes. I am completely unable to move which leads to him pushing me to the ground, yelling for me to keep moving. I don't get the chance to stand on my own.

The guard rips me from the ground by my upper arm. I hiss in pain as my shoulder pops and I try to tear my arm from his grip. Instead of letting go like I wanted, the guard grips my upper arm hard enough that I start to lose feeling in my fingers and drags me to the pedestals. He spins me and shoves me against the pedestal adjacent to the one they force Alaric against. The force with which he shoves me into the pedestal leaves me winded and gasping for air. He ties the main rope tightly around my midsection, before he takes another rope and secures my hands together in front of me. Alaric has been quiet and obedient this whole time, not putting up the fight that I can see blazing in his eyes as they find mine. His face screams the fury that is close to boiling over, he is one more hint of pain from me away from losing control.

My hands lose circulation with how tightly they tie my bonds. I look at Alaric as the breeze picks up, causing the loose strands of my hair to flutter around my face. The smell of rain is heavier now. The sky is darkening, but not releasing its contents yet. This is it. I knew this moment was coming and even though I know I survive, I am not prepared for the panic and intense terror that grips me. My breathing is shallow, coming in short bursts, and my head swims with the eyes of everyone on me. My fingers tingle and begin to go numb.

I look out into the sea of people below at the foot of the hill and notice a few more familiar faces. Some of my father's sailors are among the few I recognize— what are they doing this far north? Among the guards is the one that found me in the west hall with Alaric, and I even notice the royal doctor lingering near the back of the crowd. The wind blows again, harder this time, and my braid starts to come loose. I am glad that at least my father and sister are nowhere to be found. The same with Peter and Anna— none of them need to witness this.

A cheer begins to rise up among the people as Lucas makes his way to the top of the hill. He pauses at the bottom, clasping a man maybe ten years older than us on the back, and tousling the white blonde hair of the little boy standing in front of him. Both bear crowns of gold on their brows, and I piece together exactly who they are. The co-conspirators in league with Lucas— the King of Modiva. The little boy stares at me curiously, his head cocked like a snake debating whether to strike. He is dressed in fine clothes that show nobility, but in a style that is unfamiliar to me. He must be the crown prince and heir of Modiva. What an event to bring a royal child to: the execution of the current king and queen of the neighboring kingdom they claimed to be allies with. Perfect way to raise the next king and negotiator.

Lucas spins as he strides up the hill, walking backwards to face our people. Once at the top, he holds his hands up, grinning, and the crowd goes quiet.

"Thank you all for being here on such short notice. It means a great deal, and I'm sure my dear brother appreciates it too." He throws his head back and laughs.

How can no one else see how insane he really is? I understand at one time he was thought to be the better choice for King, but how can't they see the man he truly is? The man he is showing them now? He has everyone eating from the palm of his hands. Lucas continues to talk, but I tune it out. I watch the people that are supposed to be our subjects. They watch him avidly, curiously— seemingly awestruck. I don't notice exactly what he says to bring forth yet another cheer, instead, I notice Peter. He sneaks into the crowd unnoticed near his parents who remain near the treeline. The people are too enthralled by Lucas's tirade and captivating demeanour to notice someone moving amongst them. Peter's parents finally meet my gaze. Lord Gold nods his head and then continues to act like he has been. His face is morose, and Lady Gold stands stoically beside her husband. Somehow, I knew they wouldn't betray their king, betray me.

I watch Peter snake his way through the people until he is close enough that I can tell that he has sustained no injuries in his escape. I see the green of his eyes, and I want nothing more than to scream for him to run. My mouth opens to do just that, but he catches my gaze and puts a finger to his lips. His eyes slide from mine to scan the crowd and the hillside, trying to find a way to get to Alaric and I. I lose sight of him in the throng of people, and I hope that maybe he finally regained some sanity and left. I glance over at Alaric, and his eyes track movement in the crowd, and when I look back out in the sea of faces that have arms raised and are chanting words that are nothing more than a roar in my ears, I spot Peter. He has managed to get even closer to the hill and pedestals. He stumbles forward, accidentally pushing a woman to the ground, and unfortunately, I don't seem to be the only one to notice.

"Peter!" Lucas doesn't even bother with his title, demeaning him to nothing more than the man himself. "Welcome to the celebration! Would you care to join us up here please?" Lucas extends a hand, and a dozen guards that were waiting on the outskirts and the bottom of the hill rush the crowd to get to Peter. My breath leaves my lungs as I helplessly watch Peter duck through his fellow nobles and try to break free of the nobility blocking his movement. Every step he takes is two steps backward as the people push back against him and block every free space that was there moments before. He shoves, jumps, ducks, and does everything he can possibly do to get through, but is stopped every time. While the people block his movements, they allow the guards through. Peter spins, his head turning every direction to find another way to either get to me, or escape, I'm unsure which. He turns, his wild eyes finding mine as he uses his elbows and feet to force people out of his way on his mad dash toward the hill, towards me.

Everything slows down, and somehow I break eye contact and glance toward the monster that now steps in front of me while drawing his sword. The hiss of the steel releasing silences the chaos that ensues below. Lucas turns slightly, looking back at me with a smirk that sends pure ice down my spine. His eyes are the darkest I have ever seen blue eyes become, and the pure hatred that emanates from him is enough to make my breath catch. Lucas begins to laugh, in a way that cuts through everything until it is all I hear. He glances back at Peter, widening his stance as he waits for him to cross over the precipice. My eyes find Peter. I can tell that Peter is shaken, and almost desperate in his attempts to reach me. I want him to notice the danger and forget me, but his face is set and his own sword is drawn as he finally breaks through the crowd and races to the top of the hill. His eyes are focused with deadly precision on Lucas.

"Peter, NO!" I scream, but it is too late. He doesn't listen or he doesn't hear, but either way, my cry comes too late. Peter doesn't have time to dive out of the way of Lucas's blade as he rushes forward as he meets the top of the hill. The cries from the crowd disappear as the wet gasp and grunt of pain escapes Peter's lips as Lucas's sword runs him through. Peter falls to his knees as Lucas withdraws the sword and lowers it to his side. Peter's eyes meet mine. *I love you*, his lips form the words as he crumples to the ground. His blood seeps into the grass where he lies. I scream, the sound shatters everything inside of me as I slump forward against my bonds, sobbing hysterically. The ropes are the only thing keeping me standing. I lose control of everything. My emotions, my willpower, everything. Lucas stands there laughing at my pain, and I imagine ripping his heart from his chest, the same way he has done to me.

In that moment, I sense something shift within me. All of the visions I've had flash before me. Alaric haunting me, Lucas and his plans, the child standing alone in the road, the King's death, and finally my mother's vision I found in the journal, the pedestals, the girl and her lover. I close my eyes against the pain and grief. When I open them, I am no longer in my own body. I look down at my hands that move freely, and step forward spinning to look back at the pedestals. My body remains slumped forward, held up by my bonds, seemingly unconscious.

A breeze ruffles the unbound tendrils of my hair as I glide my way over to Lucas, momentarily forgetting about the crowd and Alaric. My skirt whispers against the ground— one of the only sounds that registers in my mind other than my own heartbeat. A deathly calm resonates within me, and I take a moment to center myself, and look over my shoulder at Alaric. His mouth is agape as he stares at Peter's crumpled body on the ground in front of Lucas. Alaric's eyes are blank, but tears streak down his face. He glances over at my slumped body, and he strains against the bonds holding him tight to the pedestal. His breathing is ragged, and I know he longs to get to me. I turn back to Lucas's back as the first raindrops fall from the clouds above.

I approach him, hesitating long enough to glance out into the crowd below. Mr. Gold holds his wife in his arms as she screams hysterically. She tries to break free from her husband and run to her son, but he holds her tight enough that she can't break free. Tears stream down his face, and I know it takes everything in him to not run to his son's side. I turn away, wanting to end this pain. Anger and numbness fills the void that was ripped open the second the sword entered Peter's body. Lucas stands triumphantly above Peter. I walk around them, facing Lucas head on. He keeps the sword in his hand, and lifts it into the air. Even though I can't hear the cries of the crowd, I know they occur by the triumphant grin that twists Lucas's mouth. He doesn't see me, but that is fine with me. I try to avoid looking at Peter now that I am so close, but I can't help but see his closed eyes, those long lashes resting against the now pale freckled skin of his cheek, and the pool of blood spreading underneath him before seeping into the grass.

With a mixed scream of fury and agony, I thrust my hand forward through Lucas's chest. My fingers find his heart. I clench my fist, still screaming my pain and fury and feel his heart start to ooze through the cracks between my fingers. Lucas begins to cough and reaches to hold his chest, dropping the sword to the ground as his fingers grasp at where my hand entered his body. He starts to stumble toward me, but I stand strong, unwilling to let him go. Since I know I am doing damage, I squeeze harder feeling his heart turn to mush. He gasps, trying to catch his breath or cry out, but he is unable to. The fire in his eyes fade into nothing and I pull my hand from his chest as he slumps to the ground, dead. I close my eyes, feeling the wind and rain against my body, and when I open them again, I am me.

CHAPTER 28

I am sorry.

Soft murmured voices bring me back from unconsciousness. I open my eyes. The ceiling is unfamiliar, and I feel as if I am laying on a cloud. My fingers grope at the soft blanket that covers a majority of my body, as I take in the space around me. The room is just as unfamiliar— the room is sparse. There isn't much furniture aside from the bed I currently occupy, a chair pulled up at the side of the bed, a small dresser, and a table with a wash basin. Alaric lingers at the doorway, talking in hushed tones with someone in the hallway. He is disheveled; his hair is a mess, as if he sat with his head in his hands and has run his fingers through the strands until they no longer went to their normal position. His clothes are rumpled, and his face is drawn and pale, making the dark circles under his eyes stand out.

I push myself up to lean against the headboard, sitting with my legs outstretched. A litany of questions cross my mind as I wait for Alaric to notice that I have woken up. Where are we? How long have I been unconscious? What happened? The last thing I remember is the feeling of Lucas's heart in between my fingers, and Peter…I gasp as a fresh wave of pain and grief washes over me, and every breath I take feels like fire in my lungs. I draw my knees to my chest, making myself as small as possible as Alaric's head whips around to find me. His eyes are wide as he looks at me. He abandons the conversation he was having and has his arms around me within seconds.

The bed dips under his weight as he sits beside me and holds me close. With one hand, his fingers are tangled in my hair as he holds me to him, and the other is wrapped around my shoulders. His lips are in my hair, and I feel his body shaking with the tears I feel wetting my hair. I feel completely empty. No tears moisten my eyes, and while each breath burns, there is a sweet emptiness that I cling to. Alaric clears his throat, and leaves a kiss on the top of my head, but doesn't release me. I sink into his arms, and he settles back against the headboard. I rest my head on his chest, and my hand curls itself into his shirt. His breathing evens out beneath me and I know he wants me to say something, but I can't. I don't even know what I would say if I could speak.

"It's been three days. Three days where you did nothing but sleep. I prayed to anything that would listen that you would wake," his voice is quiet, raspy, and broken. His breath hitches, and he continues, "I am so sorry, Kat. So unbelievably sorry." He trails off, and I hear his sniffles as he chokes down more tears. I remain silent. My throat is raw, and I don't trust myself to speak.

For the first time in almost a year, my mind is blissfully blank and there is no hint or sign of a vision. Alaric's fingers trace random shapes on my upper arm as we sit in comfortable silence. He doesn't push me to speak, and remains a comfort while I work through who I am without Peter in this world. I knew the two of us were done, I made that choice over a month ago, but I can't help but wonder how things will be with him gone. Did I do enough to make things right? Did I do everything I could? Who will take his place at court, who can fill the hole that he leaves behind?

I can't believe he is really gone.

Anna is quiet when she is around, but then again, so am I. I haven't spoken more than short greetings, or assurances for those who ask that I am okay. She keeps her eyes averted when she does speak, and I pin it on her own grief. There was more than one death that day, her brother being the second. I can't imagine the pain that both her and Alaric must feel in regard to their brother. Despite what he had become, he was still their brother.

The only thing I feel is relief, but I would never admit to it. They are grieving the same as I am, and one could say that they have more right to than I do. The guilt is tearing me apart, and I can barely stomach what I have done, let alone the food they constantly badger me to eat. I know I need to for the baby's sake, but what little I do choke down turns to ash on my tongue, and I struggle to keep anything down. The first few days after I woke up, the doctor was frequently in my room, checking my vitals, confirming my pregnancy, and ensuring that I and the baby are healthy. Aside from the emotions that battle for permanence, I am perfect.

No one seems to understand the swirling depth of the things that are just beneath the surface, and I hide it from everyone— or at least I try to. It is not an easy task, and I long for some sort of release from the pain that occurs with every inhale, or the burn with every exhale. I am unsure whether it is guilt or grief that occupies the most space, but either way, they demand to be felt in an all consuming manner that I don't know how to survive.

We linger at Lightspire a couple more days to recover from the hard journey here, and from the events of the past week. Anna keeps disappearing, and when she is around, she is unusually quiet and withdrawn. She has this ever present look of guilt that seems sewn onto her features. She has avoided me since I woke up. She checked in on me once she heard I was okay, but has not spoken to me since then. Even though I notice, I find I don't mind the distance between us. I am a shell of myself, and I know Alaric and Anna worry, but I go through the motions of everyday life. Things will get easier as time passes. Things will get easier, they have to. I plaster on smiles that don't quite reach my eyes and while I know everyone can tell how broken I have become, I continue on as I always have. I avoid Peter's parents, and send my condolences and gratitude before we leave, but I cannot face them and remain haphazardly put together. I would fall apart, and it isn't fair to anyone. It is my fault that their son now lies in the fresh grave in the Gold family graveyard. I have visited the site daily since I woke up. I missed the burial while I was unconscious, and a part of me is grateful that I was not there. I don't think I could have handled that with the grace expected of me. Occasionally Alaric comes with me to Peter's grave, but more often I go alone. I find peace in the space within the woods, and I wish I could have one more moment with him— to tell him everything and to say goodbye.

I visit his grave one final time the morning we are set to head home to Aurellia City. The air is growing chilly as the late summer turns to autumn; the weather is cooler here than back home due to the higher elevation. The heavy scent of pine surrounds me as does the misty fog that fills the small wooded area. I am glad for the light cloak that I threw over my shoulders as I headed out this morning. I draw it closer around me as I suppress a shiver. The morning may be crisp, but the cool air makes me feel more like myself as it cuts into my skin. I close my eyes briefly; allowing myself the freedom of becoming one with the world around me.

This is the part of his home he always wanted me to fall in love with, and I can finally understand why. It reminds me of the freshness I feel with the sea breeze, the clean breath that clears my mind and soul. The air here is similar and I hate to leave it behind. I open my eyes again, and spy the fresh grave at the far end of the plot under a willow. He lies at one side, while his little sister Rose lies to the other side. I situate myself in the spot that hugs my frame as I sit on the damp ground and lean against the tree. I look out over the grey morning, and I whisper everything that I never got the chance to say.

The journey home seems to go faster than the one here. We take one of the carriages that the Golds offered, and we take our time. We are each quiet, mourning in our own ways, and allowing the same for each other. When we are two days out of Aurellia City, and have rooms in the inn we stayed in over a month ago, the quiet is finally broken. Anna is in a room of her own, and Alaric and I share another. He paces in the space just inside of the door, his boots clicking on the wood planks of the floor with each step. I sit on the edge of the bed, combing through my hair as I ready myself for bed. I avoid eye contact, and I have for a while now. The guilt continues to eat at me, and I am *drowning*. I can't let go. I stole the life from Peter when I got him involved. I am to blame for his death, and I can barely look at myself in the mirror let alone see the way Alaric looks at me.

"Kat, look at me."

I turn my face toward him, but look at his boots on the floor. They are scuffed and worn from the journey to Lightspire, and there is dirt that has fallen to the floor from the soles with his relentless pacing. I hear him sigh and his feet still as he turns to face me.

"Kat, please!" His voice is broken and desperate. Guilt punches me in the gut again, and it takes everything in me to keep breathing. I take a deep breath, closing my eyes as I feel my lungs expand before I release the breath. I finally look into Alaric's face and meet his eyes. They are just as wild as I can imagine mine to be.

His grief, confusion, and pain swirl in his blue eyes and the haphazard wall I have built and hidden what I could behind, starts to crumble under the weight held there in his eyes. "I can't stand this anymore, I am hurting too." His eyes gloss over with tears that he doesn't try to hide. He allows them to fall, and I watch the muscle in his cheek twitch when he clenches his jaw. I remain silent, what is there even to say? I know I am hurting him as much as I am hurting, and it *kills* me, but I can't breathe, can't sleep, can't speak for fear of what will spill forth. No one knows the truth of Lucas's death. No one. And I can't tell them. I murdered Alaric's brother in cold blood. In retaliation for everything that he had done, and while I know he would have died eventually, it was by my hands. I held his heart in my hand, and I squeezed until it oozed between my fingers. I literally ripped the heart from his chest. How does someone come back from that? How?

Alaric spins, his hands in his hair before he spins back to face me. His eyes are wild. "Katerina! Just talk to me! Please!" His voice rises, and cracks as he runs his hands through his hair again. "Please."

"I can't." My own voice scratches as it breaks free. I shake my head before leaning forward and resting my face in my hands. "I can't." Can't he see how broken I have become?

"Bull shit. I am here. I am right. Here. Have been, but you refuse to see it." His arm flings out, he turns to the table behind him, gripping the edge with both hands and bowing his head. "I am right here."

"Alaric," I bite, pushing to my feet. "I killed him. How do you expect me to come back from that? Everything that happened? My. Fault. I am to blame. Not anyone else, me." I shake my head, and my entire body shakes in anger I can't control. But the anger is better than the emptiness that has been gnawing away at me, and I cling to it. "I held his beating heart in my hand, and I destroyed it. Is that what you want to hear? That I am a murderer?" My tone is cold, and I watch Alaric freeze against the table, before turning to face me. He keeps his face devoid of emotion, and I can't exactly read what he is thinking. Usually I am able to at least get a sense of his thoughts, but not now.

"Yeah, I do, because you know what? It is better than the complete silence that has been there since everything happened." His eyes are dark, but from the set of his shoulders, I can tell that he is more relieved that I finally spoke than anything.

"Losing Peter unleashed something in me and I became something," I shake my head, my hands balling into fists at my side. "or someone I never wanted to be. In that moment, when I stood outside of myself, I lost control. I felt nothing but seething hatred, unimaginable pain, and the desire to *end* him. I didn't care that Lucas was your brother, I didn't care about anything." My voice shakes and I don't attempt to stop it. I shake my head again, biting my lower lip hard enough that I finally feel a twinge of pain underneath the boiling anger that is on the brink of burning me alive. My throat is raw, aching with the truth of what happened, and the flood of things I have hidden the past few days. I am drowning, and I can't tell which direction is to the surface.

"I don't know who I am anymore. I don't know how to come back from this ledge that I am precariously situated on. One misstep and I go tumbling into the abyss that I am not sure I can claw my way out of." Alaric's eyes soften as he looks at me. He takes a step forward, but I raise a hand and he stops. "I can barely look at myself in the mirror, let alone attempt to see myself through your eyes. I can't imagine you see anything worth anything when you look at me," I pause, nodding my head at him, and my voice lowers to a whisper. "That look in your eyes right now? It nearly kills me to see, because I don't deserve it."

"Oh, Kat," he breathes and ignores my protest as he takes me in his arms. I try to break free, but his arms are steel and my nails bite into the flesh of my palms as I clench them harder. "You may not know who you are, Kat, but I do. You are still the woman that I fell for, that hasn't changed. You care deeply for everyone in your life, and it shows in everything you do. You have sacrificed so much for everyone else, it is time for you to let go and live." I shake my head again, and my body is so tense that my fight or flight instinct kicks in, and I can't tell if my muscles are coiled to spring and hit him, or if I want to run. Alaric maintains his hold on my waist, and meets my fearful gaze. "You can take it out on me, I can handle it. Kat, I am not going anywhere. I am right here."

I shake my head, refusing his gaze again as the anger shifts and I am blinded by the sadness that fills me. My fists bury themselves in my gut, and a sob escapes my lips. His arms act as a blockade to the world beyond them, and I allow myself to feel the weight that finally demands to be felt. I loosen my fists, and wrap my arms around Alaric as I press my face into his chest. The tears that evaded me finally fall, and he is the one thing keeping me grounded. He eases my pain, and comforts me when I need it. I finally calm down enough to tell him everything, and he listens. There is no judgement in his eyes, he asks questions when appropriate, and I feel heard. He sees me, and I am grateful that my mother stepped in by giving the book that led him to me.

Six months have passed, and everything seems to have gone back to as close to normal as it can. I sit in the large oversized chair in front of the warm fireplace in Alaric and my shared sitting room, watching the snow fall outside of the balcony doors. My father returned to the castle a couple of months ago, leaving my sister with an aunt we didn't know we had in Aouela. She is training with the seers, and we have sent a few letters back and forth. She plans on remaining there for the foreseeable future, but has agreed to take our little girl, should we have one, once she is older to train among the seers. She says she is happy and has found her purpose.

Things haven't slowed down since we arrived back at the castle. Alaric and I have regained our titles, and have worked diligently to seek out all of the traitors that took off when Lucas collapsed to the ground. The majority of them have been taken care of, but there are a few that are still on the run. We have filled all positions that were vacant from the massacre at Lucas's hands, and we are confident that we will have a better council than before. Ian survived the attack, as did Hayden Conway and Samuel Fairvein. Samuel's wife and newborn son have joined him at court now that any immediate threat has ceased to exist.

There were a couple of council members that ran once Lucas died, and we suspect that they are in Modiva. We have some negotiations there that need to be done to settle the promises that were made by Lucas that are now null and void. The king of Modiva is supposed to make his arrival after the baby is born and Alaric returns from negotiations that he is currently conducting with Arrowhelm. Anna has agreed to a marriage contract with the heir of Arrowhelm, Simon, but waits at home with me for Alaric to return with Simon. They are to be wed by spring.

Anna is still distant, and seems to be watching and jumping at shadows. I understand her fear, it took several months to feel comfortable entering the ballroom, and I have avoided the wing where the council resides. I miss the relationship that Anna and I had before everything, and I hope that we can move past whatever keeps her mind occupied and alone. She evades conversation with the councilmen with whom she used to flirt, and even conversation with me is stilted and off kilter. I've asked her what is going on, but get simple responses and tight smiles; thanking me for my concern, but she is fine. I worry, and I know Alaric has noticed the differences in her, but she gives the same responses when Alaric has approached her.

With Alaric gone, I handle any of the political obligations that arise. Before Alaric left for Arrowhelm, he promised that I was capable of running things on my own, and he has been proven right. The guards follow my lead and listen when I speak. My people speak highly of me, and the whispers I used to dread are becoming something good. The people come to me with any problems or crimes they suspect. They trust me, and I hope in time they will do the same with Alaric. The people are still wary, but they are slowly starting to come around. He is finally comfortable showing everyone the man that I saw beneath the façade that he put forth a year ago, and they are learning that he is truly there for the people.

He wants peace, happiness, and trust on all fronts. I know he will be a great king, but I am glad that I have found something I enjoy and feel that I am actually good at— leading our people. Whenever Alaric is home, almost every minute is spent together. We have made a small nursery in our chambers, and he obsesses over every movement the baby makes. He is completely wrapped around their little finger. It has made me fall even more in love with him. We have worked hard to move forward together, lingering in moments that make us feel alive, but still reflecting on the ones that tear us down. There is a lot of pain to sort through, but we are doing it together. I have found the place where I belong, and it is here, with Alaric.

Alaric promised to be home in time for the birth, but negotiations are moving slowly, and it is likely that he will miss it. I lay his letter on the small table sighing as I carefully lift myself out of the chair, and head out onto the balcony. The room is stuffy from the heat of the fireplace. The snow swirls in the light breeze around me, but the cold air feels good on the exposed skin of my neck and face. The wind makes my hair fly behind me as my hands cradle my swollen belly. I'm due any day now.

I watch the sun slowly start to sink into the horizon, and I find my thoughts circling around my child. I hope my child has Peter's green eyes, but my auburn hair. I hope that they have his charisma, his kindness, his strength, his love. While I hope my child is a boy for the sake of not inheriting the seer gene, I don't at the same time because it isn't fair to Alaric. I know Peter is watching wherever he is, and that thought comforts me more than anything else. I smile, thinking about the laughter-filled moments, and how much I loved him as we grew into who we became. The baby kicks, and all I can think about is how I can't wait to have some part of him back, to hold, cherish, and watch grow into the sort of person that I hope he can be proud of.

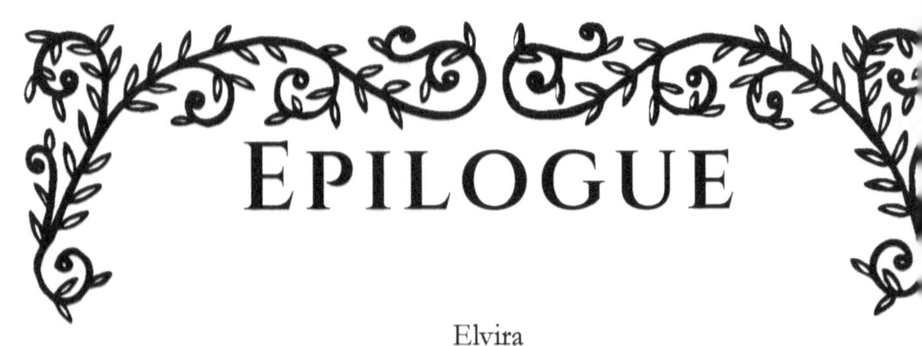

EPILOGUE

Elvira

21 Years Later

The past few nights have been rough. Hell, it has been rough ever since the visions started. I rub my hands over my face as I sit in front of my mirror at my vanity, sighing, not wanting the glow of the evening to fade but knowing I need to take the time to write and analyze the visions I've had so far so I can figure out what is going on. I always thought the visions would be like I was on the outside, watching things unfold, but so far I have seen and been in the body of whoever is the focal point of the vision. I didn't know this was possible, but even though I am seeing through their eyes, I cannot see or feel their thoughts, just see, feel, and hear as they do. With a sigh that deflates my shoulders as I roll my neck to ease some of the tension the visions offer, I glance back into the mirror, and find myself looking into eyes that aren't my own.

I stumble backwards a couple of steps, and ignore the nausea rising in my gut. Wind whistles through the trees around me, and I shiver with the sudden chill. Where the hell am I? *Who am I?* I glance around. I am in the same wooded grove that I was in my last vision. The same small pond is in front of me, the ridiculously tall pine trees almost a perfect circle around the small clearing. There is a small pack leaning against the reddish brown bark of one of the trees to my left. I stumble over to it, grimacing against the shooting pain in my gut. Every breath hurts, and the effort it takes to draw them, makes me question the worth of each one. It is nearly impossible to breathe deeply, and I don't bother to try.

I pause when I reach the tree, bracing myself against it with one hand as the other reaches down to grab the bottom of my torn, dirty tunic. Panting, I lift it carefully, groaning when the shirt sticks to the large wound just to the middle left of my belly area. I carefully tug the fabric free, and there is a gash that is around four inches long cutting through me. My fingers lightly graze over my battered skin to feel my back, and I hiss as my fingers find the wound there, as if whatever caused the gash on my front ran completely through me. My back is bandaged, but I definitely need a fresh one, and one on my front.

I have bled through— my fingers come back wet with blood that has seeped through the back bandage, and my front is oozing which caused the fabric to stick to the wound. Based on my own knowledge, and the knowledge granted by the person I inhabit, I know that it isn't long before the wound will fester and grow infected. I fall to my knees by my pack, groaning with the jolt of fresh pain that tingles through me. I hiss through clenched teeth, holding in the growl and shout of agony that I wish I could release. I search through the pack, fighting through the pain. I find nothing that I can use as a fresh bandage- there aren't even fresh clothes. The pack is empty aside from some food scraps and a canteen, but nothing of any use otherwise. I groan, lowering myself to sit leaned back against the tree and stretch my legs out in front of me.

I wish I knew what he was thinking, how the wound occurred, or who he even is. I have an idea, but it is impossible. He died twenty-one years ago. Instead of focusing on the impossibility of the person that I have become during this vision, I linger on what is happening around me. I don't know if this wound is something that happened in the past, or something that is currently happening, but I do know that this is a serious injury that needs assistance now before it is too late.

If I am feeling the kind of pain that he did, I know this is agony for him. It is taking everything in me to keep from passing out from the pain. Who knows when the last time he ate or drank something was, and I wish I could help in some way, but I can do nothing but watch as things unfold. I watch the sky through the break in the trees for a few minutes, trying to breathe through the pain, but each breath is more of a gasp than anything.

The snapping of twigs in the woods to my right breaks me from the reverie that I find in the clouds I see through the trembling leaves overhead. I know I am easy prey as I am, but I am far too weak to rise, or try to protect myself. I brace myself for an attack, and hope that whatever it is, makes it quick. Instead a voice that is as familiar to me as my own mother's rings through the small clearing.

"Peter?"

ACKNOWLEDGEMENTS

I want to start by thanking everyone who played a role in getting me to where I am today.

To my parents- your guidance through life has helped shape me, your support has given me the courage to get up and keep trying after every step backwards. You have helped me learn, grow, and evolve into the woman that I am today. Your push to follow my dreams helped solidify that drive, and look! I did it!

To my husband- thank you for being my rock. My venting place and the push I needed to kick my ass into gear. You have helped more than words can even express, and I thank you from the bottom of my being (I'd say heart, but it isn't big enough), everything you do makes life a little easier and brighter. I love you so much.

To my kids- you guys are my light in the dark, the guiding light leading me home. You make my world spin on its axis, and I hope you always know how truly LOVED you are. You are both my everything. I love you sooooo much!

To my siblings (every single one including in-laws)- you have all supported me in this endeavor, and have proven to be rockstars and cheerleaders on the sidelines of making all of this happen. I appreciate all of the time, effort, love, and cheering you have provided me with over the years. Nico and Bee, thank you both for taking the time and putting in the effort for merch ideas as well as character art for this. It means the world to have you both included in different areas for this book.

To Bluebonnet Books– thank you for taking a chance on me and my work. It has been amazing working with you, and I look forward to working on book 2! Your insight has been so helpful, and some of your suggestions were seriously the best thing that could have happened to the story and the book as a whole. Thank you!

To Rebecca–Thank you for working so hard on the map, and listening and adapting to each critique. What we created is the perfect representation of the world within these pages. You are a rockstar! Can't wait to work on the map for book 2!

Daniel de la Fe– Thank you for making my cover and characters come to life! From the first sketch to what you created, THANK YOU! Are you ready for book 2?

To my friends and family- you guys have seriously helped alleviate stress and been encouraging since day one. That's exactly what I needed when I would spend days working on this project. Draft after draft, endless feedback and suggestions, and an available ear has meant the world.

To everyone else: my readers, professors, supporters, THANK YOU. Seriously, I couldn't have done it without any of you.

ABOUT THE AUTHOR

Alexandria Long is from Erie, Pennsylvania. She has her BFA in Creative Writing with a minor in English Literature from Pennsylvania State University; The Behrend College, and her M.Ed in Educational Leadership from Edinboro University with both a Teaching and Principal Certification. She is currently a high school English Language Arts Teacher in a Charter School in the city of Erie. She loves sharing her love of literature and writing with her 11th and 12th graders! She loves everything that she does in education, and has helped spark and foster writing in her classes when she isn't being involved in everything on campus.

She has served as the poetry genre editor on an international literary journal, and the copy-editor for a student-run newspaper while in college. She has always loved working toward making writing the best it can be, and offers editing services as well as beta reading services through Fivver.

When she isn't writing, reading, teaching, or editing, she is a photographer. She started Long's Enchanting Images back in 2021, and has been blessed to meet many wonderful people and capture the beauty of their families. She loves capturing the beauty and magic of the world around her, whether that be in words or images.

She is married to a wonderful, supportive man, and is a mom to two bright little kids- one little girl who has as big of an imagination as her mother, and a little boy who loves to curl up in someone's lap with a book. Their solid black German Shepard, Hawkeye, drives everyone crazy with his hyper antics, but he makes the family complete. Whenever Alexandria isn't writing, she can be found reading, seeing live music, dancing in the rain, or singing karaoke. She is beyond excited to share her first novel, the first installment of the Bound by Sight series with you!